RED HUGH,

THE

BACKWOODSMAN

BY SILVERSHOT.

x

THE SPECTRE WARRIOR.

CHAPTER I.

THE SPECTRE WARRIOR.

THE years rolled slowly past, and four times had Tim Delany and I visited the blasted and withered plane-tree that stood in the centre of that vast prairie near a portion of the western bank of the father of waters, the mighty Mississippi.

The hunters' oath taken four years previously had not been forgotten, and we went year after year to ascertain whether any of our six companions had survived the dangers of the chase or the unerring weapons of the untamed red men.

Four times had we visited the spot and there was no sign; so with rifles in our hands we sought for the surviving six to avenge them if dead, to liberate them if they were captives to men who knew not the meaning of the word mercy.

To those who have not read the story of "My Adventures amongst the Prairie Indians," a brief explanation of the parting of the eight hunters may not be uninteresting.

It was midnight when we drew lots for the choice of companions, and good fortune allotted Tim Delaney for mine.

For we went in pairs, one to the east, one to the west, one to the north, one to the south, and before we started a solemn and binding oath was taken—

That all who were alive that night twelve-months were to meet at the old plane-tree on the prairie.

And each pair as they went their way were to leave "hunters'" signs to mark their path, a broken stick or a notch in a tree; this was to be done to guide the survivors to the spot where the absent had disappeared.

Then we swore that those who survived should avenge those who had fallen, swore if even seven were missing the last man should avenge them, or die in the attempt; and we were men who would keep our word.

We alone of the eight had survived, for at the expiration of the first year we followed the western track taken by Dick Crosby and Paul Morgan, and this led us among the prairie red men, and to the adventures I have related in my former story, yet we fell across no sign of our two comrades.

The second year we were at the plane-tree, and kept solitary vigil during the whole night. The next morning we started on the northern track, and for six months kept it, then turned back, and reached the tree, our minds sadder than ever, for we knew four of the gallant band had fallen.

The third track was to the south, and in following this, and returning to the tree at the expiration of another year we were melancholy indeed, for there was no doubt now but that we were the only survivors; and our oath compelled us to wander far from the haunts of men, for there was a faint hope that a "sign" might be found to tell the story of the fate of two at least; this "sign" once discovered, speedy retribution would follow.

   .　　　　.　　　　.　　　　.

The hunter, however brave he may be with mortal foes, is one of the greatest cowards upon earth when anything appertaining to the supernatural crosses his path. Your servant, Silvershot, was not braver than his class, or the strangely fearful story I have to tell would never have needed telling; and but for the superstitious feelings that overcame the judgment possessed by Tim Delaney and myself we might have nipped an atrocious villain's career in the bud—nay, earlier, when the first leaf was visible.

We were upon the western track from the old plane-tree, the track that led to the mouth of the River Yahana.

We had been about a week toiling through the thick wilderness of the eternal and mighty forest, when, thoroughly worn out by our long march, I threw myself beside a rippling stream, and unfastening my leather mocassins, began to bathe a serious scratch I had received a few days before.

"It's an ugly place, Silvershot," Tim Delaney remarked, as he leant upon his rifle and watched the operation. "Bedad, it's my opinion we needn't push on so fast, for we shall never meet with any sign of poor Paul Morgan or Dick Crosby."

"I anticipate a different conclusion, Tim; have you forgotten the hatchet mark we saw on the mora-tree?"

"No, Silvershot; but that mark was made by an Indian's tomahawk, not a hunter's axe."

I was too tired to argue the point, for Tim was a good woodsman; still, I thought he was mistaken.

"Perhaps you are right," I said, "still; your story of the spectre warrior would make me go forward if it was only to catch a glance of his ghostship."

Tim looked cautiously over his shoulder, and a slight shiver came over him as he said—

"Then you don't believe it, Silvershot?"

"No."

"But, man alive, I've seen it."

"I've seen dozens of spectres, Tim, and so have you quite as much as you have seen this one."

"I've! Devil a one, Silvershot, before this, and I hope I may never see him again! But, man alive, where have you seen the dozens? Bedad, one's enough for me!"

"Do you remember Ohola? Was she not a spirit until the mystery was cleared up?"

"True for you, but that's only one, and you say you have seen dozens?"

"I've seen them, Tim, and felt a bit queer until I found out what they were."

"Ghosts?"

"No, Tim, the stumps of trees, low bushes, and large stones; all these things in the grey light of the coming day assume a strange appearance and seem to make me feel as queer as the Indian chief's shadow made you feel."

"I've seen these sort of things too," said Tim, slowly, "but I never fired at any of them."

"Did you fire at this fellow, then?"

"Bedad, I did," whispered Tim, and the bullet—the bullet, Silvershot, was thrown back to me."

"Nonsense!"

"Faith, I wish it was. Look here."

Tim took a bullet from the pocket of his leathern jacket and handed it to me.

I closely examined the globe of lead, and recognised it as one of a batch I had cast before leaving the last settlement.

There was the mark of the ramrod upon it—Tim's ramrod—and one easy to know again, for the end was slightly damaged. Looking closer I saw the bullet was clouded by the explosion of gunpowder.

Having made these observations I gave the ball back to Tim, and said, not without a peculiar feeling creeping over me:

"It's very strange, Tim, but don't you think the ball may have fallen short of the mark you aimed at, and striking a stone rebounded back to you?"

"The devil a bit, Silvershot; for the ball was fired back by the spirit, and there was no noise from his rifle——"

"He carries a rifle, then?"

"Shure, man alive, do you think a redskin would be without that piece of furniture, alive or dead?"

"Perhaps not, Tim; but I never heard of a ghost having a rifle before. You say there was no report when the ball was returned to you. How do you know the ghost fired it?"

"Well, I'll tell you. After I had let go at him, and sure as faith when I did I thought it was a Sioux and not a ghost. The Lord be good to us and preserve us——

"Go on, Tim, for I am getting curious to know the end of your story."

"Well, then, when I fired and thought to see the Sioux jump up, and then jump down dead, a voice—such a voice, Silvershot, said—

"'Take back your bullet, pale face. Remember, should I cross your path again, that all the powder and shot belonging to the Western nation cannot hurt me. Look in the trunk of that tree and you will find your bullet; keep it, for the Sioux are alarmed, and the pale faces have cause for fear.'"

"Saying this in a voice that made me hair stand bolt upright," Tim continued, "the spirit vanished in a blue flame; and when I got out of the shaking that was upon me, sure enough round I turned, and with me knife picked out from the tree the very ball that I had shot at the ghost."

"Why did you not tell me this before?"

"Because," Tim replied, "it's always ready you have been with a laugh when I said a word about the spectre."

"I won't laugh again, Tim; for there is something in this more than I can understand. When did you see the apparition last?"

"The very last night that was. I saw him pass close to where we were sleeping. Bedad,

it was the cowld wind that he brought with him that woke me up."

"Last night, when we were among the cypress trees?"

"Yes; the same, Silvershot."

"And the dogs, did they not notice him?"

"The devil a bit; they had their noses on their paws, and only blinked a little when the varmint passed. Bedad, Silvershot, that ought to prove that he is not a mortial man, a red man anyhow, for neither Jip nor Ben would let one of their stinking carcasses come nigh us without giving mouth."

There was some truth in this, for the faithful hounds we had with us were not at all friendly towards the Indians.

What was I to suppose after this? Either that Tim had been dreaming of the spectre warrior, and awaking suddenly had fancied he saw the shadowless form pass our camp fire.

If this was not the case, there was no conclusion to arrive at but the acceptance of my companion's story as an undeniable fact.

Before coming to the latter conclusion, I asked Tim—

"Have you made a mistake; don't you think you were dreaming?"

"The devil a dream now—not a bit of it. I saw him as plain as I see you, and——"

Tim was interrupted by Jip, the largest of the two dogs, sweeping his tail to and fro, and looking towards the brushwood as though expecting some one to emerge therefrom.

The dog's instinct was always true; there was no cause to prepare for the coming of a foe; no, whoever it was, we knew must be a friend. Still it was as well to be prepared, and we placed our rifles across our knees and turned our heads in the direction of the dog's gaze.

Presently the dry twigs began to crack under the comer's feet, and a few minutes after, the bushes parted, and a young fellow we had made acquaintance with in the Comanche country came towards us.

CHAPTER II.

RED HUGH.

"Hugh Howard, by the mortial man!" said Tim; "well, I'd never thought of seeing you down here."

The new comer advanced with extended hand, as he laughingly replied :—

"I knew I should find you both here, for I've been upon your trail for a week."

I shook hands with the new-comer, and bid him welcome; and an incredulous smile passed over my face when he said he had been upon our track.

He saw it; and as he seated himself upon the trunk of a fallen mora tree, said—

"You surely believe me, Silvershot?"

"It seems very strange," I said, "that you should be able to strike a trail that has deceived even the most cunning of the Sioux warriors."

"Not at all strange," was the answer, "for I have been taught in the Red Skins' school; and a white man's brain is surely better than an Indian's."

"True for you," said Tim, "and an Irishman's senses are the best of the lot, an' that's why I'm such a good woodsman."

Paying no heed to Tim's words, I turned to Hugh, and asked—

"What school do you refer to, comrade?"

The hunter's eyes blazed with sudden passion, and between his teeth he hissed rather than spoke the single word—

"Vengeance!"

"A man would do much," I said, "to carry out this passion——"

"And his eyes would be keener and his thirst for blood greater," Hugh said, "if to the passion engendered by hate a great wrong is added."

"Surely you have not suffered a great wrong, Hugh? When we met in the Comanche country you were the merriest fellow of our set; and when the cowardly Crows had us pinned in a corner your jest was the lightest, although death seemed inevitable."

"A few days will sometimes work a change in a man's destiny, and I——" He stopped suddenly, as though afraid to say too much, and added: "never mind; my troubles must always be a secret. So we will change the subject. What have you for supper? I am hungry."

I emptied the contents of my bag upon the ground, and Hugh said:—

"Buffalo steaks. We must have a fire. Come, Tim, let us get some wood. Silvershot is on the sick list."

"It's a bad foot he has," said Tim, "so come along, and we'll leave him to nurse it."

Unfastening their hatchets from their belts, my companions began to lop off the driest boughs from the adjacent trees; and while so engaged, I nursed my foot, as Tim termed it, and watched Hugh Howard's movements.

He was, without exception, the handsomest man I have ever seen; and his features, except when disturbed by angry emotions, were almost feminine.

The short black curling locks that graced his well-shaped head, and his large dark eyes would have given him that pallid sickly hue so general among dark people but for the peculiar hue of his skin, for he was as nearly as red-complexioned as a Comanche Indian; and it was this peculiarity that had gained him the appellation of Red Hugh.

The buffalo steaks, though rather dry, were not bad eating after undergoing a good scorching from the pine branches; and when our supper was over and the pipes lighted, we rolled ourselves in our blankets and lay near the blazing fire, chatting of our exploits when hunted by the Crows from their territory.

Tim Delany suddenly changed the conversation by starting up on one elbow and clutching his rifle as though he had detected the snake-like advance of a rascally Sioux.

"What's the matter, Tim?" I asked; "a redskin in range?"

"Faith, no, Silvershot; but I was thinking the ghost of one might come this way."

"The ghost of one!" said Hugh. "Surely you don't believe that nonsense about the Spectre Warrior?"

"Faith, I do," said Tim, "seeing as how I've seen him twice."

Red Hugh laughed at Tim's earnestness, and looked towards me as though inquiring whether I believed in the supernatural presences.

"I suppose you will laugh at me," I said, "for I believe that story, although I have not had the honour of seeing his ghostship."

Red Hugh did laugh, a prolonged roar, that made me feel anything but pleased.

"Don't be riled, Silvershot," he said; "really I could not help laughing at the idea of an old hunter like yourself taking in such nonsense."

"It's no nonsense," I said, "that is if Tim Delaney has spoken the truth, and I have no cause to doubt his word, never having discovered any of his statements to be false."

"His imagination, perhaps, has made him fancy he saw the shadowless warrior, eh, Tim?"

"The divil a bit!" answered my Hibernian friend; "it's no fancy when a man fires at a spirit and his bullet is sent back to him."

Red Hugh looked very grave as he asked—

"Has this really occurred to you?"

"Faith it has, and here's the bullet."

Hugh examined the piece of lead carefully, and handed it back to Tim, saying—

"This is very strange, and shakes my faith a little."

"Have you heard it before?" I asked.

"I have," Red Hugh answered, "and I have the story that caused the spirit's appearance."

"The cause!" Tim and I exclaimed.

"Yes, it's known at all the settlements round about here; and many's the time the warrior's ghost has been hunted by both whites and Indians."

"And they never caught him?"

"No," said Hugh; "the phantom has returned the bullets fired at him, and admonished those who felt bold enough to follow after——"

"He spoke to them, ye mane?"

"Yes, Tim, admonish, which means he told them to keep out of——"

"The same as he told me, by the powers! Well, and did they?"

Red Hugh gave a merry laugh, as he said—

"Yes, the cowards ran like skeered cattle, and hid themselves until the ghost had left their vicinity."

"Where was that?" I asked, for I knew our friend could draw the long-bow very freely.

"Pine Valley, for one place," he said; "there are several others, both white settlements and Indian villages, I could name; but this one will suffice for the strange and terrible events connected with the Spectre Warrior's appearance."

Red Hugh shuddered as he spoke, and a sad light shone in his dark eyes.

I was, to use an Americanism, "pretty considerably" interested in my companion's statement by this time, and felt quite as eager to hear the remainder of the story as my friend, Tim, who sat open-mouthed listening to every word that fell from Hugh's lips.

"What events do you speak about?" I asked. "Surely, his spectreship does not fly away with women and children when it vanishes in a cloud of blue smoke?"

Hugh looked up, and an expression of surprise covered his face as he asked—

"Surely, you have heard the whole of the story?"

"Considering we have been two months out on the track of two of the six of our fellows who so mysteriously disappeared, I don't know how we could hear anything of the doings amongst either settlers or redskins."

"True, I had forgotten that. Light up again, and I will tell you."

We refilled our pipes, took an extra turn in our blankets, and prepared to listen.

"I think it was about nine months ago," said Hugh, "that a gang of horse-stealers turned up at Pine Valley, and after securing all the cattle that were worth taking, they set fire to the dry grass and made for the prairie, but a heavy shower of rain came down and saved the settlement, so the men made tracks after the thieves, and falling in with a village of friendly Indians, borrowed their horses, and were soon close upon the filcher's heels."

"They came up with them near the rocky hills, and there was a fight, in which the settlers got the worst of it, and had to return, leaving a third of their number on the field.

"The horse thieves had their women and children up among the hills, so when the settlers had gone there was a drunken carouse in honour of the victory.

"Whisky did its work; and during the night the settlers, aided by a party of Indians, fell upon the drunken brutes, and wiped them out, men, women, and children, not one was spared.

"Surely," I began, but Hugh cut me short by saying—

"You are about to say the red men did this devil's work; you are wrong, it was done by both. Aye, the whites were the worst, for in their savage frenzy they imitated the Indians by scalping the slain."

"Horrible!" I remarked. "Most horrible!"

"The Lord preserve us from such devils!" said Tim, "for devils they must have been."

"Fiends incarnate!" Hugh answered; "but not worse than many others. Well, amongst the women who were so pitilessly killed was a young girl famed for her good looks; she was shot through the throat and scalped.

"This girl had two suitors, so the story goes, one an Indian chief, the other a young hunter, and when the news reached them of the Rock Hill massacre they started to put the body of her they had loved under the earth.

"Chance brought them to the spot at the same moment, and instead of mourning over the poor girl's death, they turned upon each other like tigers, and fought with knife and tomahawk over the dead bodies that were lying around.

"One was killed. The story says the Indian's body was found most frightfully mutilated when a party of the settlers came to bury those they had murdered."

Red Hugh paused, as though the recital of the horrible story had unnerved him.

I handed over my flask; and after a sip of the vile spirit it contained, he resumed :—

"They saw the young hunter went mad after he had killed his former rival, and was never heard of after. But, stay; I had almost forgotten the most horrible part of the story. On the young girl's neck there was the marks left *by human teeth*."

Hugh paused again, and shook as though attacked by the swamp fever.

My flask restored him a second time; and Tim and I had a taste of the spirit, for our companion's story gave us a chill.

"It seemed," continued Hugh, "that a white or red savage had not been content with the bullet and scalping knife, but, in their eagerness for revenge, had tried to tear the poor girl's flesh. My goodness! Silver-shot, it seems too horrible to be true."

"It does; but go on, for I feel rather queer, and shall be glad when the story is over."

The Lord be good to us!" muttered Tim, "and keep us from such monsters."

"I am near the end," said Hugh. "Well, the hunter went mad, and perhaps devoured by wild animals, and the Indian dead; so there was no one left to avenge the girl's death. So the settlers and the Indians thought. When lo! the spectre of the Indian chief suddenly made its appearance, and every place it visits, no matter whether it is the red man's wigwam or the settler's village, some of the community are sure to be found lying stark and stiff, a bullet-hole through the throat, the scalp gone, and the marks of a set of teeth on the throat. Now, Silver-shot, I have done, and I hope you will sleep well after hearing my story."

I drew a deep breath, and was about to reply, but Tim jumped from where he was sitting, and came over to my side.

"Silvershot," he said, "it's no wonder the dogs didn't see the ghost, and it's a mighty wonder we hadn't the hole in our throats, and our scalps gone, and the teeth-marks in our throats. Do you hear that, Silvershot?"

"I do, Tim Delany, but if it is ghost or devil the first time it comes within range of my rifle I will try a shot at it."

"So will I," said Red Hugh; "that is the very reason of my being in these parts, for I don't believe a word about the ghost being but thin air."

"The devil a trigger will I pull," said Tim, as he cast a fearful glance over his shoulder; "the devil a shot will I try again. Ugh, scalped and shot through! But, I say, Hugh, why don't the spirit keep to the place where the settlers and the Indians live, not come here and wander about worse than any ghost?"

"That's the mystery," said Hugh; "but it is supposed the spectre means to wipe out every man, woman, and child that's now living, and the course he has taken seems to warrant this belief."

I heard Tim's teeth chatter as I turned over on my side to try and sleep off the weight of horror that oppressed my brain.

CHAPTER III.

I TRY A SHOT AT THE SPECTRE.

I MUST have slept some time before I awoke with a sudden start, and a peculiar sensation creeping all over my body, a feeling I can only liken to a stream of cold water trickling down my back.

I lay perfectly still for a few seconds, and the distant cries of the solitary night birds and the demoniacal yells of a tribe of monkeys, which were perched upon an adjacent tree, did not improve the agreeable sensations I experienced.

"This is childish," I thought, and I tried to shake off my nervousness, "quite childish."

I raised myself upon my left elbow and looked keenly, and I saw Tim Delaney fast asleep near the trunk of the large pine, and within a few feet of the spot I reclined upon Hugh Howard was seated.

It was too dark at that moment for me to see whether Hugh was asleep, for the moon had become obscured by a mass of black clouds.

"Are you awake?" I asked, and stretched forth my hand to touch my companion.

"Yes," he answered; "and marvelled very much how you could sleep during such a storm."

"A storm!" I repeated, sitting up. "Yes, you are right. Why, I'm soaked with the rain."

"And to judge from appearances," Hugh said, pointing to the place I had just risen from, "you have been in the way of that peaceful stream the rain has caused to flow down the incline."

I placed my hand upon the ground, and felt the muddy water trickling past within a few inches of my back, and laughed outright.

"What are you laughing at?"

"Because I was fool enough to imagine a cold sensation was creeping over me, all through that confounded story of yours, when, after all, it is the rain puddle that has found its way between my collar and my skin, phew! Where's the rifles, they will be useless if they are wet?"

"Tim has them under his blanket, so they are——"

Hugh paused, started to his feet, and listened intently, then answered—

"Did you hear that?"

"I heard those infernal monkeys," I said, "and the rain dripping from the trees, that's all."

"All! Hark, there it is again. Man, you must be deaf; it is a woman's scream. Do you hear it now?"

I did, and most inexpressible was the sensation that followed. Ugh, it was like the wail of a human being in its last agony.

"My rifle," exclaimed Hugh; "they are scalping a woman, and I——"

He snatched his piece from under Tim's blanket and fled, crashing his way through the thick underwood, and beating down the long grass with the butt of his weapon.

"The Lord preserve us!" said Tim Delany, sitting up; "what's the matter, Silvershot?"

"You are as wise as I am, Tim," I answered. "Hugh Howard has rushed away like a lunatic because he heard a noise like—like——"

"What, Silvershot? Man alive, speak out!"

"Like a woman screaming out."

"And did you hear it, Silvershot?"

"Well, I did, Tim Delany."

"And standing there all this time without putting a foot—— Oh, holy moth——"

Tim rolled over as a prolonged war whoop came upon our ears.

"My rifle, Tim. Come on, we must see what devilment the Sioux are up to."

"Give me your hand, Silvershot," said Tim, "for the blanket has got twisted round me legs, and get up I can't."

"I assisted Tim, and in so doing discovered the cause of his sudden somersault. It had been his intention to jump to his feet when the unearthly war whoop rang out, but the wet blanket being around his ankles had caused him to make an undignified descent.

Protecting the locks of our rifles from the rain drops that fell from the trees, we started in the direction of the savage yells—the dogs Ben and Jip trotting on in front.

Most of my readers, I have no doubt, are pretty familiar with written descriptions of an American backwood, to such I would say skip the next few sentences; to those who are not, read and remember what you read, and you will have a tolerable idea of a bit of wild country.

The place where we had rested for the night was the side of a small hill, overgrown with the most luxurious vegetation.

When the moon shone out for a few minutes the view of the country below was so magnificent and enchanting that the most material and ambitious of human beings could not fail to become meditative when thus face to face with God's wondrous work.

To the right was a mighty forest where the masses of the stately pine and the gigantic maple intermingle and formed a shelter for thousands of wondrous birds and strange animals.

On the left the waters of two large streams met bubbling and seething, as though striving for mastery, then the waters mingled and swept along in majestic beauty.

Bounded by the forest on the one side and the river on the other was a large plain, covered with long grass and fragrant shrubs, the former growing over six feet high; and by the movement of the spear-like blades of grass on various parts of the prairie we knew that several prowling beasts of prey were creeping about in quest of food; but worse still for us, the crafty red men were at their evil work amongst the long grass.

We kept clear of the open ground by strik-ing a path within the outer belt of trees, the trunks of which would serve as an additional means of defence should an attack be made by the enemy.

So far we had struck no sign of the path followed by Hugh Howard, so I began to feel some anxiety respecting our comrade's fate.

"The divil a red man's hereabouts," said Tim, suddenly, "for I have watched the dogs ever since we started."

"I have watched them, too," I said; "either their scent is at fault, or the wind takes it off——"

"Nonsense, man alive," and Tim held up his head, "that wind comes straight from the prairie to here."

So it was, and I began to feel something, puzzled to account for this phenomena.

"As for Hugh," Tim continued, "it's little fear we need be after feeling for his safety, for he's as cunning as a Sioux, and as brave as a Comanche; besides there hasn't been a report of a rifle yet, so he's all safe."

"I hope so," I answered, "but did you not see the prairie grass waving about as we came down the hill?"

"Faith I did, and that's a sign the beasts are out looking for their supper. The divil a red man——"

A shrill scream came from the plain, then a loud shout, the report of a rifle, and a shriek of despair.

Old hands as we were, we stood petrified, and gazed in each other's faces, as though a spell had fallen upon our faculties.

"Silvershot," said Tim, in a low voice, "there's some divil's work going on amongst the prairie grass. Send the dogs forward, and we'll follow."

I gave the dogs the signal to go on, and they ran forward, and were soon lost amongst the thick vegetation.

As a precautionary measure we put fresh priming to our rifles and awaited the return of the dogs.

There was a rustling amongst the grass, and Ben, the oldest of the pair, ran to my feet, and began to whine piteously.

"Come on, Tim, the matter is getting worse; and ghost, man, or devil, I'll see the end of it."

My blood was roused, and I waited not to ascertain whether Tim followed me or not, but he was close to my heels, and as we struck a path through the high grass I heard him growl—

"There's no Indian there; Ben gives mouth at the sight of a red skin."

The clamour made by the old dog as he led the way was answered by Jip.

We were within one hundred yards of the place when—ugh!—a shudder comes over ne when I think of it—the ground became clear of grass or shrub and in the centre of the cleared spot stood the weird form of the Spectre Warrior.

I heard Tim's cry of horror as we both instinctively came to a halt.

My terror was but momentary; the next, my rifle was at my shoulder, the muzzle covering the ghastly warrior's breast.

Was the figure mortal, a man assuming the disguise to frighten the settlers, his last moment had come.

Such were my thoughts as I held my breath to take a surer aim; then the hammer fell; there was a flash and a mocking laugh from the spectre, who stood erect and defiant within forty paces of the muzzle of a piece that never missed.

Following the demon's mocking laugh a voice said—

"Take back your bullet and beware, or your life will pay for this."

A hard substance struck my breast as the figure spoke, and stooping mechanically I picked up the bullet that had so recently left the rifle I held.

CHAPTER IV.

BUCKSKIN BILL, THE TRAPPER.

DAZED by the spectre's words and the return of the bullet, the yelling of the dogs, who were by this time together at the place we were making for, sounded like the mocking yells of a legion of demons, and I put my hand to my forehead and reeled like a drunken man.

"He's gone," I heard Tim exclaim; "and may the curse of the crows go with him."

I looked in the direction of the clear space, and grasping Tim's arm, said—

"Come, come, let us go forward; do you hear the dogs?"

"I do" (my companion held me back as he spoke); "but, man alive, you mustn't go."

"Were there a legion of fiends hidden among the priarie grass, I would do. Do not hold me, Tim."

"But, Silvershot, you are mad. Let us go back."

"I am mad. Good Heavens! what fearl thing was that we saw?'

"A ghost, Silvershot; so let us——"

The yelling of the dogs ceased for a while, en recommenced with redoubled vigour.

I wrenched myself from Tim Delany's nervous grasp, and plucking my long knife from its sheath, started forward.

"I'm with you," exclaimed Delany, drawing his tomahawk from his belt; "go on, Silvershot."

I could not repress a shudder as I passed over the ground where the spectre had ap-

peared, and to keep up my courage, I heard Tim's teeth chatter audibly.

Not a braver or a better man ever lived than Tim Delany, nor was I without a certain amount of pluck; but I am not ashamed to confess that the pair of us were at that moment in as great a "funk" as ever were two schoolboys crossing a country churchyard after dark.

The dogs left off barking when they heard us breaking through the long grass, and for a moment we were at fault as to what direction to take.

"Where-away, Ben?" I cried. "Whereaway, good dog?"

The animal heard my voice, and replied with a piteous whine—

"This way," said Tim, as he ran forward, and the tall vegetation closed over him.

The next moment I heard a cry of terror, and the words—

"This way, Silvershot, this way, for the love of heaven!"

The moon shone out with spectral brilliancy as I dashed to Tim's side, and when my eyes fell upon the spectacle that had caused his hurried exclamation, I felt rooted to the spot—where the grass had been beaten down by the blood-bedabbled form of a young girl.

She was dead, and the white face looked whiter under the pale light that stood upon it.

The neck-partings of her dress were torn open, and about an inch above the collarbone the blood was oozing out from a bullet wouud.

Her forehead was besmeared by the red stream; and as I stooped over the ghastly form, I shook with horror, for the girl's long hair had been shaven from her head.

She had been scalped, and to complete the soul-stirring sight, there were the marks of teeth on her neck.

The demon, or whatever it was, had added another victim to avenge the well-hid massacre, and the strangely-horrible story of the Spirit Warrior's mission upon earth was complete in every detail.

There was a faint hope in my heart, that the girl I thought so fearfully mutilated, might still have life enough left in her to tell us how she came to that wild spot, for her appearance was as mysterious as her death.

My mind filled with this thought, I knelt beside the yet warm body; and before raising her head, I placed my knife upon the ensanguined grass.

"She breathes!" I exclaimed, but the next moment I allowed the ghastly hand to fall back as I added—"No, it is but the air coming from her throat

"Poor girl!" said Tim, "she is dead enough, but the wonder is how she came here."

"That is strange, very strange," I answered, mechanically, "for there is no settlement near this part."

"There's a Cherokee village somewhere beyond the wood yonder, but she is not a Cherokee."

"No, Tim, her parents are Whites, and she must have been very handsome. Ugh!"

I started back, for the closed eyelids opened by the contraction of the severed muscles of the head, and the glassy fixed horrible stare of the girl's blue eyes seemed to rival that upon my face.

"This is awful," said Tim, in a suppressed voice; "it seems as if she was looking at us."

"It is horrble, Tim, and I pray Heaven I may never behold such a sight again."

"Amen! The Lord be good to us! Come, Silvershot, let's get away, for we can do no good now. Poor girl, she's past that."

"We can bury her, Tim; so off with your jacket, lad, and we'll make her last bed."

We selected a spot about a dozen yards from where the body lay; and cutting down the grass, threw it aside, and, with our tomahawks, began to fashion the grave.

We worked for some time in silence. The events of that night had unstrung our nerves.

Suddenly Tim paused to rest himself, and, wiping the perspiration from his brow, exclaimed—

"Where's Hugh?"

"I had quite forgotten the backwoodsman until that moment; and resting from my toil, I repeated—

"Ah, where's Hugh?"

"There's no roads about here," said Tim, "so maybe he's in amongst the grass, now lurking about; send Ben after him."

I whisted for the dog, and to my surprise the call was unanswered.

I whistled for the younger animal with a similar result.

Tim stepped out of the grass and went to look for the dogs, and I saw him standing with his back turned towards the dreadful object that lay upon the trampled grass.

"The dogs are not here," he called out; "sound the whistle, Silvershot."

Attached to a hempen cord I had a small whistle, made from the tip of a buffalo horn, and this blown hard could be heard for nearly half-a-mile.

It was very rarely I used this, for the Indians had by some means found out who was the whistler, and their memory not being relieved from the silver button business, I did not at all times deem it prudent to apprise them of my whereabouts.

"Most likely," I said, "they have gone to meet Hugh Howard."

"Maybe," said Tim, "so we will wait and see if he comes, for there may be some rascally redskins hereabouts who would hear the buffalo whistle."

"Most likely," I said, "so come back and we will finish this poor girl's grave."

Tim had begun to return and by the time he had taken half-a-dozen steps he increased his pace to a run and exclaimed—

"Did you hear that Silvershot?"

"I do not hear anything, Tim, except——"

"Listen, man alive, listen!"

I did so by placing my ear close to the ground.

"What is it, Silvershot?"

"I could almost swear the wind brings with it a sound very much like the tramp of a body of men."

"Scarcely that, hereabouts," said Tim, stepping into the half-formed grave. "Maybe it's a buffalo or two going to their feeding grounds."

"Perhaps so," I said rising. "Oh, here's the dogs."

The animals broke through the grass as I spoke, and began jumping around me.

"Down! Down! what's the matter, Ben? Hey, Jip, good dog. What's the matter?"

The animals turned in the direction of the sound I had heard, and ran to and fro.

"Buffaloes, Tim," I said, "or these brutes would not be so pleased."

"Or Hugh Howard, coming this way," said Tim; "for they are remarkably fond of Hugh."

"Hugh Howard," I answered, "wear mocassins. Even if he wore long boots, h could not make the noise I first heard."

"Maybe not, but he's coming, or the dogs wouldn't be wagging their tails so. No matter what it is, they are friends, so let's get this job over before they come, for I shan't be aisy until that poor thing is under the turf."

We fell to work again, and soon scooped out the earth to the depth of four feet at least, for the wolves were capital resurrectionists, and the poor girl's body would have been scratched out of the earth in a very short time.

The morning was fast coming when our task was concluded, for we had to loosen the ground with the blades of our tomahawks, and scrape out the earth with our hands.

We were glad when the mournful business had got so far, for the sight of the mutilated body would, we knew, be more horrible to look upon when the golden sunshine shone above the prairie, and the light streaks in the eastern horizon warned us that the dawn of day was near at hand.

"Silvershot," said Tim, as we stood over the body, "maybe it would be as well to search the poor creature's clothes, and see if there is anything in the pockets that will tell us where she came from, for it's mighty strange her being here."

"A good thought, Tim."

With a gentle hand I drew forth the contents of her dress pocket; they were few and simple.

A white pocket handkerchief, a small leathern case containing needles, thread, and a thimble, and a Prayer-book, with a metal clasp.

I opened the book, and after some difficulty made out the inscription written inside the cover. It was this—

"Jenny Heywood,

"A birthday present from her father."

I had just finished reading this to Tim when the tall grass all around us was torn aside, and twenty rifles were levelled at our breasts.

"Catched, anyhow, this time, ye varmints."

I knew the owner of the voice; it was Buckskin Bill, the trapper.

CHAPTER V.

AN UNPLEASANT PREDICAMENT.

WILLIAM WALTERS, or Buckskin Bill, so called from the rather unusual nature of the nether garments he wore, which were nothing more or less than an old pair of buckskin breeches—no doubt once the property of an English fox-hunting squire.

Buckskin and I had travelled many a long mile together up the Missouri some six or seven years before this unpleasant renewal of our acquaintance.

I was but a youngster then, a kind of apprentice to the trade of catching animals and selling their fur, and Bill, though my master, was a jolly companion, and very partial to his pupil.

Remembering this, I turned so eagerly at the sound of his voice, and said—

"Old Buckskin, as I'm alive!"

The trapper lowered the butt of his rifle and extended his hand a little way, then quickly withdrew it, saying—

"No, lad; old Bill never gives his paws to one of your kind, no matter if it was his own brother; still, he's sorry for you, lad, But, cuss yer! you ought to know better."

I looked at the old fellow, and there was such a peaceful expression upon his face that I could not help thinking something was wrong.

I looked from him to the crowd of men who formed a circle round Tim and I, and saw them furiously gazing at us.

They were strong-built men, and from their garb I imagined they were settlers going out westward.

Buckskin Bill's presence warranted this supposition, for I had heard he often gave his services as a guide to the new-comers, and to make this supposition a certainty, I saw the men lower their rifles when he lowered his.

He was not only their guide, but their leader; that was very evident

It was but the work of a moment to understand all this, and I was about to ask old Bill the meaning of his strange words, when a half-stifled sob caused me to start and look round, and a suppressed cry of vengeance to come from the lips of the hitherto silent group of settlers.

Looking towards the dead body, I saw a man's form stooping over the remains of what had so recently been a beautiful girl.

I saw a lock or two of his gray hair beneath the brim of the settler's hat, and my heart ached at the sight, for instinct told me the kneeling figure that shook so with silent agony, was the poor girl's father.

I made a step toward's Buckskin Bill; it was my intention to ask him to take his companions out of sight of the father's agony; but ere I could speak, he raised his rifle, the muzzle in line with my forehead, and sternly exclaimed—

"Keep back, young fellow, don't move an inch, or by the Great Father I will save the rope a job; you too," he added, turning to Tim, "keep quiet, and don't stir till I tell yer, that won't be until we see whether deer-hide thongs will hold fast and strong. Don't forget; keep still."

"Man alive!" said Tim angrily, "don't you know us?"

"Aye," replied Buckskin Bill, "I knew ye both when ye were good and honest men, but I know ye not now ye are thieves and murderers."

"Bill Walters," I exclaimed, raising my rifle by the muzzle, "if you repeat those words I'll beat your skull in with the butt end of this piece."

"Take their guns away," said the old trapper; "case we have to do the business with a bullet instead of the rope."

Resistance was out of the question, for the angry men closed upon us, took our weapons away, and under old Bill's directions bound our limbs with deer-hide thongs.

"Now, ye varmints," the old man said, "will ye deny this work, eh, when we've caught you in the very act?"

I staggered when the meaning of the trappers came to my brain, and Tim Delany gave a howl of rage, and said—

"Holy Mother, do ye mean to accuse us of this poor creature's murder?"

"Well," said old Bill, "if ye are not guilty without trial, no men ever were; that's

Buckskin's opinion. What do you say, lads?"

He beckoned towards the group of settlers, and they responded with a vengeful cry.

Matters were getting very serious, for I saw more than one of the men examining the priming of their pieces.

"Buckskin," I said, "listen to me."

"Aye; every man ought to have a fair hearing afore he's strung up. Go on."

"We are innocent."

"Aye, it looks like it; your hands are all over blood."

"Of course they are," said Tim. "Didn't we take up the poor girl's head when the dogs found her here?"

"Most likely," Buckskin Bill said; "but how comes this here?"

He picked up my knife from the grass, and I shuddered when I saw the blade was covered with blood.

"I placed it there," I said. "Good Heavens, you do not—"

A cry of rage came from one of the settlers and interrupted my speech, and to the horror of all present, the man held up the girl's long auburn hair with the scalp adhering to it.

The settler had picked up the ghastly trophy about six or seven yards from the body, so close that we must have passed within a few inches of it; but the morning light had not come to show us where it lay.

"Curse ye, for a lying dog," said old Bill. "Will you deny it now? Your hands red, your knife-blade covered with blood, and the scalp close by—"

"We are as inno——"

The trapper turned savagely upon me, and grinding his teeth, said—

"Open yer coward mouth again, and I'll stop yer tongue with this."

He clutched his rifle, and knowing the man so well, discretion kept me silent.

"What's that over there?" he exclaimed, when his eyes fell upon the newly-made grave. "A hole! to hide the girl's body in. Well, by the eternal, I never came across such a pair of devils in all my days. "Well," he added, turning to Tim, "I suppose ye didn't dig that hole, did ye?"

"Faith we did," was Tim's answer; "and there's our tomahawks lying beside it now."

"Oh, ye did that. What were ye going to put in it, eh, my young gallows bird?"

"Don't answer him, Tim," I said, "for every word you utter will only add to our seeming guilt."

"Ay, seeming guilt," sneered the trapper. "Well, I hope ye will get clear of it, but it won't be with my consent, and I've pretty much sway with these chaps here."

The girl's father rose from beside the corpse, and in a broken voice said—

"Her pockets have been rifled."

"Sure to be," growled old Bill. "What else do you think the varmints murdered her for?"

I writhed under the mental agony I suffered, and Tim Delany I saw was white with suppressed passion.

"Which of you," Buckskin asked, "has taken the things from the girl, eh, ye varmints?"

I made no reply, but Tim, turning upon the trapper, said—

"By the powers, old man, if my hands were loose, I'd choke you for those words."

"Aye," Buckskin Bill grimly retorted "no doubt of it; but the choking will be done another way, ye varmint. Now, then, which of you robbed the girl?"

The state of mental excitement I was in quite drove the recollection of the articles I had taken from the murdered girl's dress pocket being in my possession.

"Search 'em," the trapper said to the men who were near him. "Shake the varmints up."

The command was instantly obeyed, and when the prayer-book and other articles were found in the breast-pocket of my hunting jacket, a yell came from the settlers, and but for old Buckskin, Tim and I would have been sacrificed on the spot.

"Keep back," he said, "keep back; let the varmints have a fair trial. Surely ye needn't trouble about killing 'em no, for we've got enough ag'in 'em to string up a dozen such wolves."

"Buckskin Bill," I said, "surely you would not help to put the halter round the necks of the innocent, for we are as innocent of this atrocious deed as any among you. Will you listen to me, and hear how we came to this accursed spot?"

Buckskin gnawed the ends of his shaggy moustache, and crossing his hands upon his rifle muzzle, said—

"Well, there's no harm in hearing what ye have to say, so while the chaps are making a litter to convey the body you can speak. Go on."

With the exception of the four men engaged in the construction of the litter, the settlers crowded around, anxious to hear the defence a man could make who had been seemingly caught red-handed in the commission of a most atrocious crime.

I spoke slowly and calmly, and gave every word its just emphasis, as I told the story of the spiritual vision and our finding of the body; and when I had concluded the old trapper threw his rifle over his shoulder, and tersely said—

"Bring 'em along, lads."

CHAPTER VI.

SENTENCED TO DEATH.

THE settlers, I afterwards learnt, came from Franklin, a town westward of the Missouri; and the place towards which we were going was a small valley leading to a fork on the Red River.

They had chosen this spot for their home, and a lovelier abode could not have been found in those majestic regions.

It was but a mile to the valley from the spot w'ere the murdered girl was found, but to Tim and I the distance seemed twenty times as far.

We had been in many strange and perilous positions during our wild life, had stood face to face with the grim tyrant, but never before had we experienced the sensations that occupied our minds during that short walk from the prairie to the new settlement.

To die battling hand to hand with the untamed but gallant red men was a fitting end to a hunter's life.

To fall under the claws and fangs of a ferocious animal was to die horribly; but death in the form that now threatened us was too horrible to contemplate, that I could not bear its approach with that fortitude that had supported me in other trials.

If guilt could be read in the dejected countenance and drooping form, both Tim and I were guilty: for two more wretched-looking subjects than we were would have been hard to find, even amongst those whose evil deeds had brought them to the scaffold.

I essayed several times to draw the men who guarded us into conversation, but no heed was paid to my words. They seemed not to hear me, but marched on with a slow and solemn step in accordance with the gloomy determination apparent upon their faces.

It was a mournful procession. In front was the bier and its ghastly load; behind this a grey-haired man, with lowered head and drooping gait.

A group of the settlers followed the stricken father, then came the guard and their prisoners.

Old Buckskin Bill brought up the rear; and I could hear him talking to the dogs who followed us.

"Never could have thought it was them as did it," the old trapper said. "My dogs, you will want a master soon. You shall have one, a good one, too; I'll be your master when we've rid this part of the Prairie of these two varmints."

After a little time he resumed:—

"I liked the lad once, and thought better things of him. Well, there's no telling how the tree will grow—no telling; for he promised well as a sapling. Free of foot, ready and keen with his eyes, and would as soon face a red man or a jaguar as trap a beaver. Well, women-haters is a queer thing at the best. Back, dogs! Keep here, or you'll taste this bit of a deer-hide thong I always carry with me."

After he had journeyed about a quarter of a mile farther, Buckskin broke out again with these characteristic words:—

"Well, after all the trouble I took with that lad, that he should come to this. Skin his ungrateful hide! Why, I made a man of him. The end of it is to be a yard of rope, if they've as much; only—hem!—if they ain't, I've as much deerhide thong as will do the business."

The reader will be kind enough to imagine the state of mind I was in during the time my old friend Buckskin Bill was so coolly speculating upon my disgraceful exit from the world.

"The divil take the old man," Tim said. "What a mercy it would have been had he been scalped before he turned guide to these settlers, who only come to disturb the game, and——"

"It will not matter to us, Tim, who disturbs the game; our days are nearly ended."

"You think so, Silvershot?"

"I do."

"Well, I don't, for we've been in worse fixes than this, and always got clear."

"Never in such a fix as this before, Tim."

"Maybe not, taking it altogether; but, anyhow, I'm thinking we shan't want old Bill's deer-hide thongs."

A drowning man will catch at a straw, so says the musty proverb; and I believe it, for I caught eagerly at the hope shadowed forth in Tim's words—

"Tim," I whispered, "tell me, old comrade, what causes you to think this?"

Well, Silvershot, I'll tell you, and I think you will say the same as I do."

"Quick, man; come, out with it."

"It's just this, Silvershot; there's our friend Hugh Howard, and if he doesn't turn up at the right moment and clear us of this scrape, he's not the man I take him for."

My heart fell, for I knew the excited settlers would not believe a word uttered by one whom they could regard as a companion, who would say anything to clear our two necks from the halter.

"No, Tim," I said; "the hope you hold forth is without foundation; besides the improbability of the settlers believing his statement. How is he to know the road we have taken, for this spongy ground does not show a footprint?"

"Hold your tongue, Silvershot," said Tim. "Now, man alive! do you think I've come

"CATCHED, ANYHOW, THIS TIME, YE VARMINTS."

all this way without leaving a trail for Hugh to follow ?"

I followed Tim's downward glance and saw him dig his heel into the ground at every third step.

This was the danger mark; and I knew if Hugh saw it he would follow us; aye, to the risk of his life.

My hope of freedom again rose within my breast, but as soon fell when I reflected how utterly useless would be the efforts of one man to release us from the hands of those who were so determined upon our destruction.

Had we been nearer the Comanche country—the lands of those splendid Indian cavaliers, whose spears and axes would have reeked in blood to save us—there would have been a chance of escape.

But, alas! we were far from the Comanche hunting grounds, and the remains of the tribe I knew had gone upon the war path in quest of the Bonnaxes.

While my mind was filled with these wretched thoughts, a confused sound struck upon my ear, and looking up, I beheld a group of old men, women, and children, hastening towards us.

We were climbing the valley, and I saw in rear of the coming group the tilts of the settlers' waggons, andsome half-furnished log huts; the axes and saws lying about, as though men had been suddenly called away from their labour.

Give me men to deal with, let the matter be ever so trifling, or fraught with the greatest possible danger.

I make this remark not as a cynical misanthrope, but as a man who has seen some ups and downs in his life.

No sooner did the gentle portion of the community behold the corpse laid on the litter of crossed rifles than they gave a yell, and before the settlers could close around Tim and I were being martyred.

Our hair was torn out by the roots and little rivulets of blood streamed down our faces, for the fair creatures' nails were long, and in some cases would have been all the better for an application of a good stiff nail-brush.

I am not a fastidious man as a rule, but I do abominate dirty nails, let the person be either man or woman.

Buckskin Bill and the dogs soon came to our rescue; the latter making sad havoc with the home-spun and cotton skirts, and the latter charging the gentle creatures with the muzzle of his rifle.

"Now, look here, you women," said old Bill, "let's have fair play; the chaps is guilty, there's no doubt about that, but you needn't fall to and scalp 'em after that fashion. Get back, will ye, ye she devils!"

By upsetting some of our assailants, old Bill forced us from their rampant attentions, and I would have given much to have rubbed my head, for the place where the hair had been plucked out smarted awfully.

Tim, I am sorry to say, was ungallant enough to kick his gentle admirers' shins, and with some effect too, for I saw several limping away as though they were hurt.

"Death! death! Kill them! Kill them if you are men! Shoot them! Hang the lot! Tear to pieces the murderous scoundrels!"

Such was the substance of the cries that came upon our ears, and to which old Buckskin replied—

"All in good time; but we can't do all the ways you ask, leastways not all at once. Suppose we hang them first?"

"No, no, no!"

Buckskin Bill crossed his hands over the muzzle of his rifle and looked at the angry women.

"Keep them back there," he said to the settlers. "Skin their hides. Fust they call out kill 'em in as many ways as there Sundays in the year, then they says 'No;' but any-how it's not for them to judge, it's for the men; so bring the varmints this way."

The varmints, courteous readers, were Tim Delany and your humble servant, Silvershot.

The settlers formed a circle, the centre of which was occupied by Buckskin Bill, Tim Delany, and Silvershot, and the women being denied admittance by their husbands, fathers, and brothers were none the less noisy upon this account; and I firmly believe, if skinning

alive had been a Christian punishment, the fair creatures would have doomed us to it.

Buckskin Bill kept his eyes averted from us as he assumed his position of judge.

"There's not much to be said about this mat-ter," he said, "We all know how the poor girl left the valley to gather the flowers that bloom amongst the prairie grass; we know too that she was a long time away—that's why we followed her trail; and we know how we found her scalped, shot, and bitten."

Old Bill paused, to nerve himself for the concluding portion of his speech.

"We know too," he resumed, raising his voice, "who did this foul work, for we caught 'em in the act—"

"It is a lie!" I began, but was checked by old Bill saying—

"We don't want to put a gag on you, we don't; but if you are not quiet, we shall."

I bit my lips in anger and mortification.

"Having got so far," old Bill resumed, "the only thing now to be done is to say how the varmints shall die. For my idea is that hanging is too good for 'em."

There was a dead silence, even the women, whose tongues had been making such a dia-bolical clatter, ceased, and they came close to the circle, and drawing themselves for-ward, listened intently.

"It's no use," old Buckskin said, "to ask 'em whether they are guilty or not, for we know all what they would say; so be sharp with your judgment, for the sooner they are out of the way the better."

One by one the men stepped forward to give expression to the mode of punishment we were to undergo.

Some were for roasting us alive, and the women clapped their hands when they heard this.

Others were for hanging, and two men who were related to the poor girl proposed we should be served in the same manner as they supposed we had murdered their relative.

Old Bill listened without making any reply to these propositions until the last man stepped forward, then said—

"You've given 'em as many kinds of death as there are wolves on the prairie, but they are none of 'em to my mind like the last man has thought of, so lead the varmints away, and we'll talk over it."

We were taken to a pile of logs, and gruffly told to be seated, one of our guards kindly remarking at the time—

"If you've any prayers to make, be sharp about it, for they will not be long settling your business."

It was quite a work of difficulty for our guards to keep the women from subjecting as to a second edition of their playful attentions.

They were not satisfied that we were sentenced to death without their having a share in the execution, so when they were beaten back from the logs we were favoured with a shower of stones that drew blood from prisoners and guards alike.

CHAPTER VII.
HEARING THE CATARACT.

THE two modes of death suggested by the last speaker were not the pleasantest that could be devised.

The first was the inverted mode. Although I make a feeble joke of it now, at the time it was far from being a subject for mirth.

To return—the Christian settlers thought if we were hung up by one leg to the branch of a tree, overhanging a precipice, we should not only die a most horrible death, but afford good practice to the unskilful shots of the party.

The other mode was quite as cruel.

A few minutes' walk from the valley there was a swift torrent that emptied itself into a gigantic basin; the fall being at the very least one hundred and fifty feet.

We knew the place well, and oft had sat on the opposite side watching huge trunks of uprooted trees borne over the waterfall, hurled into the hissing waters, bent and broken to fragments upon the points of the jagged rocks that formed the bed of the natural reservoir.

The suggestion was that we were to be tied to a log and sent adrift upon the rapids; and for fear we should escape the inevitable death that would follow, the youngest of the settlers were to pepper us with bullets as we were being carried down the stream.

Knowing that one of these kinds of death would be chosen, we sat silent with beating hearts, awaiting the summons to appear before our self-constituted judges.

The summons came—not too soon, for the hopeless anxiety we suffered was as bad, if not worse than hearing the order given for our destruction.

"Bring the varmints this way."

Polite old Buckskin Bill was promptly obeyed, and the "varmints" were taken back to the centre of that group of sullen, savage men; and another shower of stones from the gentle ones grinding the heads of our guards, and by no means improving our personal appearance, for the "ladies" were quite as good marksmen as the boys of Tipperary, who, upon Tim's authority, are called "stone throwers."

"Now," old Buckskin Bill said, "as we are Christians, and not savage red-skins, we'll put you out of your misery as soon as we can, and the way we have decided it is this:

Tim and I no doubt looked a trifle pale at these words, for the idea of quitting the world was not at the moment one to inspire us with heroic feelings.

"You, Silvershot," Buckskin continued, "will be tied to a log, and sent adrift down the rapids, and the water will soon make a jelly of your ill-begotten carcase."

I held my breath, and looked at poor Tim, whose face betrayed a foreknowledge of his doom.

"You, Tim Delany," the old trapper said, "will be hung by the leg to the trunk of the old mora tree that hangs over the cataract, and be shot at until you die. Take 'em away; and Heaven have mercy on their miserable souls."

Our executioners now divided in two parties, and were about to separate Tim and I, when Delany turned angrily, and raising his right foot, sent the man nearest him sprawling.

"Christians, are ye?" Tim said. "Ye are worse than the greatest heathens that ever lived."

"Take 'em away," said old Bill, sternly; "the sooner it is over the better for us all."

CHAPTER VIII.
LASSOING THE LOG.

STIMULATED by Tim's resistance, I burst through the men who surrounded me; and as I strove to free my arms from the thongs that held them, I turned to Buckskin Bill, and said:—

"Listen, old man: you have known me from a boy. Yours was the hand that first taught me to level a rifle; yours the hand that first showed me how to trap an untamed animal; and your lessons in handicraft showed me how to strike a trail either of a red man or a treacherous jaguar. Did you see anything in my nature to make you suppose I could be guilty of—"

"Skin your hide for ye!" the trapper replied. "What matters what your nature shows? Didn't we find you red-handed in the act? Enough has been said. Take them away, my lads."

"Hear me," I shouted, as the men thrust me forward; "if you must murder us, let us die together. Surely you cannot refuse this request?"

"Take the varmints away, lads; off with 'em."

The settlers tore us apart, and the cries of the women added to their fury, for the murdered girl's father had been led away from the corpse, and the women now surrounded it, and filled the air with their lamentations and vengeful cries.

A deer-hide thong was looped around the trunk of a plane tree, and half-a-dozen men dragged it to the bank of a stream. "Many hands make light work" was exemplified in my case, for I was thrown on my back, and lashed firmly to the log.

Old Buckskin stood near, directing the men to make the loops fast; and when it was prepared for my last journey, the trapper pointed to a tree that overhung the cataract, and said—

"There's your companion all ready to hoist when we set you afloat. Are you ready? Have you said your prayers, Silvershot?"

I made no answer; my eyes were fixed with a strange fascination upon the prostrate form of my gallant friend.

Ugh! it was a horrible sight, and one that will never be forgotten.

I thought not of my impending fate; I saw not the clear waters rushing past; heard not the sullen roar of the cataract; for my eyes and ears were all for my comrade.

He lay upon the ground, held down by three strong men. There was a rope, or thong, thrown across the projecting bough of the tree; one end was fastened to Tim's right leg, just above the ankle, the other held by a group of settlers, who waited but Buckskin Bill's signal to haul poor Tim above the seething waters.

His face was towards me, and the ghastly look upon his features told how much he suffered.

"Good-bye, Tim," I shouted, and my voice was husky with emotion. "Good-bye, old comrade; may we meet in a better world than this. Thank Heaven, old fellow, we die innocent of this atrocious crime for which we are to suffer."

He heard not my words, for we were too far away from each other; but I saw his lips moving either in prayer or in giving utterance to a farewell.

"He can't hear you," old Buckskin said, grimly, "so it's waste of breath. You had better have used it to say your prayers, for the time is up. Now, as you are upon the brink of the unknown world, I ask you to confess your guilt, and tell us the motive that caused you to commit such a devilish crime."

"I am innocent," was my reply, "as innocent as yourself, Buckskin Bill. I have told you the truth; more I cannot tell."

"Heaven have mercy upon your black soul!" responded the trapper. "Send him adrift, lad."

I stifled the cry of horror that came to my lips as the log was impelled forward, and thrust into the current.

A shriek came from Tim Delaney at the same moment; and as the rushing waters whirled the log onward, it brought me in view of Tim's form as it rose through the air.

I saw a party of the settlers standing in line, about eighty yards from the tree, and heard the crack of their rifles as they tried to cut the thong that suspended my ill-fated comrade.

My brain then became dizzy, as I was whirled down the current; and the roar of the falling water sounded like a death knell upon my ears.

The distance from where I had started to the cataract was greater than I had supposed.

This was owing to a bend in the river, and, as I believed, around this my course was suddenly checked by the log coming in violent contact with a dense mass of uprooted vegetation and fragments of trees that had collected at that turn in the current.

The water rushed past me, and the serf caused by the obstruction rolled the log over and over, bruising my face and limbs as I bumped against the branches of trees and other waifs that stemmed the rushing waters.

Bruised and torn as I was, a wild hope of rescuing life sprang up in my breast. I sought to free my hands of their bonds and cling to the branches of the floating trees.

This hope became stronger when the log became motionless, and I lay face uppermost, my conveyance wedged firmly amongst the mass of timber.

I had not enjoyed the respite from death many moments when a shout from the left bank of the current caused me to turn my head, and to my horror I beheld several of the settlers running towards the brink, some of them loading their rifles as they hurried forward.

A puff of smoke and the plash of a bullet within a yard of the log told my fate if I escaped the cataract.

A second bullet came nearer the mark, and did me a service, for I found my right hand free, and impelled by a sudden desire to escape the merciless butchering, I pushed aside the impediment to my progress down the current, and once more swept onwards.

I had not gone many yards when the log was dashed against the right bank of the stream, and I felt as though every bone in my carcase had snapped in twain.

The bullets now began to fly plentifully around me, and but for the rolling of the log I must have been riddled like a sieve.

Again I was borne onward, but not before I became sensible that something was closely following me.

I heard a subdued breathing, then a yelp, and I knew that one or both of my dogs were following their master to destruction.

My heart filled at the knowledge of the poor brutes' devotion, and I was about to call out for them to swim ashore, when a puff of smoke came from the centre of a bush on the right bank of the current.

Following this came the report of a rifle, then the bush parted, and to my astonishment the lithe form of Red Hugh stood on the brink.

In his right hand he held the coils of a lasso, and as I swept past he made a "cast."

The thing cut past my head with a hissing noise; the next moment I felt it cutting my legs, and the log was brought to a standstill, the water bubbling and dancing over my face as though angered at losing a victim.

Strong and steady was the pull upon the stout lasso, and its progress towards the bank was hastened by the assistance I gave with my right hand.

I heard the yells of the settlers, who were by this time on the opposite bank, and nearly in a line with my unfortunate body."

"Quick, quick, Hugh! quick for God's sake! or I shall be perforated."

The backwoodsman put forth his strength, and the log went faster towards the bank; but it seemed slow to me, for the shots were coming in pretty fast.

"Pull at the lasso, old fellow," said Hugh, cheerily. "Never mind their plugs. Excited men seldom aim straight, and these fellows are babies with the rif—eh?"

"What's the matter?"

I was close to the bank now, and for a reply Hugh turned the log over, and I found myself in danger of being suffocated, for he threw himself flat upon the ground, as he gave me such an unpleasant immersion.

I heard his defiant laugh a minute after, and the log was righted. A few nicks with the hunting-knife, and bruised, half drowned, and scarcely able to crawl, I was dragged up the bank, and placed behind the bush from which Hugh had emerged.

My senses then forsook me; and when consciousness returned, the backwoodsman was kneeling beside me, my head on his knee, and the neck of a bottle was being forced between my teeth."

"That's right," he said, "open your eyes, and your mouth too. A swig of this will do you good."

I gulped down some of the fiery fluid, and felt much better after it."

"The dirty-minded old rascal!" Hugh continued. "But for my quickness, Silvershot, he would have put a pellet in your skull. Curse him! but I'll be quits with him yet, or my name's not Hugh Howard."

I was able to raise myself on one arm; and looking at the backwoodsman, I feebly asked—

What's the matter, Hugh?"

"Nothing particular," he replied, "but there might have been something not very pleasant had I not turned you over."

"I wondered why you put me face downwards in the water."

"I daresay you did. Well, it was just this. I did not care the flapping of a prairie hen's wing for those fellows who were firing at you; but when I saw old Buckskin Bill about to try a shot, I thought it time to dodge out of the way.

"He's a good shot."

"Yes, curse him; but he needn't have kept his practice up by making a target of you."

"It was through him I was sentenced to be carried over the waterfall, and Tim—but where's poor Delany? Surely they have not——"

"Tim is all right by this time, I hope: for I cut the string that suspended him over the current, and as he is a good swimmer, he will make for the bank. He's sure to see the sign."

"Sign!"

"Did you think I would have left him to drown, after seeing him into the water? You must think me a novice at woodcraft, Silvershot!"

"There's not a better woodsman," I said, "east or west of the Big Prairie than yourself, but how you came to our help in the nick of time, puzzles me."

Red Hugh laughed as he said :—

"Does it, old comrade? Well, I'll soon explain the matter. You remember when that woman's cry was heard?"

"I do."

"I made for the open prairie, and as I crossed the timber, and when I was clear of it, I saw the form of an Indian warrior standing in my path."

"The spectre!"

"Yes. I thought not of the ghostly tradition at the time, so clubbed my rifle to knock him out of the way, for we were so close that it would have been waste of time to use powder and shot."

"Exactly; I understand."

"Well, I made a sweeping blow at the redskin, and my rifle butt meeting with no opposition, struck the ground——"

"Passed through the shadow?"

"I suppose so; but I had not time to ascertain, for I found myself flat-face downwards upon the ground."

Red Hugh gave a strange, discordant laugh, and his eyes had in them an expression of terror.

I attributed this to the effect that his meeting the spectre had had upon his mind. Judging by myself I knew the recollection was not pleasant.

"You know, Silvershot," he continued, "I

am about the last man to believe in ghosts, so looking upon the fact of my rifle having passed through the spectre as a creation of my brain, I jumped to my feet and gave chase to the warrior, who was just passing through the outer belt of timber——"

"Hark, what was that?"

He listened, and looking through the bushes, said—

"A good omen."

"It was a rifle or two spoke."

"True, Silvershot, but still a good omen, for they are firing at Tim Delany, and that proves he fell into the deep water, as I anticipated he would when I cut the thong that—"

"Listen, do you not hear the shouts of the settlers?"

I tried to rise, for the voices seemed so near that I thought they were upon my track.

Lie still," said Hugh, "quiet will do you good; it's those vagabond emigrants who are yelping, and old Buckskin at their head; flay him alive, the old devil! Yelp away, ye curs," he added, as the voices became nearer, "there's a wide current to cross before ye can get here."

"But," I asked, "is there no way of getting across without breasting the current?"

"Yes; there's a portage about thirty miles down the stream, but the yelpers won't try that, for the Bonnaxes are near it."

"Thank God for that. But what about poor Tim?"

"He's safe enough, so I will go on with my yarn, and if you don't interrupt me I shall not tell you one thing twice over. Where did I leave off?"

"The spectre was entering the timber."

"Yes; so I gave chase, and a long and unprofitable one it turned out, for the abominable thing danced about like a will-o'-the-wisp, and I pursued until I was fairly knocked over—"

"One moment, Hugh; what do you think of this affair? the spectre, I mean?"

"What do I think?"

"What is your opinion; do you think it possible there can be such a thing as a ghost?"

"I never did until now, Silvershot; but if this is not one, I should like to know what it is."

"So should I, but go on with your story."

"I made my way back to the prairie, and saw the grass trampled down, and blood stains in several places; I looked farther, and saw a newly-made grave—"

"Tim's work and mine."

"Don't interrupt, there's a good fellow; I shall soon be done."

"All right, Hugh; proceed."

"I wondered what all this could mean, and wondered what had become of Tim and Silvershot, so I followed the tracks, and soon saw by the 'signs' that you were in danger."

"Thanks to Tim," I remarked; "his forethought suggested the danger signs being made as we went along."

"So I soon found out. Well, I got pretty close to you, and when the settlers' women gave you a specimen of their amiable disposition I was hidden in a bush, and saw all that took place."

Hugh indulged in a long fit of laughter at the recollection of the sorry figure I cut when scratched by the women.

"I can't help laughing, old fellow," he said, "when I think of the way in which you tried to butt at them with your head. I suppose you would have used your hands had they been at liberty, eh?"

"I never yet struck a woman," I savagely answered; "but I'm afraid, had my hands been free, I should have floored a few of them."

"I should have done so, I know. Never mind, old chap, you will soon get over the marks of their delicate fingers, and your hair will grow again."

"Yes, yes; that does not trouble me," I pettishly answered, for I saw by the twinkle in Hugh's eyes that he was mightily amusing himself at my expense. "Get on with your story, comrade, for I am anxious about Tim."

"As I told you before, I was very close when the trial was going on, and after you and Tim were sent away, I heard that old cuss Buckskin Bill talking over your punishment; so as soon as I knew what was up I made the preparations that turned out so well."

"In my case, but poor Tim?"

"He's safe, I'll wager my rifle against a redskin's bow and arrows, for I tumbled a couple of logs over the pool he would fall into, and they would keep him up, and by using his hands he will be able to paddle to the opposite side."

"And when he reaches the opposite side, what then?"

"He will see an old tree, the trunk of which I have marked with my tomahawk, the mark he will follow until he reaches us."

I did not feel very much satisfied with Hugh's programme, for there were twenty chances to one against Tim getting safely over the pool.

There was every probability of a stray shot striking Tim, or he might be so weakened by his sufferings while hanging to the tree, that his strength would not be sufficient to keep him afloat after he reached the water.

"Don't be uneasy," said Hugh; he saw by the expression of my face how anxious I felt. "Tim is allright, I'll stake my life upon that, for he was alive when I fired at the thing. Poor devil, he must have felt queer when they were trying to shoot him as he hung."

"Queer, it must have been most horrible agony."

"Aye, it must have been, and——"

"There's one thing surprises me," I said, interrupting Hugh, "that is how you got across the stream so soon."

"Does it. Well, I did not cross the stream, I ran to the precipice, that overhangs the pool beyond the waterfall, and dropped from shrub to shrub until I reached the water, then I crossed."

"Hugh!" I exclaimed, "Buckskin Bill will bring them over the same way."

"The devil. Yes, I'd not thought of that. Lie still, comrade, I will be back soon."

He picked up his rifle, and parting the bushes disappeared, leaving me alone, bruised, weak, and helpless.

CHAPTER IX.

THE YOUNG RAVEN.

HUGH left his spirit flask beside me, and as I felt almost sure my sanguine friend's opinion about everything turning out all right would be exactly the reverse, I took the liberty of transferring its contents to my mouth.

The stimulant restored my shattered system, and I soon felt able had I been in possession of a rifle to use it, but being totally unarmed I felt I could not do better than follow Hugh's advice and lie quiet.

I called the dogs nearer to me, and bidding Ben lie in such a manner that I could use his body for a pillow, I placed my head thereon, and making Jip stretch himself over my feet, I pointed in the direction taken by Hugh, and aroused the dogs' vigilance by saying—

"Watch their guard, dogs, watch them!"

The animals understood me, and having cocked their ears they fixed their eyes in the direction pointed out.

I was safe now from any sudden attack, for the faithful creatures would not have allowed even my companions to break through the bushes without giving me timely notice of their approach.

Everything remained quiet for some time, and, overcome by the potency of the contents of Hugh's flask, I gradually closed my eyes and fell into a deep sleep.

I must have remained a couple of hours unconscious to all that had so recently troubled my mind, for when I awoke the sun was at its zenith.

I started up before my eyes were well open, and felt for the handle of my tomahawk, for the cause of my awakening was the pressure of a hand upon my throat.

My belt was without a weapon, and to my relief I found there was no present need for one, for the hand, as I supposed it to be, was the heavy paw of my favourite dog, who was trying to arouse me, and sniffing the air at the same time.

"What is it, boy?" I asked, "what is it, good dog?"

Ben got up when I raised my hand, and joining his companion, they ran a few yards from me, then returned, growling angrily.

Life seemed sweeter than ever after the narrow escape I had had of losing it, so, seeing the dogs' bared fangs were turned towards a party of the settlers whom they had by this time began to look upon as foes, I jumped to my feet, and despair giving me strength I tore a stout branch from the nearest tree, and hastily tearing off the leaves and young shoot I resolved to sell my life dearly.

There was one thing surprised me—the dogs, instead of going in the direction taken by Hugh, faced exactly opposite, and this made me imagine a party of the angry men had crossed the current and outflanked Hugh, whose rifle would, had they crossed the pool here, despatched many of the foe ere they could reach the opposite side.

I was well aware his piece had not spoken, had it done so I should have started up immediately.

It was an anxious time for me when the rustling of the leaves told the close approach of my foes.

I stood with my club uplifted, ready to brain the first man who came within its reach, and the dogs crouched lower and lower, uttering short angry cries.

Another minute and they would be upon me. My heart beat faster as I saw the tops of the bushes moving, then they separated, and to my astonishment an Indian chief advanced towards where I stood.

I called the dogs to keep back, and lowering my club extended my right hand, which was immediately grasped by the young savage.

"The young Raven," I said, "is welcome to his white brother's eyes—very welcome."

"Silvershot," said the Indian, "is no less welcome to the young Raven; but why do I find him thus?"

He saw I was bruised, and that my face bore marks left by the gentle interference of the settlers' women.

I told him the cause of my defenceless condition, and of the scars I bore, and the young brave shrugged his shoulders, and said:—

"The white hunter, who is the brother of the chief of my tribe, must wipe out the marks left by the hands of the squaws. Ugh!"

He placed his gaily-ornamented tomahawk in my hands, and seeing I was about to refuse, pointed to the long knife that hung from his wampum belt.

"The young Raven," he said, "does not require arms; he is scouting, and being fleet of foot, can keep clear of the Bonnaxes."

These words explained his presence, the Comanches were near at hand, and in all probability driving the Bonnaxes from their village.

I had not seen the young Raven since I left the Comanche country, and at that time he had not been upon the war path.

He was young, very young, to wear the eagle's feathers in the circlet that bound his long silken locks, but I remembered he was related to Uwato, and gave such promise of being a good warrior, that he was no doubt placed among the fighting men of his tribe earlier than usual.

A brave, handsome lad he looked in his picturesque dress, and every movement he made as he listened for any sound that could be heard above the dull roar of the cataract, reminded me of the lithe and stealthy movements of a tiger.

I had told him of our escape, and Red Hugh's errand in search of Tim, he soon became anxious that we should go and ascertain what had become of my companion.

"But the Bonnaxes," I said. "Does the young Raven forget it is his first war path, and how necessary it is for him to track the enemy, that his braves may know of their coming."

"The young Raven," he answered, "does not forget the Bonnaxes, they are sleeping in their wigwams above the cataract. I have seen them, and was on my way back to Uwato when——"

"Uwato! is my Indian brother with the young men?"

"Uwato is with his warriors, and they but rest their horses at the foot of the mountain that dips into the water before they sweep down upon the lying Bonnaxes."

I knew the place he mentioned, knew it was at the very least six hours' journey from the cataract, knowing this my hopes of succour from the Comanches died away.

"My brother's fears betoken a change in his spirit," said the young Raven. "Does he wish the warriors of my tribe were nearer?"

"I do; for the settlers are many, and are well armed. And should they cross the water there is but little hope of our escape."

"I am sad because my brother is sad; but it cannot now be different, for the young men of my tribe have ridden day and night to come up with the Bonnaxes, and they stayed not until their horses began to droop and lose their swiftness. No, my white brother, Uwato and his braves must remain where they are, until their cattle can fly over the Bonnaxes' country. But why is this my brother is at war with the people who have but now come to rob the red man of his hunting grounds?"

I told the young brave the story of the spectral warrior, and saw, despite his attempt to command his facial muscles, more attention was perceptible when I related the finding of the poor girl's body.

"The old men of my tribe had wisdom on their tongues when they spoke and told our braves to go upon the war-path, for a Bonnaxe is a coward, and makes war upon women, and hides his face from the sight of a warrior."

I was too well skilled in the peculiar mode of speech used by the red men to interrupt the young brave's preamble to an astounding piece of intelligence that, to use homely parlance, quite gave me a turn.

"It is now six moons since," the youthful warrior continued, "a cowardly Bonnaxe passed the watch dogs of the young men who were in charge of the wigwams wherein our tribe slept; the morning came, and the horsekeepers coming to arouse the warriors, passed three of the sentinels whose spirits had gone to whence they came; in one of the wigwams slept the daughters of an aged warrior, their souls departed, and all that were left bore the cursed marks you have seen upon the body of the white man's child. Yes, my brother, they were scalped, their breasts bitten by the coward's teeth, and the mark left by a rifle bullet through their throats. Now, does my brother wonder that I tell him it is the work of a Bonnaxe—not the doings of one whose spirit don't come back to earth?"

Staggered as I was by this intelligence, I did not overlook one circumstance connected with the death of the young men and the women.

"The young Raven is wise for his years," I said, "can he tell me how it was possible for the Bonnaxe to fire his rifle six times in the midst of the Comanche village without being heard?"

"Silvershot but repeats our chief Uwato's words when he asks this, but the old men made him answer, and said the Great Spirit was angry with his red children and clo d their ears while the reports of the enem 's rifle rang out; but come, my brother, let us go to the falling waters, for here the noise is too great to hear the war shout of your companions."

We made our way cautiously through the thick brushwood, and my mind was completely mystified by the strange story the young Indian had told me.

The reasoning of the old men had no

weight with me, for I had but little faith in the anger of the Great Spirit closing the Indian's ears against the report of a rifle.

Yet I could not in any way account for the strange circumstance, and the more I thought of it the greater was the mystfication I felt.

But for the bullet wounds I should perhaps have believed a Bonnaxe had something to do with the murder, for we were very close to their village.

Against this reasoning there was the fact of the spectre returning the bullets Tim and I had fired.

All attempt to solve the inexplicable mystery was fruitless, so I tried to dismiss the subject from my mind.

We soon cleared the brushwood and came upon a jutting piece of rock that overhung the waterfall, here the roar of the leaping water was so great that I could not hear a word my companion said, for he was speaking, and energetically, I could see by the movements of his lips and the expression of his face.

I soon understood that something of great import troubled the young brave, for he placed his hand upon my shoulder, and forced me down, and as I lowered my body, he followed my example, until we were hidden by a large boulder.

"The noise of the falling waters," I shouted in his ears, "is more powerful than my brother's voice, let him now speak."

"Beyond where the waters hiss and bubble," he replied, "there is a quiet lake; high rocks rise up from the still waters, and down the rocks I saw many men descending; they creep down like a sleuth, and one old man with a white beard tells them where the path is safe; he stands at the edge of the rock."

"Buckskin Bill!" I exclaimed, "directing the cursed settlers down the side——"

"I have not told all. Listen, my brother. On this side of the still waters there is a rifle. I saw it shoot a jet of smoke, and one of those who was coming down the rocky side gave his death cry. I saw him fall as the bird falls when stricken by an arrow."

"Red Hugh defending the passage."

"My brother's words are backed by wisdom, but it is not wisdom to walk the path we have been walking, for the white men are many on the opposite side, and their rifles carry across the waters. Behold!"

He placed his finger upon the sleeve of my hunting jacket, and I saw a bullet-hole through the loose part round by the bend of the elbow.

"Sharp work, Raven," I said; "how are we to join Red Hugh?"

"Let my brother follow."

Reared from his earliest boyhood to all the devices of Indian warfare, the young brave soon hit upon a plan to cross the rocky grounds that lay between us and Red Hugh.

With his hunting knife he cut down a number of bushy shrubs, and with the bark from the longest stems he bound three or four together.

This operation was repeated, and pointing to the one I was to use, he said—

"The ground is covered with the green trees, let my brother be cautious, and he will reach his friend. Come!"

Lying at full length face downward, we wriggled our bodies along the ground, and holding the shrubs upright with our left hands we were well hidden from those on the opposite side.

Our progress was slow, and the wily Indian stopped every few seconds and held his screen perfectly steady in order to better carry out the delusion that the small trees were stationary.

The numberless shrubs that covered the ground (kalmias), aided the young Raven in his device, and we were able to creep across the clear space unnoticed.

When we reached the broken ground the shrubs were cast aside, and bending ourselves nearly double we kept behind the fragments of rock that were scattered about.

The dogs behaved well; a word or two from me and they kept side by side and near my right hand, thus keeping behind the screen of shrubs that concealed my body.

Unobserved we reached a clump of tall vegetation, and about thirty yards from this we could see the occasional puffs of smoke from Hugh's rifle.

Looking through the branches of the dwarf trees we had a good view of the enemy's movements.

Buckskin Bill was standing on the edge of the rocks directing the movements of the settlers who were descending cautiously by clinging to the tufts of rank vegetation that grew in the crevices of the rocks.

Old Bill had a bandage round his left arm, and by the savage manner he from time to time pointed towards the spot where Red Hugh was concealed—I knew the backwoodsman had put a bullet through the trapper's arm.

Hugh seemed to have lost his unerring skill with the rifle, for during the time we stood watching the proceedings of the settlers, he fired at least a dozen times, and I did not see more than two of the foe roll down either dead or wounded.

We stayed long enough to see the men who reached the bottom immediately run behind the fallen boulders, and protecting their bodies by the bulwark of stone, fire at the post where Hugh was concealed.

"The old man," the young Raven said, "is

used to the war path, and he is a brave. Would I had my rifle, he would never more teach his young men the way to come upon the track of his foes."

"Buckskin Bill," I said, " is a good trapper, and was once a friend of mine, but had I my rifle I fear I should forget the ties that have held us together. Does my brother see the motive of these men hiding like squaws instead of swimming across?"

"The old man is crafty," said the Raven. "The white men fear to go to their Great Spirit, or they would cross where but one rifle defends the passage, but the old man tells them it is not good; he wishes them to get together, and when all are crossing the pool, there will be less danger."

"The young Raven is right," I said; "but my companion has grown merciful, or he would have picked them off like so many vultures, as they descended the—"

"My brother is at fault, his companion is wounded, and every shot tells he is getting weaker. Behold!"

The Indian was right, his learning told him the cause of the last shot fired by Hugh feebly striking against the trunk of a tree, and then harmlessly falling down the rocks.

"His arm has not cunning sufficient to ram home the bullet, and his hand has lost its steadiness, for half the powder has fallen to the ground in place of the rifle. Does the young Raven speak truly?"

"I fear he does," I said, "for there is no other cause to which I can ascribe such feeble shots, but we will go to him. The Raven is strong, and he can use the rifle."

The young brave's eyes sparkled at the prospect of picking off several of my worthy friends opposite; youth as he was, war was a pastime, and killing his fellow men was the shortest and best way to the happy hunting grounds when he died, and while he lived, the more scalps he could hang in his wigwam the greater warrior he would be amongst his tribe.

"The young Raven," he said, pointing to the men who were lying wounded or dead on the opposite bank, "will return to take those scalps to his tribe, and there will be rejoicing——"

"The young Raven," I said, fearing he would carry out his purpose, "is a brave, and would not scalp any but his enemies; these men are not his foes."

"They would have put the Comanches' white brother to death. Even now they thirst for his blood. My brother's foes are my foes, my foes are my brother's foes. I have said."

And I could have added, " mean to keep my word to."

CHAPTER X.

OVER THE PRECIPICE.

I AM afraid the young Raven and myself very much compromised our dignity as we crossed the few yards of level ground that intervened between our post of observation and the place where Hugh Howard was concealed.

Old Buckskin sighted us as we emerged from the rear of the bush, and the settlers who were near him began to blaze away with a hearty good will to do us as much harm as possible, and to escape this unwished-for attention we were guilty of the useless but reasonable impulse of ducking our heads as the shots whistled around.

"Good," said the young Raven, when we had crossed the open ground; "the white man's powder has been wasted."

"So much the better for us, Raven. Confound that old Trapper, he seems determined to do his best to kill me."

"The old man with the white head," said the warrior, " lives because the young Raven has left his rifle; the Raven is sorry for this."

So it seemed by the vengeful glances the Indian lad cast at old Buckskin and his companion.

We were now in the rear of a tangled mass of brushwood, and the Indian raised his hand warningly, and stood as motionless as a statue.

I motioned for the dogs to keep back, and stood beside my friend, who said:—

"My brother has ears, let him listen."

I did so, and recognised the voices as of Red Hugh and Tim Delany.

"I can't hold out much longer, Tim," Hugh said; "the last four bullets I have fired with only one charge of powder between them."

"Have you none left, man alive?"

"Only a pinch, Tim; not enough to carry a ball across the water."

"What shall we do?" But you can go, Hugh; never mind me, you go and look after Silvershot."

"I never deserted a companion in distress, yet," answered the backwoodsman, "and never shall, I hope. Now try if you can stand, Tim."

"The devil a stand, Hugh; me ankle is as big as a panther's body, and the pain is like ever so many pins and needles all red hot, sticking into me. Bad luck to old Buckskin! What a pity it be you didn't wipe him out with that bullet, Hugh?"

"I don't want to shed the blood of a white man," said the backwoodsman. "I tried to wing him, and succeeded."

"You did, avick, but it would have been better to have breken his leg, the old reptile. What are they doing now?"

"Nearly all down the rocks, and will soon begin to swim across."

"May the divil sink the lot. Ah! what's that, Hugh? Man alive, there's some of the divils got over and coming this way."

Tim heard the young Indian approaching their covert, and Hugh clubbing his rifle, turned from the contemplation of the settlers' movements, and confronted us.

"Silvershot, he said, "and a Comanche. You are welcome. Would be more so had you rifles in your hands."

"It's glad I am to see ye, rifle or no rifle," said Tim, grasping my hand, "for I'd given ye up when I sees the log going through the stream. Good luck to Hugh, for the nate manner in which he lassoed the beastly thing."

"He saved my life, Tim," I said, "and yours, too.

"That's true, Silvershot, and saved it when I thought it was all up with me, for my foot began to feel as though it was coming out by the root. Sit down, Silvershot, ye don't look very well."

"I am all right, Tim, but you are hurt very much. What is the matter with your leg?"

"Just a bullet-hole, that's all, me friends gave me when I was swimming across the pool. It's lucky it be not my head instead."

"It is, Tim, can you stand?"

"The divil a stand, and worse luck, them vagabonds will be over here soon, for Hugh's powder is clean gone."

"The last shot," said Hugh, at that moment, "here it goes now, my friends, we shall have to clear out, or a deer hide thong will do our business."

He fired as he spoke, and the young Indian said—

"Good, the Raven has another scalp for his wigwam."

I ran to the look-out hole in the rock, and saw one of the settlers being carried away from the water's edge, and Buckskin Bill, who had just advanced, was giving orders to the men to emerge from behind the rocks where they had been sheltered from Hugh's rifle.

Led by the old trapper, the settlers waded into the water, and holding their rifles above their heads with their left hands, they struck out for a level piece of ground just under where we stood.

"A rifle," said the young Indian, "or a bow and arrow would stay the coming of those angry white men, but a knife and tomahawk can do but little. My friends must be like the beavers, whose cunning finds a place of refuge when his foes are near. What does my brother with the Indian's skin say?"

The query was addressed to Hugh, whom the Comanche had known some time before.

Hugh watched the settlers as they swam across, and saw their progress was greatly impeded by the necessity of keeping their rifles clear of the water.

"In ten minutes," he said, "they will stand where we now stand, but ten minutes is a long time to the hunter to clear from his foes. Has Silvershot no plan?"

"Only flight," I answered, "it is no use to stay here, and but little use to try and get away, for Tim cannot stand."

"Never mind me, Silvershot. Quick, take to your legs, all of you, and leave me to——"

"Hold your tongue," I said, "you shall escape with us, or we die together."

"Silvershot speaks like a brave," the youthful Comanche said, "but it would be better if his tongue had a little of the serpent's cunning. To die like wolves in a trap, or squaws caught in a wigwam, is not to die as warriors."

The settlers were slowly making their way across, and by this time a third of the distance had been passed.

I began to feel anxious, and wished my Comanche friend would omit the preface to the plan he was about to place before us.

"The Raven," he continued, in his slow measured tone, "is very young, but the warriors of his tribe have taught him wisdom. Let my brothers listen, and say if this is good."

"By the mortial men!" said Tim, suddenly, "if you don't tell us what's the best thing to be done, we shall have the divils over here."

The Comanche gave a contemptuous glance at the settlers and said:—

"The thieves who come from beyond the big river to rob the red man of his land have not limbs that will carry them across the water. See, my brothers, they are already tired swimming with one arm so long, and but for the old hunter whose hair is white with age they would return."

"The old reptile!" muttered Hugh; "I'd like to put a plug of lead in his carcase."

The settlers paused, and trod the water for a few seconds; then they were enabled to relieve their left arms from the weight of their rifles, and bringing them into their right hands, began to move forward, using the left arm to swim with.

"By the mortial man!" said poor Tim, trying to rise to his feet, "I'd like the divil to suddenly rise up in the middle of the water, and fly away with every mother's son of them."

"The young Raven," I said, addressing the Indian, "has a plan; let him speak."

"My brother is right; the hunter with the

Indian skin (pointing to Hugh) will stay with the young Raven until the Silverbullet has taken his wounded brother from here. There is a mighty chasm in the prairie; let Silverbullet go there. I have said."

"Brave Indian," said Hugh, "here, give me a hand to lift him upon Silvershot's back."

"Aisy, man," said Tim, "and mind how ye lift me, for me carkis is all egg-shells, and I shall break to pieces."

I shouldered my comrade; and before making for the chasm, where I knew there would be plenty of hiding places for us; I said to the young Raven—

"My brother has spoken wisely, yet I would like to know why he stays with Hugh Howard."

The youth pointed to Buckskin Bill's party, and answered—

"The white thieves will soon be under the rocks. Here are stones; our arms are strong, and——"

"Hurrah!" said Hugh, seizing a huge stone with his brawny arms; "let's begin, and if we don't crack some of their skulls, we can make such a splashing that will damp their powder."

"Go it, ye divils," said Tim; "keep 'em back until we get to the snug little place the Raven has mentioned. Go on, Silvershot, or your back will soon ache with me sticking on it. Go on, man alive."

I whistled to the dogs, and turned to leave the place, and as I did so Hugh launched the huge stone down the rocky side of the river.

I could not resist a shudder passing through me as the fragment of rock fell against the projections, tearing down the brushwood and shrubs, and finally falling into the water with a loud splash.

Red Hugh gave a yell of joy, and the Indian a defiant whoop, when the murderous missile reached its destination.

They were answered by an angry shout from below; and Hugh, running to the assistance of the young Raven, gleefully said:—

"Go it, Comanche, that wiped two or three of them out and spoilt the powder in the rifles of as many more."

Pushing my way through the brushwood I soon came to the open prairie, and bidding Tim look out for the chasm, hurried forward.

"Go on, man alive," said Tim, "I'll look out for the illigant place—by the mortial, but that Indian is a good friend at a pinch, but it's better he would have been had he brought a few of his tri——what's that, Silvershot?"

"Rifles at work," I answered, staggering on under my load, "and a sign old Buck-skin and his party have gained this side of the river."

"Bad luck to them, yes," said Tim, "but the boys, Hugh and the Comanche, will keep them from coming this way."

"Not for long, Tim."

"Eh? Why not, Silvershot?"

"Because they can dodge the stones, Tim, and our friends cannot dodge the bullets."

"That's true, every word, worse luck—do you feel timid, Silvershot?"

"Not a bit—do you see anything of the chasm?"

"By me soul no, unless that's it straight in front."

"What does it look like, Tim?"

"A great black place, but the sun is in my eyes, so I can't see as plain as I should if the sun was not in—— Do you hear that, man alive?"

"I do, Tim. The settlers have nearly gained the top of the rocks. Their last shots were nearer."

"True," said Tim, and twisting himself round to the danger of dislocating my neck, he added, "by the mortial, there's the smoke from the rifles puffing out from the bushes."

I was so weakened by the severe handling the settlers had given me, that my legs began to totter, and I felt as though I should be obliged to succumb under my burden.

"How far is it, Tim?" I gasped, as my tongue dry, and the perspiration dropped from my forehead. "Not much farther, I hope?"

"We're close upon it, old son, but if ye are done up, drop——by the mortial, here they are!"

A bullet whistled past my ear as Tim spoke; then I heard the vengeful shout of our pursuers, and running blindly forward I reached the edge of the yawning gulf.

There was no foothold to be seen, and my heart fell, for I knew I must die—should I fall into the settlers' hands after all I had gone through to escape them.

"Can you see a little track down the chasm, Tim?"

"Not one. The sides are as level as the back of me hand."

"Look back, and see how far the devils are——"

I was answered by a voice that caused my heart to leap to my throat; it was the voice of my relentless foe, Buckskin Bill.

"Seize 'em! Seize the varmints!" he shouted. "Take 'em alive!"

I heard the deep bay of the dogs as they turned upon our pursuers. I cast one glance behind me, and saw the faithful animals had dragged Buckskin Bill to the ground, and were trying to get at his throat.

I saw, too, several of the settlers with drawn knives running to old Bill's assistance;

LASSOOING THE LOG.

and preferring death by my own hand to again falling into their power, I gripped Tim closer and said :—

"Good bye, old comrade, we will die together."

"Yes, yes, Silvershot, the Lord receive our souls. Over with you, man. Good-bye."

"I felt a hand touch my shoulder, and ere the fingers could tighten upon the collar of my jacket, I gave a cry of despair and defiance, and leapt over the precipice with Tim on my back.

CHAPTER XI.

AT THE BOTTOM OF THE CHASM.

Down, down, it seemed into the very bowels of the earth ; I felt my body strike against the shrubs that grew out of the bank ; felt them bend beneath our weight. I heard large stones loosened by the contact of our bodies during the fearful descent, thunder down the abyss, and strike against the bottom with a fearful crash.

My brain became dizzy, my heart stopped beating, and my senses became a blank, except for the knowledge that death had claimed me for its own.

Consciousness returned just when the glowing hues of the setting sun shone upon the prairie, as I opened my eyes upon a scene that caused me to think of the Indian's belief in the happy hunting grounds of the future.

I was lying upon a grassy bank, and the ground near me was covered with short grass, above which the beautiful wax-like flowers of the magnolia raised their rich blossoms.

The branches of a cotton wood tree formed a canopy above my head, and at a little distance a clear stream rippled past.

Beyond the running waters were mighty boulders of reddish stone, and looking down the stream I beheld splendid arches of a similar substance spanning the water.

An antelope was drinking peacefully within a dozen yards of where I lay, and numberless birds of rich plumage were hopping about from bush to bush, shaking the red and yellow leaves and the scarlet blossoms.

There was a peaceful quietude pervading this scene, such as I had never experienced before, and the light tinted with the sunset's glow was mellowed, and the air that swept across my face impregnated with the most delicious perfumes.

I raised my head, and the scene was pure, chaste, and sublime ; my senses were steeped in a dreamy ecstacy, which was not marred when I found I was alone.

Perhaps, I thought, this is the portion of the happy lands beyond the grave that is allotted to me, and thinking thus, I placed my hand upon my brow, and fell into a tranquil sleep.

From my belief of the enjoyment of paradise, I was aroused by a hand being placed upon my shoulder, and the joyous barking of my dogs mingled with the well-known voice of Tim Delany, who said, " More power to the old dogs for finding ye out, Silvershot."

" Where am I ?"

" Well, that's a pretty question to ask, considering ye come all the way here by yourself. Can ye get up, man alive, for it's my belief every bone in your body is broken."

" I thought I was either in the Indians' or the white men's ' happy land,' " I said, sighing to find myself still alive, " surely it can't be a dream that fearful leap over the precipice."

" A drame, man, not a bit of it; get up, Silvershot, quick, and find out if your bones are all sound."

I arose, and to my surprise my body and legs felt as though they had been pommelled with a dozen cudgels, and my joints were so stiff that I could scarcely move them.

" No bones broken," said Tim, " that's a good thing anyhow. By the mortial, I thought you would have been jelly before getting here."

" Here, where am I ?"

" At the bottom of the big hole, Silvershot, that's where ye are, and it's a power of a way here from where ye left me ; for I've been ever since walking about on these two crutches, trying to find yer, and but

for the dogs the divil a find it would have been."

I saw Tim was supporting himself upon two branches that had been torn from a cotton muna tree, and the forked ends of which made capital substitutes for crutches.

" I'm all in a fog, Tim," I said, " for I remember nothing since I jumped over the verge of the chasm with you on my back, until I awoke on this bank, and thought myself in paradise. Pray explain, there's a good fellow."

Tim looked very haggard and ill, and I could see, by the nervous twitching of his facial muscles, that he was undergoing the most acute pain through his exertions to find me."

" I'll just take a sit down, Silvershot," he said " for me leg does pain me a bit."

Seating himself upon the grassy bank, he gave a sigh of relief, and looking into my face, said :—

" I've heard of an Indian having as many lives as ten Tom cats ; but, by the mortial man, I think we've as many."

" We've had a most wonderful escape from death, Tim."

" That's true, and I'll tell you how we came off so well. It's just this. When you jumped over the edge of the horrid place you knew I was sitting on your back with me legs hanging over your shoulders ; you remember that, avick ?"

" I do, perfectly."

" Well, the way you held 'em was a caution, for you jumped short, and that kept us close to the side, and having our hands to use, grabbed at the bits of trees that grew out. Look here."

Tim extended his hands, and I saw they were cut severely, and bleeding from the more serious wounds.

" The little trees, good luck to them," Tim answered, " held on for a little bit, and when I found 'em coming out by the roots, I just looked below, and there, about twenty feet under us, a decent young plane threw out lots of branches ; and keeping me eyes on this, I was ready for a grab, when the little fellow gave way, and we dropped smack into the plane."

" That saved our lives, Tim."

" Sure enough, but I didn't think it would, for the branches went flying right and left, and then at length I caught a hold of them, which slipped through me hands, and cut me like this. Anyhow, we stuck in the fork of the gentleman at last, and I hollers out for you to catch hold, and just as I did so, by the powers my legs slips from between your arms, and away you goes."

I had put my hand to my head during the time Tim was speaking, and found I had received a severe scalp wound, for my hair was matted together with blood.

"I must have been stunned Tim," I said, "when we landed amongst the branches of the tree, or I should have taken hold."

"That's just it, Silvershot; you were knocked out of all sinse, and me heart came right up to me mouth when I saw you going down; but you didn't go very quick, not a bit of it; sometimes you stopped by a little tree, then the stem bent, and you slipped, and I watched you until me eyes ached and I couldn't see a sign of you, for you suddenly went round and round; and I said a prayer for your soul, Silvershot, for I made sure it was all over with you."

"Poor Tim."

"No, it was poor Silvershot then, for I was all safe perched up in the tree like a red monkey looking out for nuts; and when I thought I'd seen the last of me comrade, I began to wonder how the divil I should get down, for me fut seemed full of red-hot pins dancing all about it, and I knew I couldn't stand upright a minnit."

"But I knew it was no use to sit thinking about it," Tim continued, "so I got out at the foot of the tree, and managed to crawl further along the side which wasn't near so smooth as it was a little higher up; on I crept until I reached the bottom of the tree, and then I very soon made a pair of crutches that helped me a little when I had crawled to the cattle track, and there I was able to hobble a bit on me sticks, then I had to go on me hands and knees again, and when I was about half way down, what should I see but the two dogs trotting along ahead, and calling them we travelled on together nntil I found you, and mighty glad I was, for I couldn't have gone another yard."

"You seem done up, Tim, I said; "I know I am tired, bruised, thirsty, and hungry."

"We can rest down here, "that's one good thing," said Delany, "and that will soon make us right about the tired part of the business; as for the thirst, there's plenty of water, the Lord be praised, but about the hunger, that's another thing, Silvershot."

"I saw an antelope drinking at the stream a short time since."

"You did, where?"

I pointed out the spot and Tim struggled to his feet and began to hobble away when I stopped him.

"What's the matter, man alive?"

"You remain here, Tim, I will go—"

"What nonsense, avick, you look more fit to be in a soft bed than here; and for the matter of going to trap the game, I don't believe you could walk as far."

I essayed to disprove Tim's words, but to my dismay I found I was not able to move one foot before the other.

I sank back, and Tim hobbled away, saying—

"It's hard enough to have two big ankles, bad luck to old Buckskin for that same, and it's bad, too, to have a bullet hole in the leg, but all this put together is not as bad as Silvershot is, for the divil a tinder foot he'll be able to move soon."

Tim went to the margin of the stream, and finding the antelope's footprints, followed them until the side of the chasm became too difficult for him to ascend.

He soon returned and brought his fur cap full of water, and the draught for a time restored my sinking faculties.

"The antelope will not make us a supper," Tim said, "that's very certain, so we needn't stay here waiting for it."

"As well here as anywhere else," was my gloomy answer.

"Not a bit of it, avick," said Tim; "it will soon be dark, and then the dew will come down, and though it's a mighty good thing for the grass, it's bad for us."

"Ague and fever, Tim, and in our present state it only wants that to finish our business."

"That's true, Silvershot, but we needn't wait for that, there's plenty of warm holes in the side of this place, and we must get to one and stay there until the Comanche and Red Hugh find us out."

"Hugh and the Indian are dead, Tim."

"Don't say that, man; not they, depend upon it they are not the sort to be taken alive by the settlers, or for the matter of that to stay until old Buckskin's vagabonds get them under their rifles."

"I hope they have escaped," I said, "not that it will better our condition, Tim, for neither of us are able to get up the sides of this chasm."

"You talk like a big girl, Silvershot; why, man, haven't we our hands and knees? and what do you think they were given us for—why to crawl, of course, when we can't walk, so crawl we must, and the sooner we begin the better, for the night won't keep us long waiting before it's here."

There was no denying the truth of my companion's words, so with many a groan of pain coming from our lips we began the ascent of the almost perpendicular side of the fissure.

The yawning abyss into which we had fallen became more palpable as we toiled upwards, and when I glanced to its summit a shiver passed over me at the terrible distance the brink was from whence we crouched.

I saw the place afterwards, and my head grew dizzy gazing down into its depths—

gazing down it seemed into the very bowels of the earth, and I could scarcely realise the truth of a few trees and bushes having saved me from being dashed to an undistinguishable mass.

The rent in the prairie was no doubt caused by an earthquake at some period far remote from the time I visited it, and the hollow thus made had for some generations become a receptacle for the rains that fell during the wet seasons.

From the brink to the bottom of the ravine, the distance was at least five hundred feet, and the width nearly double. Its length could only be imagined, for a party of Comanches afterwards told me they rode for two hundred and fifty miles along the brink, and were unable to discover where it began.

To return, Tim and I crawled up the side until we were exhausted—the dogs following us, and evidently at a loss to understand why we should imitate their position when travelling.

Panting and worn out, we lay upon the broadest part of a rocky ledge, a sort of uneven shelf jutting out above the bed of the chasm.

We lay there unable to move, and the twilight began to deepen into night.

" Tim," I said, " we must remain here until the morning, for I cannot move."

" Bedad, that's the same with me, Silvershot, and I've left me crutches be——What's the matter, Ben, my good dog?"

There was no need to ask, for with the last gleam of daylight, and the first shadow of night's sombre mantle falling upon the earth, the sneaking, hungry wolves left their lairs, and went forth in search of food, uttering those short cries so ominous to the ears either of a hundred men or a four-footed beast

We were weak, helpless, and unarmed, and within earshot were a pack of prowling wolves.

We knew our fate if the brutes got scent of us, and neither spoke. We could not move now, without the certainty of falling from the rocky ledge into the abyss beneath.

And so we must pass the night, or, failing that, be torn to pieces by the brutes whose cries came with such horrible distinctness upon our ears.

CHAPTER XII.

A TERRIBLE NIGHT.

" SILVERSHOT," said Tim, " we're in a nice place now, just to think now that we should not have been able to get any higher, and the night getting darker every minnit. Man alive, what shall we do?"

" Roll off this ledge," I sullenly answered,

" and break our necks; it will be an easier death than dying under the fangs of yonder howling brutes."

" Look, here. Silvershot," said Tim, " while there's a little bit of life left in us there's every chance of getting a little further on our journey, so don't talk about cutting the little bit short."

I tried to roll over and put an end to my misery, but my bruised limbs refused to do their office, and I sank back, a groan of hopeless despair coming from my lips.

" Keep up your heart, comrade," said Tim, " keep it up, man, shure I am as bad as ye are, and it's only the hope of one day pinning that old divil, Buckskin Bill, that keeps me alive at all."

" Curse Buckskiu Bill!" I fiercely exclaimed, " the old man shall pay dearly for what we have suffered if I live over this night."

" Live, to be shure ye will; it's only your bones that are a little bit bruised, that's all. Shure we shall both be all right to-morrow."

" I hope so."

" That's right, by the mortial, there's nothing like——What's that?"

" What?"

" Something splashed on me face."

" I did not feel anything, Tim, it must have been fancy."

" Not a bit of it, it must have been a raindrop, but there won't be much rain, for the stars are coming out, and the moon, too, for that matter."

I looked up at the sky and saw the bright stars twinkling peacefully above us, and the silvery moon's rays began to light up the precipitous sides of the chasm.

It was a fair scene, so tranquilly beautiful, yet majestically grand, and as I gazed up I could not help thinking how many happy men and women were being looked down upon by the bright celestial bodies that were above the two bruised and broken-spirited hunters.

The night seemed calm, for it was like the treacherous lull before a tempest at sea, for as I gazed upwards huge billows of clouds rolled across the moon's disc, and the large raindrops fell more frequently.

" We shall have a fierce storm to-night, Tim," I said, " and the wind and rain will, perhaps, dislodge us from the ledge, and put an end to our misery."

" The Lord be good to us," said Tim, " and keep us alive till the morning. I wish we had strength enough, Silvershot, to get up to the next ledge, for maybe there's a hole at the back of it where we could hide."

About six feet above us there was another projection, and I saw, had our strength lasted out, we should have been able by clinging to the shrubs to have gained a better shelter from the coming storm.

"Too late, Tim," I replied. "Here we must stay until the storm or the waves wipe us out."

As I spoke, a faint moaning sound came upon my ears; it was the wind rising and sweeping across the prairie.

The moaning soon increased to a sullen roar, and, sweeping through the rent in the earth, carried with it a shower of leaves and dried turfs.

The black volumes of clouds soon disappeared, and spreading over the hitherto bright firmament, coloured the moon and its satellites; and as the rain descended, we were in utter darkness.

"I'd give all the skins I could take in six months," said Tim, "for the dirtiest old blanket the red skins could find. Ugh! the blackguards might have left us ours, Silvershot."

We were soon saturated by the heavy rain, and as the wind increased in fury, huge bushes were torn from the side of the fissure, and fell to the bottom; in their descent, the earth and loose stones falling in showers over our unprotected heads.

"It's a good job for us," said Tim, assuming a cheerfulness he was far from feeling, "we are not at the bottom, or some of these playthings might fall upon our heads; and it's a good job, too, that we have that ledge above us to catch the things as they fall, and save our heads; don't you think so, Silvershot?"

"I don't know that it matters much."

"The divil you don't! Why, man alive! if it hadn't have been for that we should have been rubbed out before this."

"A happy release."

"That's your way of thinking, man, not mine. Do you feel that, Silvershot? Why it's raining rivers instead of big drops. By the mortial, it's enough to wash us away."

It was indeed raining rivers. The earth above having become saturated, the water collected, and ran over the edge of the precipice in vast streams.

The muddy shower came leaping and splashing from every jutting piece of earth or stone strong enough to bear its weight, until it reached the ledge above us; there it was broken, and fell upon our wretched carcases.

We could hear the Storm King at work on the prairie, and in the chasm trees were being uprooted and blown away, while those who resisted crouched and groaned as though in agony.

Every now and then a weighty object would whirl past us and fall into the abyss, and once a spreading branch of a dislodged tree swept across my face, and nearly tore me from my narrow resting-place.

Thunder and lightning added to the horrors of the scene; the former filling the chasm with a deafening roar, and the latter adding ten thousand new terrors to our already overwrought minds.

"The Lord be merciful to us," murmured Tim, "and forgive us our sins."

"And," I added, "put our misery to an end at once."

I did not believe it possible we could be in a worse predicament than we were then. I had to learn that matters, however hard they may appear, can yet be worse.

As the night wore on, the tempest rose in place of abating, and the peals of thunder succeeded each other with scarcely the slightest interval.

The lightning was terrible in the extreme, and every time the abyss was illumined by the electric fluid we were compelled to cover our eyes, for it seemed impossible to escape being blinded.

Had it not been for the alarm natural upon the occasion, I should have remembered that it was a very rare occurrence for a living being to be struck by that dangerous fluid, descending in great abundance discharges itself by so many channels that simple objects are less violently hit than is the case in England.

The rain descended in such sheets that we could hear the splashing of water in the bottom of the fissure, and the wind lashing the newly-made stream until the waves beat against the rocky sides with a sullen wash like breakers on the sea-shore.

Old trees, that had weathered the storms of many years, were soon stripped of their bark and branches, and some of the latter were hurled against our bruised and numbed bodies with such violence, that used to hard knocks and suffering as we were, it was impossible to avoid crying out with pain.

At last overtaxed nature succumbed, I either fainted from agony and exhaustion, or was stunned by a falling stone, for when the hurricane was at its height, my senses suddenly left me, and I became lifeless.

When I returned to life all traces of the tempest had passed away, save the broken trees, and the gullies made on the side of the ravine by the rain. The sun was just gilding the heavens. A faint dull glow—not sufficient to render objects any distance distinct to my aching eyeballs.

As my consciousness returned little by little, as it were, I became sensible that Tim Delany was moaning with pain, and the two dogs were growling angrily.

"What is the matter, Tim," I asked, turning my face towards my companion, "has anything happened since I—I—"

"Silvershot, old comrade," was the strange answer, "what made you come to life again?"

The events of the terrible night I thought had taken an effect upon my companion's brain.

"What have I returned to life for, Tim? Because I was not dead, I suppose. What is the matter with the dogs?"

"The matter, don't you see them, Silvershot; don't you see their eyes all on fire, and their teeth grinning at us?"

"The dogs!"

"The dogs,' muttered Tim—"no, man, the wolves!"

"Wolves!"

"Aye, you may well shout this time; look at 'em, Silvershot, look at 'em, they are right over your head."

I looked up, and my blood seemed to freeze, my brain reeled, my eyes grew dim, and covering my face to hide the appalling sight, I groaned, "Heavens, how horrible!"

Terrible, most terrible, was the sight that met my upturned gaze, and never will it be obliterated from my memory. Never shall I be able to recall that scene to my mind without a shudder.

On the very verge of the ledge above us there crouched upwards of a dozen gaunt and hungry wolves.

Their red tongues were protruding through their horrible-looking fangs, and their cruel, angry eyes fixed upon our defenceless bodies.

Now, indeed, there was no hope—we must die—die the most horrible death.

Already, in fancy, we could feel the brutes' long white teeth tearing our flesh, felt ourselves being torn piecemeal by the ravenous flock, and the mental agony became so intensified, that I gave a shriek of despair.

"It's no use, Silvershot," Tim said, "that won't frighten them, it's only the dogs that keep 'em from jumping upon us; Lord, Lord, that our graves should be the stomachs of a lot of hungry varmints like this. This is dreadful, Silvershot."

"It is! it is!" I answered, frantically making an attempt to rise; "any death but this, anything but this horrible fate!"

I could not move from where I lay, and my soul sickened with dread as I fell back in the muddy pool that formed my bed.

"I've tried to move meself," said Tim, "but me legs are clean done for, until I can get this bastely log from across them."

I saw part of a huge branch lying across Tim's legs just below his knees, and felt how powerless I was to aid him.

There was a strange fascination in the sight above me, for my eyes immediately re-

turned to meet the savage, longing looks of the famished pack.

They were growling and snapping at each other, and one, an old repulsive brute, evidently the leader of the skulking crew, laid himself close to the edge, and tried to claw at the dogs, who were jumping upward in the endeavour to bite the lean shaggy wolf prowling to and fro, yet never for a moment taking his eyes from the expected meal. The brutes continued ever on the move, save now and then one would crouch as though preparing for the accursed spring, and our hearts would cease beating, for we knew that if one came upon us the remainder would follow.

Oh, for a rifle at that moment. What a priceless gem my old piece seemed to me now that I was deprived of it.

How strong was the wish to kill the brutes, when killing was out of my power, so strong that I believe I would have willingly died any death for the mere satisfaction of slaying the prowling brutes.

A ray of hope came to my heart; after I had watched my foes for some time I saw their hesitation in leaving the rocky ledge, and attributed it to the defiant attitude of my dogs.

"There's a chance yet," I said to Tim; "the brutes won't attack us while the dogs——"

The words had scarcely left my lips, when the old grizzled brute drew his legs under him, and prepared for the downward jump.

I closed my eyes as the loose stones fell, and Tim Delany gave a shriek and fainted as the old wolf left the ledge.

CHAPTER XII.

A BARRICADE.

IT was an involuntary action I made when my arms were placed across my face; it was a poor defence against the fangs of the brutes that I felt sure were springing upon us, and the respite from them was only owing to the bravery of my dogs.

How quiet the deadly struggle between the noble animals and the prairie prowler was being carried on, for there was scarcely a sound came to my ears except the snappish growls of the wolves, and that seemed to proceed from above in place of within a few feet of where I lay.

But the dogs will soon be slain and then——

"By the mortial man, Silvershot, the varmints made a mistake that twist."

I opened my eyes and saw Tim, his body raised upon one arm, and his face as gleeful as could be expected under the circumstances we were in.

There was no wolf upon the ledge, neither

were the dogs, and I looked interrogatively at Tim.

"Ben and Jip," he said, "waited for the old varmint to come down; the old varmint jumped too far, and in place of landing forenenst he went clean down to the bottom."

"And the dogs, Tim?"

"They went after him, and are worrying his life out in the water."

That fact soon became apparent, for the splashing of water and the angry yelp of old Ben could be plainly heard.

I had no fear for the dogs, together they were a match for any skulking wolf, but I feared for ourselves, for we were now left without the little protection the dogs could give us.

I looked up at the snarling crew above and saw them still leaning on the edge of the rocky projection.

As cunning as Satan is the prairie wolf, and the fate of their leader had deterred the others from imitating his example.

"By the mortial," said Tim, "I think we are pretty safe from the varmints now, there's not one cares to come down; you should have seen them put up their backs when the old fellow tumbled over."

Tim was getting quite sanguine over the ugly business. I was not so, for I knew our enemies would not be long before they found a safer mode of reaching us.

So far they seemed undecided, and appeared to hold a conversation. I say appeared, although like most men who have had much to do with animals, I firmly believe the brute creation have a mode of communing with each other, but whether by an understood code of mute signals or a succession of low cries I cannot state.

The wolves drew back from the edge except one, who turned his hateful head from side to side as though measuring the distance that lay between us.

His scanning lasted about two minutes, and then as though having satisfied himself that a successful attempt could be made, he withdrew, and the others gathered around him.

This debate did not last long, for the brute returned to his old position, and after surveying us for a moment, slowly and cautiously drew himself to the brink.

"By the powers," exclaimed Tim, "do you see that?"

I saw the cunning brute, in place of jumping from the ledge, was about to drop, and from where we crouched his body would fall within a foot of Tim's head.

"It's all up with one of us now," I said, "for if this prowling thief succeeds the whole pack will be down."

"Me arm," said Tim, "is as strong as ever, the Lord be praised, so just throw me over that tomahawk, Silvershot."

"Tomahawk?"

"Yes, man alive, that illigint little thing hanging at your waist."

I had forgotten the young Raven's present until that moment, and my heart beat joyfully as I unlooped it.

"Here, Tim, drive the blade well home, lad, if you get a chance."

"Never fear," said the gallant fellow; "while there's an inch of it left neither Tim nor Silvershot will be hurt, that is if they only come one at a time—look out."

Thump; down came the wolf, and as though a little undecided which of us to attack, he backed from one to the other, and I, in my desperation—what thoughts desperation will give!—rose to a sitting posture, and seized a jagged piece of stone; for what purpose I can scarcely tell, for I was too weak to knock a rabbit over.

Tim Delany seemed the most plump eating, for the wolf advanced warily; he had no doubt seen a tomahawk before.

"Come on, ye skulking devil," said Tim; "here a lad who'll live to be buried in a better place than a stomach like yours."

The brute cast an upraised glance at his companions, then uttering a low growl, lowered his head, and advanced towards Tim.

My companion nerved himself for the encounter, and when the wolf came within striking distance, I saw the tomahawk flash and heard the crash of the brute's skull as the blade divided the bones. This caused a yell of triumph from Tim, and his foe rolled over, kicking in the agonies of death.

"As clane a hit as ever I made in me life," said Tim; "more power to the tomahawk, it's as good as ever. Keep your eyes on 'em up there, Silvershot, while I try to get rid of this log from me legs."

I did keep my eyes upon the brutes, whose savage instincts were by this time further aroused by the scent of their dead companion's blood.

Their eyes blazed angrily as they peered over the edge of the ledge, and snuffing the air, low angry cries from time to time broke from them.

The brutes seemed to fully realise the fate that had befallen their companion, for their eyes shone like balls of dusky fire as they glanced down upon us, and marched restlessly to and fro above.

"They're a long time making up their minds, Silvershot," said Tim; "maybe they will come down upon us in a body."

"The Lord forbid, Tim."

"Amen, comrade—but look at the devils now."

"I am doing so; they are talking over

some plan to get at us better than jumping from the ledge."

"I believe you are right; by the mortial, no one would believe the brutes had a talk of their own, would they, Silvershot?"

The wolves, however, were collected in a group, their noses together, and after remaining so for a few moments, they turned towards the rugged path that led upward from the ledge, and following each other in single file, marched slowly away.

"The Lord be praised," said Tim, "they're gone at last."

"But we have not seen the last of them yet, Tim."

"How's that, man alive?"

"We shall soon see, Tim; for, as sure as we lie here, they have made a resolution to get at us in a mode more advantageous than jumping from the ledge."

"May be so, Silvershot; thus, if we can't get away from here before they come back it's rubbed out we'll be."

"Rubbed out, old chum?"

"But, man alive, we mustn't let 'em."

"How can we help it?"

"We must get up somehow, Silvershot. If not on our feet on our hands and knees."

"I cannot move, can you?"

"The divil a pass, but I think I could if I got rid of this beastly log."

A sudden thought came to my mind. Tim was not more than a couple of yards from me; severely bruised and shattered as I was, I could roll over to him, and with my hands pull off the broken bough that lay across his legs.

I could but make the attempt; if it failed, we could not be worse off than we were; if I succeeded, why not? But at the thought there was every chance of escaping from the hungry brutes.

Raising my body upon my arms I managed to turn over towards Tim, and so great was the agony I suffered that I nearly swooned.

"Keep on, man alive," said Tim, "keep up, and it's close to me ye'll be, keep up."

"I feel——"

"Shure, I know ye do, Silvershot, I can see that by the face ye are pulling, but never mind, keep it up for a little time, and we'll be ——by the mortial, look at the varmints."

My eyes followed Tim's extended finger, and I beheld the wolves slowly descending the side of the precipice.

They were near the top and about fifty yards to the left of the ledge where we lay, and I saw by the manner in which they were moving they would reach us by following a steep path that was in a line with our resting-place.

Desperation gave me strength, and I dragged my bruised limbs close to Tim, and placing my hands across the log, rolled it over into the abyss below.

I heard the loud crash against the rocky, precipitous chasm, and before it reached the bottom a howl of pain came from some animal, and looking over the ledge I saw my faithful dogs rolling over and over into the muddy stream that filled the bottom of the ravine.

I had swept them off the side as they were ascending after killing the old wolf whose body lay upon the top of the water.

"Poor old Ben and Jip," I said, sadly, "the best dogs that ever man possessed have I killed."

"Shure it's a misfortune, Silvershot, and a big one for us just now."

"It is, Tim."

"Where are the wolves, Silvershot? you can see them better than I can."

"They have retreated," I said; "the pathway was much too steep for even their footing."

"The Lord be praised for that. Amen."

"A false hope, Tim, they have gone a little higher up, and our fate is sealed."

I rose upon my hands as I spoke, and with a face of despair sank down again, my head striking against the side of the chasm.

Just above the ledge was a strata of sand, and so soft that even the slight force with which my head came against it, left a hole.

I gazed a moment at the place, my senses dazed with joy, for above, below, and on each side of the place I had stood against was solid rock.

I knew at once the sand must be loose, not the regular formation of the side of the ravine.

My heart beat wildly at the discovery, and I called out to Tim:—

"Up, man, up, if you have any life left in you!"

"What's the matter, Silvershot?"

"We are saved," I said, tearing wildly at at the sand with both hands, "this loose stuff has been washed down the side of the chasm by the rains, and behind it there is a hole big enough I've no doubt for both of us."

Inspired by my words, Tim crawled forward, and found in the bank an excavation. How madly we tore away the rubbish that was piled in the opening of the case! Only those who have been near death and suddenly see a chance of escape can realise.

We soon made an opening big enough for our bodies to pass, and putting my head inside I beheld a hole large enough to shelter a dozen men.

The wolves were now close upon us, advancing with slow, careful steps, and growling angrily at the sight of their expected food.

"In, Tim," I exclaimed, "they will be here in less than a minute."

"Go in yourself, Silvershot, you are the heaviest of the two."

There was no time for argument, so I dragged myself inside, and Tim followed, and turning quickly round he said :—

"By the powers, here they are."

Two of the brutes were upon the ledge, and the others coming quickly in, and as Tim gripped his tomahawk, and lay near the entrance, one of the hungry, gaunt brutes gave a savage cry, and darted to the opening.

I saw the light of the young day shut out by the animal's body blocking up the entrance. Saw the small eyes gleaming like dusky balls of fire; and just when I expected all was over with us, the sickening sound of the blade of the tomahawk crashing through the animal's skull came to my ears.

The warm blood bespattered my face and hands, as the howling brute collapsed, and fell in a heap, partially blocking up the entrance to the cave.

"Faith," said Tim, "that's a beautiful stroke, for I've not only rubbed one of them out, but I've stopped the way intirely, but here comes another."

"We want one more," said Tim, "to fill up the hole properly. Then we shall have as safe a barricade as can be put up."

The second wolf thrust his head and shoulders in the opening, and savagely tore at his companion's body to get it out of the way, and while thus engaged, the young Raven's weapon came with unerring aim upon his head.

"The barricade's made," shouted Tim, "for the hole is as nately stopped up as though we had a mason to do it."

The barricade was made, we were in total darkness, and my mind was tortured with a fresh horror.

Who was to remove the bodies of the dead wolves? We could not do so, even if the others went away.

Our joy was but short lived, for we knew we must die—and such a death—and the choking effluvia that would soon arise from the bodies of the slain animals would increase our misery.

CHAPTER XIV.

BURIED ALIVE.

WE could hear the wolves sniffing at the carcases, and the pattering of their feet as they ran to and fro, evidently at a loss to know how to act.

So closely was the opening to the cave filled up that not a ray of daylight entered, nor was there any ventilation.

The place soon became hot and stifling, and so close that we could scarcely breathe. Hunger and thirst we had often suffered, and were suffering then, but the pain was not one hundredth part as bad as inhaling the fetid atmosphere of the cave.

The disgusting effluvia from the dead wolves and the smell of blood added to our sufferings, and we wished ourselves dead. Surely death would have been preferable to prolonging our miseries.

"Silvershot," said Tim, "this is awful; it's worse, I feel, than when I was tied heels upwards to the tree."

"It is awful, Tim, but it will soon be over."

"Faith, I'm glad to hear you say so, but it's not Tim Delany's opinion."

"Why so, comrade?"

"Because it's a slow death. We shall die choked in this hole."

"Let us try and clear the opening, and the wolves will make short work of us."

"No, Silvershot, that's worse than dying here. Ugh! man alive, fancy feeling the brute's teeth tearing your flesh. No, comrade, it is best to die easily if we have to die."

I sank back, and pillowing my head upon my arm, answered—

"Had I a rifle, Tim, I would soon settle the business."

"The wolves' business, ye mean?"

"No, ours."

"Glad I am ye haven't one. Mortial man, what are they doing now?"

The wolves set up a howl at this moment, and we could hear them crowding round the entrance to the cave.

"They are trying to get in, Tim. See, the brutes are dragging the dead bodies away."

"Not that, Silvershot, it's cunning enough they are, but not enough to pull out the carcases of these varmints."

The howling changed to sharp angry cries, and the dead wolves were moved violently.

"By the powers!" exclaimed Tim, "the bastes are eating one another."

I started up, and never shall I forget the thrill of horror that passed over my frame when I heard the crunching of the dead brutes' flesh as they were being torn piecemeal by their living companions.

"That's one way," said Tim, faintly, "to get the obstruction out of the way; there won't be much of the doorway left for us to eat, Silvershot."

"Not much of us either," I said, "when the brutes have done."

"Tim Delany won't make these brutes a dessert, anyhow, while he has this illigant little tomahawk."

The uppermost carcase, or rather that uneaten, was suddenly jerked out from the narrow opening, and a streak of the glorious sunny air flowed into our dark prison.

In a moment we felt the living influence of the pure atmosphere, and our senses, which were rapidly failing, became restored to something like their former tone.

"All right yet," said Tim, "and wide awake, my darlings."

The brave fellow squatted in front of the opening, and with raised tomahawk awaited the coming of the boldest of our unwelcome victims.

The fore-quarters of the brute were soon devoured, and with much less snarling and snapping than when the repast was begun.

"Here's one," Tim said; "he thinks he'd like a little Christian flesh before he begins the other gintilman."

I saw we were pretty safe while one of the stinking carcases remained; unless they disposed of it in the same manner as the other there was not more than sufficient space there to admit the head and neck of any of the prowling brutes.

Possibly their hunger was a little satisfied, for Tim, from his post of observation, kept up a running fire of comment upon their movements.

"It's setting down they are now, Silvershot."

"May they grow to their seats, Tim."

"Faith, I wish they would, but there's no such luck, for here's one big varmint coming in this minit."

I raised my body upon my hands as the brute placed his fore feet upon the carcase, and with an angry growl, thrust his nose within the cave.

Thud! Down came the tomahawk, and our victim's nose was split in twain; bone and cartilage separated as cleverly as a good strong arm and a sharp weapon could do it.

The brute gave a shriek of pain, for I cannot compare the unearthly cry to anything else, and backed out reeling from side to side.

"More power to the young Raven," Tim said, "for keeping his tomahawk in such illigant order."

The appearance of the wounded animal—had we possessed any pity for such skulking brutes—would have touched our better feelings.

He stood for a few seconds on the edge of the rocky platform, looking helplessly at his companions, and raising his off fore leg to the gaping wound rolled over into the muddy bed of the ravine.

"Another gone," said Tim. "By my soul, we should make a good bag if these varmints were worth skinning."

"Or," I said, correcting him, "if we had strength to take off their hides."

"There's something in that, Silvershot

Look here, man alive, and tell me what the brutes are up to now."

The fate that had befallen the venturesome wolf was not without its weight of warning, for the remainder of the pack, after passing over the spot where the brute had disappeared, squatted in a circle before the entrance to the cave, and began sniffing the air.

One of them then rose to his feet, and trotted slowly to and fro, keeping his nose elevated, and giving expression to a low guttural growl.

"They are scenting something," Tim said, "and whatever it is, whether man or beast, it is coming down the side of the ravine, and crouching down ready to jump. Heaven forbid, it is our comrade Hugh, or the dacent fellow, the young Raven."

"Something more formidable than either," I said, "for they are becoming uneasy, and seem to wish to leave the ledge."

The evident disquiet exhibited by the wolves caused us much speculation. We knew they were strong enough to face a man, and for that matter a panther, if driven in a corner, as they were, or seemed to be, from the manner in which first one then the other ran to the only place of exit, and then returned, peering over the edge into the void beneath, as though meditating the consequences of escape that way.

At other times the cunning brutes' manœuvres would have amused us, but under the circumstances the probability began to arise that a more dangerous enemy than the wolves was approaching.

"By jiggers!" said Tim, who had crawled close to the hole; "it's a fearful brute, anyhow, that's coming. Do you hear that, comrade?"

I heard huge stones falling down the face of the precipice, and after a few minutes' pause the gruff angry grunt of an animal well known to every hunter—better known than liked.

"A bear, by the mortial!" said Tim; "a grizzly, by the powers!"

"So much the better," I said, "he will drive the wolves away; then, Tim, we shall have a chance of escape."

"But, man alive, suppose he should want to get into this hole?"

"We must keep him out."

"With this?"

"Yes, with the tomahawk."

"Well, well," said Tim, "to hear a man that knows so much about every animal say such a thing. Shure, there's a mighty difference between a bear's snout and a wolf's."

"True, Tim. There is also a difference in the size of their bodies; a wolf could get through that opening if it was clear, but a bear could not."

"Couldn't he then, by the mortial! there's nothing could get in easier; sure, man, you must have forgotten the bear that trapped us down by the Red River."

I had until Tim mentioned it, and the recollection was not very agreeable, for the bear in question scented our resting-place out, and finding the entrance not large enough began to make it so by using both paws, and would have got in and hugged us to death, but for our awaking just before the business was concluded.

We stopped that gentleman's career by a couple of bullets; should this one try a similar dodge, we had not similar means of defence, and as Tim said the young Raven's bright tomahawk was not much good.

"Here's the gintilman," exclaimed Tim, as the bear landed amidst the wolves. "Look at the varmints' tails, Silvershot; by the powers, they are trying to hide them for fear the old chap should bite 'em off."

The grizzly stood at the end of the ledge to prevent the wolves from escaping; then rearing himself upon his hind legs he growled defiantly at the skulking crew.

"Puts me in mind," said Tim, "of a big chap squaring up to a lot of little ones."

We became rather interested in the movements of the bear, for we were tolerably safe from him unless he tried his paws at excavation.

He must have had an especial spite against the wolves. "Maybe," as Tim suggested, "the skulkers have made off with the old fellow's wife's cubs."

The wolves most politely declined the bear's challenge to "come on," and if their assumption of meekness could have arrested his anger their appearance would have done so.

The grizzly waited for a few minutes to ascertain whether any of the pack were open for a set-to, but finding they still continued to sneak about with their tails between their legs, he gave a growl and went to work with his huge paws, knocking the brutes right and left.

Three were tumbled over into the bed of the ravine in less time than I have taken to write this sentence, and while he was thus engaged two of the enemy slipped past and made their escape.

Bruin gave a grunt of displeasure when he saw this, and turning fiercely upon those who remained, caught one up in his paws, and, despite the wolf's attempt to turn upon his captor's neck, hugged him to death.

"Whurra!" said Tim, "the old one is giving 'em something."

As my companion spoke one of the wolves made an attempt to enter the cave.

He wriggled his head and shoulders inside and would have joined us but for the tomahawk that played about his ugly head, and caused him to retreat as quickly as he entered.

Foiled in the attempt to get away from the bear, the wolf scrambled up the side of the ravine, and his big advancing form stopped our further view of the proceedings.

"By the mortial," said Tim, "the grizzly is after him."

So we soon found out to our misfortune, for bruin in his descent clawed at the rocky side and dislodged some large fragments which fell right into the opening of our prison.

"Trapped, by the powers!" said Tim, "it's all up with us now, Silvershot."

So it seemed, for we were safe from the bear, but that safety was dearly purchased.

We were buried alive, and as effectually as though in a leaden coffin with the cover soldered down.

CHAPTER XV.
IN THE TOMB.

In the darkness of our tomb we heard the growling of the bears and the scratching of the wolves' feet, as the shaggy animal pursued the few who yet lived.

By degrees these sounds ceased, and an awful stillness succeeded. A terrible silence it was to us, whose thoughts were so gloomy.

A single ray of light shone into the cave, a small streak that came from a crevice where two pieces of the dislodged wall met.

The orifice was not large enough to admit the handle of the tomahawk; and the beam of sunshine that straggled through was not sufficient to render us visible to each other.

Yet it was welcome. We watched the motes dancing about, and felt there was yet a bright and sunny world beyond our sepulchre.

The hours passed slowly away, and the sun was at the meridian before we exchanged a word.

The hopeless despondency that had taken possession of our minds forbade even the cheery interchange of words.

"The bear," said Tim Delany, in a hushed voice, "has gone, and the wolves are gone too, Silvershot."

"Yes," I cried absently, "and we remain to perish liked caged rats."

"We have only to die once," said Tim, "and I suppose it matters but little how we pass away from the world."

Tim's voice belied his words. Poor fellow, he thought it was in his power to console me; fancied he could render the approach of the grim monarch less terrible by his attempt to cheer my spirits.

"It matters much," I replied bitterly. "I do not fear death, old comrade. We have been so many times nearly in his clutches, that much of the terror most people would feel is unfelt by us; yet I would have liked to die as a man should die, not in this——"

"It's better not to think of it, comrade."

"Do you not think of it, Tim?"

"Faith, I do, Silvershot, and it makes me flesh creep all over, so I try not to think of it at all, and wait patiently for the end that will come, whether we think about it or not."

"Aye, it will, but we have to suffer before being set at rest for ever.

"I suffer now," said Tim, "me throat burns for a drop of water, and me tongue feels as big as the tongue of a buffalo."

"Poor Tim."

"Poor Tim! Sure, man, ye are no better, I know; but it's like ye, the divil a word of yourself, it's all for Tim ye feel."

"God help us both, for we are beyond the aid of our fellow-men."

"Aye, as far beyond as if we were at the bottom of the say, and that's what makes me feel so grievous when I think about it."

"About what?"

"About being shut up in this hole and dying bit by bit, and then our bodies going to pieces, and all sorts of varmints creeping about our——"

"Tim," I exclaimed, horrified at the mental picture he was creating, "stop this; let us not add to our agonies by dwelling upon the horrors that will ensue in this place. They cannot affect us in any way. What matters what becomes of the senseless clay when the spirit has fled?"

"Not much," said Tim, in a plaintive tone, "not a straw, but it's a bit of a relief to think about it. Fancy, man alive, when this cave is opened, it maybe ye know some day, and they'll find a heap of bones, a tomahawk, and the fools will perhaps fancy we were the last of some animal—the last of a tribe—species, I think ye call it, Silvershot, and ho, ho, ho, ho!"

The wild laugh rung out horribly shrill upon my ears, and I shuddered, for I knew Tim Delany's reason was leaving him.

"Tim," I said, soothingly, "do not excite yourself; let us die calmly, and leave to futurity what may become of our bones."

"Calmly, ye must be a worm, Silvershot, not the man I've taken ye for; not the man who has stood up against a swarm of redskins, and fought them all; not the man who fought the panther, the bear, and clipped the head off a rattlesnake with your tomahawk when the varmint's body was twisted round your own. To the divil with such a snip of a man as ye are now. Ye may die calmly, but Tim Delany will die as he likes, and as a Delany should."

"Tim, my poor old comrade, would I had strength to crawl over to you and grasp your hand."

"Bedad, if you did, I'd knock your brains out with the tomahawk. Don't try it, Silvershot, don't interfere with a Delany about the way he intended to die, or——"

"I do not wish to, Tim, there is but one way we can die, and——"

"It's a liar ye are, Silvershot, do ye hear that?"

"I do."

"And isn't it true?"

"It is, Tim."

"Then hold your clacking tongue, any one would think ye were a bit of a girl, and not—. I say, Silvershot, man alive, do ye hear that?"

"I did not hear anything."

"Ye are a liar again, bestir, here it is again, do ye hear it now?"

"No."

"The devil fly away with ye for a fool as ye are; it's the spectre calling out for Tim Delany, he wants to scalp us, Silvershot, he wants to bite our throats, ye varmint; and old Buckskin Bill, the curse of St. Patrick and all the Delanys fall upon him, is laughing and telling the redskin's ghost that he can't scalp Tim Delany seeing that he's now living again."

"Tim, for Heaven's sake, be quiet."

"Quiet, ho, ho, ho, quiet!"

"I'll tell ye what, Silvershot, if it was not for losing this tomahawk, I fling it at your face. Ye are laughing at me, I can see ye."

"Tim, this is dreadful."

"Maybe it is, maybe it isn't, that all depends how ye take it; it is not dreadful to Tim Delany, for he knows how to cheat old divil Buckskin Bill, do you know that, Silvershot?"

"I do; but old Buckskin has nothing to do with us now."

"What next, he shut us up alive here, isn't he laughing at us because he thinks we shall die like a pair of trapped varmints, but he's mistaken, Silvershot, do you hear that now?"

"I do, every word."

"And do you know how I'm going to cheat him, avick, do you that?"

"I do not, Tim."

"Well, I'll tell ye, but mind, not a word to the red ghost, not a word to the thing that is not mortial, not a word to the spectre who sent Tim's bullet back."

"Not a word, Tim."

"That's right, ye'll keep your word I know, that so I'll tell ye all about it; now listen."

THE LEAP FOR LIFE.

"I am listening."

"Well, avick, I've a tomahawk here, do ye know that ?"

"Yes."

"That's good anyhow, for it's but little ye do know."

"True, Tim."

"Of course it's true, or Tim Delaney would not say a word about it. Well, man alive, I'm going to knock me brains out, with this nate little Indian hatchet, knock 'em clane out the very next time I hear old Buckskin laugh —that would chate the old divil skin, Silvershot."

"It will, but mind you wait until you hear him."

"That I will, avick, and——"

The sharp report of a rifle rung out at this moment, and I heard the tomahawk fall from Tim's hand.

"Saved"' I cried, frantically, "saved? Tim; do you hear that ?"

My words seemed to restore Delany's fleeting reason, for he spoke quite calmly in reply.

"Saved !" he said; "what is the matter, Silvershot ? Ugh ! I know now ; we are shut up alive."

"Yes, yes. Did you hear——"

A second shot was fired, then we heard the dull thud of a heavy body falling into the abyss.

"What is it, man alive ?"

"The bear, Tim; the bear has been perched somewhere on the ledge, and the rifle balls have knocked him over."

" Serves the old divil right ; but who is it fired the shot ?"

" Hugh Howard," I said, " so come, Tim, use all your strength, and let us give a shout that will——"

The completion of my sentence was checked by the sound of footsteps outside the cave, and a strange voice saying—

" You knocked him over pretty clean, old Bill."

" Aye, and the old man can use one arm as well as two when he has a place to rest his rifle upon."

" Tim," I whispered, and my blood seemed to curdle in my veins, " it is Buckskin Bill and the emigrants."

" Curse them, yes. Whist, they are talking about us now."

They were, for old Bill, in reply to a remark from one of his companions, said—

" No, lad, we'll not go down any further ; it's no manner of use, for the varmints must have been knocked to pieces before they got to the bottom of this place."

" I should like to get their bodies, anyhow," was the rejoinder, " if it is only to hang 'em up to a tree near our camp."

" Better let 'em be, lad," the trapper said, " for the bottom is full of water, and they won't be a nice sight to fish out."

" They are fellow-Christians," whispered Tim. " Had we but a rifle apiece, Silvershot ; had we but a rifle, even one."

I made no answer ; I was too enraged to speak.

" We ought to have shot 'em," said one of the settlers ; " it would have been some satisfaction for our people."

" I'd have shot the varmints myself," said old Bill, " and would now if they were alive. I'd have wiped 'em out, lad, if it had not been for Hugh Howard."

" Curse him and the Indian to."

" Aye, always cuss a redskin, my lads, and always give him a plug of lead, for they ain't no manner of good any way, and if they gets the upper hand at any time, you'll find out they are about the cruellest reptiles out."

" There's no manner of doubt about that," another now said, " so we will always be ready to plug 'em when we get a chance."

" Never mind the Indians, now," said another ; " there's plenty of time to settle them when we get a chance ; let's come to some arrangement about this affair. Are we to go and fish out these fellows' bodies or not ?"

" I say not," old Bill answered, " for it's no use, for they are as dead as these wolves long before this."

" That's settled, then, so we had better turn back, or the women will be in——"

A distant hallo came upon our ears, then old Bill said :—

" It's one of the young fellows we left behind to look after the horses and the women. Be very keerful, young man," Buckskin continued, as the new comer descended the ravine. " That's right, boy, hold on, for it's no easy work for them as isn't use to it."

The man reached the ledge ; and though faint from his exertions, placed his back against the stones that closed the entrance to our tomb.

" Speak out, young fellow," we heard old Bill say, " and don't stand making faces in that queer manner."

" I'm out of breath," was the reply, " and so horrified with last night's affair that I can——"

" Last night's what ! Come, out with it, lad. What has happened since we left ?"

" My companion," the settler said, " and three of the women were served the same as poor Jenny Heywood was——"

" SHOT !" roared the old trapper.

" Yes."

" SCALPED !"

" Yes."

" AND BITTEN IN THE NECK !"

" Yes, just the same as poor Jenny."

" Then by——these varmints are not dead ; they must be hiding somewhere hereabouts. Follow me, lads, we'll root 'em out, and skin their hides for 'em."

" Stay a moment," said the bearer of this horrible intelligence, " I have not quite done."

" Give it mouth, lad, for neither sun nor moon shall see us stop our search until those reptiles are caught, and cut up in little pieces. Say on, lad."

" One of the women," the messenger said, " saw one of the murders committed."

" Aye."

" She was under the tilt of a waggon when it was done."

" What does she say ?"

" That it was not done by anything mortal !"

" What ! not by them skulking coward. One of 'em, rot his carcase, was like my own boy to me. Go on."

" She says it was an Indian, all feathers, and like a ghost, for the thing must have been a spirit, for the woman says it passed her like a shadow ; there was no sound of footsteps, and when it fired there was no noise from the rifle, and the——"

" Woman is a fool," said old Bill," " and you another to love her."

" I am not ; this is the word of the spectre, we heard about it——"

" Hold your tongue, lad, it's the work of

these reptiles, and may I not live to see another sun rise if I don't find them. Come on."

We heard the hasty movements of the men's feet, their angry, vengeful oaths, as they moved away in search of two men who were guiltless of the slightest crime.

Men who were doomed to a terrible death, and dared not call upon their fellow men for release from a living tomb.

CHAPTER XVI.

UNEARTHED BY THE DOGS.

"So they are Christians, are they," said Tim, and they think that red men ought to be rubbed out whenever a chance offers, isn't that it, Silvershot?"

"It is, Tim."

I sat with my face buried in my hands; the reaction that had taken place when my hopes were so suddenly blighted by the coming of old Buckskin, had quite broken my spirit.

The reflection that so many of our fellow creatures had been so close to us, and we should have died a much more painful death than by remaining in this cave, was in itself sufficient to make a strong man feel crushed in both body and mind.

The pangs of hunger and thirst too were slowly increasing, and such was our experience of the preparatory symptoms of dying by starvation and thirst that Tim said—

"It's a pity, comrade, we didn't let them know we were here, a bullet would have been better than this."

"A bullet would have been better, Tim, much better, but there was something more violent in store for us than such a swift end to our miseries."

"Maybe you are right, Silvershot, but there is no way so dreadful as this."

"Perhaps not, but I felt it impossible to face the cruelty those vindictive vagabonds would have shown, had we again fallen into their hands."

"It was hard, very hard to see they were going away, and we left to perish here."

"It was," said Tim, "but we have nothing to fear, soon our passing away will be like falling into a deep sleep."

"The Lord send it may be so, but I begin to feel the horrible torments of thirst."

"I have felt it creeping on for some time, Tim, let us bear it like men, no matter how much we increase our agony by dwelling upon all we have to undergo—did you hear the men's account of the spectre's visit to their camp."

"I did, and me blood all turned cold surely, Silvershot, the ghost can be——"

A large stone, evidently detached from the top of the chasm, tumbled down at this moment, and the faint sound of men's voices could be heard above us.

"They are keeping upon their search," I said; "what do you think, Tim, about letting them know we are here, that is if they come down near us?"

"Let us die quietly," said Tim, "for it's far from a quiet way they'd put us out of the world."

"Be it so, comrade."

How we suffered during that wretched day, no words of mine can express.

We had the terrible pangs of hunger and thirst, added to the prospect of a lingering, horrible death, and when the sun set we were completely worn out in mind and body.

Tim Delany slumbered like a cradled infant, and much as I wished to hear his cheery voice—cheery even under the appalling condition we were in, I refrained from arousing him from his blissful respite from the dark hour that was upon us.

I watched the solitary stream of dusky light that came into the cave. Assuaging my burning thirst by chewing a piece of my deer-hide leggings, and while thus attempting to smother my agony my eyes closed, and I too fell into a tranquil sleep.

I had dreams, too, such dreams as only visit those who are suffering from hunger and thirst.

I revelled in a glorious feast of the rich and juicy beef of the buffalo, and cooled my parched lips at the clear, running clear.

I laved my face with the water, stripped off my garments, and sported in the stream as I had often done when a boy.

But the dream soon had its reverse, for as I swam to and fro laughing with boyish glee, I heard the snorting of a huge animal.

I turned and struck out for the bank, but I could make a stroke a strange feeling of suffocation came over me, then a faintness, and my arms dropped powerless to my sides.

I felt myself sinking, going down slowly to the bed of the stream, and as I tried to tread the water a heavy weight came upon my breast.

My brain seemed bursting, my heart swollen, and my tongue clove to my mouth; the sensations were horrible, most horrible, and my attempts to cry out only increased the pressure upon my breast.

Down, down, until I reached the pebbly bottom of the stream, then I seemed to rock to and fro, as though uncertain whether to fall or not.

Then strange and horrible things came floating about me; there was the murdered girl pointing towards me with one hand while the other was placed upon her recking scalp.

There was a horrible monster near her; all

of which save the head was like a man, and the form was that of a crocodile's with long jagged teeth, which kept snapping at me so close, that I could see the huge red mouth and throat from which issued volumes of sulphurous smoke.

Other monsters there were near me, brutes whose forms defy description. The end soon came, I felt myself seized by the crocodile's jaws, I heard the snortings of the brute as his teeth pierced my flesh, I felt my bones crunching, then the spell that had been upon me broke, and I gave a piercing scream, and opened my eyes.

"It is a dream, thank God!" I murmured, "only a dream!"

"And a fearful noise you've been making over it," said Tim Delany. "Why, you've been groaning and moaning, and——what's that?"

"I do not hear anything," I said, placing my hand upon my breast to feel if the pressure was still there. "What do you hear, Tim?"

"'Faith I don't know what it is, if it's not some of the wolves come back, for there's a lot of scuffling going on outside there."

I listened, and distinctly heard the paws of a four-footed animal at work tearing at the entrance to the cave.

Then I heard a "snuffing" noise similar to that made by a dog, when tearing a rat hole.

"It's the wolves, Tim," I said. "Worse luck, the old bear did not wipe them all out."

"Hark, Silvershot!"

"What do you hear?"

"Listen, man, listen."

"I am doing—and—and——"

"What! what! Don't spake it, unless you are sure it's true, don't comrade, don't."

"It's the voice of Red Hugh!" I screamed, "a voice of a friend.

"That's what I thought, but I wouldn't speak it; but how are you sure it's them and the wolves together?"

"It's the dogs," I said, "that's good old Ben's note, and there follows Jip's. Hark! Tim. We are saved! saved! saved!"

"Glory be to him who has looked after us to-day," said Tim, and dropping from his half-bent posture, he swooned.

CHAPTER XVII.

UWATO'S WAR WHOOP.

MY brain swam with delirious joy, and I tried to call out loud enough to be heard beyond the cave.

But my voice was weak—so weak, that it scarcely filled the narrow place we were caged in.

I crawled forward, despite the maimed and bruised state of my body, and placed my hand close to the stones, that blocked up the entrance to the cave.

Every limb thrilled with joy, and my heart beat painfully, for all doubts were now removed about the identity of those outside

It was Hugh Howard and the dogs. I could hear him speaking to them. I listened for the voice of the young Raven, but heard it not, and the idea that he had been slain by the settlers repressed my joyous feelings at the prospect of being restored to life.

"What's the matter with the dogs?" I heard Hugh say. "There's nothing there except the carcase of a dead wolf, and that is not very tempting. Hi! Ben; this way, old man. We are only losing time here."

I tried to make my feeble voice reach his ears, for the thought of him leaving us to our dreadful fate gave me the most excruciating agony.

"Hugh, Hugh Howard, I am here, Silver shot. We are here, Tim Delaney and Silvershot."

He did not hear me.

"Come, Ben; this way, Jip. We must try and find all that remains of your master and his chum. This way, dogs, and try and recover the scent."

"We are here," I screamed as loud as I could, but my voice was not more powerful than a puling girl's. There has been a landslip, Hugh. Do not leave us; for goodness' sake do not."

The dogs' keener sense of hearing must have detected and recognised my voice, for they began yelping, and tore the ground with their fore-feet.

"It's strange," said Hugh, "very strange. What the devil's the matter with the brutes? There cannot be anything inside the rocks, and——"

He paused for a moment, then added, savagely—

"Old Buckskin Bill and his crew, by all that's infernal!"

I heard a distant hallo, then the reports of several rifles echoed down the ravine.

"Curse ye," said Hugh fiercely. "Had I my rifle I would wipe you out one at a time like so many carrion; but as it is I must slink behind this stone, to save my body from the bullets.

Our last hope was gone. Hugh could not escape the settlers and old Bill, and when he died our fate was sealed.

By a superhuman effort I drew myself close to the stones; the bear had departed, and putting my eye to the crevice, through which the single trace of light came, I obtained a view of the rocky ledge.

I saw Hugh Howard crouching behind a a huge stone, his right hand grasping a knife, and by his side lay the dogs, Ben and Jip, their white fangs gleaming in the failing daylight.

I heard the reports of the settlers' rifles, and the bullets pelting against the rocks; heard Red Hugh's dire oaths of vengeance against the party, headed by old Bill.

" 'The Lord take me safely out of this,' he said, " and I'll wipe every mother's son of them out, as sure as my name is Hugh Howard."

The settlers were rapidly descending the rocks. I knew that by the deep growl of the dogs, who were being set on by Hugh.

" Watch 'em, good dogs, watch 'em."

A deep growl, and the faithful animals settled down for a spring when their foes should come near.

The brutes, no doubt, had sufficient intelligence to know the men who were approaching had been the cause of their masters' destruction.

The position taken up by Hugh was a good one; the boulder had fallen near the end of the ledge from which there was no outlet, shutting off a corner as it were of the rocky platform.

The opposite end, as I have before stated, was approached by a zig-zag path down the side of the precipice.

The width of the ledge could not have been more than three feet, thus the settlers would not have been able to approach Hugh more than two at the time, and knowing how skilful he was in the use of the knife I felt assured that some of our implacable foes would fall before he was rubbed out.

" Now for it," said Hugh, as the party neared the ledge; " watch them Ben, ready, good Jip, or it's all over with Hugh Howard the backwoodsman."

Old Buckskin led the settlers.

He was the first upon the ledge, and levelling his rifle with one hand, for the other was yet in a sling, he called out—

" Come out of that, ye varmint, and tell us what has come of Silvershot and his mate."

" Come and take me out, you old thief," answered Hugh ; " come by yourself and see what will be the result."

" Ye varmint," said old Bill, " it's my belief ye are one of the———"

" Indians, Indians," said one of the settlers, " they are on the top of the chasm."

I looked up, and to my joy beheld a party of mounted Indians reined up on the very verge of the precipice, and I gave a feeble shout of triumph, for I knew by their gay trappings they were my friends the Comanches.

Yes they were the chivalrous Comanches, and as they sprung from their horses, and began to nimbly descend the side of the precipice, I heard the clarion-like war-whoop of Uwato, the handsome chief of the tribe.

CHAPTER XVIII.

A CHANGE OF AFFAIRS.

" IF they were the devil's imps," said old Bill, angrily, " we'll have this reptile's blood —come on, lads."

" Back," said Hugh, keeping within shelter of the boulder, " back, old man, or your scalp will dangle from the wampum belt of one of yonder warriors, a fate from which I alone can save you."

" I'd be cut to pieces," said old Bill, " before I'd give in now you've saved them varmints from the punishment we gave them, and we'll have your blood."

" Take it, then," shouted Hugh, as he sprung from his place of shelter, " take it now."

He had Buckskin Bill by the throat, and the long-bladed knife held aloft ready to plunge in the trapper's breast, and the dogs, as though excited by the scene, jumped forward and savagely attacked two of the nearest settlers.

" Place a finger upon a trigger, any of ye," shouted Hugh, " point a rifle towards me, and by Heavens I'll plunge this knife blade into Buckskin Bill's heart."

Inexperienced in the deadly struggles that were of daily occurrence on the prairie, the settlers paused and looked irresolutely from one to the other.

" I've done ye no hurt," Hugh continued ; " yet you seek my life ; no, dogs that ye are, it's my turn, for here come my friends."

As he spoke he cast the old trapper from him, and Uwato, followed by a dozen Comanche warriors, sprang upon the ledge. Every one of the settlers would have been slain but for Uwato.

" My warriors," he said, " are braves, not women. Disarm these men, and bind them ; it is for my white brethren here to say how they shall die."

I had a good view of the Comanches' attack, and could not help remarking the utter prostration of the settlers when they found themselves so easily discouraged and arm-bound.

It was a matter of every-day occurrence with the warlike band, and when they had finished, and gathered the white men's arms, Uwato advanced from Hugh Howard's side, and addressing old Bill, said—

" Hunter of the white head, we have met before."

" Ay,". replied the old trapper, " we have, ye redskin thief. Had I my arms at liberty, skin yer hide for ye, I'd stake my life we'd never meet again."

I saw Uwato's handsome face flush as the trapper spoke; the angry expression was but transient, for he said calmly, in reply to old Bill's words—

"An old man's tongue," he said, "is forked. Well for him of the forked tongue that he is old, or Uwato would throw him into the water beneath, for he owes the old trapper no good will."

"Skin your hide for ye, it's less you would have had I my way."

"Hush, old man, my braves have ears, and they are angry when they hear an old man threaten their chief. Surely age should have taught you wisdom? Let me hear it is so, for I have much to ask you."

"Say on, ye redskin devil," replied old Bill, savagely. "I can hear all you have to say, and whether it is answered or not is a matter for myself to decide."

"The old man will answer," said Uwato, "or his grave will be in the water course. Listen. What has been done by you with those men who have come from beyond the big river? What has been done, I ask, with my white brother, Silvershot, and his companion?"

"Nothing, worse luck," said Old Bill. "Skin 'em alive, they got away, through that varmint yonder."

He pointed to Red Hugh as he spoke, and the backwoodsman said:—

"You are a liar, Buckskin; you know what has become of our friends."

The young Raven came forward from amongst the warriors in obedience to a signal from Uwato.

He looked sternly at Buckskin Bill, and his small hand instinctively sought the hilt of his hunting-knife as he told the story of the doom to which Tim Delany and I were consigned by the old trapper and his companions.

I saw, by the vengeful glances the group of warriors cast towards the settlers, how well I was liked by them.

The young warrior modestly kept in the background his share in our adventures, and when he concluded, Uwato said:—

"Old man, you have heard the words of a Comanche, you know they do not lie. What have you to say in answer to the wrong you have done two brave hunters, who have never harmed thee or thine?"

"Indian," said old Bill, with less anger in his manner than he had hitherto shown, "you know me well, you know how I could have shown the greedy Mexicans where the Comanches kept the gold they dig from the earth and use to ornament their saddles. I could have shown the Mexicans all this and more, and the reward would have been a waggon of the precious metal. You know this, Comanche; say, do I lie?"

"The old man speaks the truth," said Uwato; "but what has the gold to do with the lives of those the braves of my nation love so well?"

"Not much, perhaps," said Buckskin. "I only alluded to it to show you that I would not do an unmanly action, even for the possession of the share of so much wealth that I could have left the western prairies and become a prince among my fellow-men. If I would not do this, do you think I would have harmed the gallant fellow whose eye and hand I trained to make him what he was?"

The trapper was well versed in the Indian customs, so he paused when he thought his speech had reached a telling climax.

"You have not lied, old man," said Uwato; "we are grateful for your fidelity, and the remembrance of it will not be overlooked when your life is at stake for the evil you have done to Uwato's white brother."

"I have done him no evil, Indian," said old Bill. "He was caught red-handed in the murder for which we demanded his life. Look here, Indian, I ask you if you would not have done the same?"

"Not with Silvershot," was the prompt reply, "unless he said his hand had been reddened with the woman's blood, and he told you he was innocent. Did he not, old man?"

"He did," said Buckskin; "but we had our eyes, Indian, and they told the truth."

"You lie!" said Uwato. "My white brother does not speak with a double tongue; had he scalped that white woman, he would have said so, even if his hands were red with her blood, and her scalp hung from his belt. Is it fit a brave hunter should die because he has killed a woman? Of what value are a dozen women's lives—not equal to one brave's?"

"Not by your customs," replied old Bill. "With us one life is as much as another, even to the smallest child."

Uwato gave a gesture of contempt and pity to old Bill, and said:—

"Take the old man and his companions to where the horses stand; let my braves be careful they arrive there without the loss of a scalp. I have spoken. Go!"

The caution was necessary, for the Comanche warriors looked very much inclined to scalp the whole of the settlers and their leader.

About half a dozen of the Indians remained with Uwato, and the latter, Hugh Howard, addressing, asked—

"Has the trail been struck?"

"Not yet," he answered; "we have yet to find their bodies——"

Tim Delaney had recovered from his swoon, during the time Uwato and Buckskin Bill were speaking.

I had time to briefly explain all that was heard since the arrival of the dogs and Hugh. I also told him that unless we succeeded in making ourselves heard by the party outside we were doomed to linger out another wretched day before death put an end to our misery.

"Me voice," said Tim, "is but a squeak just now, Silvershot, maybe yours is not much better."

"Alas, not even a squeak, Tim."

"Suppose we put the two together, and who knows but they may hear us? Of course they will, don't we hear them speaking plain enough, man alive?"

"Quite so, but remember you hear the voices of men whose tongues are not swollen, whose throats are not parched, and being live prisoners, I don't believe we shall do it, Tim, for it's as much as I can do to make you hear me."

"That's true, and it's the same with me-self, and as we are not strong enough to hulloa—man alive, what fools we are!"

"What's the matter?"

"Matther, avick! The tomahawk, to be sure."

Tim seized the weapon, and just as Hugh Howard was telling Uwato our bodies had yet to be found, Delany began hammering against one of the stones that choked up the entrance to the cave.

"The dogs were right after all," Hugh joyfully exclaimed; "our friends are shut up in the earth, how, Heaven and themselves alone can tell."

Ben and Jip, who had not ceased smelling about the place, except for a few minutes after the arrival of Buckskin Bill's party, then began to yelp and scratch at the entrance to our prison.

"Silvershot's manitou has been good to him," said Uwato, laying his rifle upon the ground, and stripping off his deer-hide jacket; "come up here, use the strength the Great Spirit has given you."

Hugh Howard and Uwato worked as though they had found the strength of a couple of giants.

We could hear the largest of the stones hurled over into the precipice, and the Young Raven and two of the Comanches shovelled away the loose earth with their hands.

Gradually the crevice became larger; a head was thrust through, and as quickly withdrawn, for at the same moment a warning cry came from Red Hugh, then there was a swift dispersal of our deliverers out of the way of a mass of earth that fell when the stones were removed.

We tried to utter a cry of horror as we were covered by the earth that forced its way into the cave; in a moment we were suffocated by the heavy weight upon us, then all became a blank to our senses.

Uwato afterwards told me he quite despaired of saving us, for not only had the roof of the cave fallen upon us, but the greater part of the ledge was choked up, and they found it a long and severe task, seeing that they were without tools of any kind, to clear sufficient space to get near us again.

When I returned to consciousness I was lying comfortably wrapped in several blankets; it was night, yet I could not see either moon or stars, so I put out my hand and soon found the place where I lodged was a tent made from the skins of various animals.

Satisfied so far that all was well I began to feel about to ascertain if the party who owned the tent had left anything drinkable never at hand, for I was consumed by a burning thirst.

I had not felt far to my right before I grasped something which to my confused senses seemed like the handle of a drinking vessel.

CHAPTER XIX.
GOOD FOR EVIL.

I WAS very feverish and anxious to slake my thirst, so my thumb and finger very tightly gripped the handle, and to my astonishment the vessel gave a yell, then spoke as follows—

"What the divil, man alive, are ye doing with me nose?"

"Is that you, old fellow?"

"Faith it is, and none the better for being lifted up by the nose."

"I'm very sorry, Tim——"

"Don't say a word about it, avick, don't spake at all, only to tell me how you are."

"I do not feel very bright."

"Bedad, no, it's a wonder you can feel anything at all, after the long time you have been coming to."

"Long time coming to!"

"The same, man alive! this is the second night we have been out of the cave, and the divil a sign you have made until now; it's my opinion if it had not been for Uwato you would never have spoken again."

"What has been the matter with me?"

"That's more than anyone of us could find out," said Tim, "but it's my opinion you got a crack on the skull, for when they dug us out, there was a large stone lying over on your head."

A peculiar thumping on the top of my head caused me to raise my head, and I found my my hair had been cut away, and a plaster, no doubt of the leaves of one of the many healing plants that grow upon the western hills.

I understood it all now. The terrible excitement I had undergone in the cave, coupled with the blow from the stone, had caused a stupor from which I had but just recovered.

"Maybe so," said Tim, when I told him my opinion; anyhow, I thought it was all over with you, so did Uwato; and as for the other Indians, it was all the chief could do to prevent them from rubbing out old Buckskin and his party."

"Where is Uwato?"

"He's gone to his tent to sleep, for he wants a sleep, considering how he's been sitting by your side ever since you and I were dug out of the cave."

I was touched at this proof of Uwato's love for me, and mentally resolved to become a member of the Comanche nation as soon as I began to tire of a hunter's life.

"What has become of the settlers, Tim?"

"Bedad, they are safe enough, and praying for you to get well, I'll wager."

"Why so?"

"Because Uwato told them if you died they'd all be strung up by the neck. The young Raven is in charge of them, so there's no fear of even one getting away, for the Raven is as sharp as a hawk, and——"

"Hallo there! what time is it? What are you fellows talking about?"

The voice came from the left side of the tent.

"He's awake, Hugh," said Tim, " and barring the twist of the nose he gave me, he's as sensible as ever."

"I'm glad to hear it," said Hugh. " Give me your hand, Silvershot. Never mind, go to sleep, and we'll talk in the morning."

I fell back in my comfortable bed, and was soon asleep. Quick as I was, my companions were ahead in the race, for I heard them as my eyes closed performing a well-sustained nasal duet.

In the morning I was able to leave the tent, and, supported by Hugh's powerful arm, went to the encampment, in the centre of which stood Uwato and two hundred and and fifty of his choicest warriors.

It was a gallant sight to behold. The gaily-accoutred Indians formed three sides of a square. Neither eye nor head moved as they stood proudly out, leaning upon their rifles.

In the background stood the fiery horses, champing their golden bits and impatiently pawing the ground.

When I entered the square the braves raised their eyes and glanced at Tim Delany's and my ragged figures, and when they saw our pale, pinched faces, there was more than one hand sought the haft of the scalping-knife.

The act was parent to the thought, for I knew they longed to wipe out the indignities we had undergone by scalping old Buckskin's party; and so great was their animosity that I found I could, had I been so vengefully disposed, have had the whole of the settler's slain.

The young Raven was anxious to leave the ranks and speak to me, but the strict rules of the Indian laws forbade even the oldest chief amongst them to move a pace forward until their prince, the handsome Uwato, had given them permission to do so.

My gallant friend had not yet joined his band, he was standing at some distance from the horse lines, talking to an old chief, and by their animated gestures I knew that something extraordinary had or was about to occur.

Their conversation lasted for nearly half an hour, then Uwato came towards the savages, and the old chief took his place in the ranks.

Every spear point was lowered to the ground when the Comanche King entered the open space.

He acknowledged the salute by a slight gesture, and the spear points were raised, and the ranks became as stationary as though they were composed of the best drilled soldiery in the world.

"Welcome, my brother!" said Uwato, grasping my hand. "Thy spirit has been near the hunting grounds of thy race. Uwato is glad thy Manitou has been so good to thee."

"Silvershot," I said, adopting the Indian mode of speech, "rejoices to be able again to speak to his brother. He had not thought of having so great a joy when his spirit was broken, and his body lay in the cave at the side of the precipice."

Uwato shook hands with Hugh Howard and Tim Delany, and bade them welcome because they were my friends. He told them, with Indian generosity, that all the tribe possessed was at their service, except the warriors' arms and horses.

"Let the old trapper," he said, addressing the young Raven, " and his companions, the men from beyond the great river, be brought here."

A dozen warriors followed the Raven, in obedience to a signal from the chief, and in a few minutes the settlers and old Buckskin were brought before Uwato.

Old Bill looked angrily at the immovable groups of Indians, and the settlers seemed anything but at ease.

"Before the sun reaches the tops of yonder mountains," said Uwato, "the Comanches will be upon the war-path; they will take with them the white hunters," he pointed to Tim, Hugh, and myself, "but the men who have come from beyond the big river will remain behind."

"That's a good thing," said old Bill, "for we don't want to go with those who——"

"Silence, old man! I have not done speaking. Listen. My braves, the Great Spirit has sent down from the happy hunting grounds the shade of a warrior whose mission is to carry out the Manitou's will, and for the doings of this spirit my white brother and his friend have been blamed. I ask was this right, and I read in your faces that it was not."

He paused for a few minutes, then resumed—

"Were the white men Shoshones, Arapahoes, Comanches, or Bonnaxes, we should know how to punish them, but they are whites, and we will leave it to our white brothers to say what shall be done. Let my brother Silvershot speak."

Thus appealed to, I was led forward to pass punishment upon those who had so recently sought my life.

"Comanches," I said, "brave children of the Great Serpent, I am but a stranger amongst you, yet my voice has often been heard at the councils of your nation, and my rifle has been used side by side with the rifles of my brothers here. Have I spoken with a single tongue?"

I paused, and a general murmur of approbation came from the Indians' lips.

"When the rascally Crows," I resumed, "left their hiding-places on the mountains and the holes and fissures of the earth, and sought to take the scalps of a party of Comanche braves, I, thanks to the Great Spirit, and my companion here, Tim Delany, prevented the Crows from falling upon the tired hunters. Many of you were foes of that party, and all, from the youngest brave to the oldest chief, told me when I had a favour to ask any of your nation to ask it, and it would not be denied. Comanches, I now wish you to redeem your promise. Let these men go free; they have erred, but their motives were prompted by brave and manly feelings. Comanches, I have said."

There was a few minutes' silence, then Uwato said—

"Silvershot has spoken. What say my braves? shall we hearken to his words, and give them up their lives? or shall we make them suffer, as they made our white brothers suffer?"

Gne by one the chief warriors came forward and gave their opinion; and the majority of them being in favour of my wishes, Uwato turned to them and said—

"We have heard the voice of one who is dear to us, old man; and those who came from beyond the big river to rob the Indian of his land, are free. Go; leave us before the Indian forgets this clemency and wipes out the wrongs of those who never did them harm."

Neither Buckskin nor his men uttered a word while the thongs that bound them were being cut; but when this was over, the old trapper turned to Uwato and said :—

"Indian, it is many miles from here to our lodges. Are we to go unarmed?"

I thought I detected a sinister gleam in the trapper's eyes as he spoke; but being in communication with the Comanhe chief at the time, I did not take much notice of it.

This negligence nearly proved fatal to me, as the next chapter will show.

CHAPTER XX.

EVIL FOR GOOD.

"The old man wan have his rifle," said Uwato; "it will be sufficient to provide food, the others must be left with us. We have need of them.

"My young men," old Bill said, "will have need of their rifles, Indian. Are they to starve upon the prairie? Are their huts to be left undefended when the Bonnaxes go upon the war-path?"

"Silence, old man," said Uwato sternly; "speak not with the tongue of the serpent, for Uwato can tell what is within one of the waggons the white men brought from beyond the big river."

The waggon alluded to by Uwato, I afterwards found, contained cases of rifles and ammunition, brought out, no doubt, upon the spec of selling them to the Indians.

Buckskin made no reply, possibly he thought one of the cases would be confiscated by the Comanches, many of whom were in want of rifles.

Let the old man have his rifle," continued Uwato; "let him also open his ears and listen to my words, if he has the brains his grey head ought to have, he will keep out of the path of my young men, for they are angry. I have said. The old man can go."

One of the braves brought Buckskin's rifle, shot-bag, and powder-flask, and flinging them at his feet, said—

"Our chief has spoken, do not forget his words."

Buckskin Bill bit his lip angrily, but made no answer.

I watched him take the rifle from the ground, and try whether it was loaded; having ascertained this, he slowly placed the ramrod in the pipe, then raising the weapon to the firing position, put a new cap on the nipple, and before any one could divine his purpose, the butt was brought to his shoulder, and the muzzle in line with my head.

"Skin your hides," he said, "do ye think old Buckskin cares for his life so much as to leave that varmint alive after what he has done? No; take that——"

The young Raven dashed forward and beat up the rifle as old Bill pulled the trigger, the ball flew right in the air, and for all I know may be lying among the long grass to this very day.

The young Indian then flung himself upon the trapper and bore him to the ground; one hand gripped the fatal scalping knife, the other was upon old Bill's throat.

He would have been stabbed but for Red Hugh, who rushed forward and caught the young Indian's upraised arm.

"Let him get up, Raven," said Hugh, "the knife is too easy for him to die by. We'll find another way more suitable for the old varmint."

The Indian reluctantly relinquished his prize, and rising, said—

"The old man is a dog, he must die."

"All in good time," Hugh said. "Listen, your chief speaks."

Uwato thrust the tomahawk back in his belt; he had plucked it forth to destroy old Bill, and pointing to the emigrants, who stood tremblingly awaiting the issue of their leader's rash act, he said—

"The Raven is young, but he is a warrior, and can be trusted; let him take a dozen of the young men with him and see the white men back to their lodges; the old man must stay with us."

The men were forced to obey, so the settlers, under the escort detailed by Uwato, left the camp.

An Indian stood on each side of old Bill, tomahawk in hand, and ready at the slightest movement to bury the keen blades in his skull.

Uwato motioned for them to bring the prisoner forward.

"Old man," said the chief, "you are as ungrateful as the serpent, who seeks a refuge in the Indian's blanket, then stings the man who has sheltered him from the cold winds; what mercy do you deserve, after the evil you have returned for the good done you by my brother, Silvershot? Why should I not have your life, and throw your body to the dogs? Answer me this, old man?"

The trapper looked sullenly at Uwato, and compressed his lips tightly, fearing his angry passions would cause him to make an answer.

"Your heart is brave," said Uwato—angry as he was, he could not help admiring the old

fellow's stubborn pluck, "but your white hairs have not brought wisdom; you deserve to die, old man, and I should be no longer worthy to be the chief of so many braves and mighty warriors were I to let you live. You must die, but your death will not be the easy passing away from this world by the swift bullet or the keen knife. No, you must die slowly, bit by bit. Death must be welcome when it reaches you, for the sufferings that come before will be worse than the fleeting of the spirit to the unknown world.

Buckskin Bill's face paled slightly; he, no doubt, thought the torture was to be his fate.

"It is but just," said Uwato, in continuation, "that you should suffer, only just that you should feel the agonies you have caused my white brother to feel. Listen, Comanches; listen, my friends, whose hearts are with our nation; and if any of you have any words to say against my wish, let him speak."

There was a dead silence, and the Indians leaned their necks forward to catch the next words.

They came slowly, distinctly; every syllable uttered with that peculiar distinctness of which the Indian language is capable.

I could feel for the old trapper, whose doom was now about to be pronounced, and who, despite his immense courage, could not prevent a slight quivering of the lip and an anxious, wistful glance towards the handsome chief.

"Old man," said Uwato, "I have said you must die. Hear my words: my braves will take you to the cave from which we brought my brother and his companion; there, old man, you will be walled in until the Great Spirit releases you from this world. Comanches, I have said."

A suppressed guttural exclamation of pleasure broke from the Indians' lips, and I saw whatever merciful plea I ventured to put in would be overruled.

"Let the old cuss taste what you have tasted," said Hugh; "it will do him good."

There was something else to be done, for several of the Indian braves surrounded Buckskin Bill, and turned his face in the direction of the big prairie.

The old trapper recovered his firmness, and endeavoured, as far as the deer-hide thong that bound his arms would permit him, to strike at the men who were about to lead him away.

"Curse ye for a lot of copper-coloured devils," he said; "ye may kill me, bury me alive; but when the old man is dead, the voice he leaves behind him will speak and tell the Mexicans where the Comanches have hidden their gold."

"Go, old man," said Uwato, "meet thy death like a brave, not like a squaw who uses hands to terrify the child she carries in her arms."

"It's no idle boast, Indian," retorted old Bill, "for I left at St. Juan Compestrano sufficient to guide the greedy Mexicans to your treasure. I left it there, Indian, with orders that the deer-hide case should be opened if I did not return in six months' time. Four months have gone by; there are two left; and I should have returned in time but for you. Now, Indian, do you think my life worth saving or not?"

"The old man is cunning, but his cunning will not save him. He has sealed his doom by his own mouth, for who would suffer a double-faced liar to live?"

"I am no liar, Indian; I am no traitor. I was, perhaps, when I marked down the bearings of the cave where your treasure is hidden, but the way in which you behaved to me when I lay wounded in your village changed my mind towards you, so when I returned to St. Juan Compestrano I left the piece of deer-hide in a safe place, intending, if I returned, to bring it away and place it in your hands, but as it is it will be opened, and the Mexicans will find what they have so long coveted, so think twice, Comanche, before you shut me up in the side of the precipice."

"Uwato has spoken," said the chief; "the old man must die, and the lies he utters will not bear him quicker to the happy land beyond the earth."

"It's no lie, Comanche," said old Bill. "I tell you the Mexicans will be upon your village unless I return to St. Juan and——"

"Enough; the Comanches are able to keep this country from the attacks of a nation of liars. I have spoken. Let the old hunter be taken away."

Uwato's gesture was sufficient for the braves, so they hurried their captive forward, and were soon out of sight, for there was a swell on the prairie just beyond the horse lines.

"Now, my brethren," said Uwato, turning to me, "we have but a few hours to rest, before going on the war path. Come hither, my father," he added, turning to an old man who stood on the right flank of the gallant band; "come hither, and try if thy skill can restore the brave Silvershot to fleetness of limb and strength of body."

The venerable Indian, whose hair was as white as the drifting snow, came forward, and placing his hand upon my shoulder, said—

"Does my son fear to trust his life in the hands of the old medicine."

"I do not," I replied, "for the medicine men are far above those of my nation who profess to relieve our bodies from pain."

"My son speaks well, let the old man's deeds prove how much he deserves such praise."

The old medicine examined my wounds and bruises, also those of Tim Delaney; then he left us, and speaking a few words to a couple of Indians, they placed their weapons upon the ground and left the camp.

I guessed their errand, they had gone to search for herbs, and in less than half an hour returned, bearing in their hands bunches of yellow leaves and long grass.

By this time the fire had been lighted, and the old medicine placed an equal portion of the medicine herbs in a small iron pot, and boiled them to pulp.

This he laid upon our wounds, and desiring us to drink as much as we could of the liquid, ordered us to return to the tent we had so lately quitted.

Before we arrived there our limbs began to feel pulseless, and by the time we sank upon the buffalo robes which served for our couch, a strange numbing sensation began to creep over us.

I tried to master it, so did Tim, but the spell was too potent, our eyes closed, and we sank into a dreamless slumber.

CHAPTER XXI.

ANOTHER MYSTERIOUS MURDER.

I WAS the first to awake from that death-like sleep, and it was some time before I could collect my confused senses sufficiently to understand all that had befallen me.

I felt for the dressing of leaves the old medicine had placed upon my wounds, and discovered they were gone, I touched the wounds and found all sense of pain had left, and the ugliest gashes were closed and the edges drawn firmly together.

My limbs, too, were free from pain, and rising from my couch I found I was once more restored to health and strength.

Tim Delany slept soundly by my side, and I was about to awaken him when the old medicine softly entered the tent, and seeing my intention respecting Tim he placed his hand gently upon my arm, and said—

"My son must not be impatient; let him remember if his brother awakens before the medicines have done their work it will be fatal."

I stepped back, for I knew the old Indians at times employed the most violent poisons as antidotes to wounds.

I knew also that these desperate remedies required a certain time to operate upon the system, and during this period the mental senses must be in a state of quietude.

"My father is wise," I said, "Silvershot thanks him, and will once more breathe the fresh air, if it will not interfere with the——"

"My son," the old Indian said, interrupting me, "the pure air that sweeps so swiftly over the prairie is sent by the Great Spirit for the good of His children. Come."

I followed him from the tent, and great was my surprise when I looked around and saw that the Comanches, except a dozen of the younger warriors, had disappeared.

The shields and spears belonging to the young braves were placed outside the tent, a sign that they looked upon Tim Delany and I as their chiefs, and would follow us wherever we wished to lead them.

It was a graceful act of Uwato's, and I fully appreciated it, for it was an honour only conferred upon the greatest chiefs.

"My son," the old man said, "looks around for the Comanche braves. Does he not know they are upon the war-path?"

"I knew they were going in quest of their foes, father, but knew not they had gone until now. How long is it since the camp was broken up?"

"Two suns have gone down beyond the edge of the prairie," the old medicine said. "since the Comanches went upon the trac of their foes. My son's ears have been closed for many hours, or he would have heard the braves assembling."

I had indeed slept many hours, and soundly, too, or I should have heard the departure of the tribe upon their warlike mission."

I asked the old man concerning the fate of old Buckskin Bill, and heard that Uwato's sentence had been carried out.

I could not repress a shudder when I thought of the agony the old man must have endured in his living tomb, and the thought that all must be over by this time, caused a sensation of remorse, for I knew I had not done as much as I ought to have done to have saved him.

However, regrets were useless, so I tried to dismiss the matter from my mind, and saluting the young warriors who stood awaiting my commands, I re-entered the tent to look after Tim Delany.

I found my chum sitting up rubbing his eyes, and looking rather perplexed at the walls of the tent.

"That's you, Silvershot," "well and strong on your pins again, that bates all."

"How do you feel, Tim?"

"Bedad, that's just what I was trying to find out," he said, "for the leg seems all right, so does me skull, and I was wondering whether it was a drame or not when you came in."

"It's no dream, Tim, thank Heaven and the old medicine, we are as well as ever."

"By me soul, I belave we are, and it bates all the doctors in the old country to nothing. Don't you think so, man alive?"

"There's one question about that, Tim. Of course we are very different to a European doctor's patient."

"How do you mane, Silvershot?"

"I mean what I say, Tim."

"Yes, yes, but spake plainer, man alive.'

"Well, the old medicine has no interest in keeping us from getting well, so he cures us at once; but where a man has to live by another's illness, you cannot blame him for making the affair profitable to himself."

"That's true, avick, and it's glad I am sometimes that we are on the prairie, and not living in any of the big settlements among the doctors and lawyers."

"You and I have good reason to feel so, for misery and death follow in the track of the doctors who flock to the new villages; and endless litigation and strife are the inevitable consequences of a lawyer's appearance."

"To the divil with both of 'em," said Tim; "it's not worth troubling our heads about the lives of such varmints."

"True, Tim, so get to your feet, and we'll have a turn on the grass."

"Bedad, and so we will."

Tim was profuse in his thanks to the old medicine, whom we found outside the tent.

"It's a fortune you'd make," Delany said, in conclusion, "if you were to go to any of the towns beyond the paths of rivers. Wouldn't he now, Silvershot?"

"I'm afraid not," I answered, smiling, "for it's the women who are the doctor's best friends, and I don't think they would believe in the medicine's attentions. No, Tim, he's better where he is, for he is neither young nor handsome, or the proper colour for the fair ones."

"Bedad, that's true. Well, anyhow, I'm mightily obliged, and I know you are Silvershot."

"I am, and have already expressed myself to that effect."

Tim declared he felt as well as ever he did in his life, barring a little bit of pain in the leg.

"But that,' he said, "will soon go away. Then, Silvershot, we'll be able to go after the Comanches, and who knows but we may be in time for the fun?"

"A good thought, Tim. I was just thinking it would not do for us to remain here, for these young braves are eager to join their companions."

"Of course they are; so what do you say? Let me see. One, two, three, four, five, six——"

THE BONNAXES REINED UP AT THE SIGHT OF THE LEVELLED RIFLES.

"What are you counting, Tim?"

"Their horses, man alive; and as sure as my name's Delany, there's two more, and they are for us."

I motioned for one of the Indians to join us, and he did so quite as respectfully as though we were chiefs of his own tribe.

"Stormy Weather," I said, calling him by the name that had been given him by his tribe, "will be glad to join his brave companions, who are now upon the war-path."

"The white chief, with an Indian heart," he answered, "speaks well. He utters the thoughts of the Comanche warriors."

"Let us go, then," I said. "My brother will see the tent taken down."

The Indian's joy was expressed by the way in which he communicated the welcome order to his companions, who at once took up their arms and went to the picket lines.

Assured by the old medicine that our recovery was certain, Uwato had before his departure, left us arms and horses, and one of the latter, when they were led to where we stood, I saw was Uwato's favourite steed, his black mustang, that had carried him through many a fierce fight.

The bridle of the black horse was placed in my hands; at the same moment another Indian came forward with a couple of soft deerskin hunting jackets, beautifully embroidered with coloured quills.

Not a single article that we stood in need of had been forgotten by the thoughtful chief.

Fur caps, covered with black eagle's fea-

5

thers, shot pouches, game bags, waist belts, new blankets, lassos, knives, rifles, tomahawks, and pistols.

Well dressed, well armed, and splendidly mounted, we rode at the head of the gallant band and travelled until nightfall.

There was no lack of provisions, for my dogs, Ben and Jip, foraged about during the day's march, and every "bit of eatable game" they started was brought down by the Indians.

We were in the Bonnaxes' country, so as a prudent measure we refrained from making a fire of logs, not but that it would have been very acceptable, for the night was chilly and the dew very heavy.

The tent was pitched near the horse lines, and the old medicine, whose property it was, wished us to take possession of it.

This we stoutly declined; we wished to keep up our prestige with the Indians, and to do this it was necessary to sleep as they did, our blanket and buffalo robes forming bed and covering.

We feasted right royally on a young antelope baked in clay. The fire to cook this was made in a hole; and after the clay and its contents were placed upon the crackling wood, the orifice was carefully covered to hide the light from any prying foe.

Before rolling myself in my blanket, I placed sentinels around our camp; then, seeing the old medicine to his tent, I prepared to pass the night in a greater state of luxury and comfort than had fallen to my lot for some time."

"Bedad, Silvershot," said Tim, "this is something like old times come back again. Better than being amongst the wolves, eh, avick?"

"Much better, infinitely better than being on the ledge during the storm."

"That's true for ye. Good night, comrade."

"Good night."

The dogs were coiled at my feet, and we were within three yards of the old medicine's tent.

But for the dogs being so near, I should have placed a sentry over the old Indian's tent, for I knew that the Bonnaxes were bold and cunning enough to penetrate our camp, if any of them were near.

The tent bore the symbol of the Comanche chief; this alone would have been a sufficient incentive for a Bonnaxe to risk the chance of being discovered in an attempt to scalp the supposed leader of the hostile tribe.

"The dogs," I thought, as I drew my blanket over my face, "will give the alarm should a foe pass the sentinels."

Satisfied with this, I soon fell into a deep sleep.

Something disturbed me about midnight, I thought a cold hand drew down the blanket that enveloped my head, and starting up I looked eagerly around.

I must have been dreaming, so I thought at the time, for the dogs were still in the position they had taken up before I slept.

The sentries, too, were passing slowly to and fro, or leaning against the trunk of a tree, their bright arms flaming under the starlight.

"Confound that antelope," I muttered, "it was not sufficiently cooked, so I am in for a lot of disagreeable dreams."

Tim Delany awoke at this moment, and putting his head outside his blanket, said:—

"Is that you, Silvershot? What's the matter?"

"Nothing. Only underdone antelope does not agree with me.

"You needn't have taken the trouble to wake me up, for all that."

"I wake ye up?"

"Yes, you. Shure didn't ye pull the blanket off me face, just now."

I started bolt upright.

"No, Tim, I did not. What a singular thing, I was awakened by the same thing happening to me."

"The divil you were."

"But I attributed it to a dream, for everything is quiet, and the dogs show no sign of uneasiness."

"That's true; so it must have been a drame a-piece, Silvershot, for if it had been a Bonnaxe, we should not have been talking now."

"Right, Tim, so good night for the second time."

"Good night, avick."

We were astir with the first gleam of the new day, and while some of the Indians were busy with the horses, others collected pine nuts to cook our breakfast.

We had no fear now of being seen, for the prairie was wide, and our nerves were to be depended upon if a *retrograde movement* was necessary to save our scalps.

The horses were ready, and the birds that had been cooked were getting cold, by the time Tim and I returned from the brook, where we had been taking a morning refresher.

"It's glad I am," said Tim, "that we are not last, for it wouldn't do for the braves to think we are late."

"I think we are the last," I said, "for the horses are bridled, the men armed, and the morning meal none the better for expecting our arrival."

"Maybe all this," Tim said, "but there's one not yet put in an appearance.

> "Who's that?"

"Why, the old medicine, don't you see his tent hasn't been unfastened yet?"

"You are right, Tim, then we have saved our character—confound it, what are we to do? I'm as hungry as a wolf, and etiquette will not allow us to feed, until the old fellow puts in an appearance."

"Send one of them to wake him up."

"That's against etiquette too," I said, "so we have nothing to do but to admire these birds. It will increase our appetite, Tim."

"Maybe so, but I'd prefer to pitch into them."

"So would I. Here comes Stormy Weather; I'll ask his opinion upon the matter."

The Indian saluted me as he came up, and in reply to my question, said:—

"Silvershot is a chief. It is he alone who can disturb the slumbers of the old medicine."

I was glad to hear I had this privilege, so at once acted upon it, and went to the tent, and rapping the hide with my open hand, I called out :—

"It is late, my father, and the young men are ready."

CHAPTER XXII.

THE BEGINNING OF AN INDIAN BATTLE.

THERE was no answer, so I beat the dried hide until it sounded like a bass drum, and repeated my summons.

Still no answer.

"The old man sleeps sound," I said to Tim; "so I suppose there is nothing for it but shaking him out of his dreams."

"That's the only way, avick; so the sooner you do it the better, for me stomach is beginning to cry."

I gave a scream of horror, and fell back, and poor Tim, catching my arm, said—

"What's the matter, comrade? Have you trodden upon the head of a snake?"

I could only point to the interior of the tent for a reply, and Tim advanced and looked through the opening, and I heard him gasp—

"The Lord be good to us, and the devil fly away with the spectre!"

Our strange cries brought the Comanches to the tent, and when they saw the ghastly spectacle they gave a yell of rage and despair.

There lay the old medicine in a pool of blood, his scalp gone, the bullet hole in his throat, and the horrible teeth marks, which so fatally distinguished the spectral warrior's victims.

The old man was so well liked by the tribe that I feared there would have been an extra display of feeling.

Such was far from the case : for the men, strong in their belief that the old man's death was caused by the Great Spirit's anger,

bowed meekly to the will of their deity, and getting round the body, chanted the death song.

This over, they buried him where he had been found ; then setting fire to the tent, and all that belonged to the good old man, returned to the horse lines.

I gave the signal for the men to mount, and, putting our horses in motion, we rode gloomily away.

I was deeply grieved at the old man's death ; so was Tim, who rode apart from me, his face gloomy and abstracted.

I called him to my side, and said—

"Tim, do you think it was a dream now that our faces were uncovered last night?"

"Faith, I do not !" he cried. "And that's what puzzles me."

"To think that the ghost shouldn't know who was under the blankets without looking at us."

"And do you think it is a ghost, Tim?"

Delany looked up in surprise, and asked—

"What is it, then?"

"Our wisdom upon this matter is equal," I said, "for I cannot fathom the hellish mystery."

"Nor I. But it can't be a mortal, Silvershot, for there's none of the young men seen anything moving about the camp last night; besides, there is the shot, for the old medicine was shot, and there was no report when the rifle was fired."

"The strangeness of that," I said, "has puzzled me, Tim, and will do so, I suppose, until the mystery is cleared up."

"Cleared up? Man alive, do you think it ever will be cleared up? Sure, hasn't you and I and Hugh Howard come many a mile to clear it up, and we are as far off as ever?"

"That's true, Tim; but time and perseverance will yet solve this inexplicable affair."

"Faith, I hope it will; but I'm afraid it won't be in our time, Silvershot."

"Think not?"

"I do. It's of Hugh's belief I am, and everything that turns up makes my belief the stronger."

"What is Hugh's belief, Tim?"

"Just this. The ghost has a certain time to walk about the earth, and when that time is over there will be an end to all these horrid murders."

"Certainly Hugh Howard's belief is worthy of being followed, for I don't know a man who would follow up anything with more resolution than Hugh. By the way, where is he?"

"Stormy Weather," Tim said, "told me that Hugh had gone with Uwato, and is in charge of the scouts."

"Uwato could not have a better man for the duty."

"Barring yourself, Silvershot."

I smiled at Tim's compliment, and was about to reply, when one of the two braves who were in advance of our party came galloping back.

We had left the level prairie for some time, and had struck a path, dangerous and rugged, that led to a chain of high hills.

There was a cattle track between two of the hills, and to this we were making, for our advance guard had been told to follow the route taken by the Comanche braves.

It was when our scouts reached the cattle track that they turned back; one reining his horse under the shelter of a palmetto, the other retiring to report the strange sight visible in the forest below.

The Indian pulled his horse sharply up, and, lowering his spear, awaited my command for him to speak.

"Ready-Hand" I said, "has eyes. What is there in the bend beyond the hills that causes him to leave the trail of his tribe?"

"Beyond the hills," answered the Indian, "there is a plain. On each side of the plain the timber grows thickly. In the timber on the right hide the Bonnaxes; in the timber on the left the mighty Comanches await the coming of their foes."

"Ready-Hand has spoken well," I said; "let him return to his companions."

The Indian wheeled his horse and sped back. I saw him draw rein when he neared the foot of the cattle track.

Then he walked the snorting beast gently up the hill, keeping well under the shadow of the trees.

I raised my hand as a signal for the Comanches to halt, and when they were drawn up in double line, I rode to the front, and said—

"Brave warriors, children of the Great Serpent, listen to the words of one who is of thy nation in everything except the colour of his skin; that we cannot help."

A buzz of applause came from these horsemen, and I proceeded.

"Uwato, the chief of a mighty nation, has left some of his bravest warriors to my care. Now, listen. I know my young men, when they hear the rifles crack, and behold their brothers in the fight, will lose their prudence, and wish to join them. Is it not so?"

"The white chief speaks the Comanches' thoughts," said Stormy Weather. "He is a brave and skilful warrior, and a lion in the fight."

"I want my brothers," I said, "to obey me, for the Bonnaxes are as numerous as the leaves; and the Comanches, though brave, are but few. Will my young men keep with me? They shall join the fight, but not with

their chief. No; they must wait and see how fares their tribe, then I will give the word."

The Comanches knew by this time my motive for keeping them from rushing headlong into the fierce melee, and with one voice they said—

"The Silverbullet is our chief, him alone will we obey."

I bowed in reply, then giving the signal, we resumed our march towards the hills.

"Bedad!" said Tim, "if ye were to colour your face, comrade, there's no one would know but you were a redskin, for your tongue is more Indian than anything else."

"To you, perhaps," I said, "but I'm afraid my bungling speech must make those fellows grin, although they are too respectful to do it before my face."

"Well, then, it don't matter; for no one cares what's done behind their backs."

"That's a matter of opinion, Tim; for I believe anything that is done openly, no matter what it is, creates less mistrust and pain than if it is done out of one's sight."

"Maybe you're right."

We were upon the cattle track, and slowly ascending the foot of the hill, when one of the scouts came down and met us, saying—

"The Bonnaxes are crawling from their lairs."

He wheeled round, and returned to the shelter of the trees, and I called a halt.

"My young men will dismount," I said, "and stand by their horses until I return."

I got out of the saddle, and Tim followed my example, and giving our horses to the nearest Indian, we began the ascent of the hill on the right.

"It bates me," said Tim, "what ye are after."

"Does it? Come on, and you will perhaps find out."

The summit of the hill was as flat as a table-top, and fringed with short vegetation; so, when we reached it, I threw myself down, and crept towards the edge.

Tim was at my side giving vent to anything but polite speeches, because he every now and then put his hand upon a prickly cactus.

Looking through the bushes we had a splendid view of the valley below and the wooded country on the right and left.

"As nice a place for a fight," remarked Tim, "as ever I saw; for those who get the bating, can run away and hide in the wood."

"I'm afraid," I said, "those who will be beaten to-day will not run away."

"Shure, man alive! you don't think the Commanches will get the worst of it?"

"I do."

"The divil! How's that?"

"Because the Bonnazes are five to one, and you know they are good fighting men."

"Faith, that's true! but—— Hallo! that's the first shot."

The report of a rifle came from the wood on the right, then a party of Bonnaxes emerged into the open space, yelling like demons.

They were, no doubt, tracking the Comanches, none of whom had yet appeared.

We began to feel interested, for the enemy ran boldly towards the wood on the left, and seemed about to enter it, when a volley stretched many of them on the ground, and the remainder retreated.

Following this discharge, about fifty Comanches spurred out from the timber, and, spreading themselves out like a fan, couched their long lances, and gave chase to the foe.

Many a Bonnaxe warrior bit the dust before the Comanches were driven back by rifle bullets and arrows from the wood.

Both parties were soon under cover again, and the valley, save for the dark forms that were lying stretched out on the grass, and several riderless mustangs galloping about, resumed its quietude.

The skirmish that had just taken place would be termed in European warfare an affair of pickets, for it was evident the main bodies of the two powers were not yet ready for action.

Everything remained perfectly quiet for some ten or fifteen minutes, and Tim began to grumble at the loss of time.   er the

"For," he said, "the sooner it is ov better."

He had scarcely spoken, when a horseman spurred out from the Comanches, and made straight for the spot where lay the only one of his party who had suffered from the Bonnaxes' fire.

"That's Hugh Howard," said Tim. "Surely he's not going to scalp any of 'em?"

It was Hugh Howard, and I began to wonder why he so fearlessly faced the enemy.

His object was evidently to gain possession of the fallen Comanche, but why he should not have left that to one of his men I was at a loss to understand.

The Bonnaxes were not slow in discovering his intention; for two of them, evidently chiefs, shot out from the wood, and with spears at rest, galloped across the valley.

"Bedad, ye are late," said Tim. "Go it, Hugh! Ah, that's it! Look, Silvershot, he's off his horse. Make haste, man alive, make haste, or they'll——By the powers, it's Uwato!"

It was indeed the gallant chief who lay so prone upon the grass. We could recognise

him now, for when Hugh raised his body the setting sun shone upon the silver disc Uwato wore upon his breast.

I thrust the barrel of the rifle I carried through the bushes, and stopping my breath as I glanced along the sights, took a careful aim at the Bonnaxes.

Another moment and the bullet would have been released; but ere I could press the trigger Hugh threw Uwato's body across the saddle; then, springing on the horse's croup, dashed away.

He was only in time, for the Bonnaxes' lances grazed his hunting shirt, as the Indians dashed past him.

The Bonnaxes wheeled with the intention of cutting off Hugh's retreat.

The movement cost them their lives, and added two horses to the Comanches; for the young Raven and another chief galloped out, and, couching their lances, charged the Bonnaxes.

Truth compels me to state that the latter were taken at a slight disadvantage, for the Raven and his companion caught them as they swept across Hugh's front.

"Well done, me boys," said Tim. "Bedad! the Bonnaxes are clane rubbed out, and their horses are being taken to the other side."

"True, Tim; but there go some of the Bonnaxe warriors to avenge the death of their——"

"Bedad! they are late, then," said Tim, "for Hugh has got amongst the timber. The Raven is being joined by——Mother of Moses! did ye hear that?"

It was the war whoop of the opposing tribes as they swept out of the timbers, and, with levelled spears, rushed to the conflict.

"This is the beginning of the battle," I said. "What the end may be, remains to be seen; for the foe is five to one against our friends."

"More's the pity," mused Tim, "since Uwato is wounded——"

"Wounded, Tim?"

"Yes, man alive! I saw him meself catch hold of the saddle."

CHAPTER XXIII.

I MAKE A CAPTURE.

WE had no time for further conversation, for the conflict had begun in earnest, and the valley, which had looked so peacefully beautiful, became covered by dark clouds of horsemen.

From the depths of the wood where the Comanches had been mustering, there came the clear ringing note of a bugle.*

---

* The Comanches, Utahs, Apaches, and other powerful tribes have long adopted European military tactics in conjunction with their Indian mode of fighting. The Comanches especially possess a complete military system that would do credit to a Continental army, for they not only charge in line but manœuvre in obedience to the bugle call.

I knew the meaning of that sound; it was the "advance," and a few minutes afterwards the gallant band swept out from amongst the trees.

Red Hugh was at their head, and with as much coolness as though the five hundred Bonnaxes were twenty miles away in place of galloping furiously across the valley, he reined his horse sharply round in front of their band and waved his tomahawk as a signal for the dusky bugler to sound "Form line."

The Comanches had issued from the timber six abreast. When they heard this sound the leading files halted, and those in rear dividing to the right and left, spurred madly forward to form before the Bonnaxes should come upon them.

The latter, confident in their superiority of numbers, rushed forward, and, from our post of observation, it seemed they must reach the Comanches before their formation was complete.

Had such been the case nothing could have saved my friends from utter annihilation.

The Bonnaxes advanced in two irregular lines, distant from each other about a hundred yards, and by the time the Comanches had formed for battle, the first of those lines was about a hundred and fifty yards from them.

There was no time to lose, for the coming red men were well mounted, and at every stretch made by their mustangs the distance was lessened.

I could fancy by Hugh's gestures that he was addressing the Comanches; so it afterwards proved. He was explaining to them the necessity of keeping their horses well in hand, should they succeed in breaking through the first line of their foes.

Now the bugle rings out loud and clear its wild summons for the Comanches to "charge."

The notes seem like the effect of an electric shock upon both men and horses, for they remain for a few seconds as though turned to stone, then the mustangs tossed their silky manes, and their snort of defiance was mingled with the warriors' shout as they rushed to the fight.

The Comanche line was as like a wall as they met their foes. The shock seemed to shake the earth as the two bodies met.

There was a confused medley of horses and men—the rattling of spears and tomahawks against shields; the sharp detonation of rifles—then the wild notes of the Comanche bugle rang out above the din of slaughter.

"By the mortial," said Tim, "that was a fine charge. Shure, man alive, the ould Enniskelleen Dragoons couldn't have done it better."

Red Hugh is still in front. The tomahawk he wields no longer glitters as he hurries the warriors on—the bright blade is dimmed by the blood of the Bonnaxes.

The Comanche ranks, though thinned, burst through the first line of their foes, and shoulder to shoulder, dash at the second.

Ha! they yield. Borne down by the fiery prairie horsemen, thrust aside as though they were reeds, hurled to the earth, horses and men, the latter, before they can rise from their struggling horses, are transfixed by the Comanche spears.

The White Hawk, the crafty, cruel leader of the frontier Indians, has shown his ignorance of military tactics. His second line, in place of being the steadiest warriors, is composed of young braves, to whom the shock of battle is new.

The White Hawk sees his error. It is not too late to repair it; for his followers are numerous—still more than treble that of his foes.

He shakes his tufted spear aloft, and directs the first line to wheel, then gallops to the second, which is being re-formed by the chiefs in command.

From our place of observation we note every movement, wondering why the second line should break into two divisions, and, galloping off to the right and left, disappear from the valley.

We soon forget them; for the Comanches, having re-formed, dash back at their foes, who, in place of meeting them, open their ranks, and allow Hugh's band to pass through.

As quick as thought the Bonnaxes turn their horses round, and follow the Comanches, who are in the act of wheeling.

They meet face to face; but this time both ranks are broken, and the warriors separate into small groups, and battle fiercely for life.

So engrossed had we been by the battle, that we had not noticed the approach of the Comanche braves we had left with the horses. They had ascended the hill one by one until the whole of them had posted themselves amongst the long grass, and, by their glaring eyes, and the manner in which they grasped their weapons, I saw I should have some difficulty in restraining them from joining the fight.

"My young men," I said, "must be patient. The time has not yet come."

"The Silver Bullet," replied Stormy Weather, "speaks like a Western warrior, not like a red-skin."

"Stormy Weather forgets I am a chief."

"The Comanche's tongue speaks the thoughts of his heart. He forgets everything when he sees his brothers fighting hand to hand with the hated Bonnaxes."

"By the mortial!" shouted Tim, "here's some of the blackguards coming this way."

Following the direction of Tim's finger, I saw one of the divisions gallop out from the right of the wood, and, plunging into the cane brake, lead their horses from the rear of the hill.

I saw the White Hawk's manœuvre now; his intention was to out-flank the Comanches, who had by this time fought their way to the verge of the wood, from which they had at first emerged.

The division beneath us, sheltered by the rugged nature of the ground, hoped to make a detour round the hill, and, entering the side of the wood nearest us, at the same moment as the other division entered at the opposite end, fall upon the rear of the Comanches, and place them between two lines, each considerably greater in numercial strength than Uwato's band.

In a moment my plans were made. I had a dozen gallant fellows panting to join the fray, so I knew I could count upon their assistance.

"Down the hill," I said, creeping back. "Down, and we may yet be in time to outwit the cunning Bonnaxes. Come, my braves, follow me!"

Secure from the observation of the advancing Bonnaxes, we rushed down the hill, and I led the way to a thick cane brake that skirted the base, and formed one side of the path the Bonnaxes would have to pass—the other side was lined with large fragments of red sandstone.

The path itself was narrow, at the utmost not more than six feet at the widest part.

I had not much time for preparation, for we could hear the hoof strokes of the Bonnaxes' mustangs as they galloped over the stony ground.

"Tim," I said, addressing Delany, "take four of the braves, and get behind these stones. Quick now, or we shall be too late."

"Sharp's the word," said Tim. "Come along, me boys."

He called the four men who were nearest to him, and as they ran across the path, I said—

"Remember, not a shot is to be fired, unless you wish to alar——"

"All right, man alive. Shure, do you take us for gossoons?"

I placed four men nearly opposite to Delany's party, explaining to them as I did so how they were to act. Of course, in case of peril we had our horses close at hand, and must trust to their speed for our safety.

I took the four men that remained, and drew them up across the path. They had their rifles at their shoulders, ready at any signal to empty the foremost saddles.

Matters being thus arranged, I cut a green bough from one of the trees, and awaited the approach of the foe.

They were soon in sight, riding three abreast, and perfectly unconscious of the ambuscade.

Luckily for my scheme, the winding pathway kept my party out of sight until the leading horsemen were full upon us.

They reined up suddenly on catching sight of the levelled rifles, and uttering an angry "'Ugh," looked round as though seeking another path.

On either side they beheld the other muzzles, some pointing through the underwood, others through the chinks of the red sandstone.

Turning from this unpleasant prospect, their eyes fell upon the green bush I waved to and fro.

They saw they were trapped. Perceiving by my gestures that an unconditional surrender, or the certainty of a volley from both sides of the path, was the choice of evils, and no doubt thinking my band was very numerous, they chose the former, and then threw down their arms.

Stormy Weather and his party in the cane brake kept up the idea of an immense force being there, for the brake would rattle, and a couple of rifle muzzles appear at all points of the thick vegetation.

Tim followed the Indians' example, and with such success that I at first thought he had been reinforced.

Our prisoners were led six at a time in rear of the cane brake, and two of Stormy Weather's party aiding the four men, I had soon bound the Bonnaxes with their own lassoes.

The stratagem succeeded so well that in the course of ten minutes we had the whole band bound hand and foot, their horses picketed, and two of our party walking to and fro with loaded rifles before the captives.

"Now to horse!" I shouted; and, leaping into my saddle, spurred forward, and skirting the wood, entered it without observation.

Once in the timber, our progress was very slow—too slow for the Indians, who were excited to madness by the shouts of the combatants outside.

We pressed through the thickest part of the wood, and suddenly came upon a small glade, in the centre of which was a number of the wounded Comanches under the care of the medicine men.

"I told you so," said Tim, springing to my side. "He's right enough."

"Who?"

"Uwato, of course. Don't you see him!"

I did. My gallant friend was being assisted to his saddle as Tim spoke, and I saw the lower part of his left leg had been bound up by one of the old men.

Once in the saddle, Uwato's wound was forgotten, for he shook his spear aloft, and was about to rush to the fray, when I galloped over to him.

We shook hands, and in a few words I explained all that had happened in the path at the base of the hill.

He made no comment upon seeing me. I had been cured of my wounds; such being the case, my place was by his side.

"My brother has been wise," he said. "Had the dogs passed the hill, there would have been weeping in the lodges."

He pointed to the Indian braves, who must have fallen into the hands of the men I had left so securely bound.

"The Bonnaxes are warriors," he resumed, after a pause. "They are brave warriors, and my young men have much to do to keep their scalps, but the Comanches will never yield while there is a rifle left to send its death cry to the foe. Uwato's place is with his braves, but he cannot go, for his brother has brought great success."

He repaired to the other party, who had by this time entered the timber. They had more ground to cover than the enemies I had captured, or they would have been hopelessly run by this time.

Uwato sat for some moments in deep thought; then a smile came over his handsome face, and addressing me, he said—

"The wounded braves will lure the dogs to this place. Come, my brother, we will prepare for them.

Uwato called together all that were not actually engaged in the fight, and, ordering them to dismount and picket their horses, he made preparations to receive the Bonnaxes.

The dismounted portions of the Comanche forces were posted behind the trees, and Uwato, Tim, and I went with those that were mounted, and seeking the shelter of a row of trees, awaited the coming of the foe.

They came dashing through the trees, and upon coming into the glade, caught sight of the wounded braves and the medicine men.

The temptation to "raise hair" was too much for Indian nature.

In a moment half the number sprang to the ground, and, plucking out their scalping knives, ran forward to secure the envied trophies from the wounded men and their attendants.

They gave a yell when about half way across the glade, and before its echo had died away among the trees, there was a wild response, followed by the deadly detonations of a dozen rifles.

Some of the scalping party sprang up and fell forward, dead. Others were wounded, and struggled to get back to their horses.

Too late. Uwato's war whoop rang out, and we dashed madly forward, and charged the astounded Bonnaxes.

Taken in front by the Comanches, who were loading and firing from behind the trees, and in the rear by us, the poor devils knew not what to do, until half their number had fallen.

Then the chief who led them, after parrying a fierce blow made by Uwato, backed his horse round, and made for the recesses of the wood.

His followers went with him, and, flushed with victory, the Comanches would have followed, had not Uwato called them back.

The fight outside the timber was at its height when we galloped out from the wood, and the Bonnaxes, catching sight of us, raised a shout, for they felt sure we formed part of the braves sent by the White Hawk to take the Comanches in rear.

"Ula-ula-loo!" shouted Uwato. "Proceed, my braves. Strike, and spare not."

Five minutes' fierce battling, and the Bonnaxes, who were getting the upper hand of their enemies, began to fall back.

They had hopes yet of seeing their companions debouch from the wood. Thus it was they lingered, fighting desperately to hold the ground they had won.

Uwato saw this, and spurring forward in advance of his band, called out—

"Dogs! do you want to follow your companions to the unknown land? Do you want to see their bodies? Behold them in yonder wood——"

"Liar!" yelled the White Hawk. "You double-tongued thief! Learn how a Bonnaxe warrior punishes his foe."

Before Tim or I could prevent it, the lasso held by the White Hawk coiled above Uwato's head, and he was dragged from his horse.

CHAPTER XXIV.

I NEGOTIATE AN EXCHANGE OF PRISONERS.

SWIFT as an arrow sent from a strongbow, the young Raven dashed out from amongst us.

He threw away his rifle and spear as he went, and, armed only with his long knife, flew to his kinsman's assistance.

We could see Uwato's body being dragged along the ground, and at times bumping against the small hillocks. Ugh! it made our very blood run cold, and, for a time, deprived me of the steadiness necessary to send a bullet through the head of the exultant Bonnaxe chief.

Others of Uwato's braves followed the young Raven; so that by the time my nerves had become sufficiently steady to use my rifle, it was impossible to do so, for fear of hitting a friend before the ball could reach a foe.

The Comanches in pursuit kept up a dropping fire upon the retreating foe; but it was useless, for another lasso had been thrown around Uwato's right leg, and, closing around the ankle, he was borne swiftly towards the wood, where the Bonnaxes had by this time entered.

The young Raven seemed to bear a charmed life; for, during his attempts to cut the lasso, dozens of bullets and arrows were discharged at his body.

The last brave act I saw of the gallant youth was just as Uwato disappeared in the timber.

The fearless boy had thrown himself alongside his horse, and, holding on with his left hand, managed to cut the lasso that was around his chief's shoulders.

Attacked by a dozen of the foe, he wheeled his mustang, and galloped back to our ranks.

To follow the Bonnaxes in the fastnesses of the forest would only entail a useless slaughter, so we held a council of war.

The Comanches were for attacking the foe; but I overruled this by telling them the number of prisoners we had in the cane brake at the base of the hill.

A yell proclaimed their delight at this news, and it was as much as I could do to prevent them galloping off and scalping the poor devils.

"Listen," I said, when the momentary confusion was over, "the Comanches love their chief as well as his white brother loves him—is it so?"

An exclamation of assent followed this speech.

"Of what use," I reasoned, "are the Bonnaxes' scalps to the brave Comanches? They have as many scalps as there are leaves upon the trees. Their mocassins are sewn with their enemies' hair, and from their shields and spears hang the scalps of many braves and warriors. Again I say, the Comanche braves do not want the scalps of the Bonnaxes."

There was no response to this, for the rich harvest of hair was too tempting for my savage friends to forego the pleasure of reaping it.

"I have spoken," I said, "but the lips of my Indian brothers are closed. Will they open their ears to what I have to tell them?"

A murmur of assent came from the statue-like horsemen.

"Were every leaf that quivers in the wind above our heads a scalp, of what value would they be compared to the life of the brave chief we all love so well?" Comanches, I have spoken."

A fierce shout came from the warriors' throats, and they looked vengefully towards the prisoners.

"It is well," I continued. "Listen, my brothers. We can save the life of the brave Uwato. I will do so. Alone I will go to their chief, the White Hawk, and tell him we will restore their braves, with their scalplocks still upon their heads, if they will give us, in return, the brave Uwato. If he does not, then my young men can do their will upon the Bonnaxes. I have said."

One of the chiefs came forward, and leaning on the point of his spear addressed them.

"The Silver Bullet," he said, "has the courage of the Indian and the wisdom of the white man. How-ka-ra has had his words. I say let it be so. The young men will not touch a hated Bonnaxe's scalp until the Silver Bullet returns and states his wishes. I have said. Let my young men prove. How-ka-ra has spoken this, brothers."

"Wagh, wagh! it is good."

"How-ka-ra speaks our thoughts."

"The Silver Bullet is a wise warrior."

These and similar expressions came from the Comanches; then a voice near me said—

"Better let the beggars be scalped. Uwato's gone, and if I am not mistaken he is cold meat by this time."

I looked down and saw Hugh Howard, his handsome face covered with blood, one arm in a sling, and his right leg bound tightly with a silken scarf.

Four Comanches had just brought him in from the battle-field, and laid him near my horse.

I dismounted, and grasping the backwoodsman's hand said—

"You are badly wounded, Hugh."

"No, old comrade; a few scratches, and a broken leg, that's all."

"All!"

"By the mortial!" Tim put in, "it's enough to make you remember this day, anyhow."

"Ay," replied the backwoodsman, grimly; "but for every scratch I have received a Bonnaxe has been rubbed out."

"Bedad," said Tim, "we have done our share of that same thing, and come off with a whole skin."

"So much the better for you, my Hibernian friend," said Hugh; "but look here, Silvershot, if you intend trying to save Uwato you had better go at once, or they will have wiped him out."

"It's not by yourself ye are going," said Tim, "I must be with you; for, bedad, there's no knowing the scrapes ye may get into, if I am not there."

"I must go alone, old comrade," I said. "The White Hawk will act honourably, I sure."

"Perhaps," said Hugh Howard, as he was borne away upon a buffalo robe; "but don't trust too much to his honour, Silvershot."

"I am willing to take the risk."

So saying, I turned my horse's head away and rode towards the wood.

I carried my rifle across my back, my knife in its sheath, and the tomahawk hung from a loop of the saddle.

In my right hand I carried a bunch of white bell-like flowers—they were the nearest approach to a flag of truce. So, when I entered the wood I fastened them to the point of my ramrod.

The patter of my horse's feet upon the dry earth caused several dusky faces to appear from behind the trunks of the trees; and when the owners of the faces saw my errand was a peaceful one, they came forward.

"The White Hawk," I said, "is a great chief. The hunter would speak with him."

"The White Hunter," answered one of the Indians, "is a friend of the Comanches. Does he know our chief will not hold converse with a foe?"

"The White Hawk," I replied, "will listen to my words, for the lives of the young men he sent by the path at the foot of the mountain can only be saved at my price. If he refuses to listen, the Comanche warriors will send them to the happy hunting-grounds without their scalps."

There was a few moments' whispered conversation amongst the Bonnaxes; then one stepped forward, and beckoned me to follow him.

I obeyed, and treading a tortuous path amongst the timber, came to an open space, where the Bonnaxes had pitched their camps.

Near the centre the White Hawk's spear was stuck in the ground, and his shield bearing his totem—a white hawk emblazoned upon the skin.

Behind this I saw Uwato lying face downwards, his hands and feet securely bound with thongs, and near him were about twenty of the Comanches, who had been taken prisoners during the fight.

Turning my eyes from this unpleasant spectacle, I saw a red pest erected, and near it the greater part of the Bonnaxes.

The spears and shields lay in a heap upon the ground, and as they formed a ring round the war-post they drew their tomahawks and knives.

The scalp dance was about to begin, and I knew if it was concluded before I obtained speech with the White Hawk my friends would be sacrificed.

Riding forward, under the excitement of the moment I did not heed the savage looks that were bestowed upon me, neither did I halt until I was within a few feet of the chief.

He awaited my coming, and leaning against a tree, looked up and said—

"The White Hunter values his scalp but little, or he would not come to the Bonnaxes' camp."

"The White Hunter," I said, "has no fear of the Bonnaxes. He has met them in the fight, has fought with them as warriors, and knows they would not disgrace themselves by injuring a man who has come with news of the missing Bonnaxe braves."

"The white man has a living tongue, let him speak."

"In the Comanche camp," I said, "there is a band of Bonnaxe warriors. Their scalp-locks are still upon their heads, but the Comanches love their chief and their brothers better than the scalps of their foes. Does the chief understand the white man?"

"He listens," was the terse reply.

"The White Hunter comes to the Bonnaxes' chief to tell him his young men can return to their camp with arms, horses, and their scalps, if the Comanche chief and his braves are set free. What does the White Hawk say?"

"The white man is a liar, for here come my young men."

I followed the direction of his finger and to my chagrin beheld the fellows I had captured trotting towards us, and dangling from the spears of the two foremost horsemen were two reeking scalps.

I understood all that had happened, the prisoners had risen upon their guards, scalped them, and returned to the camp.

The White Hawk laughed long and loud at my surprise, and making a signal to his men, they gave a whoop and sprang upon me.

Resistance was out of the question. I was dragged from my horse, my wrists and ankles bound. The four Indians carried me to where Uwato lay, and pitched me beside him.

The Bonnaxe chief followed us, and striding to Uwato kicked the young chief savagely.

"Open your eyes, chicken-hearted dog," he said, "and behold, your white brother has come to hang his scalp beside that of the Comanche chief's."

He struck Uwato sharply across the face as he spoke. The blow was not a heavy one, but it succeeded in its object.

Uwato writhed like a poor wretch upon the rack, and compressing his lips to prevent a sound escaping, then looked steadily at his tormentor's face.

Never shall I forget that look. Fierce as was the White Hawk, he quailed under it, and turning upon his heels forced a laugh and rejoined his companions.

I spoke to Uwato when our captors were out of hearing, but he paid no heed to my words. It was not the time for sympathy; the thoughts of my companion were far away with his fair and lovely bride.

CHAPTER XXV.

THE PRAIRIE WOLVES.

I HAVE no kindred ties, no beloved wife, no prattling babies, to leave, yet I liked not the prospect of the cruel death to which we were doomed.

The Indian warrior, who lay with closed eyes by my side, had both wife and children to mourn his loss, and it was for them his heart bled, and his manly breast rose and fell with agony.

What he suffered, save for this sign, was hidden, for his face was calm, not a muscle moving to reveal the mental anguish he endured.

With horrible yells and fierce gesticulations the Bonnaxes danced around the fatal red post, and ever and anon one of the warriors, carried away by excitement, would run to the emblem of war, and go through the motion of scalping a foe.

Until the red sun began to sink behind the tree tops, the dance was kept up. The scalps that had been taken duriug the day were suspended to the top of the post.

The sight of these ghastly emblems caused a gnawing sensation to pass over my scalp.

This feeling was not lessened when I heard the frantic yells the appearance of the reeking trophies caused the Bonnaxes to give us they danced, hand-in-hand, around the post.

Exhausted, at length, by their wild gestures they, one by one, withdrew from the dance, the war paint upon their faces smeared and partially removed by the perspiration that trickled in big drops from their foreheads.

At any other time I should have been inclined to laugh at this grotesque appearance, but now my thoughts were too sad to admit of even a smile upon my features.

While watching the dusky devils, the chief came towards us, a cruel, triumphant expression upon his face.

He stood near Uwato, and, kicking the Comanche's prostrate form, mockingly said—

"There will be another scalp-dance to-morrow—that will be when my young men have taken the hair from the Comanche dogs and his white brother. But no," he suddenly added, "the Bonnaxes are braves—they are not a nation of women. They care only for the scalps of those who are as brave as themselves. These are squaws we have here, and only fit for the skulking wolf or the hungry prairie dogs—to the wolves and dogs they shall go. What say my young men?"

A guttural murmur of approval came from the lips of the men who stood near.

"My braves are pleased," the White Hawk resumed. "They care not for scalps of dogs to-night. The prairie wolves shall feast upon the stinking carcases of these chicken hearted men, who would try and make us believe they are Indians."

It was a relief to me to find that my scalp was safe for the present. But this feeling did not exist in the minds of my companions.

They would sooner have been scalped twenty times had it been their reward for the fate shadowed forth by the White Hawk's works.

I saw them write in their bonds when the Bonnaxe said they were unworthy of the scalping-knife of his braves; and Uwato, who dreaded, perhaps, more than all the rest, being treated with such contempt, sat upright, and began to taunt the White Hawk.

"The Bonnaxes," he said, "are dogs and liars! They fear to take the scalps of the Comanches."

"The Bonnaxes," returned the White Hawk, "do not scalp the Crows, for they are unclean, and only dogs; they do not take the scalps of the thieving white men who come from beyond the Father of Waters. No; they give the bodies of both Crows and white men to the dogs; and why? Because they are but carrion, and only fit for the food of carrion. Wagh! a Bonnaxe would be for ever disgraced in the eyes of his people were he to touch a scalp that came not from the head of a brave warrior."

"There is not a knife," said Uwato, "that can take a scalp; there is not a rifle or bow that can send us to the happy hunting-grounds. Why is it? Because the Bonnaxes are sqaws; they know not the use of a warrior's weapon. They are brothers to the Cherokees, who cannot fight. I spit upon them—they are not braves."

The White Hawk was stung by Uwato's words, and once I thought he would have plunged his spear into the chief's heart.

By a powerful effort he subdued this inclination and answered—

"The Comanche is cunning, but his words will not cause a great chief to treat him like a warrior.. No; he shall not go to the happy land beyond the big mountains until the wolves have fed upon his body. He shall not die like a brave, leaving his scalp in the nands of his foe; for he is not a brave, and the

Bonnaxes despise those whose hearts are like the heart of a fool."

The Bonnaxe chief turned his head contemptuously, and, motioning for his warriors to follow him, left us to our wretchedness.

The discussion that took place amongst our captors was carried on too far away for us to hear a word that passed.

It was evident some of the band longed to "raise our hair;" but in the end the chief had his way, and we were to be treated unlike brave warriors.

However much this may have gone against the inclination of my Comanche friends, your servant, Silvershot, was not at all ambitious to die like a brave. If I must be rubbed out, I most certainly preferred to have my head covered by its natural covering.

I said nothing of this to my fellow prisoners, who were, by this time, cursing the Bonnaxes and deploring the cruel fate that had willed they should die so unworthily.

I watched the last gleam of the sun fade away, and wondered if I should see the god of day again.

While doing so, the sharp, hungry cry of a wolf came from the margin of the trees, and my soul sank within me.

Our captors heard the cry, and the White Hawk, followed by his braves, came towards us.

"It is time," he said, "the wolves were fed. Heard you their cries? They thirst for the blood of the squaws, whose bodies they will so soon devour."

At a sign from the chief the thongs that bound our ankles were cut, and we were dragged to our feet.

Uwato and his companions refused to move. They expected their foes would give them a spear thrust, and thus put an end to their lives.

The Bonnaxes knew this, and the chief said—

"The Comanche squaws are cunning. They would die by the warriors' spears. Let my young men convey them to the wolves' covert."

The Comanches were dragged along by their exultant enemies, who, in mockery of their despair, began to chant the death song.

I walked quietly to the place of execution, which was at the back of the wood, where the prairie opened out and extended for miles beyond our vision.

A few minutes sufficed for the preliminary process, and we were tied to the outer row of trees, our faces turned towards the open prairie.

Securely fastened by the deer-hide thongs, it was impossible to move a limb that was lashed to the tree trunks, and, to the inexpressible rage of the Comanches, the Bonnaxes began a song, the tenor of which was, "A number of chicken-hearted squaws were given to the wolves, because they were unworthy to die as warriors."

When this quaint song was ended the chief said, pointing to a swell on the prairie—

"The White Hawk and his braves will stay and feast their ears with the screams of the squaws when the prowling wolves begin to tear their miserable bodies to pieces.

With a swift noiseless pace the whole of the band passed over to the high ground, and disappearing behind it, waited patiently for the appearance of the skulking brutes.

I soon began to understand how much more preferable death by the tomahawk and scalping-knife would have been to that to which we were doomed.

We suffered as no pen can describe.

The fall of a leaf, the rustling of the branches sent the blood back to our hearts, and causing a cold perspiration to ooze out from every pore in our skins.

Twice had the horrible cry come upon the wind, and we strained our eyeballs to catch sight of the shrieking forms.

Better, ay, ten times, the hungry brutes should advance and put an end to such intense agony of mind.

Slowly the silver moon rose in the heavens, shedding its soft light upon as fine a scene as ever mortal eye dwelt upon.

Soon the mental torture we endured affected our vision, so that every shadow that crossed the prairie was magnified into a drove of our executioners; and dreadful as the thought was that we must die by their fangs, there was, perhaps, a little relief to the overtaxed mind that all would soon be over.

Such was not our fate. We were doomed to suffer for hours, doomed to such torture that the cords of reason seemed as though they would snap and leave us drivelling idiots.

Not a sound the whole of this weary time from behind the swell on the prairie, not the sight of a waving feather from the Bonnaxes' hiding-place.

It seemed sad to believe that behind the mound there were nearly a hundred of our fellow creatures exulting in the misery we suffered, and not one would give us a drop of water to cool our parched and swollen tongues.

Higher rose the heavenly disc of light in heaven's blue vault, and more distinct became the sheen that flooded the undulating land.

It must have been nearly midnight before the Bonnaxes showed any signs of disquietude. They knew how we suffered, and delighted to gloat over it. The distant cries had buoyed

SCREAM OUT, YE DEVILS, AND THEY'LL THINK YE'RE BEING TORN TO PIECES.

them with the hope of the wolves' speedy advance; but at last, finding the sounds did not approach any nearer, one of them imitated the whistling noise made by a deer when alarmed.

For a few moments I was deceived, and fully expected to see a stately buck cross my vision; but the sound being repeated, revealed its source.

So still was everything around us, that the sound be heard nearly as far as we could see.

It was! Oh, God! Never before had I felt such a sudden suspension of my faculties, as when I descried three dark forms skulking towards us.

They were the advance guard of a hungry drove. There could be no doubt of this; for some two hundred yards in the rear, I saw a black mass making for the timber.

Nearer and nearer! I closed my eyes to shut out the horrible sight. Nearer still; so near that I could plainly distinguish the outlines of their gaunt forms.

Ten minutes more and all would be over, unless the brutes were lured by the scent of the Bonnaxes, and tried to attack them.

No, that was impossible; for the cunning red devils had tied us in the wind, and the quarter from whence the wolves came was where the scent was carried.

How the fiends must have rejoiced when they saw the skulking brutes advance—how they must have grinned at their own cunning in placing themselves out of the direction of the night breeze.

Nearer yet? still with the same measured pace. Why do the brutes linger on the way? Is it because they are not certain of the scent?

Is it that they are too cowardly to advance without the larger body that lingered so far in the rear? Have they gorged upon the slain in that day's fight so that they cared little to advance upon their living prey?

Heaven is more merciful than our foes; for a dark cloud sails over the moon, shutting out from our horrified gaze the prowling brutes as they near our quivering bodies.

I hear them—feel them near me; something touches my leg; then a cold nose is placed against my hand; then the hot breath of one of the brutes fans my face. A pair of heavy paws are placed upon my shoulders, and my brain reels, and the closed lips that have so long held back a cry of agony, now part, and give vent to a scream of wild, pent-up despair.

CHAPTER XXVI.

A TRANSFORMATION SCENE.

"THAT'S it, avick! Shout like the devil! Go it, old son!"

Am I mad? No; it is the voice of honest Tim, and I open my eyes, and behold his good-natured face close to mine. Above the welcome sight hangs the head of a wolf. I see it all now. I am saved; but what are these brutes, whose tongues are licking my hands.

"The dogs," says Tim. "Scream out, ye divil, and make 'em believe ye are being torn to pieces."

I do scream, but it is the scream of joy. I scream louder when I hear the snick of a knife cutting the thongs that bind me to the tree.

"Where are the divils, Silvershot?"

"Behind the swell, listening to my agony."

"It's something else they'll listen to directly. Scream out again, ye divil!"

"So I did, pressing Tim's hand and caressing the dogs, and listening greedily to his words, as he says—

"It's right in the shade of the trees where they can't see us. I'd have come before, but that thafe of a cloud wouldn't go across the moon. Hallo out, avic; but not so loud."

"That's it; now drop down, and take this knife. Keep behind the trees, and set those poor divils free; the dogs will go with you. Tell them to scream out, Silvershot, while I go and fetch the other wolves."

"The other——"

"It's the boys, every man of 'em playing wolf. Bedad! the Bonnaxes will get it directly! Go in, avick, before the cloud clears away, in case the divil should spy us out. I am not a regular hunter."

I grasped his hand, then clutching the knife he held towards me, slipped behind the trees and soon reached Uwato.

The Comanches were chanting their death song; and, brave as they were, the mournful tones ceased when I sprang upon their chief.

A few words told the story; and, in obedience to my wishes, Uwato gave a yell of affected agony, while I severed his fastenings.

"The Manitou is good," he whispered, "and his children are grateful for his goodness; for it is not a warrior's death the cowardly Bonnaxes would have given us."

When the dusky band behind the wood heard Uwato's cry a subdued exclamation of satisfaction came from them.

"The dogs!" said Uwato, fiercely. "When the scalpless hunter returns with the Comanche braves, it will bring mourning to the lodges of the Bonnaxes."

So far all had gone well with Tim. He had passed the mound without the device being detected, and was within twenty yards of the disguised warriors.

I still kept behind the trees, fearing the moon would suddenly burst effulgent from behind the bank of dark mazy clouds, but so far all was well.

The dogs I played with, causing them to jump at my breast, and the rustling of the dry leaves under their feet caused our hidden foes to believe they were tearing Uwato piecemeal from me.

The young chief, to carry out the ruse, kept up a succession of groans that seemed to be forced from the lips of one who was in the most poignant agony.

I could have given a hearty hurrah, when I saw Tim join the dark forms on the prairie, and the whole body come swiftly towards the trees.

The yells of agony from the Comanches distracted the attention of their foes from the advancing crowd of wolves.

This was fortunate, for the moon shot out with unequalled brilliancy just as the Comanches came opposite to the mound.

"Now," I said to Uwato, "now my brother's war-cry can cause the hearts of his foes to fall."

"Uh-ula-loo!" shouted Uwato. "Uh-ula-loo!"

The wild cry was repeated by the Comanches, and, mingled with the Indian rattle, I heard Tim Delany's voice yelling—

"Ireland for ever! Hurroo, my boys, let 'em have it!"

The recumbent forms started erect, the wolf skins were cast aside, knives, tomahawks, and rifle barrels glittered in the moonlight, then, with savage, triumphant cries the braves rushed to the mound.

The White Hawk and his braves must have been rather "skeered" by the sudden change in affairs, for the Comanches swarmed over the mound before their foes were sufficiently recovered to use their weapons.

This indecision did not last long, for the device was so in keeping with the Indian nature that after the first few moments of surprise they felt the only thing to be done was to make a bold stand and rub out so many of their clever foes as they could under the circumstances.

The Comanches' attack, impetuous and determined as it was, failed to scatter the Bonnaxes. True, many fell before the White Hawk had recovered from his surprise, but now, fired with rage at being so cleverly outwitted, they return blow for blow and yell for yell.

It was the work of a very few minutes to cut the bonds of the remaining captives; this done, Uwato snatched the knife from my hand, and, calling out for his braves to follow, rushed to the fight.

We were unarmed, save for the knife Tim had left with me, but when we reached the mound there was no lack of murderous weapons.

Tomahawks, rifles, spears, and knives were lying about, their late owners either dead or wounded.

We were armed in a moment, and Uwato's blood being fired by the rascally treatment he had received from the Bonnaxes, he sprung into their midst with the fury of a tiger.

We were not slow in following his example, and so deadly was the strife, that scarcely a cry was heard until the Bonnaxes began to retreat.

Then the Comanche war-whoop rang out, and the warriors, excited to fury by the cry, threw themselves upon the foe.

It was not the rush of an undisciplined body of savages, for the Comanches had formed in two lines—those with spears in the front rank—and shoulder to shoulder, like a European regiment of infantry, they swept upon the foe.

Since that time I have seen the gallant 88th Connaught Rangers at the charge; I have heard their wild, warlike shout, "Faugh-a-Ballagh!" and without casting any discredit upon this famous corps, I can conscientiously state the charge of the Comanches was as good and equally as destructive.

The Bonnaxes were broken—hurled aside as if they were mere balls instead of stalwart men—and, like a herd of startled deer, they fled across the prairie.

Satisfied with the slaughter, the Comanches did not pursue, and soon the scalping knives were at work, the excited braves yelling like so many demons.

I turned from the sickening sight, and, with Tim Delany, sat under one of the trees awaiting the conclusion of the horrible scene.

"There's but few of the varmints," said Tim, "who tree'd you will ever have the chance to do so again."

"Ugh, I wish the Comanches would dispense with their savage work, Tim."

"So do I, but it's no use. You know Indian nature is Indian nature, Silvershot."

"True, old comrade, true; but I thought I had seen the last of it."

"When you were tied to the tree, you mean?"

"I do."

"Faith, it was lucky they thought of tying you up."

"So it seems. But how did you find it out?"

"Just this way, comrade. About half an hour after you left us, we began to feel rummy; so the young Raven—good luck to him!—offers to scout and find out what had become of you. He's a plucky fellow, that same Raven, Silvershot."

"He is."

"So he creeps to the place where the Bonnaxes were having their scalp-dance, and hears all about the way you were to be served. So he wanted to attack the Bonnaxes at once; but Stormy Weather and one or two more would not hear of it——"

"What are you stopping for?"

"Do you hear that?"

I listened intently, and heard the sharp cry of the prairie wolves.

"It's one of the old ones," said Tim, "calling the varmints together."

"It is," I answered. "They scent the blood of the dead Indians. Never them them, Tim; go on with your story."

"Well, there's a lot of jaw about the matter," resumed Tim; "for the Comanches were awfully savage at losing the prisoners we had taken."

"So I suppose."

"The Young Raven and Stormy Weather put their heads to work, and the plan was for us to track the wolves to their lair, kill 'em, and take their skins. Faith we did too! We found a hole full of 'em, and when Ben and Jip started 'em out, we knocked 'em over, skinned 'em—and you know the rest."

"Except how you came to find out where we had been taken."

"That was easy enough; for, while we were killing the wolves, the Raven came after you. So we searched round, and saved ye, avick."

"You did, and bravely."

"Don't say a word, me boy, for you've done the same to me, and many times. Here comes the chief, looking as pleased as though he'd just had a good dinner."

"My brothers," said Uwato, "we have, thanks to the Manitou, driven the lying Bonnaxes to their caves. Come, our horses await us."

We left the battle-field to the dead and the prowling wolves, whose dark forms were visible about half-a-mile from the belt of trees.

Once more we were mounted and well-armed, and the rising sun saw us on our way to the Comanche country.

"My brother," said Uwato, as we rode side by side, "shall see the Comanche treasure."

CHAPTER XXVII.

THE COMANCHE TREASURE.

I HAD heard of the tremendous wealth possessed by the Western Indians, had heard that heaps of glittering gold lay concealed in some secret spot, known only to a few of the chiefs.

The Comanches had not valued the precious metal until the greedy Mexicans had opened the Indians' eyes to its wealth.

They liked it because of its colour, roughly wrought into grotesque designs, the dross for which men strive so much had hitherto only ornamented the horses, braves, and the women of the tribe.

But of late they had awakened to the fact that the yellow dust, procured so plentifully in the gullies and rivulets, would purchase the best weapons of defence—the swiftest horses and the softest furs—yet they had no idea of melting it into small pieces; in fact, to organise a system of currency amongst themselves.

If a Mexican or white trader had blankets, arms, or ammunition for sale, he was paid by a certain amount of the metal—paid, perhaps, a hundredfold.

I must confess my heart fluttered a little when Uwato said I should behold the treasure —no wonder it did so.

The peculiar sensation that stole over me must have been an ill-understood foreknowledge of the dangers and adventures the accursed metal was about to lead me into; but of that anon.

Six days' travelling brought us to the beautiful tract of country over which the Comanches held sway.

There can be no doubt about the Comanches being the richest and most powerful of the Indian nation.

They have countless herds of horned cattle sheep, and horses, who find rich pasturage upon the Great Prairie.

The greater portion of their country abounds with copper ore. The right of working these valuable mines that they have has long been sought by the Mexicans; but all attempts to corrupt the chieftains have failed.

"We have thousands of horses, sheep, and cows," said an old chief to one of the Mexicans who came to negotiate. "We have gold lying in profusion around the San-Seba Hills; see, the bracelets, diadems, and armlets worn by our squaws are made of the yellow metal; see also the bit yonder mustang champs is of gold; of what use, then, are the offers the pale-faces make to us? I have said."

"But," urged the Mexican, "the Comanches require arms, ammunition, blankets, and the waters of fire for the young men to drink, one draught of which will make them braver than the lion, and their foes will be as a cloud of dust before the spirits of the air."

"Pale-face," replied the chief, checking with a gesture the advance of two or three braves, "my young men are angry when you mention the accursed fire-water. Go and seek in the lodges of the Sioux, and ask what has become of their warriors, and the Great Spirit will whisper, 'They have drank of the fire-water and died;' go to the wigwams of the Minnelego and the Osage, and ask where are the young men, and the Great Spirit will say, "They also have drank of the accursed stream. Such shall be the fate of all the forest children whose lips are defiled by the poison.' Say it not again, pale-face, or my young men will slay thee."

Abashed, but not beaten, the envoy said—

"There's the rifles, knives, blankets, powder, and lead. Will these "——

"The pale-face has done well his master's bidding. Let him return, and say the Comanches do not want these things; they have gold and rich furs to exchange with the traders who came from beyond the big river."

This was the last attempt the Mexicans had made to get a footing in the Comanche country, and so savage were they at being foiled, that a secret conclave was held, and a resolution was passed that any man who succeeded in discovering the cave wherein the Indians kept their gold should receive a sum of money that would enrich him for life.

Old Buckskin Bill had found the cave and taken its position, and, but for the kindness he received during his stay in the country he would have betrayed the secret to his employers. Unfortunately, the roughly-drawn chart was in St. Juan Campestrano, and this was the cause of the rapid march of the Comanches.

The village was situate on the bank of a wide, clear river, and the wigwams extended for upwards of a mile.

There were three rows of dwellings, and

the lines were straight enough to please the most fastidious quartermaster in the British service.

The horse lines were in rear of the lodges, the horses' heads pointing towards the river, thus securing the Comanches from any sudden attack from their foes on the Mexican frontier.

The other side was well defended by nature. A thick belt of timber formed a half circle, the ends of which touched the water.

Outside the belt of timber the naked prairie extended far beyond the range of the unassisted vision.

Well might the Comanche chief fondly boast that his village was secure from the attacks of his red-skin foes, or the more disciplined but less brave forces of the Mexicans.

In the centre of the village stood Uwato's lodge, a large and handsome dwelling. In front of the entrance five hundred spears were stuck in the ground.

They were the weapons of the best and bravest of the Comanche warriors, whose spears were placed before their chieftain's tent to show they were ready at any moment to follow him, either in the chase or upon the war-path.

The old men, the boys, the young children, the dogs, and the women had turned out to welcome the warriors' return.

There was the song of joy from those whose relatives had safely returned from the war-path, and the song of sorrow for those who had fallen.

There was the huge bonfire, the interminable scalp-dance, the old medicine-men, and the women squabbling about the possession of the wounded warriors.

Outside this strange scene of noise and bustle the stalwart sentries stalked to and fro, keenly watching the river, for a runner had brought the young chief some important news about the movements of a party of Mexican guerillas.

I stood by my horse's head, watching the scene, and smiling at Tim Delany, who was making violent love to a pretty Comanche girl.

I saw my chum attempt to kiss the dusky beauty, and heard the smack on the cheek she gave him.

I joined in the laughter that ensued, and was about to turn to the horse lines to picket my weary steed, when a light hand was placed upon my shoulder.

I turned, and saw Uwato gazing somewhat sadly at the pale face of Red Hugh, who was lying upon a pile of buffalo skins, one of the medicine men attending to his wounds.

"The Comanches' friend is very ill," said Uwato. "Has my brother seen his wounds?"

"I have; but the medicines say there is nothing but what they can cure in a few days."

"Uwato is glad that it is no worse. Come, my brother, the lodge is open to you."

Leaving the tribe to their amusements and sorrows, I went with the Indian warrior to his lodge.

His fair-skinned bride, the lovely Oholoa, welcomed me at the doorway.

"It is a long time," she said, "since Silvershot has been near us. Does he intend to keep his promise now, and stay with his friends?"

I smiled at the recollection of the promise I had made to settle amongst the only true friends—Tim excepted—I had ever had, and answered—

"Not yet, Oholoa. I cannot break the vow I made at the old plane tree."

"You will never find your companions, Silvershot; they have either passed beyond the frontier, and found a charm in civilised life, or perished amongst the wild animals they were so fond of hunting."

"Still," I said," my vow remains the same. I must search until I hear news of them, and——"

"I am acquainted with the nature of your strange compact," said Oholoa, "and, for your sake, wish it had never been made. Be seated, and rest, for you must be tired after your long ride."

Seated upon a pile of rich skins I watched my hostess prepare the meal, and saw she was still in the bloom of her singular beauty.

I did not marvel at the Indian chief's love for his wife, and a thought stole into my head that my life would, perhaps, be brighter had I a loving helpmate to cheer my lonely condition.

This feeling soon passed away when the recollection of the hunter's vow came to my mind, and I knew how much better it was for me to be untrammelled while upon my dangerous mission.

Uwato was sad and thoughtful during the repast, so sad that his wife failed to elicit more than a feeble smile in return for her endeavour to arouse him.

I also tried, but his answers were brief, and quite at variance with the remarks I made. I told the story of the old medicine's death, and he lowered his head, and told me it was the Great Spirit's will that the ghostly murderer was let loose upon earth.

When the meal was over, Oholoa left the lodge, and Uwato, after walking round the exterior to ascertain that none of the warriors were near, reclined at full length upon a pile of furs.

I was soon made aware that some business of importance troubled my friend's mind, for he filled the bowls of two gorgeously ornamented pipes, and holding one to me said—

"My brother will join me in the pipe of reflection."

"I will."

We ignited the fragrant weed by a spark from a flint and steel, and smoked for some time in silence.

"Silvershot," said my companion, breaking the silence, "has wisdom. His Indian brother needs counsel—will he give it?"

I bowed my head affirmatively.

For nearly half-an-hour the young chief's voice rose and fell as he detailed the troubles that hung over him and his nation.

He told me the Mexican President had supplied a band of guerillas with arms and money.

This band of desperadoes were at that moment marching towards the San-Seba Hills, there to effect a junction with a hostile tribe of Indians which had long been at war with the Comanches.

The young chief's lips curled scornfully when he mentioned the Mexican guerillas. He felt assured of an easy victory over them.

But the matter was more serious when the Mexican power was joined to the Umbiquas, whose warriors far outnumbered the fighting men of the Comanches at that time in the village.

"I have listened," I said, "and my brother's words are words of trouble to my ears. Yet I think there is hope."

Uwato shook his head.

"The Comanches," I said, "are fleet of foot. Why does not my brother send runners to the nearest villages of his nation? and before the Mexicans or their allies can reach here, there will be bands of Comanche warriors more numerous than the leaves upon the forest trees."

The Comanches, I may as well inform my readers, are many thousands strong—so numerous that their villages are miles apart; thus it occupies many days to assemble the whole of the warriors.

"Swift runners," said Uwato, "are now on their way to the villages of my people; but before they can deliver my message the Umbiquas and the pale-faced cowards will be here; but this is not what troubles my mind. No; the warriors are here, and our village will be safe from the enemies' feet as long as Uwato has a dozen warriors at his back. No; we care not for Mexican or Umbiqua. We can fight them with cunning, with rifle, with spear and tomahawk; but

we cannot fight the greedy men who will come after these."

"You expect another——"

"My brother heard the words spoken by old trapper who dwelt so long within our wigwams?"

"Buckskin Bill?"

"My brother's words are true. This man has left a chart, showing the position of the cave wherein the red men hide their treasure. The time will come when this chart will be found, and——"

"There is yet time," I exclaimed, as the old trapper's words came to my mind; "plenty of time to obtain the chart. I will go to San Juan Campestrano, and if the hiding-place of this precious paper is to be discovered, I will discover it."

"Uwato is grateful"—the young chief grasped my hand as he spoke—"and the name of his white brother shall not be forgotten during his absence. His praise shall be sung at the council, and the women and children will pray to the Manitou for their friend's safety. Come, my brother, you shall behold the cave."

Quick in his movements, the chief arose, and bidding me to follow, we left the tent, and, passing through the horse lines, came to the decayed trunk of a mora tree.

The tough remains of the forest giant stood at least twelve feet high, and was destitute of the smallest branch.

Its diameter could not have been less than twenty feet, and was to all appearance without crack or blemish.

When we halted at the base of the old tree I noticed Uwato had a lasso coiled in his hand, and before I could ask any question concerning its use, the loop was circling above our heads, and soon it belted around the top of the old trunk.

"Come," said the chief, "let my brother follow."

Placing his feet against the trunk, and firmly grasping the deer-hide thong, he quickly reached the summit.

Here he released the end of the lasso, and I in my turn followed, and when I reached the top my surprise was great to find the massive-looking trunk perfectly hollow.

Inside were several flat pieces of wood placed horizontally, and by stepping from one to the other of these we reached the bottom.

Cunning hands had fashioned several pieces of the gnarled root, so that they seemed to form a portion of the old tree.

This cover Uwato removed, and we descended the root, forming a safe hand and foothold.

"Now," said the chief, pausing, "we will have a light, for we have yet some distance to go. Is my brother tired?"

"I am out of breath," I answered, "for the descent is by no means easy."

Uwato struck a light, and ignited a pine torch. This done, we resumed our journey.

A few minutes' climbing brought us to the termination of the roots, and to the beginning of a flight of steps cut out of the rocky ground.

The steps led to an arched vault, and scarcely had I placed my foot inside than a cry of horror immediately came from my lips. Uwato paused, and holding the torch aloft, the light shone upon such a ghastly spectacle that it made my flesh creep and my heart beat faster than its wont.

Suspended from the roof were the blackened corpses of seven men. Four were Indians—three by their dress white men.

The bodies were in perfect preservation. This I accounted for by the fact of the absence of the outer air.

"My brother is not afraid," said Uwato, grimly. "These are the bodies of spies who came to find the Comanche treasure."

"I never feared the living," was my reply; "therefore, do not fear the dead."

Uwato turned and passed under the tensile figures, and in following him I had to stoop to avoid my face coming in contact with their stiffened extremities.

The vault led to a more spacious excavation, and Uwato, holding the light so that its flickering gleams fell upon the treasure that was piled around, said—

"My brother's eyes behold the metal, for the possession of which the white man would slay the forest children."

It was a sight that would have driven a miser mad with avaricious joy.

Heaps of the dull-looking yellow ore lay about the cave, and in baskets, made from grass and short reeds, the precious dust gleamed and sparkled.

I had not until that moment believed there could have been so much gold in the world, and to assure myself I was not dreaming I plunged my hand up to the wrist in one of the baskets, and allowed the many grains to sift through my fingers.

The peculiar thrill that passed over me I cannot explain, but I could fully realise the eager, trembling, delirious joy of those who hoard their gold when they seek their treasure and glut over its possession.

"My brother," said Uwato, "will need some of this dross to carry him through the country of the lying, chicken-hearted Mexicans. Let him take this."

He handed me a small pouch, made from the skin of the red fox, then, taking up the torch from where he had stuck it, in the bottom of the cave, he led the way back.

I must confess to giving many a wis

look at the yellow heaps as the Comanche stalked forward.

Soon all thoughts of the treasure were dispelled, for we came to the weird-looking objects suspended from the roof of the first cave.

Ugh! my soul sickens at the recollection. In returning I did not stoop low enough, and my fur cap, touching one of their feet, there was a slight crack like the breaking of a dried twig, and the bones, first lodging upon my shoulder, fell to the ground.

CHAPTER XXVIII.

A NIGHT WITH THE DEAD.

WHEN we emerged at the top of the old trunk I shook off the horrible feeling that had held possession of me since the moment the dried portion of what had once been a living being fell at my feet.

We reached the ground by the same means used to ascend the entrance to the treasure cave.

I was the first to descend; Uwato remained to cut the loop of the lasso. This done, he placed the thong across the top of the trunk and slid down.

When he reached the ground a jerk at one of the ends removed the lasso, and the old gnarled, grim-looking sentinel stood alone over the secrets beneath the wide-spreading roots.

Crossing to the horse-lines a horrible suspicion flashed to my mind, and I felt angry with myself for allowing my feelings to get the better of my courage when I stood before the ghastly forms of the treasure seekers.

I ought to have examined the horrid relics of humanity, and there, in that subterranean vault, in all probability, I should have beheld two or probably three of my missing companions. The more I thought of this probability the more certain it seemed that I had found a clue to the mysterious fate that had befallen Dick Crosby and his comrades.

I asked Uwato when the unlucky prisoners were caught. He could not tell me. All he knew was they had been dispatched during the absence of the tribe upon the war-path.

"But when? How many moons since?"

He could not say, but knew it must have been many moons, for the cave was but rarely visited—not more than once in twelve moons, and the time before this he had descended the old trunk he found the men hanging there.

So he asked no questions; they were dead, and a few lives was not of much consequence.

I could have quarrelled with the Comanche chief. My fingers tingled to clutch him by so certain was I that I had at last discovered what had become of the gallant fellows with whom I was as a brother.

A few minutes' reflection showed the folly of my anger. What could I do to avenge them, situated as I was in the midst of a powerful tribe of warlike Indians?

Besides, there was still a doubt about the correctness of my surmise, and, until I could clear that up, it would be madness to interfere.

I must try and learn when those hapless wretches' lives paid the penalty of their greed —learn that before I left the village to go upon my long and dangerous journey to the interior of Mexico.

There was not much time left to do this; for, with the rising of the morrow's sun, Tim and I would be mounted, and on our way to the frontiers.

A handsome lodge had been erected for the Comanche's pale-faced brothers; at the door of which Uwato left me, bidding me rest my limbs, for I should soon have need of all my strength.

My parting with him was colder than usual, for I could not dismiss the horrid picture of the cave beneath the old tree from my mind.

After placing my weapons and saddle in the lodge I went in quest of Tim Delany. I needed advice, and knew of no one better than my old comrade to consult with.

I found him heart and hand with the young Comanches, who were making merry on the smooth greensward in front of the village.

Tim's partner in the dance was the dusky beauty, whose hand had caused his cheek to tingle but a short time before.

Perhaps Tim was right when he gravely told me it was all for love, for the girl seemed happy enough with her partner, and her father, a venerable looking warrior, smiled approval when the pair rather over-did their parts in the by no means delicate dance.

I do not mean to say the Comanche maidens were guilty of any indelicacy. It was their manner of dancing, and as they knew no sin they knew no shame.

When the dance was over, I called Tim, and he came hot, flushed, and panting towards me.

"What did ye think of that, Silvershot?"

"You seem an apt pupil," I said; "but no wonder under such an instructor."

"She's an illigant little girl, Silvershot—don't you think so?"

"She's very pretty, but surely you—"

"Faith, I do though, and I mean to ask the old chap about it to-morrow."

"To-morrow," I said, "will see us on the frontiers of Mexico; so—"

"Bedad, it won't see me, unless I can take the little dear with me."

"Come with me, Tim. We have something more serious to attend to than your love-making. You can do that when we return; that is, if ever we do return."

I found Master Tim very difficult to manage until I told him the ghastly spectacle I had seen in the cave.

"By the mortial," he exclaimed, "and it's very near getting married I was to one of them. It's lucky you saw that same sight, Silvershot, so that the end of poor Dick Crosby and—"

"I am not sure it is the lost—"

"Man alive! I thought you were certain of it. Well, perhaps, after all, it may be a false alarm."

"It may be so, Tim, but I am afraid not."

"What were you doing with your eyes, man alive, not to see the faces of the poor divils? Shure, that would have been easy enough when you were there!"

"It would, Tim; but the appalling sight came so suddenly upon me, that I forgot all about our old companions, and it was not until I had left the cave the thought came to me about poor Dick and his comrades."

"Well, it can't be helped now, Silvershot. There is only one way to settle the doubt.

"That—"

"To go back to the cave. You know the way there. We can have a good look at them, and should they turn out to be our ould chums, we must keep our oath of revenge, although we shall have to kill our friends.

"It is death to anyone who is caught near the cave, Tim; death even for a Comanche!"

"What the divil about that? Sure, we can manage that without being caught."

"We can try."

"That's right, avick! So, as soon as it's dark we will go."

"So be it. What do you intend to do now? I think you had better come to the lodge with me."

"The divil a lodge! It's making love I mean to be until the dancing is all over!"

Tim turned away and joined the dusky maiden, who had been watching our conference, and soon he was capering to the Indian music, evidently shutting out from his mind that the fact that our expedition to the cave might end in the death of one or both of us. The law upon this matter was very stringent, and, much as I was liked by the tribe, I knew they would not spare me if caught.

Soon after sundown the murky group separated, and went to their wigwams; and as the darkness spread over the village, there was not a sign of life to be seen, except the sentries, who were pacing slowly to and fro.

We had nothing to fear from these dusky warriors, for they kept their faces from the camp. They knew there was no danger to be apprehended from their friends. Their eyes and ears were only for the expected foe.

The night was all that could be desired for our purpose. The moon kept behind the clouds, and the few stars that were visible failed to light the earth.

Armed only with our hunting knives and a lasso, we crept from the tent and stole softly towards the old tree, and, with the aid of the lasso, were soon at the summit.

"Wouldn't it be as well," suggested Tim, "for us to take the lasso with us, in case anyone should pass, and see it dangling here?"

"A good idea, Tim. We will do so."

I found it required our united strength to remove the heavy mass of interwoven roots that covered the entrance to the cave, and when we had done so, we placed the cover on end to allow as much fresh air as possible to find ingress to the stifling vaults below.

"A queer place," said Tim. "Make haste with the lights, avick!"

I must have been unnerved by the thought of the grisly forms suspended from the roof of the first cave, for I succeeded in knocking the skin off the fingers of my left hand before obtaining a light.

Tim uttered an exclamation of horror when the pine-torch blazed and crackled as I held it aloft, and revealed the row of ghastly figures.

"Shure, it's a dreadful sight," he said; "and no wonder ye didn't think of looking at their faces. Make haste, comrade, and let's get it over."

Ugh! what a fearful sight it was!—the distorted faces, blackened tongues, and eyeless sockets of five of the dead men. The other two were yet more appalling, for their bodies had dried to powder, and yet were so entire that every fearful distortion of face and limbs was visible.

What a subject for a horribly-sensational picture the scene in that murky cave would have made had there been one of the old school of painters there to have transferred the figures of the living and the dead to canvas!

The grisly, horrid forms, the flaming pine-torch, our pale, horrid faces, and the surrounding darkness forming a background sombre enough for such a scene!

Our examination was long and minute; but, in spite of the perfect state of preservation the bodies were in, we could not make out any resemblance to what the features were when the hapless wretches were living beings.

"It's not much like poor Dick or any of the boys these poor devils are," said Tim. "Not a bit like, in my opinion, Silvershot."

"It is impossible to form an opinion," I answered, "so the Comanches will have the benefit of the doubt."

"There's no doubt at all," Tim said. "It's certain I am that not one of these was ever known to us. Look at their shoulders, man. Shure, they are not half as broad as any of our old comrades' shoulders. I'll tell you what it is, Silvershot, avick, these whites are Mexicans, the divil a doubt of it."

I gave in to Tim, for argument was useless when he had once formed an opinion.

"Perhaps you are right," I said; "so we will return."

"But about the gold, Silvershot? Shure, it would be a mortial pity not to have a peep at it, particularly when—"

A sudden noise, like a peal of thunder, stopped his speech, and caused us both to start, and, unfortunately, my nerves were so unstrung that I dropped the pine torch and extinguished it.

"What's that?" said Tim. "What the divil is it? Where's the light?"

"The torch it here, Tim; but about the nature of that noise, I am as wise as yourself."

"Never mind. Light the pine-torch again, and we'll soon find out."

Easier said than done; for I had left my flint and steel on one of the steps that led to the vault.

I told Tim where I had placed them, and he started forward to get as far as possible from the dead.

"Which step, Silvershot?"

"The second from the top."

"The divil a flint or steel's there, avick. Make haste, man alive, and help me to find them."

Guided by Tim's voice I mounted the steps, and to my horror the flint and steel had disappeared.

"What's the matter, Silvershot? What are you swearing about now?"

"You must have knocked the flint down."

"The divil a bit—maybe it's fallen, for there's part of the step gone."

Passing my hand over the step I found Tim's words were true—a portion of the earth had broken away.

"Something has fallen from above," I said. "That accounts for the noise we heard."

"By the mortial, you are right," said Tim, who was by this time at the top of the steps, "and as I'm a living man, Silvershot, it's the cover that has fallen over the hole."

"The Lord help us, then!"

"Why man—sure we can lift it. Come, comrade, let's put our strength together."

We did so—exerted ourselves until the perspiration rolled off our foreheads; but we might as well have tried to move the old tree.

"It's useless, Tim," I said, dolefully. "We are trapped. Uwato told me the mass of wood was so arranged, that, unless it was placed a certain way it would be sure to fall."

"And didn't you place it the certain way, Silvershot?"

"I did not know the way, Tim Delany."

"Bad luck to you for a thick-headed fool, Silvershot! It's a pretty mess we are in now!"

"We are doomed to certain death, Tim."

"The Lord be good to us!"

I felt sorry for my comrade, for I alone was to blame. Uwato had cautioned me, and I knew the penalty of visiting the cave beneath the tree.

Silent and dismayed, we sat upon the step the whole of that long night. . Such a night! it was a wonder we did not go mad.

The seven men suspended a few feet below us seemed to gibe and mock our misery.

We fancied they came and thrust their horribly distorted faces against ours—thought the eyeless sockets were furnished with blazing eyes—and, bitterest thought of all, we should soon be suspended from the fatal beam. To add to our horrible situation, cold slimy reptiles crept forth from their lairs, and crawled over our faces and hands; and from the farthest cave, where the yellow gold lay in heaps, came the monotonous tick-tick of the death spider.

"Silvershot," said Tim, when the night was half spent, "I shall go mad."

"Poor old comrade! Keep up your heart. This is not the first time we have been near death."

"True, Silvershot; but it will be the last."

"I fear so—no, no. Courage, Tim, and all may yet be well."

"What is it, Silvershot? Speak, man!"

"We have our knives—to work, Tim Delany. This accursed thing is only the interwoven roots of the tree. There is time enough yet before daylight to cut a passage through."

We forgot the grisly forms, which we had fancied were moving about the cave; thought not of the cold, clammy reptiles; heeded not the death-watch beating our fate.

To work we went. The interwoven roots were tough, but our knives were keen, and the steel well-tempered.

Hour after hour passed, and not a word was spoken. The only sound heard was the chipping of the wood, as we laboured for life and liberty.

At last—hurrah!—my knife-blade passed through the wood; then a small hole was made.

The hole became larger—larger. Then I passed my hand through, and felt the keen morning air playing upon my burning skin.

Another hour and we had cut away sufficient of the wood to admit the passage of our bodies, and just as Tim passed through, the first gleam of the rising sun fell upon his pale and haggard face.

"Thank God!" was my first exclamation, and it was echoed by my comrade.

The light that streamed through the hole was but feeble yet, so I determined to wait until there was sufficient daylight to reveal the spot where my flint and steel had fallen.

CHAPTER XXIX.
THE HURRICANE.

"It's my opinion," said Tim, as he passed through the hole, "ye want to get caught."

"How's that, Tim?"

"What the devil are ye hunting for?"

"The flint and steel; and if I do not find them, we may as well stay here as go to the village."

"That's true, comrade."

There was soon sufficient light for my purpose, and I found the flint and steel under the fallen earth.

"Now," said Tim, "the whole village will be astir directly, and long before the sun dries the dew upon the grass our trail will be discovered."

"Will it?" I said. "Well, Tim, you must imagine I have but just begun life on the prairie. Lie down, Tim, and I will show you how to deceive even a Comanche."

"Lie down—this way, Silvershot?"

"No; on your back—that's it; now raise your feet."

Tim did so, and I caught him by both ankles, and dragged him towards the camp.

"Bedad, Silvershot!" he said, "it's a mighty fine way to get rid of the marks of a pair of mocassins; but be aisy, man, when ye come to the stump of a tree or a stone, for the small of my back is not made of cast-iron."

We reached our tent a few minutes before the bugle rang out the summons to arouse the sleeping Comanches, and an hour later we were mounted, our horses' heads turned towards the Mexican frontier.

Well mounted, well armed, and followed by my faithful dogs, we were as light-hearted as though the horrible night we had spent in the cave had been but a fleeting vision in place of a reality.

"Enjoy life while you can," said Tim; "for there's no telling what will soon happen to us."

Had we known to what that journey would have led, it would never have been undertaken by either Tim Delany or your obedient servant, Silvershot.

We rode for two days through the tangled forest, starting the deer at every twenty yards, and causing the squirrels, who were thickly clustered upon the trees, to whisk off the branches, and seek shelter from the guns of the intruders.

We had brought sufficient dried deer and bear flesh from the Comanche camp to last us three days, for we expected at the expiration of this to be on the plains where the buffaloes were feeding.

Soon after the sunset of the second day's march we halted for the night on the bank of a silvery streamlet, and unsaddling our tired steeds, fastened a bell round each of their necks, and turned them loose to feed upon the rich pasturage.

The bells were to guide us in the morning should the horses stray from our bivouack.

The fire was lighted, and the meat placed on a stick above the flame.

I was attending to the culinary operations, and Tim, whistling "St. Patrick's Day," as he placed a blanket across the lower branch of a tree, to form a tent, for the night dews were heavy, and the shelter was very agreeable.

"Bedad!" said Tim, suddenly, pausing in the pointing of some sticks to peg down the corners of the blanket, "bedad, Silvershot, the sky looks mighty queer."

I looked up from the pleasant contemplation of the frizzling steaks, and saw the change that had taken place in the heavens since we had halted.

A thick haze, not unlike the fogs that sometimes visit this country, hung midway between the earth and sky.

"A storm," I said to Tim, "and unless we are lucky we shall have to eat our supper half-cooked."

"Faith! I think so too, Silvershot; but that don't matter much."

"Not much; but you had better catch the horses, and hobble them, in case of accidents."

"Just wait a minute, avick! I've only two pegs to drive in the corner of the blanket, then the tent will be——Look over there, comrade, that is not the moon, anyhow."

I looked towards the south-east, and beheld a blood-red streak shining through the haze.

My heart seemed to leap to my throat, as I jumped up and exclaimed—

"It's a tropical hurricane coming, Tim. Quick, for God's sake! and secure the horses, or they will stampede. Take your rifle, Tim, for the wolves will be startled from their lairs by that fiery omen."

I heard the tinkling of the horses' bells as

Tim passed through the timber, then turned to the shelter he had partly erected, and, drawing the tomahawk from my belt, drove in one of the two pegs.

I was about to do the same with the other, when the wind suddenly rose, and in a moment increased to such a terrible force, that the loose corner of the blanket was torn from my hands.

The pegs yielded at the other corners, and the heavy Witney was soaring above the tree-tops as though it were a scrap of tissue paper.

Instinctively my eyes were turned in the direction I expected Tim to return, and, to my dismay, saw the trees bending over as though a giant hand was forcing them down.

Crack—crack—from all sides, as the branches were broken off; then, with a crash, the massive trunks yielded to the fury of the blast.

So rapid had the storm set in that I had not had time to seek a place of safety, and I needed one, for the bushes and tops of the trees that had been torn away in rear of me were being driven forward in the current of the hurricane.

Twigs, foliage, and heavy branches were whirled through the air, and in such masses that everything in its way was hurled asides, and soon those portions of the shattered trees as were light enough to ride in the blast helped to swell the mass, until the air was so full that I could not see beyond the moving mass.

With a roar like the falling of a mighty torrent, the flying mass was whirled above my head, and, terror-stricken, I stood and watched it pass beyond the ruined forest.

What a sight the place presented after the passing of the storm-fiend! The noblest of the forest monarchs had been stripped of every branch and leaf, and those which had not withstood the furious tempest had either been torn up by the roots or snapped across at the thickest part of the trunks.

The fury of the gale abated almost as soon as it had risen, and, although the wind yet howled in the track of the desolating current, and carried with it a cloud of small twigs and leaves, I knew there was nothing to fear from another passage of such heavy branches as had so recently passed over my head.*

Half-stupified with amazement, I looked at the spot where I had lit my fire, but it was gone, and the best portion of our food with it.

My fears for Tim's safety overcame my regret at the loss of a supper, and I began to

---

* The American papers, in their account of this storm, state that large houses were blown away, and cattle, such as sheep, cows, and horses, were carried ten miles from their pasturage. As they received their information from the trappers, there is no cause to doubt the statement.

ponder over the best way to ascertain what had become of him.

Delany was a good woodsman, and as the storm-current could not have been more than a quarter of a mile in breath, I hoped he had caught the horses, and galloped to the right of it—there, in all probability, the wind would scarcely ruffle the foliage.

If so, he would soon return, and in all probality if I went in search of him, we should miss each other—and I did not wish to give my comrade any pain; for I knew if he came back to the camping ground, and I was not there, he would give me up for dead.

I seated myself upon a fallen tree, and began anxiously to examine my rifle, for this good weapon was more to me than gold or precious stones.

Whilst thus engaged, a peculiar light suddenly blayed upon the barrel, and leaping up, I observed the sky had a lurid crimson hue, and from the earth beneath my feet there arose a disagreeable sulphurous smell.

Starting up in amazement, I looked around to ascertain what was about to happen, for I had been told by the old frontier men these signs betokened an earthquake.

The peculiar tinge that overcast the heavens soon passed away, so did the disagreeable smell of sulphur, and Nature, save for the marks of the tempest, resumed her usual aspect.

My rifle was uninjured, I found, and myself, save for a few scratches, was none the worse for the tempest.

For nearly an hour I sat feverishly awaiting the return of my chum, but he came not; so, to try and allay the suspense I underwent, I climbed the moss-covered trunk of a gigantic tree, the top of which had been torn away by the hurricane.

The summit was between forty and fifty feet from the ground, and when I reached it I had a grand view of the surrounding country.

To the right and left the mighty forest was untouched, but looking in a direct line from where I sat, I could follow the course taken by the storm.

Where it had passed there was a space filled with uprooted trees, naked trunks, and heaps of shattered timber.

I could not help feeling awed by the scene, and, under the impressions that filled my mind, I exclaimed—

"Nature, thy works are indeed wondrous!"

The words had scarcely left my lips when the heavens became overcast, and a twilight gloom fell over the earth.

Following this there came a noise like the distant roar of a cataract; then the semi-darkness passed away, and the light became perfectly clear.

I clung to the broken summit of the tree, and an expression of alarm broke from my lips, for with the coming of the strange light the massive tree trunk began to sway to and fro.

"Heaven help me now, for the earthquake is near!"

It was near; and the trees began to rock to and fro, as though the very roots would burst through the earth.

The ground, too, began to rise and fall in furrows, like the sea when ruffled by the breeze.

I had heard of earthquakes taking place in these remote regions, but the reality of the dread spectacle was a thousand-fold worse than the most vivid description.

There I was alone in the midst of Nature's most dreadful workings—alone, swaying to and fro like a child being rocked in a cradle.

Holding on, my heart filled with the most dire apprehensions. for I knew not the moment the earth would open and engulph me in a depthless abyss.

This dreadful state of things lasted for some time, perhaps half-an-hour, as near as I can remember. Then the rumbling gradually ceased, and the earth settled down to its wonted appearance.

"Thank God!" was my first ejaculation. "It has passed, and I am alive."

I was about to descend the trunk—had gone down a few feet, when a sudden roar and a trembling of the earth caused me to rapidly scramble to the top again.

What new danger was I to face now?

The question was not long unanswered, for, looking through the open space cleared by the tempest, I saw that the level prairie teemed with a black, moving crowd.

Nearer came the strange sight—so near that I could make out the shaggy forms of a countless horde of buffaloes, and mixed with them were thousands of wild horses, wolves, and other animals, denizens of the forest and prairie.

On they came, with the irresistible force of an avalanche, crashing the smaller tree trunks and bushy shrubs that had out-rode the storm.

On they came, the earth trembling beneath the mighty living torrent, and as far as the eye could reach the multitude extended, and heaven knows how far beyond.

I had only time to gaze, terror-stricken at the appalling spectacle, when the horrible position I was in flashed upon my mind.

The frightened multitude were making for the space in the forest cleared by the tempest.

Coming towards it, thousands being crushed to death by being hurled against the unbroken timber.

THE GLARE OF THE TORCH FELL UPON THE BODIES SUSPENDED FROM THE ROOF

I threw up my hands in despair, and shouted aloud in my agony, for the tree upon which I sat stood in the centre of the cleared space.

I closed my eyes, as I thought, for the last time, and grappled the tree, which I knew in another moment would be overthrown.

Never did I experience such a sensation as when the first shaggy beast thundered past me, making the very earth tremble under his ponderous hoofs. My brain was in a whirl, and as the herd followed on I lost all consciousness until a shock awoke me, and I felt myself thrown with a jerk upon some warm substance.

I clung tenaciously to whatever it might be, and it was well for me I did so.

I soon found I was on the back of a huge beast, who was bearing me with whirlwind speed across the prairie, and, to add to my discomfiture, my face was towards the rear.

My first thought, however, was of being released from my unpleasant position. At present I could not dismount without encountering a fearful death.

Fear caused the herds to fly for hours and days, I had been told by old hunters; and thinking of this caused me to wonder how long I should have the strength to keep my seat.

Onward still—until the queen of night rode high in the heavens, and the plain was as light almost as though the daylight streamed from above.

I began now to detect signs of my shaggy charger's speed slackening. I did not feel any change, but the fact of several of the herd passing me, told the circumstance.

My heart filled with joy at the prospect of having a clear space in rear, for I could then leap or roll to the ground.

The hope was a false one, for although many thousands of animals rapidly swept past, there was no diminution of the dark mass in rear.

The deers, the antelopes, the mustangs, and I could almost swear I saw several lithe panthers, were the first to pass.

Then came the younger buffaloes, and a swarm of wolves, and I was thankful their fear was so great that my presence was unnoticed.

Forward still. Hour after hour passed, until the grey tints of the coming day began to replace the paling moon.

During this time myriads of untamed animals had passed me, as far as I could judge I was in the very midst of the moving mass.

Although the old bull's pace was slackening, I knew it would take some hours yet before the dense mass in rear would pass, and being shaken in every limb by my uncomfortable mode of riding, I determined, if it were possible to alter my seat, it should be done.

The motion of the buffalo was not unpleasant, being more of the see-saw kind than the regular jerk of a horse.

Under these circumstances, and having plenty of room to turn, I thought it would be as well to begin before I was too much exhausted.

Stretching my legs out towards the bull's shoulders, and tightly grasping his tail, I laid full length along his back, the sides of my feet and the grip of my hands preventing me from dropping off.

My next motion was to place my left hand as far as I could towards my steed's head, and grasping a tuft of hair near the hump, dropped my feet down his near side.

The tuft of short hair was naturally strong, it would have given way when I freed my right hand, and passed my left well over the bull's off side.

In this position I remained for a few moments, and was nearly tumbled off, for the buffalo, evidently thinking an opportunity had come to rid himself of an encumbrance, made a couple of side jumps, and would, no doubt, have succeeded in dislodging me, had I not quickly released my grasp on the back

of him, and, throwing my right leg over, obtained a firm seat on his haunches.

The change was worth the risk I had undergone, for the pace was much easier, and I could see ahead, a boon that I soon discovered was not so pleasant as I at first anticipated it would be.

The scene around was wild in the extreme. As far as the naked eye could reach the level plain was covered with the terrified brutes, and the air was filled with their cries.

There was the snort and neigh of the untamed horses, the bellowing of the buffaloes, and the snarl of the skulking wolves.

Soon the ground bore evidence of the effects of the stampede, for the noble animals dropped panting and exhausted at every step.

I began to dread this accident befalling the buffalo upon which I rode, for there were yet countless thousands in rear. Therefore, the chances were a thousand to one that I should be trampled to death were the old bull to give in.

The sun's ray's began to shoot out from the leaden sky, and soon dispelled the morning mists.

Onward, for another hour, until the plain was flooded with the brilliant light.

I was wondering when the brute's mad career would end, and looking anxiously around, fearing every moment that I should see the dark outline of a forest in the distance.

This was a danger quite as terrible to me as the hoofs of the crowd in the rear, for I knew the fear-blinded animal would rush against anything in his path. Should this be a tree and my skull make acquaintance with the trunk, there would be an end to my adventures.

Reflecting upon this, I did not for some time notice the circumstance that soon caused a damp and cold perspiration to ooze out from every pore.

The plain, as I have before said, was perfectly level, the absence of even a low-growing shrub gave the prairie more the appearance of an immense sea than anything I can compare it to.

I saw the animals in front were gradually lessening in number; yet ahead of the leading crowds the prairie was perfectly deserted.

Less and less, until there remained scarcely a hundred dark forms before me, and these soon began to diminish, and, like the lightning's flash, it came to my brain that I was fast nearing one of those fearful chasms so common in the prairie.

My blood curdled in my veins at this appalling thought; for I had no idea of judging by the depth of the place, which had sucked in its devouring jaws the multitude of animals in such a short time.

I looked back, and, despite the fearful spectacle, determined to risk a leap from my steed in place of being dashed to atoms by falling over the edge of the precipice.

Too late—the brute, missing his companions, started out to overtake them, and when I turned my head I was upon the verge of the precipice.

I can remember giving vent to a wild cry; then I became dizzy as I whirled downward; then came a sudden shock, my body rebounded, and all became a blank.

CHAPTER XXXI.

A NARROW ESCAPE.

THE gloom of the dusky sunset fell upon the strange scene when I regained my consciousness.

I was lying at a short distance from a huge pile of dead and dying animals, a heap the base of which was at the bottom of the chasm, and the apex level with the edge.

How many thousands of carcases were in that gigantic pile defies calculation, for the bodies were so closely packed that even the wildest guesses would have been eminently short of the total.

The pile formed by the carcases had served for a passage for the remainder of the herd, and the countless hoof strokes had crushed the upper strata as level as though the slope had been of earth.

It was a pitiful sight, for many of the poor brutes, although every bone was broken and their bodies trodden into the palpitating mass beneath, still showed faint signs of life, and the upturned eyeballs and parched tongues showed how intensely they suffered.

I must have been carried over when the pile was half formed, and the lightness of my body falling upon the soft heap had caused me to rebound and roll to the spot where I found myself upon awaking to life.

Animals of every description had passed over me, for my body, when I attempted to move it, was in such pain that I yelled out. A few moments' careful manipulation assured me that no bones were broken, but many were most terribly bruised.

Luckily my knife and tomahawk were safe in my belt, so was the little pouch containing the gold dust; not that the latter was of much service at the time, but I did not know how soon it might be.

I lay for some time cogitating over the matter, and resolved not to die where I had fallen if there was a probability of regaining sufficient strength to crawl a few yards.

Within this distance was the carcase of a buffalo, and that carcase not only contained the luscious and highly-prized hump, but a certain cure for my bruised body.

Life was at stake; so, despite the agonizing exercise, I crept towards the carcase, and soon had the satisfaction of being beside it.

My knife soon put me in possession of the tender hump, and a fire being a luxury I did not care about indulging in, I sucked at the dainty, and felt not only refreshed but much stronger for the operation.

The sun went down, the moon rose, and I could hear a pack of ravenous wolves busy among the carcases; but I heeded them not, and went busily on with my work.

I was stripping the buffalo of its hide. I had separated the upper half when the thought occurred that I should not be able to succeed with that portion beneath.

Pausing for a few seconds over this difficulty I came to the conclusion that my bruises could be quite as well cured by ripping open the bison as by rolling myself in the hide.

The thought was put to the test, and a slit was made sufficiently large for a portion of the entrails to be removed, then I stripped off my buckskin hunting suit, and, taking my knife with me, crept into my warm, and, I must confess, somewhat horrible couch.

The Indian remedy for surface wounds and bruises is the best in the world, and acts so quickly that all sensation of pain soon leaves you. The feeling—I refer to my own sensations at the time—was as though the warm flesh gradually absorbed the pain, and brought on a drowsy slumber.

I must have slept some hours, for I awoke completely restored, and was about to emerge, when the snarling of my old foes, the wolves, caused me to reconnoitre the position before I placed my flesh in the way of their fangs.

It was well I did so, for a gang of eight or nine gaunt wolves were busy finishing the portion of the buffalo I had removed before taking up my lodging for the night.

Guided by the scent of the blood that led to the bisons, two of the pack came disagreeably close to my place of observation, and began sniffing about as though there were something more than dead buffalo at hand.

I grasped the hilt of my long-bladed "butcher" knife, and waited for the next proceeding.

Leaving their hides, the brutes came to within two feet of my face, and would, I have no doubt, made a closer acquaintance with me had I not given a yell that would have done credit to the strongest of strong-lunged Indians.

Such a diabolical sound proceeding from the stomach of a dead buffalo was more than the astonished wolves could stand, for after pausing a moment in astonishment, they dropped their tails and scampered off as fast as possible.

"That's a narrow escape," quoth I, "and to prevent further accidents, I will leave this delightful place as soon as possible."

I was soon out of my warm bed; and going to a water hole that was near, I was able to have a refreshing bath.

All pain had left me before I bathed, and the cold water was so refreshing that I felt a new man, and when I had donned my clothes I cut the throats of half-a-dozen wolves that were lying near the carcases of the buffaloes.

The brutes had gorged to repletion, and were lying stretched out incapable of action.

It was not yet daylight, but there was sufficient light from the stars to guide me to the track made by the herd in their ascent of the chasm.

I was soon upon the prairie, and plodding steadily forward, my guide the morning star, for I was almost certain a settlement was to be found in that direction.

I had not gone more than a couple of miles when the feeble glimmer of a light from the window of a log hut confirmed my expectations.

I was thankful for the pouch of gold dust now, for a small portion of the yellow dross would purchase a strong-limbed horse, and I was anxious to be once more in the saddle, and on the way to the place where I had parted from my comrade.

I was rather disappointed when I reached the log-house, for I found it was a solitary dwelling, of somewhat larger dimensions than the ordinary dwellings that are to be found in the wilds.

In the dim light of the coming day the building had more the appearance of a small fort than a dwelling-house, for there was a turret of stout logs erected on the flat roof, and judging by its bulk there could be little doubt but that it was shot-proof.

I did not like the appearance of the place and was debating in my mind the prudence of arousing the inmates when the neigh of a horse, followed by several others, drove away my scruples.

I thought of poor Delaney—that was enough. Then I drew my knife from its sheath, and hammered at the door with the haft.

In reply to my summons a wicket flew open in a line with my head, and the bright barrel of a rifle was thrust through, and a voice said—

"Hallo! What are ye? White man or Injun?"

I started back at the sound, for I recognised the voice as that of one swivel-eyed Dick, a member of a band of white men, desperadoes who were the terror of the trading caravans that crossed the prairie; and it was said more than one emigrant train had totally disappeared after being attacked by these robbers.

Retreat was totally out of the question, for a bullet from the rifle would have soon brought me down. So trying to feel that I had nothing to fear I answered—

"I am a white man."

"What's yer following?"

"Hunter—sometimes trapper."

"Come a little closer this way, and let's have a look at yer mug."

I advanced a couple of paces, the rifle was withdrawn, and a strong ray of light streamed from the wicket direct upon my face.

"All right," I heard, "I'll be down in the whisking of a squirrel's tail."

So he was, and not without a little inward qualm I passed through the door into the tiger's den.

And while doing so, I took the precaution to hide my knife inside my hunting shirt.

CHAPTER XXXII.

PLEASANT COMPANY.

WHEN I entered the log-house the interior was so dark that I could scarcely see a yard before me.

"Just mind the chaps' shins," said the man who had opened the door; "if yer don't maybe a bowie or two will be stuck into you."

After this caution I was very careful in stepping towards the huge chimney, where a small heap of wood ashes faintly gleamed out of the surrounding darkness.

"Tired," I suppose?" said my new acquaintance, interrogatively; "find a corner over there, and I'll give you a buffalo hide in a minute."

I had had sufficient of buffalo hides for some time, nevertheless I thanked my querist, and found a corner where no shins or the owners belonging to the shins were in the way.

I must have been completely done up, for when I laid upon the soft hide my eyes closed, and I remember nothing more until I was awakened by feeling a heavy hand fumbling about my doublet.

Instinctively the recollection of the place I was in came to my mind, and caution being one of the essentials a hunter first learns, I lay perfectly still, as though undisturbed by my friend's hand.

"This bag," said he of the swivel eye. speaking to his companions, "feels heavy. I think I ought to look inside. Who knows what may be in it?"

" That's true, Dick. Injun's teeth, or shells most likely."

" Old nails," said another. " These chaps have queer things sometimes in their——"

" Hold your bellowing !" said Dick, in a fierce whisper. " Cuss you for a fool ! These hunters sleep like foxes."

" This one don't," replied the previous speaker, " for I just dropped some hot ashes from my pipe on his face to see if he was foxing, and not even an eyelid winked."

" That accounts," thought I, " for the smarting sensation I feel."

" Didn't know that," growled Dick. " I might, though, for the varmint seemed quite knocked over. Should say he'd footed it considerably before he came here."

" Very likely. Feel the bag, Dick—then let us know all about it."

My heart throbbed when the ruffian placed his hand under the bag, and raised it so that he could insert his forefinger and thumb inside without my feeling his touch.

The bag fell from his hand when he felt the heavy smooth grains sift over his skin.

" It's gold !" he hoarsely whispered. " Gold! real gold !—real gold dust !"

" Gammon," said a voice. " That won't do for us, Dick."

The gentleman with the swivel eye left me, and partly unclosing my eyes, I saw him approach the table and drop the crumbling particles of the precious metal in the palm of his left hand.

There was a dead silence for a few moments, and seven greedy pair of eyes were fixed upon Dick's hand.

Then seven forefingers were thrust forth to feel the grains of dust, and suppressed whispers followed.

" That bag," said one, " is worth more than the caravan that crosses the prairie on its way to Santa Fé."

" Twice as much, ever so many times as much, and we must have it if we are up to anything."

" Murtough is right; so the sooner we take the lot the better."

" I say now," said Dick. " Let's have it before the captain and the others come back, for there will be the less to share it."

" Dick's right. Who has a sharp bowie, for it won't do to give him a second stroke; he's a tough customer, I know. He has sinews of iron."

I turned over and moaned as though in my sleep, thus lying upon the bag, and by the change of position, getting a better view of my pleasant friends.

The action was so natural that it threw the ruffians off their guard, and one of them, in reply to a query from Swivel-eyed Dick, said—

" Not he. He ain't foxing; if he had been, he'd have stayed quiet, and not rolled over."

I had a good view of the gang, and must confess that my feelings were not pleasant, for a greater set of desperadoes I had never seen before.

I cursed my folly in entering the log-house, and my want of forethought in not concealing the gold ; and fearing they would make a sudden attack, I gripped the handle of my knife, and as I did so I espied a tomahawk lying close to my side.

I made up my mind to possess myself of the weapon, and while trying to settle on a plan to do so, the vagabonds began to whisper, and so low that I could only catch a word or two of their conversation.

They had determined to cut my throat while I slept, and the honour of slaying me was to fall to the man who drew a marked bullet from a hat.

There were seven bullets placed in the lucky bag, and the lucky man was he of the swivel eye.

" Just my luck," he said, " and my knife as blunt as the hoop of a tar barrel."

" Grind it," suggested Murtough. " Come on, I'll turn the grindstone for ye."

There was a small stone in the corner of the house, and to this the two men went; the others meanwhile speculating upon the weight of the gold dust.

So intent were they that I was enabled to draw the tomahawk towards me unnoticed, and, covering it with the corner of the buffalo robe, awaited the next move. While doing so, a thought came to my brain that I might stand a better chance for a fierce fight if I was upon my feet, and following up the mental suggestion, I pretended to suddenly awake.

The ruffians started, and when I had thrust the weapons under the folds of my hunting shirt, I sat up, and, rubbing my eyes, said—

" It's long past sunrise, ain't it ?"

The grindstone was deserted by Dick and his companion, and the knife hidden by the former as he came to the rough table.

It was not pleasant to find oneself in the company of these desperadoes, to calmly watch the sharpening of a long-bladed knife and know there was every prospect of the keen edge making an early acquaintance with your throat.

Yet I did not despair ; for I had been in situations quite as dangerous and had managed to get clear, but I must confess when I gazed at the rascally assemblage I felt anything but assured of my safety.

" Yes," Dick of the swivel-eye replied to

my query, "it's long past sunrise. You seem knocked up a bit, mate!"

"I am," I said; "for I have had a long and a rough ride."

"Come far, then?"

"Yes, from the Comanche country."

The vagabonds started at this, for the Comanches had threatened to tomahawk every one of the robbers.

Comanche country, eh! Are the Injuns on the war path, then?"

I was quite ready with a lie, for it struck me had the vagabonds an idea that a body of Indians were on the buffalo grounds, it would conduce to my safety.

"Yes," I answered, "there's a hunting party afoot on the plains, and for all I know they may be on my track, for I missed them when the storm came on."

"Storm, mate?"

"Yes, a fierce hurricane."

I told them of the scene in the forest, the loss of my horse, and my buffalo ride.

"Well," Dick said, "that beats Banagher, and Banagher beats the Devil. Should say you were a bit skeered."

"A little."

"I should say so. Suppose you get to work—here; you must be hungry."

I was, and the smell of the bear steak that was frizzling before the fire added to my appetite.

I declined the seat pointed out by Swivel-eyed Dick, but in such a manner that it excited not the ruffian's suspicion, for I pretended not to notice the place indicated, and seated myself near the door.

I chose this seat because there was less danger of being suddenly attacked in rear, and fell to work upon the smoking meat with a vigour that told how much I needed food.

"You are hungry, mate," said Dick. "Been long without work for the grinders?"

"Nigh four-and-twenty hours," I answered, with my mouth full. "Thought one time I should never have to use them again."

"Been long amongst the Comanches?"

"Yes, a long time."

"Oh, maybe a week?"

"Longer than that at times, but not so long when I last left them."

"They do say the Comanche country is a good one."

"It is."

"Plenty of cattle?"

"Thousands."

Dick gave his villanous knife-grinding companion a significant glance, as he said—

"Suppose it ain't true that the rains wash the gold dust down from the mountains?"

"Quite true," I replied, "for there is plenty of gold there."

"Lumps or dust?"

"Dust," I said, "until they melt it."

"Suppose you never saw any—eh?"

"Yes, seen plenty."

I had made up my mind to tell them of the contents of the bag that hung at my waist. I knew it was of no use to conceal the fact that was so well known to the gang, and possibly my apparent sociality would cause them to be less on their guard when the moment came for me to make an attempt to escape.

"Saw plenty," repeated Dick. "But didn't get any, I reckon, though you were the totem of an Indian chief."

"I am a chief of the Comanches," I replied, "so the gold is as much mine as any other chief's."

"Good!" said Dick. "Wish I were a chief too. Sure, I'd help myself. Did you say you have some of the yellow stuff?"

"I did not say so. But I have a little. Here it is."

I poured sufficient from the bag to cover the palm of my hand, and never shall I forget the greedy expression of the ruffian's eyes.

"Gold, and no mistake," said Dick, bending over to examine it. "Should say there was three hundred dollars' worth there."

"Quite," I replied. "And if you have a good horse to part with, this is yours."

The ruffians looked at each other, and Dick said—

"Well, we have a horse to spare, at that price. When do you want it?"

"Now."

"It wouldn't be exactly the best thing for you to leave just now."

A sardonic grin was upon the man's face as he said this.

"Time is an object," I said, "for I have left a comrade in the forest, and "—

I stopped short, for it struck me this would not tally with the story I had told about the Indians being on the buffalo ground.

"And," I went on, "unless I join him very soon the Comanches will be upon my trail."

"Well, that may be all right enough," the swivel-eyed ruffian said. "But, you see, we cannot part with a horse until our mates come back."

"Where are they?"

"Well, just seeing a party of settlers safe over Injun ground, that's all."

I felt sorry for the settlers, for I knew they would, to a certainty, be robbed of all they possessed, and perhaps murdered by their protectors.

"Very well," I said; "I must only commence the journey on foot, trusting to the

A ROUGH RIDE.

chance of falling in with the Comanche hunting party.

"You must do no such thing," Dick said. "No, mate, we ain't redskins, to let a fellow-crittur go away when he's knocked up like you are. Take a little more rest, and by the time our chaps come back you will be right enough, and able to ride the horse we can let you have."

I still demurred, and the ruffian cunningly said—

"Suppose you do go now, mate; you won't cover much ground before night, then you will be dead knocked up, and won't be able to go any further."

"Still I shall be on the road."

"That's true; but if you wait maybe only a couple, or at most four hours, you will get a good bit of horseflesh, and can go on until you fall in with your mate or the Injuns."

As there was no combating the truth of this statement, I pretended to be perfectly satisfied, and soon after the gang separated, some to chop wood, others to dry skins, others to fetch water from a stream about a mile from the hut.

I noticed, despite the men's occupations, and the earnestness with which they were pursued, that I was never left alone for a moment—one or the other looking in to see if I still lay upon the buffalo hide.

CHAPTER XXXIII.
A FIGHT FOR LIFE.

THERE is no doubt my over-anxious friends fancied I slept, and I began to wonder why an attack was not at once made upon me to gain possession of the treasure.

I had not wondered long upon the subject before I was enlightened by hearing a conversation between Swivel-eyed Dick and a burly ruffian he called Black Tom.

They were outside the hut, and standing close under the open window near to which I lay.

"I don't think we ought to touch the fellow," Dick said. "Supposing the Injuns should come upon his track, then it would be all up with us."

"—— the Injuns!" said Tom. "Do you think we are going to lose this little bit of luck because of the redskin varmints?"

"No occasion to lose the yellow stuff," said Dick. "We are sure of that, but I think we can wait and see whether the Comanches come up here. If they do, we will tell them we have taken him in, and they will perhaps let us off the throat-cutting and scalping they have promised."

"Not they, the varmints! They won't forget the way we trapped the caravan after it had passed through their country."

"I know them better than you do, Tom;

no, they won't touch one of us, now we have befriended one of their gang—for this chap is one of 'em, that can't be denied."

"Well, do as you like; but if I had my way, I'd slit his wizen now, and collar the stuff. That was the plan you first thought of, and why you don't carry it out I don't know."

"Because I thought better of it."

"Well ?——"

"So you will say when I tell you."

"Go on."

"You know how the captain has set his heart on getting hold of the stuff the Comanches have buried somewhere in their country ?"

"I've heard him speak of it."

"Well, when I heard this chap say he was a chief of the Injuns, and saw he was a white man, I thinks it wouldn't be much trouble, perhaps, to get him to tell us when to go to the Comanche country."

"You talk like a fool, Dick. The Injuns are too many for us."

"That's just it," said Dick; "if we went when they were at their village."

"You wouldn't——"

"Wait a bit. This chap can tell us where the stuff is; for it would be no use going there without knowing that."

"Well."

"Then we could fix upon a time when the braves are upon the war path or hunting, and go to the village, slit the necks of all the red varmints, women and children, and take the heaps of stuff they have."

"That's not a bad idea," Black Tom said, "if the fellow will guide us a little; if not, I daresay we can make him."

"Should say so. He aint the first we have made open their mouths against their will."

"No; nor won't be the last."

The amiable pair moved away, and feeling a little safer from their weapons, I rolled over and went to sleep.

I started up about mid-day, aroused by the hoof strokes of a number of horses.

The hut was empty; and, looking through the doorway, I saw them standing in a group, and heard their rough shouts of welcome to a body of horsemen who were coming rapidly from the direction of the forest that formed a background to the view from the door.

The new-comers numbered about twenty; and at their head rode a man of powerful frame and appearance, quite the reverse of pleasant.

I had seen the man once before at a settlement near the Mississippi. He was then leader of a gang of horse thieves, and I had heard something of his fierce and brutal nature.

The expedition the greater part of the gang had been upon was a profitable one, for when they dismounted and the horses were led away to the rear of the log-house, I saw four white-tilted waggons slowly approaching.

I knew the use these had been purchased for by their unfortunate former possessors, and the sight of the white covers gleaming in the sunlight told a sad story of robbery and murder.

"Cleaned 'em out," I heard Hiram Smith, the horse thief, say, "and sent every mother's son to the devil."

"Hs—sh—sh!" said Dick, warningly. "There's a cuss inside we don't want to hear too much, just now."

He jerked his thumb in the direction of the hut, and Hiram, with a coarse laugh asked—

"What is a missionary preacher? I shouldn't have thought another of 'em would come this way."

"Something better than that," Dick answered. "Worth forty of them preaching varmints, who are not up to the value of their hides—cuss 'em! But come this way, captain, I want to talk a bit."

The gigantic leader gave his rifle to one of the band, and followed his worthy lieutenant, who had gone out of earshot of the men.

Their conversation was kept up for ten minutes, and by the looks that were cast towards the hut, I knew I was the subject of their kind consideration.

I must plead guilty to a slight tremor about the region of the small of my back when I saw the pair walk towards the hut, and this feeling was not lessened when they entered and seated themselves on one of the rough settles.

Hiram, or Captain Hiram Smith—I suppose I must give the gentleman his full rank—opened the conversation by saying—

"Hi, stranger, wake up."

The voice was like the roar of a young bull, and had I slept it would have instantly awakened me.

Throwing off the buffalo skin I arose, and said—

"I am awake, and at your service."

"H'm," muttered the giant, "a clean-built fellow; could do with a few like him." Then added he, aloud, "This cross-eyed cuss tells me you want a horse."

"I do, very badly."

"And you are willing to give that little bag for him."

"I am not."

"Phew, you don't forget to speak up."

"Why should I not do so?"

"That's it, why shouldn't you? Well, I can tell you one thing, you can't have the beast under the price I have said."

"Very well, I will take my chance, and return on foot."

"Perhaps."

"Surely you would not attempt to detain me?"

"Why not?"

"Why should you? If I were amongst a tribe of Blackfeet or Arapahoes, I might expect to be made a prisoner. I certainly do not look forward to such a thing when with men of my own colour."

"You, will be, then, unless you give up the bag; for we are scarce of that sort of thing hereabouts."

"I shall not do so while I have the strength to keep it."

The giant eyed me from head to foot, and he said—

"The right stuff, I see, so we will say no more about the bag until you have answered me a few questions."

"I am listening."

"Dick tells me you are a sort of chief amongst the Comanches?"

"I am."

"Know all about them?"

"I do."

"Where are they now?"

"The tribes are scattered all over the country from beyond the high hills to the waters of the ocean."

"I know that. I met the red devils belonging to the tribe who infest this part of the country."

"Some are at the village, others are on the buffalo grounds."

"How many?"

"Of the hunting party?"

"Yes."

"About a hundred braves."

Captain Hiram Smith grinned as he looked towards his band and said—

"Think those boys a match for them, eh?"

"I don't know. You had better try."

"Don't be so free with that tongue of yours, or it may be slit."

"You ask me a question—I have answered it."

"I know you have. Don't do it in that fashion again, or maybe we shall fall out, and it's not a good thing to fall out with Hiram Smith, I can tell you."

"I have no wish to fall out with you."

"So much the better for you. Now, just tell me this. When do the Injuns leave the village?"

"About the fall of the leaf."

"Good. How many fighting men are left behind?"

"None, unless an enemy is on the war path."

"Good again! And you know where the yellow stuff is hidden?"

"I do."

"And would show us, if we acted square?—for, of course, you don't care anything for the copper-coloured varmints."

"I do care much for them, for they have always befriended me, and often saved my life when I have been in danger."

"Still, for all that, you would not mind turning round on 'em if it paid?"

"I should mind it, for "—

I paused, and, bending my head, pretended to listen.

"What's up?" Hiram Smith asked. "Hear anything?"

"I fancied I heard a whoop like the Comanches give when—— Do you hear that?"

"I can't say as I do," said the captain, "not being so used to their yells as you are; anyhow, we'll see if they are near."

He rose, and, going to the door, said a few words to the ruffians that were lying about on the grass.

"Here, take my rifle," he said; "there's six or seven of the pieces choked up with mud, so it's no use taking them. Now then, off with all of you that has shooters, for there's Injuns about."

The men were on their feet instantly, and I could not help smiling contemptuously when I saw them enter the timber, for they were screaming and halloing to each other, when the greatest caution was necessary in opposing the imaginary Indian foe.

There yet remained six of the gang, besides Dick of the swivel eye and Hiram Smith, and when I saw they were without firearms, I felt there was yet a chance for my life.

"The boys," said Hiram, when he returned to his seat, "don't care for Injun or devil, so the redskin varmints will find if they are caught."

"Which they certainly will not be," I said, with a sneer; "for your men made noise enough when they struck the timber to frighten the red men."

I don't believe Captain Hiram Smith understood the meaning of my words, for he indulged in a loud laugh.

"Ay," he said, "the sound of their voice is next to death to the redskin varmints. I can tell you, it's a pretty considerable lot we have rubbed out down here."

"Not Comanches," I said, "for they never cross as far."

"Comanche, or any name you like, they are all varmints alike, and if I had my way there shouldn't be one of 'em left."

I made no reply, so the giant resumed his self-glorification, and wound up by saying—

"I suppose you intend to show us where the varmints keep the stuff?"

"When?"

"When we get there, of course."

"I shall have no objection to do that, when you reach the village."

The captain looked at me, and, as though conscious that my words had a double meaning, he said—

"You'll just take a nice little oath we give to all new members of the band."

I kept my eyes turned towards the forest during this speech, for matters had arrived at a crisis, and I knew the only chance of escape would be during the time the greater portion of the gang was away.

"You form hasty conclusions, captain," I said. "Although thanking you very much for the honour you would confer upon me, I must decline it."

Hiram Smith crossed his legs, and attentively regarded me for a few moments. The expression of his face was not pleasant to look upon, but that did not trouble me much, for I returned his menacing stare with a haughty defiance that added considerably to the scowl with which he favoured me.

"Do you mean to say you will not join us, eh?"

"I cannot at present."

"Now, look here, I don't want any shuffling, so just tell me your reason."

"The chief reason is, the life would not suit me."

"What do you know of our life?"

"Not much from actual experience, but I prefer to be as I am."

"Well, look here, young fellow, you'll either join us, or you'll give up the gold dust and tramp off as soon as you like."

"If I refuse to yield, what then?"

"Why, we'll——soon make you."

"That remains to be seen."

As I spoke I moved rapidly towards the door and cleared it at a bound.

The ruffian had been prepared for this, for at the first movement I made he gave a hideous whistle, and the men who were outside instantly drew their knives and confronted me.

"Let daylight into his carcase," roared Hiram Smith, snatching up a rifle; "the varmint knows too much to go away."

I stepped quickly aside, and avoided the blow from the clubbed rifle, and placing my back against the hut, drew the weapons I had hitherto concealed under my doeskin shirt.

The sight of the long butcher-knife and the tomahawk stayed the sudden rush they were making, and all, save the burly leader, paused.

He came at me with uplifted rifle, and

made a blow that would have smashed my skull, had not the handle of the tomahawk proved an effectual friend.

The next moment Captain Hiram Smith gave a yell and staggered back. He had received a prod in the ribs from my knife that gave him sufficient employment to stay the bleeding.

I was cool and determined; the gang were hot and excited, and a little cowed by the manner in which I handled my weapons.

"You will find it no child's play," I said to them. "So, if you value your skins, stand aside and let me pass."

"You infernal cowards," yelled Hiram. "Give it to him. If he gets away with the yellow stuff and a whole skin, we shall have a herd of the red varmints down here. Let him have it!"

The ruffians bounded forward, and for a few seconds there was a desperate struggle between us.

Three of them wielded clubbed rifles, and more than once I staggered under a heavy blow. Then one of my assailants, with a howl of rage, would fall back gashed by the tomahawk, or bleeding from a knife-thrust.

I had worked my way towards the door, and in the midst of the fray found myself opposite the opening.

Forced back by my more wary antagonists, I was compelled to retreat inside, and to my joy found that by standing in the opening I could defend myself better than in the position I had first taken up.

Three of the gang were too seriously wounded to do more than yell out to their comrades to finish me, a request they did all in their power to obey.

I found the tomahawk a very effective weapon now, for I had only to step back to avoid a blow from a clubbed musket, and before my assailant could get out of reach he received a swinging blow.

The gang began to understand the improvement in my mode of defence, and Hiram ceased swearing at the wound in his side, and called two, who were slightly wounded, away from the fight.

His instructions to them were conveyed in a few words, and they ran to the rear of the log hut.

The attack in front was not so vigorous after this, for the ruffians guessed the cause of their companions' disappearance, and I was not long kept in doubt of their purpose, for I heard a couple of axes at work on the logs in the rear.

They were cutting an opening, and should they succeed I should be taken in front and rear.

The perspiration began to gather upon my forehead at this new danger, and when the splinters began to fly, I looked eagerly round for something to place against the hole.

My eyes fell upon a small keg of powder. The top was off. There was yet a heap of smouldering wood in the fire-place.

Quick as thought my mind was made up. I knew I had no mercy to expect should I be overpowered; so I determined, if I must die, my enemies should share my fate.

The retreat to the fire-place was the work of a moment, and as the ruffians came after me, I snatched a handful of the glowing charcoal, and, despite the pain it caused me, I held it over the barrel.

"Now!" I cried out triumphantly— "n ow!"

"At him—at him!" shouted Hiram. "Brain him quick—quick, pals!"

There was no time to be lost, for I saw the gang returning from the forest, and I knew one shot would settle the business in hand.

I dropped the red embers upon the powder, and fell with my face to the earth.

There was a roar like the explosion of a dozen pieces of ordnance—a stifling smell of sulphur—then a heavy substance fell over me, and I was stupified by the blow.

Then all became a blank.

CHAPTER XXXIV

THE FUNERAL PYRE.

THE low hum of conversation came upon my ears when I awoke to consciousness, and passing my hand over my heated brow, I endeavoured to recal the events that had caused me to be plunged into darkness.

They came one by one, at first disconnected and vague, but soon the fierce fight in every detail was brought vividly to my mind.

The powder barrel, the terrible explosion, and the sudden blow that had seemed to press me into the very earth, all occurred again, and putting up my hand I found out the cause.

A portion of the roof had fallen over rather than upon me, and the log that lay on my back had no doubt formed part of one of the sides of the hut.

With the return of life came a numbing sensation all over my limbs; my face and hands, too, smarted, and were filled with shooting pains that resembled red-hot wires being passed through them.

I soon found out the cause of this, for skin was scorched and blistered by the exp sion, and I had no doubt such parts as w numbed were black and charred.

The pain across my back was accounted for by the weight of the log and the portion of the roof that lay above it.

There was a strange feeling, too, about the upper part of my left arm, and when I placed my hand upon it, I felt the sleeve of my hunting shirt was saturated with blood.

I must have been wounded.

A moment's recollection brought to my memory the recollection of a knife thrust I had received when backing into the doorway.

It took but a few minutes to make these discoveries. Then I strained my hearing to catch the tenour of the men's conversation who were near.

I soon succeeded in this; and by raising my head I was enabled to see a portion of the ruined hut.

Save for a few broken and scorched uprights, there was not a vestige of the building left, and the voices I heard came from the men who were seated on the fallen timbers.

They were speaking of me when I could distinguish their conversation, and it appeared that my assailants had all escaped death, although they were fearfully scorched by the powder.

"What has become of the varmint"—I knew the voice, it was Black Tom's—"is a puzzler. I suppose he is blown to little pieces; for there is nothing of him left hereabouts."

"Not even a tooth," said another, "for we have turned over every bit of wood big enough to hide a rat."

I was surprised at these words, for I knew the log, the portion of the roof, and my body must have caused the hut to stand up far above the fragments that lay on the ground.

"No, there isn't a bit of the old den," said Black Tom, "but what lies as flat on the ground as a newly-felled tree. I suppose the reptile has put off to the forest, if he's not blown to pieces."

A new light suddenly dawned upon me, as the fragments were all lying flat on the ground. I must be in the excavation caused by the powder turning out the earth near the barrel.

I groped about with my right hand, and soon found out this was the case, and very thankful I felt for the strange accident that had so well befriended me.

With some difficulty I dragged myself cautiously forward, until I could rest my chin upon the edge of the hollow.

In this position it was much easier to see and hear all that was taking place amongst the gang.

"I am sorry," remarked Swivel-eye, "that the varmint escaped us by being blown to pieces."

"We couldn't have done more," said Murtough; "anyhow, we couldn't have done the job quicker."

"Quicker," said Swivel-eye, "that's just it; we wanted to do it slow, flay the cuss alive, a little bit at the time."

I knew the fate in store for me now, and devoutly hoped I should not be discovered. The prospect of being skinned was infinitely worse than dying by the knife or bullet.

"I suppose if the captain dies," said Black Tom, "we shall have to draw for a new leader, and as we've nothing better to do we might as well do it now."

This proposition was strongly dissented from by the others, and Black Tom, with a coarse laugh, said—

"What's the use of being squeamish about it? He's sure to turn up his toes."

"I don't believe it," said Dick. I've seen him worse than this many a time; for, barring the dig in the arm, he's only scorched."

"Scorched!" repeated Murtough. "Why, from his skinned hands and feet, the devil such a sight I never saw before."

"So are the others for that matter," said Dick," and were it not for the cave I don't krow what the poor devils would do, for there's no shelter from the sun anywhere else."

"That cave," said Swivel-eye, "has been very useful to us. Thanks to that we got away from the Yankees the last time they hunted us up."

"We shall want it again," said one of the men, who had been upon the marauding expedition, "for one of the settlers got away, and —curse him!—he took the road to the Yankee fort."

"Was he on foot?" Swivel-eye asked.

"No, worse luck!" replied the man. "He was across as good a bit of horseflesh as was ever crossed."

"If that's the case," said Swivel-eye, "the sooner we make a bonfire of these logs and find our way to the cave the better."

I shivered from head to foot, for should the ruffians carry out this suggestion I must be roasted alive.

"The sooner we begin the better," said Black Tom, rising; "for if the fellow reaches the Yankee station, we shall have the blue coats down upon us before we can look twice."

"Tom is right," said the squinting lieutenant. "So to work, lads, and burn the logs. It will be better than letting the Yankees carry them away for firewood."

Within a yard of where I lay the gang began to pile up the charred remnants of the hut, and after a few minutes' work, the base of the heap overspread the pieces of shingle I was under.

One of the men caught hold of the corner of this, and but for Swivel-eye, it would have been torn away, and my fate sealed.

HIS COMPANIONS' KEPT WATCH WHILE HE SHARPENED THE KNIFE.

"Let that alone, long 'un," said the lieutenant. "It will burn with the rest."

My blood seemed to freeze, and a dry, choking sensation came to my throat at the approach of the horrible fate to which I was doomed.

It was nearly an hour's work to collect the scattered fragments of the hut. When all was ready, Swivel-eyed Dick asked one of his companions for a pine knot.

I could hear the flame of the torch hissing and seething as it caught the resinous wood.

"Now," said the lieutenant, "for the funeral pile and good-bye to the old crib where we have spent many a jolly day."

He must have applied the flame to the dried wood as he spoke, for immediately afterwards I heard the crackling of the destructive element as it began to leap upward.

"What a pity," said Black Tom, "we have not got a barrel of powder to throw on the top !"

"Here's something that will do as well," said Murtough.

"What is it ?"

"A barrel of oil. Here, lend a hand to break the lid."

I heard the blows and splintering of the

wood, and the hissing of the inflammable liquid as it was poured upon the fire.

My agony became intense, and to prevent a cry escaping from my lips I was compelled to bite at the earth.

"If I must die," so ran my thoughts, "I will suffer without their knowledge," for it would have added to their triumph to have dragged me from my hiding place, and thrust my bruised, scorched, and wounded body into the very midst of the blazing pile.

A funeral pyre, not only for the log-hut, but my hapless self.

CHAPTER XXXV.

THE BLUE COATS.

THE flames soon caught the oil, and the fire burned fiercely, so fiercely that I could feel the heat, although the light had been applied at the side opposite to where I lay.

The voices of the men had ceased, they had withdrawn from the hut, and I was left to perish.

Death was never more earnestly prayed for by the martyr at the stake than I prayed for it to come and release me from the horrible agony of mind I suffered.

Furious roared the flames, hotter became the air, so hot that I seemed to be inhaling imperceptible fire.

"Oh, God!" I cried out. "Am I to die thus? Be merciful—only one drop of water to cool my blistered tongue, and I shall die content."

Oh the agonising mental and bodily torture of that moment! never shall I forget it. I screamed for help, and the hissing flames seemed to leap the higher as though with glee at the puny efforts I made to free myself from their burning torture.

The whole pile was by this time ablaze. Jets of flame were leaping out from the base, and licking the dried portion of the roof under which I lay.

Soon that also caught fire, and like serpents the streaks of fire played over my neck, scorching my hunting-shirt, and blistering up my charred and blackened skin.

I bit my lips with suppressed agony, and tried to meet my doom as I could have met it in the battle-field, or at the place of torture had I been taken prisoner.

The excitement of the fight was wanting to make me reckless of death, and the wish to appear undaunted by a captive's fate was also wanting, and, in its place, I was filled with the thought that I was like a rat being burned in his hole.

Pain and terror rendered me desperate, and forgetful of the wounds, burns, and bruises I had already received, and imbued with a giant's strength, I wrenched my body from under the log at the moment the mass of flame was roaring above me.

Springing to my feet, I bolted through the sheet of fire, and rushed out to the clear, balmy air.

I was like a man overpowered by strong drink. My legs refused their office, and I swayed to and fro. My brain swam, and I fell forward to the earth, and lay panting and helpless.

The furious flames were now at their height, and the wind suddenly veering round, drove the sheets of fire over my body.

I tried to rise, but the scorching element drove me down again. I turned an agonising look towards the pile, and saw the lower part would soon be in a blaze, and unless I moved out of its reach I should be reduced to a heap of ashes.

"How could I escape the destroyer?" I asked myself. "How could I remove my ill-starred body from the sea of roaring destruction?"

Another minute and I should have been too late; but ere even that brief space of time could pass, I collected sufficient of my scattered senses to recollect that, by rolling over, I should be safe.

I was soon out of danger; and such was the impetus I had given my body, that before I knew well what had happened, I found myself rolling down a steep declivity, not perhaps more than eight feet high, but sufficient to land me in the valley.

The cool grass was refreshing to my blistered skin; the long blades overlapped my body, and formed a shelter from the sun's rays.

To me it was one of the most delicious moments of my life.

"My joy was but short-lived; for scarcely had the tops of the long grass closed over me, when I heard a rush of feet, and the voice of Swivel-eye call out—

"This way, mates. I'll swear I saw the varmint roll down this bit of a hill."

The search began, and every moment I could feel the circle they had formed narrowing around me.

Closer and closer, until one of the ruffians trod upon the back of my hands.

The torture was fearful; but I repressed the cry that rose to my lips, and the fellow, turning away, I thought myself safe.

There was a pause, then Swivel-eye, in answer to a companion, said—

"I'll swear it. There's no mistake, and so you'll find. Here, lend me your knife."

"What for?"

"I'll fasten it to the end of this stick, and we can prod the grass, and you'll soon hear the fellow howl."

"Don't believe it was him—might be his ghost."

"Ghost be ——. There don't you see the grass move?"

In my terror I had involuntarily withdrawn the hand so lately trodden upon, and the ruffians, like a pack of wolves, rushed towards me.

Already the grass was being torn aside, and I expected to see the knife before my eyes, when the gentleman with the swivel eye said—

"Let the cuss lie still. The grass is dry. Let's set fire to it at four points, and if he attempts to move out we'll knife him."

A brutal laugh followed these words, and I could hear the footsteps of those who were hurrying to the fire to fetch the torches.

They were not long gone; then I could distinguish the crackling of the grass, and the thick smoke blew across my face.

"Guess," said one, "which he'll take—the fire or the knife?"

"Knife, I say."

"Fire, I say."

"Some of both," said Swivel-eye; "but I think the best plan will be, before the fire closes in, for one of us to ease him of the bag of gold-dust."

I did not move a muscle, or utter the slightest cry while these fearful words were being spoken. My mind was by this time so overwrought by the great excitement I had undergone, that death, a swift death, would have been welcome.

"The stuff won't melt," said Black Tom, "so let him alone—the miserable wretch. I hate to hear a fellow yelping for mercy. He's safe to do that, if we disturb him."

"He can howl until he is blue," began the swivel-eyed ruffian, "then he will not—— By Heaven, here's the blue coats!"

The sudden pause, followed by those startling words, produced an effect upon my nerves perfectly indescribable.

I forgot the fire that was rapidly closing around me, forgot my wounds and bruises, and in the excitement of the moment, I jumped to my feet and feebly cried out—

"Hurrah for the blue coats!—hurrah!"

I caught sight of the yellow facings of the American horse as they galloped out of an opening in the forest in pursuit of the cowardly ruffians.

I heard the sharp reports of the long-barrelled cavalry rifles, and shouted my feeble cry to cheer them on to the good work; then, gathering all my strength, I ran forward, hoping to come within sight of my preservers.

The sound of horses' hoofs, the shots, and angry cries of the combatants went further from me; then came a fitful discharge of firearms I recognised as the sound of the ruffians' pieces.

They were making a stand against the horsemen. My frame shuddered as the firing grew furious, for the thought came to my mind that it was quite possible for the ruffian band to ensconce themselves behind the trees, and hold the mounted men in check, and in the end drive them off.

This feat was by no means impossible. I had seen a dozen Comanches on foot, and sheltered by the trunks of large trees, hold two hundred of the Crow horsemen in check until the night set in, when the Comanches made good their retreat.

These thoughts had scarcely passed through my mind when the firing ceased on both sides.

I stumbled forward, my heart beating with the hope that the blue coats had won the victory.

CHAPTER XXXVI.
A DOOMED RACE.

I was some time reaching the timber, for my legs were but of little use to the bruised body they supported.

I had followed the hoof prints of the horses until the trail became dispersed, in consequence of the blue coats being separated into three bodies.

I hesitated a few minutes which to follow before I took the track directly before me, and soon the pathway became so narrow between the trees that only a single horse could have passed.

Here I beheld the first sign of the fray. A bullet had cut away a strip of bark from the trunk of a tree.

Farther on, the bushes were trampled down, as though a fierce struggle had taken place, and there was a gleaming knife lying on the ground. The steel had snapped close to the haft.

I saw dark spots upon the blade, but did not stay to examine whether the weapon had belonged to the American troopers or one of the gang.

The forest became more entangled every moment, and but for the pathway made by horses I should not have been able to have dragged my tired limbs through the bushes and rank grass.

Suddenly the trees grew wider apart, and an open space was visible not twenty yards ahead.

I hastened forward, for at that part I became aware these trails joined, and it needed no sorcery to tell that the struggle took place in the glen.

I reached it at last, and, looking round, my eyes encountered a fearful spectacle, for nearly every tree that surrounded the glen bore fruit that Nature never intended they should bear.

The fruit was the limp bodies of the gang of robbers. The troopers' justice had been quickly meted out—not a man had escaped.

The horrible expression of their faces caused my blood to curdle, and, glad to escape from such a place of horrors, I followed the track of the horses, hoping to come upon the bivouac.

The soldiers must have had other work of a similar kind on hand, for they had not stayed anywhere, except at a little stream, the water of which was yet muddy from the horses' hoofs stirring up its bed.

The troopers had followed the right bank of the stream, and I walked on until my strength was entirely exhausted, then I dropped at the base of a majestic tree.

"This, then, must be the end," I thought, as I buried my face in my hands. "Far better to have died by the raging flames, or the villains' knives, than to drag on another day's wretchedness."

I suffered the horrible pangs of thirst, the gnawing sensation of hunger, and the acute smarting of my charred skin.

I was weak, too, in addition to this—so weak that I could not even make the attempt to catch one of the many animals that passed me.

The forest abounded with game, and, starving as I was, the sight of them was an additional pang to my misery.

In my haste to overtake the soldiers I had not paused to drink at the stream, and, with swollen tongue, how bitterly I regretted this oversight.

The water was above two miles from where I lay, and I knew I had not sufficient strength to crawl back to it.

Exhausted and overwrought nature at length succumbed, and my head falling forward I swooned.

I was awakened just as the sun was gilding the tree tops—awakened by the pressure of a heavy hand upon my breast, and, opening my eyes, I saw a group of Indians standing near me, one of whom was trying to ascertain whether my heart still beat.

They were strangers to me. I had never before seen the tribe to which they belonged, and the absence of fire-arms and horses told they were some of the many small bands who roamed about the forest and prairies.

An old man came forward with a calabash of water, and applied it to my lips, and one of the young women, whose entire costume consisted of a strip of grass-cloth around her loins, busied herself in bruising some large leaves of the cæther tree.

They spoke the language of the Sioux Indians, and from the old man I learnt that the two same men and women I saw before me were all that remained of the once powerful Ethotauni Indians.

Continual warfare and the ravages of disease, brought on by drinking the vile spirits the fur-traders had supplied the tribe with, had brought them down to their present condition, and as I looked at them I could not help drawing a contrast between their meagre and half-clad forms with those of the proud Comanches, who never drank the accursed fire-water.

"You are a chief of a mighty tribe," said the old man, touching my totem reverently. "Do not tell your people we have not done the best we can to aid a distressed warrior. We are under the anger of the Great Spirit, and when we have done his will we shall be taken to the far-off land of our people who have gone before us."

The sad tone and the words sank into my heart, for I was grieved to behold the shattered fragments of a once powerful nation.

"Father," I replied, "a good action can only be done at the prompting of a good heart; but tell me, father, how it is the Ethotaunis have so dwindled away from a nation of warriors and sages?"

"It is the will of the Spirit, my son. Listen: you must know our nation worshipped two spirits, a good one and a bad one; and the bad one poured poison in the ears of our young men and our squaws."

"That was in the time when our braves were many, and our lodges numerous—the time when the white men came first to our villages, and gave the fire-water to the braves, and took the young girls to work in their fields; but that is long ago, many moons more than I can count. So it went on, until a few months since; then a strange and terrible spirit—an evil demon—came upon our path, and shot and scalped all who lingered away from our people."

My thoughts were upon the spectre warrior, as I asked—

"You have young men. Could they not go upon the trail of the wicked spirit?"

"They did, my son, but always returned less in number. It is the Great Spirit's will that we should be punished."

"Does my father say his young men have never seen the evil spirit?"

"They have seen it—the figure of a warrior, armed with a silent rifle."

"Ah!" there was no doubt now about the identity of the spectral warrior being seen upon the trail of the doomed race. "Has my father any knowledge of the offence his people gave the demon?"

"He has," was the low-voiced answer, "too much knowledge, my son, listen. Listen."

The aged Indian told me a story I was

quite prepared to hear. It was his people who assisted at the massacre of the horse stealers.

That fearful tragedy that had brought upon the earth that fearful mystery, the Spectre Warrior.

CHAPTER XXXVII.
A VOICE FROM THE RAPIDS.

DURING the old Indian's recital the younger portion of the band were busy collecting dried leaves for my couch.

The old man had commanded them to do so by a simple gesture, for he saw I was too weak to leave the place I had sunk upon.

The heap was a large one, much larger than I should require, and as I watched its growing bulk, I wondered what could be the cause of the young men searching so diligently among the trees and long moss, and then, bending down the young branches, and allowing them to fly upwards again.

Several trees were visited and subjected to a similar process, until, at last, they came to a gigantic species of fern, the fronds of which grew on stems at least twelve feet in length.

The Indians cut down three or four dozen of these, and, stripping them of their leaves, came to the heap of dried vegetation.

With their knives they made a row of holes along one side of the leaves, and inserted one end of the pliant stems in the ground, treading the earth firmly around each stick, until they were able to bear the pressure received by bending the points over to the other side.

I saw their purpose now. The sticks formed an archway over the leaves, and to make the roof rain-proof young shoots of the surrounding trees were cut down, and with their foliage interleaved with the hoops.

The ends were secured in the same way, excepting a small space in one, just sufficient to admit the passage of my body.

To enter this forest hut I should have to crawl inside, for there was scarce room enough to admit a man's shoulders.

I was grateful for this kindness, and as the evening chill began to descend, I signified my wish to accept the shelter.

"There will be an opening of the clouds to-night," said the old man; "see the dark, angry masses are moving across the heavens."

I looked, and beheld every indication of a storm, and, not being selfish enough to accept the only shelter the place afforded, without knowing where my companions intended to pass the night, I said—

"Where does my father, his young men, and the women intend to seek shelter from the rain?"

"There is room for us all," he said, pointing to the leafy hut. "Does my son refuse to sleep with his Indian friends?"

"I do not," I said, although if I had spoken the truth, I would rather have had a shelter to myself. "Our skins are of different colour, but our hearts are the same."

"It is so," said the Indian; "would it were always so, and the red man could live with his white brother! Would that the wind, sighing amongst the forest trees, could tell a more peaceful story than it does even now, as I hear it moan and sob like a departing spirit."

I gazed at the aged Indian, whose attitude was that of one listening with rapt attention to a distant sound, and the expression of his face was like a man suddenly inspired by feelings which were beyond his control.

"Listen," he said, in a low voice, "hear you the branches of the maple and elm, and the silvery sycamore, as they bend to the passing of the unseen spirit."

"I hear the wind," I said, strangely excited by the old Indian's manner, "as it passes through the rustling leaves."

"What does it say, my son? Listen; do you not hear the moans of the unquiet spirits of the red man and their white brothers who have fallen by rifle and tomahawk? Does it not speak of the strife and bloodshed that take place every day in these forests between those who would rob and those who would keep the land of their fathers?"

The old man ceased speaking, and as I looked towards the dark recesses of the forest, I could not wonder that my companion's brain should be confused by such a vision.

The young Indians had by this time kindled a fire, and soon a couple of birds, killed with an arrow, were drawn and plucked, ready to be roasted in the ashes.

While waiting for the meal to be cooked, I told the old man my late adventures, and to the rather long recital he listened with the greatest interest.

"You will return and seek for your companion?" he said.

"Such is my intention."

"It is not far," said the old man. "If you pass the rapids, there is a tree covers the bend of the water-course, and by going that way you will save the journey across the plain."

I was glad to hear this, for the distance I had been taken by the buffalo was the worst part of the journey now that I had no chance of getting a horse.

"How long does my father think it will take me to return to the forest?"

"Two days, when my son's limbs are strong."

"That will be many days, father; I must not wait for that."

"My son will be home by the second sunrise from this. Behold!"

I saw the women were busy reducing some leaves to a pulp, and when our repast was over I entered the hut, and the old man, assisting me to strip, covered my burns and scars with the juicy cataplasm.

He also made me drink a little decoction made from the fibres of a plant; then, covering me carefully with the dried leaves, bade me sleep.

The poultice soothed my wounds, and by the time the rain drops began to patter down, and the Indians entered the hut and coiled themselves up amongst the leaves, my eyes began to close, and, despite every effort to keep them open, I soon fell into a deep sleep.

When I awoke next morning my limbs were stiffened as though the cataplasm had become hardened into a casing of cast-iron.

The old Indian was by my side, and when I attempted to move he checked the intention by saying—

"My son must have patience; to move a limb now will undo all that has been done by the help of the Great Spirit and the medicine plant."

I understood soon afterwards that the charred skin had by this time adhered to the coating of dried pulp, and if I were to move I should tear it away, and leave the raw wound exposed, but by remaining quiet the virtue of the plant would not only detach the skin, but heal the flesh beneath.

It was with no pleasant feelings I looked forward to passing an entire day and night in my casing, for I was covered from the crown of my head to the soles of my feet, except small apertures over my mouth, eyes, and nostrils.

Necessity knows no law, so I submitted, and, under the cool shade of the leafy bower, passed the long day away in listening to the strange legends of my Indian friend.

The next morning I arose nearly well, and peeling off my armour looked round for my shrivelled doeskin hunting suit. They lay near me, and, to my surprise, beside them was a soft jacket, beautifully embroidered with quills, a pair of leggings, and mocassins of the same material, and a cap made from the beaver's fur.

These articles had been fashioned from my shrivelled garments, and when I expressed surprise at the presence of the beautiful outfit, the old Indian said—

"The fingers of my young men and girls are nimble; they saw their pale brother's clothes were not fit to touch his tender skin."

I was very grateful for their kindness, and when I parted from the peaceful little community, I electrified the old Indian by filling his palm with gold dust.

"Take it," I said. "It will purchase rifles for your young men, horses and bridles, cotton clothes for your maidens; and, with the Good Spirit's will, your nation may yet become powerful."

There were genuine tears of gratitude in the Indian's eyes, and one of the young maidens would have accompanied me on my lonely journey as my slave.

"You are weak yet," she said. "I am strong. My arm can fell wood to light your fires, and cook the food I bring down with the arrow. Let me be your slave, it is but a return for the wealth you have given to an outcast nation.

I declined the girl's generous offer, and in such a manner that the refusal gave no offence. Then, with the blessings of the simple people, I turned towards the cattle track in the forest, and, armed only with my log-knife, plunged amid the lairs of wild beasts, and, for all I knew, no less wild men

I had heard from my old Indian friend that, in the midst of the great forest, the margin of which I had to pass, a tribe of cannibals were located, an outcast nation even from their fellow red men, and so primitive in their customs that even the use of fire-arms was unknown amongst them.

Thinking over this story, I was startled by hearing a footfall in my rear, and, turning suddenly, I was surprised to see one of the young men of the people I had so recently left.

"The chief," said the Indian, "has sent me upon my white brother's track to give him this, and to ask the name of one who will be remembered in the prayers of a grateful people."

He handed me a bow and case of arrows, a gift that was very welcome, for the arrows in skilful hands were as useful in forest purposes as the rifle.

"My brother," I said, "has the thanks of the white man. Tell your chief he is known as the Silver Bullet."

"The Silver Bullet! I shall not forget. farewell. May the good Manitou guide you safely to the rushing waters."

He was gone before I could make any reply.

A distant hum, not unlike the noise made by a swarm of wild bees, suddenly struck upon my ear.

I paused and listened; then, lying flat upon the ground, discovered the humming noise was the distant roar of the cataract.

I pushed forward mile after mile, until the tribes were passed, and I reached a plateau overlooking a large expanse of rolling prairie, and, beyond this, I could see the water flashing like a belt of silver in the sunlight.

As I stood gazing upon the tranquil scene, two dark objects suddenly appeared upon the

"IF YOU VALUE YOUR SKINS," I CRIED, "STAND ASIDE AND LET ME PASS.

prairie, and as they came nearer I saw they were a couple of horses.

Wild mustangs, was my first thought; but when they came nearer I saw the glitter of polished stirrup-irons, and could define other shining objects that told my practised eye the horses were not only saddled, but their riders' arms were still strapped to the saddles.

Yes, it must be so. They are steeds belonging to a couple of the American dragoons, or, possibly, Mexican guerillas, for the sun gleamed upon the long rifle-barrels, strapped to the saddle-bows, and hanging from the cruppers was either a pistol or hatchet.

Nearer came the objects of interest, and my heart beat joyfully when I saw they were fastened together by the bridles, and two long, snake-like cords that twirled after them were evidently broken lassos, that had been used to picket the steeds.

The sun was in my eyes, so I had some difficulty in making out these matters of detail, and when I had done so my heart beat joyfully.

They were coming towards me—another fifty yards, and they would be within reach of an arrow from my bow.

I had determined to slay one of the horses. The other would be an easy prize, for being fastened together, he could not get away without breaking the bridle, and that I knew was almost an impossibility.

I had fitted an arrow to my bow, and panting with eagerness, watched the slow approach of the equipped steeds.

Two minutes more and they would be within range. The arrow head was drawn to my eye; but, ere my nervous fingers relaxed their grasp, a couple of dogs bounded out from beneath the plateau, and their loud yelps startled the horses, who at once turned and started off at full gallop towards the cataract.

I cursed the brutes with all the vigour of a disappointed man, and discharged the arrow; but my aim was not sure, and the yelping brutes that had robbed me of a rich and useful prize were soon out of sight.

There was nothing left me but to follow the tracks of the horses; so I descended from the plateau, and began to cross the prairie.

It was night before I reached the wooded flanks of the rapids, and, tired and dissatisfied, I threw myself at the foot of a tree, and when the darkness came on, ascended the tall elms, for the sounds that came from the distant forest told me the wild denizens were astir.

Suddenly I started from a state of dreamy wakefulness, for there came upon my ears the unmistakeable sounds of a human voice

CHAPTER XXXVIII.

I DISCOVER THE OWNER OF THE VOICE.

DESCENDING from the tree, I reached the shelving bank of the torrent, and placing my hands each side of my mouth, so as to form a speaking-trumpet, I hallooed—

"Hallo, there—hallo!"

The precipitous crags returned the echo a thousandfold; then a voice, apparently from the centre of the stream, replied—

"Hallo! Who the divil are ye?"

It was Tim Delany's voice, and no sweeter sound ever came upon my ears than his rich Hibernian brogue.

"Ahoy! Tim, ahoy! it's Silvershot who calls."

"Ahog! where the divil are ye, avick?"

"This side; here!"

I heard the dip-dip of a pair of paddles, and soon a large canoe ran aground near my feet.

Tim gave a genial Irish hug, and exclaimed—

"Me ould comrade! Well, I niver expected to see him again this side of purgatory."

"Don't stifle me, Tim, old fellow!"

"Bedad! 1 won't; but after finding ye, I "——

"What's that, Tim?"

"The war canoe. By the mortial! It's gone like a shot!"

It was true; the long-boat, caught by the rapid waters, was whirled away, and soon dashed over the hissing cataract.

"It's no matter," said Tim; "for now I've found ye, avick, we'll go after the horses."

"The horses?"

"The same. They are picketed beyant in the timber, and the dogs are with them."

A suspicion flashed to my mind, and I wondered I had not thought of it before.

The horses and dogs I had seen were well known to me; but the sun blazing in my eyes prevented the recognition.

"And where have ye been, avick?" said Tim. "Shure, I thought ye were carried away beyond the big river by the divil of a storm."

"Not quite so far, Tim; "but come under this tree and we will talk. What's that shout?"

"That," Tim said, "is the voice of a settler. He was with me in the canoe; but when the bastes began to roar, and the water to get near the rapids, he wanted to go ashore, so I let him. But come, avick, it's where ye have been I want to know."

We climbed up the tree, and perched in the fork. I told him all that had befallen me since the storm.

"Mother of Moses!" laughed the thoughtless fellow. "Fancy a ride on a buffalo, then a smoking from the fire ye lit yerself. Well, anyhow, I'm glad it's no worse; and if ever I meet these Indians who were so kind to ye, comrade, I'll make it up to them. Shure, it's a pity ye didn't bring the girl with ye. Was she pretty, avick?"

"Very. Your adventures now, Tim."

"Faith, there isn't much to tell compared to the mighty doings you have been up to.

"There must be something extraordinary, or I should not have seen you in the canoe."

"You shall hear, avick. After the storm passed away—ye know I was just out of its reach—I came to look for ye; of course there was no sign, so starts on the trail but missed it, and found meself near this part, and was nearly toppled over by some red divils near here, and then "——

I waited for a short time, and the conclusion of Tim's sentence was a snore.

"Tim, wake up, and finish your story."

"Eh! all right, avick. When I came here I lassooed the horses I had brought with me, and left me in charge of—ugh "——

"Asleep again—keep your eyes open."

"Bedad, I was never more awake in all my life."

"When you left the horses, you "——

"Yes, avick, I met a settler, a chicken-hearted varmint—and—yer—"

Another snore, but I aroused Master Tim, and bit by bit I managed to learn all that had befallen him since we parted, and, as I am vain enough to think the readers will prefer my way of telling the story to Tim's disjointed fragments, I will do so.

It appears from the account the settler gave Tim of the reason of his being found in such an out-of-the-way place was a desire to explore the forest.

He left the caravan—they were on their way to Santa Fe—and, thinking to overtake them on the road, shouldered a rifle and started.

He had not gone far through the forest, when the yell of a hunting party of Indians caused him to make tracks.

The man was new to forest life, so he at once fancied the red men would be upon his trail, and raise his hair.

Filled with this idea, he came to the banks of the rapids, and coming under a bush muttered—

"As surely as the bloodhound can follow the trail, so can these savages; but the water beats them."

He waded across, therefore, and descended a ravine, seated himself on the grass, and reflected on his position.

A noise in the shrubby thicket, almost before he was seated, caused him to startle with fear.

He sprang to his feet, seized his musket, and prepared for flight, when a huge bear stood right in his path.

The settler trembled as though stricken by an ague, for although the first impulse of a man of ordinary courage would have been to aim a bullet in the animal's brain, to the cowardly settler such an act was impossible.

He held on to the musket, or he would have fallen to the ground.

The bear gave utterance to an angry growl, raised himself on his hind quarters, and advanced upon the chicken-hearted foe.

The settler's destruction appeared to be inevitable. Bruin's hot breath already fanned the settler's cheek; and as he saw the long, white fangs of the bear he gave a scream of intense agony.

Fortunately, that cry was heard. A young Indian had sprang through the thicket, and, with his short hunting knife, attacked the animal.

But the craven-hearted wretch, thinking only of his own cowardly body, ran from the spot, leaving the young Indian alone to contest with the savage foe.

The Indian's skill and courage, however, championed his cause; and, used as he was to forest warfare, he plunged his weapon, time after time, in Bruin's body.

The brute fell stricken to the heart.

The conqueror, only waiting to wipe his knife, with a whoop of rejoice, ran swiftly after the settler.

The task, to a "child of the forest," one may suppose was one of comparative ease. Swift as the antelope he bounded off, and speedily overtook the settler, to whom he made signs that he was a friend, and would take him to the village.

The settler had no alternative but to obey; but it was not without a quaking heart that he accompanied his dusky guide.

Having passed through the ravine, they struck a path into the thick of the forest, when the Indian gave a piercing cry of anger.

Unsheathing his knife, he darted from his companion.

The cause of this sudden act was a mystery to the settler, but as his eye followed the flying Indian, he beheld a scene that caused his cheeks to whiten, and his body to quiver in every limb.

Within a short distance of where he stood, he beheld about a dozen savages, yelling and brandishing their weapons of war, a white man standing in the midst of this dusky circle.

The hunter, for so he seemed by his dress, which was composed of skins, was wielding a tomahawk, with which he was trying to keep the savages at bay.

The swift turns made by the savages as

they endeavoured to outflank their sturdy oppon nt gave the settler but little opportunity of judging the cause of the affray.

Sudd nly the sturdy hunter's eye fell upon the stranger's shaking form, and he cried out as he plied his formidable weapon.

"Hi, stranger! don't stand there, only look-ng on. Give a shot from your gun to help poor devil!'

The settler mechanically raised the piece to his shoulder; but before he could pull the trigger a blow from behind had levelled him to the ground.

treacherous stroke from some heavy in-strument felled this unfortunate hunter at the same moment.

The Indians gave a yell, and, brandishing their weapons, prepared to dispatch the fallen hunter.

Owing to the want of courage on the part of the stranger, the hunter was quickly in the grasp of a stalwart Indian, who at once drew his scalping-knife, and began to handle his victim's hair.

But, though the hunter had been thus savagely treated, he had not quite lost his senses; and so, when he felt the Indian's fingers at work, he formed a rather clear opinion that unless he made a struggle he should fare but badly.

The savage had taken Tim's hunting-cap off, when with a wondrous struggle he hurled his foe from him, and shouted out—

"Aisy, ye black divils! It is no baby ye have this time."

With each word he struck at the dusky group, who, taken by surprise, bore away from his muscular arm.

"Clear out, bad cess to ye!" he continued, "and leave this jintleman's sweet head alone."

This warning not being heeded by the savage in time to escape, the hunter, with his toma-hawk, clove the luckless Indian's head in twain.

Tim's eyes blazed angrily as he picked up the musket that had fallen from the settler's hands, and, raising it to his shoulder, he blew the skull of the nearest savage into frag-ments.

The report of the weapon, the smoke, and eet of fire, coupled with the death of their mpanion, struck terror into their breasts, d, with a wild yell, they fled from the place. The use of the musket and its deadly wers was unknown to the dwellers in that mote forest, and they ran as though expect-ing the strange weapon to roar again, and kill with equal lightning swiftness.

Tim watched them until every nude form had disappeared. Then he stooped over the stranger.

"It's a blessing anyhow this dacent lad come here wid that shooting iron, or Tim Delany would be eaten up by those devils long ere this. Wake up, my man, if ye are not kilt."

Tim addressed the last words to the stranger, whose head, on raising it from the ground, he found was severely injured.

Laying him on the grass, he went in quest of water.

"It's an ugly knock that, anyhow," said Tim Delany; "but it's better than being kilt outright."

He filled his fur cap up from a little stream that ran past the place where his encounter with the Indians had taken place, and threw it plentifully over the stranger, until he opened his eyes.

"Oh! murder, where am I?"

"Not murdered," was the reply; "but where you are, the divel fetch me if I know."

The settler looked strangely at the speaker, but a few minutes' reflection recalled his con-fused senses, and brought the scenes of the last few hours to his mind.

"You're alive," he said, as he rose to his feet, "I had not time to pull the trigger be-fore I was knocked down."

"Niver mention it," said the good-natured Hibernian, "we are safe from these divils now; the smoke of that old gun sent them quiet."

Tim Delany seated himself upon the long grass, and tenderly rubbed the bruise caused by the Indian's club, remarking "it was nothing, and that many a bigger one he had given him for looking cross-eyed."

The settler assented that such might be the case, "but still," said he, "that does not make it pleasanter for me to bear."

"The divil a bit; never mind it, anyhow. You're lucky as yet, for if these imps of the ould divil get over their fright and come back again, you may lose the top of yer head in a twinkling."

The bare possibility of the Indians return-ing startled the settler, and forgetting the knock he had received, said—

"Do you think they will come back?"

"They might or they might not," was the hunter's reply. "It all depends. The divil only knows."

"Depends upon what?"

"That's neither here nor there. Suppose we make tracks, then if they come they won't find us;" a suggestion quickly acted upon by the pair taking a directly opposite path to that taken by the savages.

"And now, my friend," said Tim, as they walked along, "maybe I may ax you how you came up at that minnit when the savages were belabouring my body?"

"An unforseen mishap caused it," was the reply.

" Then," said Tim, " I am indade mighty grateful for that mishap."

" I came here," continued the stranger, " to have a day's hunting, but lost my way in the forest. When I again reached the camp, the caravan had left."

" Lift ! the spalpeens ! And you here ?"

" It was my fault ; I was cautioned not to stray far from the caravan."

CHAPTER XXXIX.

TIM DESTROYS THE ENEMY'S FLEET.

" THAT alters the thing intirely ; though they might have sent for you."

" Most likely they did, but I was too far away for the men to find me."

" Glad I am for meself they didn't," said Tim ; " but sorry for ye, for this is a divil of a place to be in, anyhow."

" It is. But is there no way of getting from this place ?"

" Yes. Saving one thing, it's aisy enough to get away."

" And what's that ?"

" Well, seeing that we can't walk, anyhow on the water, it would be a trifle handy for us to have a boat ; and, bedad, a boat we'll have, when it gets dark. So let's sate ourselves on that illigant place where the flowers grow on."

Tim took a small pipe from a pocket in his skin-jacket, and said—

" We must find a canoe, if possible."

The settler's doubts respecting the finding of a canoe were very strong, and he hinted as much to Tim.

" Bedad, then," was the reply. " It is a canoe ye mean I shan't find ?"

" I cannot make out where you hope to—"

" Whist, avick. It's meself that knows where the ginteel blackguards keeps their canoes. Maybe they will be short of one before the morning. Whist ! What's that ?"

The settler and Tim both stopped—the former through fear, the latter to discover the noise.

" Be the powers," said Tim, sighting one of the red skins, " there he is, right forninst me. Hould your head down and look between the bushes."

Doing as he directed the emigrant, to his horror, saw there was an Indian squatting under a bush, and his teeth began to rattle with fear at the sight.

" Put that ould gun of yours this way," said Tim, " and be quiet, the man will not hurt you."

" Ugh ! the horrid looking brute," said the settler ; " he looks as though he would scalp anyone who came near him."

" Maybe he would any green hands," Tim said. " It's but little you would think of

these gintry if you had a season or two with Silvershot and Tim Delany."

" I don't want a——"

The Indian, who had been aroused from his sleep by the voices of Tim and the settler, suddenly sprang to his feet, and, seeing Tim handling the heavy rifle, he gave a yell and bolted.

" He's off," said Tim, " so the sooner we get up the stream and find a canoe the better."

" Is it far off ?"

" Just through the clump of trees there's an open bit of land leading down to the water, it's there the canoes are."

" Suppose the Indians should be in the forest, they will mur——"

" Never mind the Indians, man alive, but come on," said Tim, " it's here the canoes are."

The settler followed, and upon getting into the open space there were a large number of canoes, capable of holding forty or fifty people.

" Them is illigant boats," said Tim. " Come on, avick—though before we depart from this nice place let us leave our mark."

Coming to the canoes he deliberately smashed the bottom out of several with his axe.

" And now," said he, " we'll save this one from being spoilt, we'll take it for ourselves. Bear a hand."

In a minute or two the adventurers were paddling down the Indian lake.

The settler inquired where it led to.

Tim curtly answered, " The Falls."

" Did ye hear that ?" inquired Tim Delany.

The settler did hear it, and his trembling fingers could scarcely retain their hold of the paddle. It was a noise as though a crowd of demons were revelling in diabolical merriment.

Tim plied the paddle with renewed vigour, as fast, at least, as his companion's courage would permit. Tim remarking, " it was a good thing he had made his mark on the canoes, otherwise they had been after themselves like wildfire."

When the Indians discovered the havoc that had been made with their boats, and that every one sank as it was run into the water, their screms of rage were far beyond description.

After a little conversation together, nearly a hundred of them had plunged into the water, in pursuit of the fugitives.

Tim left off paddling, and taking up the settler's gun, said—

" Come on, ye divils ; I will give you a token before you leave us."

Tim marked the foremost swimmer.

When within fifty yards of the canoe he fired.

The report resounded in a thousand echoes from the woods, increased by the shrieks and yells of the terrified Indians.

Tim had aimed well, and made his foes two less.

The singular fate that had befallen the two who were stricken by the mystic weapon of Tim's awed the pursuers, and as though by one consent they made for the bank, and dashed into the woods.

Tim watched them, and, shaking his head gravely, remarked—

"By the mortial man! thim divils will be at the Falls before us."

Tim seized the paddle as they emerged from the tranquil lake into the rapids, each side of the bank was lined with the Indians.

A shower of arrows whizzed over the heads of Tim Delany and the settler. Thanks to the uncertain light, they did no injury; and, in a few minutes, the two were out of range, and, before morning, they arrived within two hundred yards of the place where Tim had left the horses.

It was while Tim Delany was searching for a landing-place that my voice was heard calling upon Tim, and the rocks echoing the sound a thousandfold, gave the nervous settler such a shock that he jumped out of the canoe, and ran to the woods.

CHAPTER XL.

THE SETTLERS' HUT.

Two hours after my meeting with Tim we had killed a deer, breakfasted, and caught our horses.

But for the dogs, we should never have succeeded in this, for the animals were as skittish as colts, and seemed bent upon enjoying their freedom.

Ben and Jip luckily caught the lassoes in their teeth, and though dragged along the ground for some distance, the horses at last allowed us to approach.

Once more mounted and well armed, we soon forgot our dangers, and were as light-hearted as on the morning we started from the Comanche camp.

We travelled very fast all day, the sun our guide, and when night set in, the rain that had threatened all day began to fall in torrents.

"Be the mortial," said Tim, "we are in for a wetting, Silvershot!"

"We are, and there is no shelter to be obtained hereabouts."

"What's that, avick?"

"What?"

"Look right ahead, and ye will see a light."

I did so, and I knew there must be a dwelling near, and I must confess I was not greatly delighted, for the remembrance of the last hut was not yet ignored from my mind.

"Shure, this will be all right!" said Tim, when I mentioned the circumstance. "Who knows but this may be one of the hotels, as they call 'em hereabouts?"

"I hope it is, for I am tired and hungry. Push on, and we'll soon see."

We did push on, through a vile swamp, our horses sinking up to their saddle-girths in the mire.

The hut was reached at last, and, to my demand for admission, the door was opened, and a cheery voice said—

"Get off your critters' backs, whoever you are, for this is a pelter. Here, Bob, and you, Jack, go, take the strangers' cattle round to the sheds."

Two strapping young fellows took the bridles of our horses, and we entered the comfortable-looking dwelling.

There were six men present, one an old fellow, tough-looking, and as well able to fell a tree as any of the five stalwart sons who were near him.

I noticed some of the young men were dressed in half Mexican fashion. This I attributed to the proximity of the guerilla bands, which swept the frontier at times, and had their ranks thinned by the band of settlers who were anything but friendly to the thieving Mexicans.

"Find a seat," said the old man, "and make yerselves at home. Hi! you Jake, bring out the sperrits; and you, Tom, put a b'ar steak on the ashes."

The glass of hot spirits and water was very welcome, and when the bear steak came on the table, we did ample justice to our host's entertainment."

"It ain't often," the old man said, "we see anybody much about hyar, except the thieving Mexicans. Perhaps you have come the way they come."

I told him I had not come that way, and I heard Master Tim mutter—

"It's a pity we are going that way, anyhow."

I found the young fellows very interested listeners to the story of my adventures after the storm, and the old man laughed very heartily at Tim's description of the cowardly settler.

"That 'ull wear off," the old man said, "after he has been out a little bit in the country. It's mighty strange how the green hands are skeered at the sight of a red man, but I never war much."

"You were skeered onc't," said one

THE COMANCHE STOOD BEFORE THE INDIAN MAIDEN AND TOOK DELIBERATE AIM.

boys, drily. "I mean the painter as cowed you up, father."

The settler pretended not to hear this, and with that open-hartedness peculiar to the old pioneers, began to talk about his early days in the forest, and I soon found by his conversation that he was a Tennesseean by birth, who had removed to the wilds of Arkansas to get clear of being crowded to death by neighbours, three other enterprising settlers having purchased lands and built their cabins within a league of him. His nearest neighbour was now many miles distant, with a thick, swampy wood between them, so that he was once more able to breathe with some degree of freedom.

In person he was tall, lank, and bony, with strongly marked features, black eyes and hair; and, as he had never been troubled with schooling when young, he was not over particular in the choice of words now, and brought them forth with a broad, hearty ring, that would have made the teeth of a perfumed city exquisite chatter.

I liked the man for his simple, unassuming, frank, and truthful nature, and soon got him interested in telling me some of his bushwood adventures.

The Indian had departed toward the setting sun before his day; but he had been a successful hunter in a country inhabited by all kinds of wild beasts, and had, in his time, been in perils from wolves, bears, and panthers—a simple narrative of which had made my blood leap, and my nerves thrill more than once.

The last adventure which he related before retiring to rest, I will endeavour to give as nearly as possible in his own words.

"Some people," pursued old Jack Sureshot, after finishing a thrilling narrative about a b'ar that he f'ot, "has a spite agin one thing and other, some agin another thing; but ef I've got a right down spite agin anything, it ar a painter. Yes, sir-ee."

"I suppose the panther at one time and another has given you a good deal of trouble, Mr. Sureshot, which may be set down as the cause of your enmity?"

"Wal, mate, he's a sneak ar a painter, and don't do things open, but slouches about and waits his chance to git the 'vantage of you, and I hate sneaks powerful.

"Now, mate, a b'ar when he does fight, stands up like a man, and pitches in; but a caterwauling painter tries to catch you off your guard, and pounce down upon you from a height that knocks daylight out of you the fust go; and if he can't do that, or cotch you a napping, he generally bolts and leaves you with a whole charge in your gun.

"Sometimes, though, you may get him riled up enough to make a pitched battle with you, and then he ain't the easiest critter to manage you ever seen. I got one into that thar fix one time, and he git me so'thing back agin that I've got yit."

"I shall be an eager listener to your story, Mr. Sureshot."

"Shall you, mate! Wal, let's take a drink."

We took a drink.

"Let me see," resumed the old hunter, running his hand through his hair. "It war in the fall of the year when my eldest, here, war a five-year old, and my youngest war a slim chance of a toddling, that I started out on a deer-hunt to lay in a small heap of venison agin winter.

"Deer in them days and in old Tennessee war a critter as could be counted on by any man as knowed how to stalk 'em, and shoot plum-centre, and sich a man war me.

"But the best will have their unlucky days, and the day I started were one o' mine.

"I got off about noon, and 'spected to be in afore night, with at least three deer hung up in the trees, waiting for me and the old hoss to come and fetch 'em home; but somehow, though I knowed they must be all round me I didn't git a sight of nothing but one old buck, and he led me a awful chase, I trying to get to leeward of him, and draw a bead on his side.

"Wal, mate, the first thing I knowed it was beginning to git duskish, and I heard a few wolves howl; and one sweating old varmint of a painter gived a scream that made my blood start and hair rise.

"I looked around me, and couldn't tell whar I war at all, nor which way my shanty lay from thar, ef I'd been killed for't; so, all thoughts of gitting home to Sophy and the young ones war drew from my head to onct, and thar war nothing left for me but to raise a fire and squat down to it, taking keer not to drop asleep and lit the painter git his clutches on to me.

"It war right dull business sitting thar by that fire all night without being allowed to drop off into dreams. Every once in a while my eyes would git so heavy that it really seemed to me that I couldn't keep 'em open nohow; and then, afore I knowed it, my head would begin to nod, and I'd begin to fancy I war along with Sophy here, and feeling monstrous comfortable; when all of a sudden so'thing would seem to say—

"Jack Sureshot—danger, Jack Sureshot! And I'd start, wide awake, only to see two eyes of fire looking right at me from the darkness; and then I'd raise my rifle keerful, and try to git a shot between them balls of fire, which would suddenly leave with a rustling in the bushes that told me plain enough the old bothering painter were dodging out of my sight. Then I'd git up and stretch myself, and poke the fire into a bright blaze, and put on more wood, and walk around it a few times, and squat down again to go the same sleep round right ovar.

"Ah, mate, it war a awful long night, I tell you, and I wouldn't go through it myself agin for a small figure, to say nothing of the consarn it gin the old woman (God bless her for a true old gal!) bekase her Jack warn't under the same roof wid her.

"But everything in this world has come to a end, and so did that night; though, as I said afore, it war the longest night that ever I seen.

"With the first streak of day I war up and a stirring, feeling powerful cantankerous, for not having no supper, sleep, an' breakfast to boot; and then I just thought to myself, ef I could only seen them thar painter's eyes agin, and git one good shot at the varmint, I'd be satisfied to put up with all my inconvenience, and call it squair.

"But nary shot could I git—not I; for the old she-devil war as cunning as a fox, and took keer to keep herself at a respectable distance, though so'thing told me she war about still, and wouldn't lose a chance to make her breakfast off o' me.

"When it got light enough, so as I could see purty cl'ar, I knowed whar I war—at least twelve good miles from home—and I war so mad to think I'd have sich a tramp for nothing and hadn't been allowed to sleep, that I swore I'd never go back till I'd killed so'thing, and I'd try desperate to make that so'thing the old buck that had drawed me on to sich a chase.

"So I set to work to find his trail, and arter about an hour I stumbled on to't, and followed on for another hour, when I come on to the old scamp, feeding quite under a holler.

"Thar war some trees to hide me, and as good luck would have it the wind was right to keep off the scent.

"I crept down awfully cautious to be sure, almost holding my breath, till I got within good bullet distance, and then I took good aim, and keeled him over so purty that he never knowed what hurt him. Down I went, broke him up, kindled a fire, and eat a breakfast that would have made any backwoodsman stare.

"Arter I'd eat my fill I felt better, though powerful tired and sleepy, and being determined the old she-painter shouldn't have a taste for her meanness in trying to come it over me, I put all in the critter's hide that I could decently take, burnt up all the rest, and set off for home.

"The first five miles of the tramp I did purty well, but after that the old buck's carcase got heavier and heavier, till at last I felt as if I'd have to take a rest or give in, and hang the critter up agin a new journey.

"Coming at last to a nice clear spring in a part of the wood where the trees growed monstrous, I throwed down my load, took a good drink, and then sat down to consider the matter. I still had an idea that the sneaking old painter war somewhar about, though I hadn't seen her nor heerd of her since morning, and I thought to myself what a pity it would be ef I should hap to fall asleep thar and git cotched at last.

"Wal, mate, I sot down, as I'm telling you, amongst the falling leaves, with my back agin a tree. I don't know how long I sot thar, for I don't remember nothing arter. I got myself easy till I heard a queer kind of rustling about my ears, and looking up quick, I found it war quite duskish overhead, and I began to think it war night again. I'd just sense enough though, not too be much in a hurry about moving, and I soon felt my hair stand up with horror as I began to understand the whole thing.

"I found a lot of leaves agin my face, and heard a rustling and stepping about, and this, what had gone afore, giv me a suspicion of the truth, and peeping up through the leaves I saw the spotted varmint kivering me over

keerful, and a smelling around me to see no part war left out to the air.

"To have stirred then would have been certain death; and I was even afeard my breathing would fotch his awful claws and fangs into me, so I kept powerful quiet, I tell you.

"I don't suppose, mate, that that varmint was at work over me a great while; but it seemed a lifetime then, I can tell you. She got through at last though, and though it was a cold day you mought have wrung out my clothes, so wet were they with the sweat of horror. I can laugh now to think of it; but I never felt less like laughing nor I done when that critter war agoing out.

"Wall, when the old she-varmint had got me kivered up to her taste, she stopped it. Through a little hole in the leaves I could see her for some distance, stopping every now and then to look back and see if I were still as she fixed me. At last she reached the edge of a thicket, and shot in like lighning.

"I knowed enough of such varmints to be sartin she'd gone for help. Eyther to kill or eat me; but for fear she mought be on the watch, I give her about a minute more, and then crawled out trembling.

"'Thar,' said I, when I once more got my rifle, and saw it was all right, 'you played your hand out, you old she-devil, and now I'll see if I can't win the game.'

"So I got hold of a good sized rotten log that war near by, put it whar I'd been myself, and kivered it over so beautiful that I almost thought I war thar still. Then I took myself up into a big tree about ten yards off, whar I could see the whole doings, got my rifle across a limb in good rest for a dead shot, and felt dreadful happy while I waited to see how the whole thing 'ud come out.

"I hadn't long to wait—not more than a quarter of an hour—afore I'd seen the old she-painter, stealing along dreadful soft, followed by two sleek-looking, spotted cubs.

"Safely the old dam stole up to within a few feet of whar she'd buried me, and then squatting her down flat on her belly she trembled all over and made one dreadful bound, lighting right plump on the old log, and burying her sharp claws and fangs right into it.

"Warn't she astonished, sure, when she found it warn't what she took it for, and that it war the poorest kind of eating as ever she'd seen. She looked that way, anyhow, for about two seconds, and then crack went my rifle, and over she dropped.

"'All right,' said I, as I slid down the tree, 'I just thought as how it would come to this, old beast, ef you didn't quit a fooling your time around an old hunter like me.'

"I'd been reckoning without my host, though, for when I'd got right near the old she-varmint, she showed me as how she were a long ways from dead by springing up right sudden, and bounding upon me afore I'd time to calculate my chances.

"I clubbed my rifle like lightning, and hit her a blow that might have laid an ox; but she only shook her head in a sort of half-stunned confusion, and made another spring.

"This time she struck me with her body and paw, knocking me down the hill, and tearing a large piece of flesh from my right thigh.

"In another second she was on me agin, and with a howl of rage, she buried her sharp fangs into my left shoulder.

"I yelled monstrous with the pain, and whipping out my knife, I struck—the Lord he only knows whar. I kind athought it hit so'ething, and then all got dark.

"When I come to my senses agin, I found my head resting quiet on that thar breast, and my knife sticking right in her heart. My chance blow had killed her just in time to save my life, and her cubs were looking awfully skeered.

"I was powerful weak; but I managed to crawl to the spring and git a drink, and arter that I felt better.

"I washed some of the blood off, found I'd got all my bones whole, and tied up the wounds as well as I best could.

"Then I loaded agin, got the cubs in range, shot them, and went to work and skinned the whole three; and then, bad as I war, I toted the three skins home, getting in about dark, acterly fainting in the doorway.

"I didn't do no more hunting for a month, I tell you.

"Yes; I hates the sneaking, caterwauling painters, you'd believe.

"Let's take another drink, mates."

CHAPTER XLI.
THE BATTLE OF THE PRAIRIE.

WHEN the old settler finished his narration, he took his own advice and another drink, without much delay.

We followed his example, complimenting him freely upon his courage and the coolness he had shown in his combat with the terrible "painter."

Tim especially was loud in his commendation. Brave himself, he admired that quality in others, and this true-hearted son of the Emerald Isle drained a full measure of *aqua ardente* to the health of old Jack Sure-shot.

"Bedad, avick! it's an Irish jintleman ye ought to be, an' it's proud I am to make yer acquaintance. Here's more power to yer elbow!"

And another horn of the fiery spirit followed its predecessor.

"Now, Tim," said I, "we had better take a snooze, for we must be up and stirring early to-morrow. The frontier is near, but San Juan Campastrana is many a long mile from us."

"Thrue, for—hic—you, avick!" replied Tim, "yer right, as usual, Silvershot, though it's mighty sorry I am, to part with the ould jintleman so airly, to say nothing of this illigant potheen."

While my comrade hesitated, I winked at the old settler. He understood me, and taking up a flaming torch, led the way into a small chamber, where a couple of shake-downs of deer-hides and 'possum skins had been prepared for us.

Wishing the stalwart sons a hearty good-night, Tim and I followed him; tired as we were, undressing did not take us very long, and the deep sonorous snores of Tim Delany soon showed that he was under the influence of the drowsy god.

I was not long in following his example, and we both slept heavily, till the loud, hearty voice of the old settler awoke us.

"Well, comrades, I reck'n you've had a tol'able spell o' sleep, hain't you? It's two hours arter sun-up, and, I guess, my lads a' got yer breakfist ready."

We started up, and, donning our simple apparel, joined our hosts, and were soon deeply engaged in discussing some savoury morsels of "b'ar" meat, washed down with plentiful draughts of diluted *aqua ardente*.

Our horses had been well cared for, and were standing, ready saddled, at the door of the hut. Taking a hearty, though reluctant, farewell of our rough and hospitable entertainers. Tim Delany and I rode off, the old settler shouted after us—

"Take care o' them h'yar painters, stranger. They're powerful sneaking cusses—they are *so*."

A last wave of the hand, a last farewell "hallo," and the friendly settlers disappeared from our view, as we rode down the forest glade.

"Now, Tim, old comrade," I said, serioasly, "we must lose no more time, but devote ourselves to the object of our journey."

"That's true, avick," replied Tim, submissively. "Shure, it's only too glad I shall be to get the job over."

"You see, Tim," I continued, "we are only on the frontier as yet, and many miles will have to be covered before we reach the central town of Mexico, San Juan Campastrana."

Tim Delany was silent for a moment; then he said, reflectively—

"They're mighty pretty gals, them same Mexicans—arn't they, avick?"

I could not help smiling at the irrepressible bent of my comrade's mind showing itself at such a moment.

"Yes," I replied, "the Mexican *ninas* are well known for their beauty; but we have something more important to talk about, old comrade."

"Thrue, avick; but every one to his taste. Faith, I'll be contint to lave the management to you, if you'll be satisfied with jist a trifle of fighting and love-making from meself."

I knew it was useless to argue with Tim upon such a point, so I dropped the conversation, and we turned our attention to our horses, which needed all we could give them, for the forest pathway was no longer clear and easy to traverse—stunted shrubs and interlacing creepers grew thickly on the ground, and made our progress anything but easy.

In a short time the forest became almost impassable. Our horses, slow as the pace was, stumbled at every step; and, by mutual consent of men and beasts, we halted.

"By the mortial!" said Tim Delany, "this is a mighty fine fix, avick! Look at them monkeys, the cratures! how illigant they're jumping on the branches o' them trees. It's meself would like to be afther changing places."

"I think the monkeys would have the worst bargain of the two," said I, banteringly.

"Arrah! be aisy now wi' that tongue o' yours, Silvershot. Be the powers, it was mighty raisonable what I said."

"What would become of the horses, Tim?"

"Shure, they might change places wid some o' thim illigant buzzards yonder."

"Enough of that," said I. "Talking won't get us out of our scrape, Tim."

"Thrue for you, avick. But——By the mortial! what' that?"

We both started simultaneously, as the quick, sharp detonations of rifles reached us. The sound came from our left, and with it we could distinctly hear the thud of hoofs upon the ground. We must, then, be near the prairie.

As if by mutual consent Tim and I jumped from our horses, and, leading them by the bridles, pushed through the thicket, and made towards the spot from whence the sound proceeded.

"What's up, avick?" whispered Tim.

"I don't know," I replied; "but I strongly suspect that it's a band of Mexican Rangers having a brush with the Indians. We're near the frontier."

"That's—— Ah! there they go again. Push on! By the mortial, they can't be far off."

As Tim spoke a second volley sent its rattling echoes faintly through the wood, accompanied by a triumphant war-whoop that could only have proceded from the lungs of Indians.

Eagerly we pushed onwards at an increas pace, for the undergrowth had become le dense, and in a few moments the thinness o the trees told us plainly that the verge of the forest was near.

Tim and I threw the reins over the branch of a tree, and cautiously moved forward.

A few paces brought us to the verge of a steep declivity, on whose very edge the forest trees still grew. Beyond lay the open prairie, and the cause of the firing was now plainly evident.

To the right was a band of Mexican guerillas, there was no mistaking them, their costume was sufficient. Their broad sombreros, the serapés and calzoneros were sufficient to convince us of their identity with the irregular troops of Mexico. They were armed, too, with lances, lazoes, and escopettes, a sort of carbine, while some wore sabres, or matchets, a weapon peculiar to the Mexicans.

To the left was a large body of Indian warriors, their dusky, naked bodies gleaming in the bright sunlight, their shining spearheads levelled, or waved wildly over their heads.

They were about to charge the Mexicans.

The two parties were about equal in force, but the superior arms of the Mexicans, if they had courage to use them, would have given them the victory; but it was evident to see, from their irresolution, that very little would suffice to rout them.

Several of their number lay lifeless on the llana, the horses galloping widly over the plain, terrified at the shouts and firing of the combatants. The Indians, too, had suffered; more than one dark form lay motionless upon the herbage—victims to the volleys from the Mexican escopettes.

It was a gallant sight to see the band of warriors, as, uttering their terrible war-cry, their bodies gleaming with black and scarlet war point, they swooped down upon the guerillas.

Tim and I watched in breathless suspense for the meeting of the hostile bands.

The Mexicans had seemingly changed their tactics, and, determined to face their foes drawn up in line, awaited the onset.

The Crows—for by their war-paint and accoutrements I had discovered the Indians to belong to that tribe—came thundering onwards, their spears glittering, their voices shouting the terror-striking war-cry.

When they had arrived within about two hundred yards of the guerillas, the warriors suddenly separated from each other, opening out like a fan upon the broad expanse of the prairie.

Before the guerillas could make a movement to prevent them, the swift mustangs had borne their riders in the rear of the Mexicans, who saw themselves thus surrounded by their most implacable foes.

Then, suddenly, it seemed to us that each Crow had disappeared from his horse's back; nothing, apparently, was to be seen but the snorting horses careering swiftly in a circle, in the centre of which were the guerillas, who had, as yet, not delivered a single shot from their escopettes.

Tim and I stared in wonder at this apparently magical transformation.

Nearer and yet more near the mustangs closed around the guerillas, seemingly as astonished as we were, at the sudden disappearance of their foes.

"By the mortial, Silvershot," said Tim, "the red devils have been carried off by ould Nick."

Scarcely had he uttered the words than a volley of arrows seemed to proceed from the horses into the midst of the band of guerillas.

Of course I well knew that it was an utter impossibility that the missiles could have proceeded from the swiftly flying steeds, and I strained my eyes in the underwood to penetrate the mystery.

Attentively regarding the horses as they sped round in that fatal circle, I saw that the Indians had not, as at first sight seemed probable, fled; they had simply adopted a *ruse* in Indian warfare, and thrown themselves behind the bodies of their horses, so as to leave no part exposed to the enemy, while they themselves were able to deliver an effective volley from under the neck of their steeds.

The Mexicans stood irresolute upon their horses; and while they did so, a second volley of arrows came from the Indians, which emptied half-a-dozen saddles.

This decided the guerillas upon a course of action. The remainder of the band levelled their escopettes, and delivered a volley at the horses. The riders were still invisible.

Not one of the shots took effect. The horses still thundered round in that swiftly fatal circle, and another flight of arrows was sent into the midst of the guerilla band.

Then fear moved them to desperation; and, with one accord, they dashed forward, spurring on their horses to break through the circle of their foes. No war cry was heard, it was with despair and fear that they made the trial.

They succeeded. So sudden had been the rush, that the Indians were taken by surprise, and the Mexicans had galloped full three hundred yards over the level llana before the Crows had resumed their seats on the backs of the mustangs, and started in hot pursuit, yelling the whoop of victory.

In a few moments both parties had disappeared from view behind a ridge that veiled them from our sight.

Tim Delany and I drew a long breath, and looked at each other; both had been excited by the view of the conflict. More than once I had clutched and half-levelled my rifle, and but little would have been required to induce me to dash forward and ride with one of the parties.

But two things restrained me,—both were our enemies, the Crows as being at war with the Comanche Indians, of which Tim and I considered ourselves, and the Mexicans as sworn foes of "Uncle Sam;" the second was, that an unlucky shot might put a fatal termination to our expedition.

I thanked Heaven when the momentary excitement was over, that I had not yielded to the impulse of the instant; but Tim was evidently not of the same opinion.

"By the mortial!" said he. "It's a pity, avick, that we didn't have a brush with those same varmints."

"Which?"

"Be the powers, both of 'em. I'd have peppered them blaggard Crows, and ye could have done the same gintaley for the yaller bellies."

I laughed at Tim's ideas of division of labour, and returned to where we had left the horses.

They were gone!

CHAPTER XLII.
THE GUERILLAS—THE FLIGHT.

TIM DELANY and I stood bewildered at the loss which had so suddenly fallen upon us. To lose a horse in the prairies of America is what it would be to a sailor to lose his sails in the middle of the ocean.

"Be the powers!" said Tim, aghast, "we're in a fix agin, Silvershot, me boy. What the divil's to be done?"

"The dogs are gone, too!" I exclaimed bewildered.

"And be all the saints in the calendar, here's blood upon the bushes!"

I looked, and, sure enough, there were the marks of a struggle. The ground was torn up, the bushes broken where the terrified horses had torn away from their fastenings, and the bushes and ground were stained and bedabbled with blood.

"Be Jabers!" said Tim Delany, suddenly, as he was looking at one of the trees, "'tis one o' them sneaking painters."

I looked, and plainly perceived the marks of deep scratches in the bark of the tree, such as could only have been made by the animal in question, for I knew well that the grizzly bear never climbs.

"We must follow the trail, old comrade; though I'm much afraid that our poor horses are useless to us by this time."

"You forgit the dogs, avick," replied Delany; "be the mortial, it would be a mighty powerful painter that could stand forninst those two illigant animals!"

Tim's words inspired me with fresh courage, and I inwardly hoped that the faithful animals had succeeded in driving off the attack of the ferocious panther.

The track made by our horses in their flight was plain enough for an unpractised man to have followed; to the eyes of Tim and I, experienced as we were in woodcraft, it was a very easy matter.

The horses had fled in nearly the same direction we had come.

Delaney and I started off at a run, for the undergrowth was now so trampled down that progress through it was no longer a matter of great difficulty.

Scarcely, however, had we gone a hundred yards than, bounding and barking, through the bush, came my two dogs, Ben and Jip, their eyes gleaming, their paws and mouths bedabbled with foam and blood.

It was a welcome sight, and we felt sure that the dogs had fought and conquered the animal which had attacked our horses.

They did not run up and fawn upon me as usual, but while they were yet several paces off, they stopped, and looked back the way they had come, barking at the same time.

I at once knew what the faithful animals meant. They wished us to follow them, and lead us to where the body of the panther was lying. To again secure the horses was a thing of which I no longer entertained any hopes. They were doubtless miles distant by this time, if the panther had not mortally injured them.

Therefore, I decided not to follow the dogs, which would have led us from the trail made by our fugitive steeds, to follow which presented our only chance of regaining them.

But Ben and Jip opposed this step violently when I would have carried it into execution, running backwards and forwards, and barking violently in the meantime, even seizing my jacket between their teeth, and attempting to pull me in the direction they wished me to go.

"Shure, it's no use, avick!" said Tim Delaney. "Let's follow the cratures; maybe they've something illigant to show us."

I consented, but more out of a wish to please Tim than hope that the dogs would lead us to anything better or more useful than the dead body of a panther, which had already done us such incalculable mischief.

What was my surprise and delight, therefore, may be judged, when Ben and Jip, trotting delightedly before us, led the way to a small open glade, where, peacefully browsing on the herbage, were our two horses, the dead body of an enormous panther a short distance from them, bleeding profusely from the wounds my two courageous dogs had inflicted on it.

Tim went fairly into ectasies of delight. He hugged the dogs, bestowing praises and blessings on them with the most remarkable volubility. Then he alternately congratulated and reproved the horses—first, for their remarkable escape; secondly, for running away; and, lastly, turning towards the dead body of the panther, he cursed and kicked it by turns, until, the violence of his wrath appeased, he left off, and turned to me.

I was examining the horses, to see what injuries they had received in the encounter. To my astonishment they had escaped comparatively unhurt, with the exception of a rather deep scratch on the fore-quarter, which my Bucephalus had received.

The panther's skin was useless, for it had been so torn and mangled by the sharp teeth of the dogs. So, leaving the body to the wolves, Tim Delany and I mounted, to proceed on our journey.

But here was another difficulty. I no longer knew which way to go. We had lost the path in first leaving it to witness the combat on the llana, and since had so frequently changed our position that it would be difficult, almost impossible, to hit upon it again.

I communicated my doubts to Tim Delany.

"Aisy, avick," was his reply. "Don't be afther troubling yourself; shure, it's as plain as the nose on the face of that ugly divil, Bill Buckskin."

"That's plain enough, goodness knows, Tim; but what's your plan, old comrade?"

"Shure, can't we ride out into the perairy yonder, and follow the trail of them yeller-bellied Mexicans?"

I was struck by my companion's idea. It was dangerous, but practicable, and likely to succeed. While I was thinking it over, Tim again said—

"Be the mortial, Silvershot, don't be afther standin' there as thoughtful as a monkey wid a rotten nut in his fisht; but come away, avick. Shure, it'll be sundown in the twinkling of a shillelagh!"

"That's all very well, Tim; but ten to one we shall fall in with the Crows, who are almost certain to have overtaken the Mexicans, and scalped the lot."

"Be the mortial!" replied Tim, "shure, ye're not going to show the white feather for a parcel of rascally Crowt? Faix! if I didn't know ye better, it's turning coward I'd be thinkin' ye are."

Seeing that Tim was bent upon having his own way, I rode out of the glade towards the prairie, guided by the tracks we made in coming.

It did not take us long to reach the spot from whence we had witnessed the fight; but here the declivity which led down into the prairie was far too steep for a horse to descend, and we were forced to ride more than a mile along its edge before safe footing could be got.

Our horses seemed as pleased as ourselves at once more putting their hoofs upon level ground, and we had hard work to restrain them from breaking into a gallop, as Tim and I cast about for tracks.

Tim was first successful. A shout from him brought me to his side. The trail was as broad, clear, and easy to follow as a foot-path.

At almost full gallop we sped over the level prairie, our ears and eyes strained to catch sight or sound which might warn us of the presence of the Crows.

Every now and then we came across the dead body of one of the guerilla band, whose horse had not proved so swift as those of his companions—a fatal fault on the prairie, where a man's life almost daily depends upon the soundness in wind and limb of the animal he bestrides.

Once we passed the prostrate form of a Crow Indian who had fallen by a chance shot, delivered by one of the guerillas in their flight. It had been dearly paid for, as, a hundred yards further on, four Mexicans lay lifeless on the prairie, their gaudy trappings glittering in the sun, where the dark red stain of the life-blood had not dulled their brightness.

Still we sped onwards at unabated speed, until we began to think that the Crows must have desisted from the pursuit of their enemies, and returned some other way, or encamped near a spring which lay near a spring which lay out of the course we were following.

After crawling on slowly through the forest, the free, fresh motion of our flying steeds over the llana was most exhilarating; we revelled in the warm sunshine, and drank in the pure cool breath of the prairie air.

Tim Delany felt the influences of the place as much as I did, and broke out with an old Irish song he had learnt, while a child, in his native country. It was a soft, plaintive melody, and as Tim, like almost all Irishmen, had a good ear for music, and a rich, full voice, the song was very impressive in that vast solitude, where, as far as the eye could see in every direction, all was sublime in its repose and beauty; the grassy herbage of the prairie, like a green, limitless sea, the blue arched vault overhead, where a few birds dotted the azure, as they circled in airy flight.

Soon the character of the llana changed; it was still smooth, but rose and fell in vast undulations, like the monster billows of the sea, so that at one time we were in a deep valley, then ascending a declivity—the descent and ascent, however, were so gradual that it made no difference in the speed of our horses, it only caused an interruption of our look-out ahead while we were in the valleys, as I may call them.

We were ascending an elevation a little higher than any we had yet come to, at the full speed of our horses, for the trail was still as distinct as ever, when from the other side we heard the unmistakeable sound of human voices.

There was not time to halt, for almost at the same moment we arrived at the top of the eminence, and beheld the cause of the sound.

It was the Crow war party, returning from the pursuit of the Mexicans. Many of them were gathered on the edge of a broad expanse of water that intersected the forest, and by their antics we could see that they were threatening some one in the distance. Following the direction in which they were discharging their arrows, we suddenly saw a raft drift out from under the shadow of the overhanging trees. There were but two persons in it, a Comanche and an Indian. The girl crouched down behind her protector with her hands clasped over her tearful face, for the savage yelling of their enemies seemed to have struck terror to her heart.

The Comanche stood before the Indian maiden to shield her from harm, and taking up a gun that lay on the raft, he took deliberate aim at one of the Crows, who was crouching down for the base purpose of sending an arrow through the trembling form of the Indian maiden, but before he had time to let go the string of his bow her companion fired and the Crow fell back dead. Tim was so delighted at this that he gave vent to a shout of encouragement; but it was unfortunate for us, as it attracted the attention of our foes, who instantly made a rush at us.

There was no time for hesitation.

The Indians were barely fifty yards from us, and I wondered instinctively why we had not seen them before.

The Crows seemed as astonished as we were, and halted; but before they recovered themselves, I shouted to Tim to dash through them.

It was our only chance, for by retreating we should have lost ourselves upon the prairie; while, going forward, we might reach some Mexican town, where the Crows would not dare to follow us.

"On, Tim!" I cried. "Give them an ounce of lead, and then ride for your life!"

"Hurroo!" yelled Tim; "hurroo for ould Oireland!"

And levelling his rifle, he fired simultaneously with myself.

Two of the Indians rolled from their saddles; and before their companions could return the fire, our horses had carried us through their midst, and were a hundred yards ahead, galloping at full speed, Ben and Jip, my two dogs, being alongside, giving vent to their full, deep barks.

A loud, ferocious yell of anger, and the thunder of hoofs upon the ground, told that the Indians were in pursuit of us.

It was a ride for life.

We had one advantage, and a great one.

Our horses were comparatively fresh, while those of the Crows were fatigued by the fight and pursuit of the guerillas.

On we sped, gaining at every stride of the gallant animals we rode, when suddenly I perceived a dark line stretching across the prairie directly in front of us.

It was not until we were within a hundred yards of it that I perceived its nature, and a thrill of fear came over me.

The dark line was a *barranca*, or natural rift in the llana, one of those deep gullies which are sometimes a hundred feet broad, and as many more in depth.

A cold perspiration broke out on my forehead. What if this one should be too wide for our horses to leap?

I wondered why the savages had not yet fired upon us. This, then, was the cause; sure of being stopped here, they did not care to waste powder and shot.

Nearer and nearer we approached the *barranca*, until at last I could see its width. It was comparatively a narrow one, not more than twenty feet wide; but its depth was tremendous.

But this was a dangerous leap even for a fresh horse, whereas ours had already had a long gallop.

"Hurroo!" shouted Tim; "faix, we're bating them copper devils illigant—ain't we, Silvershot, me bhoy?"

For all answer I pointed to the *barranca* in front. Tim's countenance fell immediately.

"By the mortial, avick!" said Tim, in a tone anything but expressive of delight, "that's a moighty powerful jump, anyhow. Shure, can't we git round it?"

"Impossible" I replied. "It stretches on both sides for miles, and before we could reach either end, the Crows would cut us off. No, Tim, we must jump it."

"All right, me bhoy—here goes. Shut yer two blissed eyes, and run the spurs in."

As Tim spoke we reached the edge of the ravine. Its width looked tremendous, now we were close upon it. The depth of its rocky, precipitous sides were terrible. I shut my eyes, and, clasping the saddle firmly between my knees, drove the spurs in up to the rowels, as my gallant horse rose to the leap.

CHAPTER XLIII.
ON THE TRAIL OF THE PANTHER.

THERE was a single moment of awful suspense, as my horse seemed suspended in mid-air over the terrible chasm beneath; then a jerk, his hoofs struck the turf on the other side, and I knew that I was safe.

I looked around for Tim Delany. He had taken the leap at the same moment as myself, and with equal success. I could not help giving vent to a joyous "Hurrah," as, checking my horse, I looked back at my pursuers.

The Crows were evidently anything but gratified at our totally unexpected escape. They had never thought we should have attempted to leap the barranca, and now were gathered on the edge, looking the very pictures of baffled malice.

There was no further danger to be apprehended from them, for their horses were too tired to have leapt a gully half the width of this one, and we had ridden a sufficient distance from the edge to place ourselves out of the range of their arrows—rifles, they had not one in the party.

"Bedad, Silvershot," said Tim, "don't they look mighty iligant there, shure, the spiteful copper-coloured divils? Faith, avick, it's a bad bargain they had of us, anyhow!"

"Yes, Tim. No doubt they feel very disappointed, especially as it seems to me that the guerillas escaped in the same way. Look, here are the tracks of their horses' feet; but there is no Indian track."

"Shure, avick, how do you that?"

"Look for yourself," I replied, dismounting, and motioning to Tim to do the same. "Here are the hoof marks of the Mexican horses all shod. The Indian mustangs could not have left a track like this."

"Thrue for you, Silvershot; faith, it's mighty 'cute ye are. Look out, avick! Down!"

As Tim spoke, or rather shouted, these last words, he threw himself to the ground, and dragged me with him.

It was a fortunate movement; for, as I yielded to the jerk he gave me, a shower of arrows whistled over our heads.

In our examination of the Mexican trail we had incautiously approached within range of the Crows, who had instantly taken advantage of it to deliver a volley.

Before they could repeat it, Tim and I started to our feet, and ran back, at full speed, to our horses, which were standing quietly where we had left them—the well-trained animals had not moved, although several of the missiles had passed dangerously near them.

"Faith, avick," said Tim, as soon as he recovered breath, "that was a mighty narrow squeak, we'd better jist give them a parting caste of our illigant rifles, and lave them to their own swate society."

My comrade loaded his rifle as he spoke, and I was not long in following his example, for the narrow escape we had just had, angered me not a little.

"Are you ready, avick?" asked Tim.

"Yes," was my reply, as I brought my rifle to the "present."

"There, thin, jist blaze away at that ugly varvint on the piebald horse, an' I'll knock over that long scoundril with the tuft of feathers in his top-knot. Fire!"

The report of our weapons was followed by a shrill cry of rage from the Crows; both shots had told effectually, and the Indians we had marked lay motionless on the prairie.

The remainder stood irresolute, divided between fear and rage, and while they checked their horses, rendered restive by the report of our rifles, Tim and I loaded again, ready to give them another taste of the deadly quality of our rifles.

It was fortunate we did so, for suddenly four of the Crows, mounted on rather more powerful horses than the others, separated from the body of their companions, and galloped towards the barranca, with the evident intention of leaping it.

"Look out, old comrade," I shouted to Tim; "aim true, and cut one out as he jumps."

"Nivir fear," was Tim's cool reply; "I'll let the blissed daylight into his ugly karkedge."

One of the Crows, mounted on a powerful black mustang, was a little in advance of the rest. Just as he was about to take the leap, and I to fire, his horse stumbled, and, with a horrible death scream, horse and rider disappeared down the yawning abyss.

The other three jumped simultaneously, and before their horses' hoofs had touched the ground on our side of the barranca, the sharp, clear detonations of our rifles rang out, one of the Crows, tossing his arms wildly in the air, fell from his horse; the second, shot through the heart, fell forward upon his horse's neck, and the affrighted animal,

landing safely, dashed past us with his horrible burden, leaving a track of blood behind him.

The third Indian, now alone, made the leap in safety; and, with the courage of despair, dashed towards us at full speed, yelling his war-cry and whirling his tomahawk above his head.

There was no time for us to relaad, neither was there any occasion for it. We had not much to fear from a single Indian, armed only with a tomahawk.

"Lave him to me, Silvershot, avick," shouted Tim, dashing forward to meet the Indian, with his clubbed rifle clutched in both hands. "I'll tache him, bedad, to molest an Irish gintilman."

"Stop, Tim," I shouted; "use your pistol." For I knew well the skill of the Crows with the weapon of their nation; but Delany, brave to rashness, spurred upon his foe with a triumphant "hurroo!"

When about ten yards from my comrade, the Indian whirled his tomahawk round his head and sent it, with deadly accuracy, full against poor Tim's head.

I thought it was all up with my old comrade; and, urging my horse forward, I prepared to avenge him.

But fortune had again favoured the rash fellow. As he swung his clubbed rifle round his head, it caught the flying missile of the Indian, and sent it whirling yards away. A moment afterwards and the heavy butt of Tim's gun descended full upon the bare head of the Crow, crushing it like an egg-shell.

"Hurroo!" shouted Tim, victoriously. "Bedad, I think that settled the blaggard nigger, anyhow. Shure, avick, there's nothing like shillelagh practice afther all."

I looked at the Crow. He lay, motionless, on the ground, quite dead.

Tim's blow, delivered with the full force of his powerful arm, had killed him instantaneously.

We looked towards the Crows on the other side of the ravine, which so fortunately presented such a formidable barrier between us and our foes. They were holding a consultation; and, from their manner and gestures, it was plain to perceive that the fate of their companions had cowed them.

"The sneakin' varmints," ejaculated Tim, in a tone of disgust. "Bedad, I'm moighty sorra. Rub out a few more, if they don't take their ugly carkages out o' me sight."

My comrade viciously rammed another bullet into the barrel of his rifle, and took aim at the dusky group.

No sooner, however, did the Crows see the deadly tube levelled at them than they spurred their horses to get beyond range. Tim's bullet, however, was too quick for them. The sharp crack of the gun was followed by a yell of pain, and another Crow fell a victim to Delany's certain aim.

Before he could reload the Indians had disappeared over the edge, leaving us masters of the field of battle, victors without a single scratch received by us.

"We are well out of that, Tim," said I, as we remounted our horses, and proceeded to resume our journey.

"Faith, ye may say that, Silvershot. It's in a fix we should have been if it hadn't been for that illigant banker."

"*Barranca*, Tim," said I.

"Well, baranker, thin, bad luck to ye," replied Delany. "Shure, it's all the same, avick."

"Now, old comrade," I continued, "we must push forward, or we shall have to camp on the prairie again."

"Bedad, it's meself that wouldn't mind doin' that same now. Be the mortial, it's moighty hungry I am, and just a trifle tired, Silvershot, to say nothing of our bastes."

I demurred to this at first, but, not knowing how far we were away from any village, I consented to stop at the first likely place where we could obtain water, and see our way to getting a mouthful of venison.

Still following the track of the Mexicans, we rode on for about three miles further, tlll I sighted, about half a mile to the left, a clump of trees, and what I fancied to be the silvery glitter of water.

We now began to feel the effects of hunger and thirst, and I was not sorry to rein up and propose to my companion that we should make that our halting place for a few hours to recruit the strength of our horses and ourselves.

"What do you say, Tim?" said I. "Shall we ride over yonder, and see if there is anything in the way of food or water to be got?"

"What do I say?" repeated Tim. "Be the mortial, avick, this is me answer!" And turning his horse's head towards the timber, he galloped off as fast as the animal would carry him.

Merely pausing to note the track, which was the only guide we had to our destination, I spurred on after and soon overtook Tim.

"My old comrade," I said, as I came up to him, "you're riding as hard as if the Crows were after you."

"Faster, avick, faster!" replied Tim; "shure the timtation's greater. Be the mortial! I'd go quicker towards a good bellyful, than I'd run away from a pack of thim copperskinned blagguards."

I thought to have reached timber in ten minutes at the outside, so close had the trees

seemed at first; but the clear, bright air of the prairie is very deceptive, and we rode at full speed for more than half-an-hour before our panting, nearly-exhausted steeds were reined up.

We had been greatly mistaken, too, in our estimates of the extent of the ground covered by the trees. What we had at first taken for a clump of thirty or trees, turned out to be a large wood, fully half-a-mile in diameter, and what had appeared to be only a small spring, increased, as we neared it, to a sparkling, limped stream, quite three yards wide, running northward across the level prairie.

So deceptive are these appearances, that a practised hunter will often mistake a buzzard for a buffalo, and a single deer for a body of mounted Indians.

In a very short space of time we had tethered our horses, and, while I collected the materials for a fire, Tim took his rifle and disappeared among the trees, in search of some savoury morsel wherewith to appease our now ravenous appetites.

I soon had a goodly pile of dry branches and withered grass, and other combustibles heaped on the ground, and, striking a light with my flint and steel, the whole was soon in a bright blaze, and I only awaited the return of Tim with something to cook.

A few momeats afterwards I heard his voice, apparently at some distance, shouting for me.

Catching up my rifle, I hurried in the direction from whence the voice proceeded, and soon came upon Tim, who was seated on the ground, his gun leaning against the trunk of a tree some distance from him, playing with a beautiful young panther cub.

The little animal was about the size of a cat, and presented one of the prettiest sights imaginable as it frisked about my comrade, now clawing and biting his mocassins and leggings, now dancing away from him, with its back arched, just as a kitten might do.

Tim was in high glee; no child ever showed a more genuine sense of amusement, and I could have watched them for hours, had it not been for the terrible danger the Irishman risked.

"Shure, Silvershot, avick!" said Delany, "is'nt it an illigant little craytur now? Faix, it is a little darlint!" he added, as the cub scratched the skin off the back of his hand.

"Get up, you idiot!" I said, angry at Tim's thoughtlessness. "The mother will be back presently, after the cub, and she won't play with you, I promise."

Scarcely had I uttered the words than a terrific roar came from the trees behind Tim, and an enormous panther leapt with a fearful bound right over my comrade's head, and instantly faced him, crouching on her stomach, her eyes gleaming in the shade like huge fire-balls, her long tail lashing her sides till they sounded like a muffled drum, the hoarse, low snarls coming from between her long, white gleaming fangs.

I had involuntarily jumped back several paces upon the appearance of the terrible monster, and now stood a little behind Tim, sharing the glances of the angry beast, who was evidently undecided upon whom she should bestow her first attention.

Delany still sat motionless on the ground, staring in terrified astonishment at the panther. He was a brave man—most Irishmen are that I've met—but the suddenness of the brute's appearance, and the consciousness that he was unarmed, unnerved him.

The cub greeted the appearance of its mother with a mew of welcome, but did not attempt to quit its playmate. It still remained playfully scratching and biting Tim's clothes, now and then uttering a low, soft purr of enjoyment.

I did not know how to act. The least motion on my part would, I feared, draw upon one of us the attack of the panther, and that was a consummation not devoutly to be wished. Its terrible teeth and claws would soon make short work of an enemy.

But it was impossible to remain long inactive, the suspense was beginning to tell upon me, and I determined to risk all for a shot before my aim became unsteady.

I cocked my rifle steadily, and raised it slowly, inch by inch, until I had it firmly at my shoulder, the muzzle pointing straight for the panther's right eye; so slowly did I seem to do this that I thought it fully a quarter of an hour before I glanced down the sight at the ferocious brute, who, now glaring and growling more angrily than ever, seemed about to spring.

Steadily I looked along the gleaming barrel of my rifle, hand and eye were sure, my aim was certain, and I pulled the trigger.

A puff of white smoke, a loud report, drowned by the agonised roar of the panther, as, making a convulsive bound forward, she rolled at Tim's feet—dead.

Oh! the joy and relief of that moment, as I sprang to Delany, and, kicking the cub aside, helped him to his feet.

He was pale and trembling from the effect of that awful ten minutes, for the whole duration, from the panther's first appearance to our lucky shot, could not have exceeded that, but it seemed as if the agony of a lifetime had been concentrated in that short period.

We returned to our fire, dragging the panther with us, after having knocked the cub on the head, lest it should, at some future time, cause some one the terror its mother had inflicted upon us.

" Be the mortial, avick," said Tim, as he wiped the perspiration from his yet pale features, " I don't wonder at the old settler cussing them sneaking panthers. Shure, I'd sooner have a fair stand-up fight wid twinty o' thim Crows, than sit forninst that div'l of a panther agin."

My comrade, however, soon forgot his fright in the discussion of some tender steaks cut from the body of his enemy; and two hours after we started again upon our journey, men and horses refreshed by the rest and food.

CHAPTER XLIV.

THE GUERILLAS AGAIN.—THE SHOOTING MATCH.

THE day was already far advanced, when we started again upon the trail of the guerillas, and we could scarcely hope to arrive at any of the frontier villages before night overtook us, unless we urged our horses to their utmost speed.

This we needed no other inducement to do, and the refreshed animals dashed along the smooth level of the prairie in gallant style, and in the pleasure of the swift motion Tim soon learned to laugh at his late adventure with the panther.

" I'm mighty sorry, avick," said my comrade, " that ye knocked the cub on the head —shure, 'twas an illigant little animal."

" What would you have done with it, old comrade ?" I asked. " The dogs would have made short work of it, once it had come within range of their teeth."

" Faith, that's thrue. But, Silvershot, avick, how was it that ye didn't bring the dogs when that ugly baste of a painter came a while ago ?"

" I left them by the fire, old comrade, settling down for a snooze. I didn't think there was any occasion to take them with me."

" Faix, then, I wish you had; it's dog's mate they'd have made of the brute in the twinklin' of a bedpost."

" I don't know that, Tim," said I, looking at the skin of the brute stretched on the earth before me.

This panther measured quite eight feet from nose to tail, and would have been a formidable opponent to a pack of hounds, much more to two.

The dusky shades of night were now fast closing around us, and we could no longer see ahead. The trail, however, being, luckily, broad and clear, we could still see to follow it without any trouble.

" By the mortial, Silvershot," said Tim again breaking the silence, after another half

"A CRY OF WONDER BROKE FROM MY LIPS—IT WAS UWATO."

hour's hard galloping, "we shall never be able to reach a place before dusk."

"I think we shall, Tim," I replied. "These guerillas we are following cannot have ridden much further; their horses must be quite knocked up. Depend on it, we shall either come up with their camp or reach a village before long."

"Shure, they must have ridden like the very divil. They must be a set of cowardly skunks, avick."

Gradually, but surely, the shades deepened, until we were obliged to bend from our saddles towards the earth to discern the track of the guerillas.

"Faix, Silvershot, we shall niver—Hallo! what's that, avick? Look ahead."

I looked up from the ground, and peered into the gathering darkness. There, faintly glimmering, I saw a distant light, not the flickering blaze of a camp fire, but a light evidently proceeding from the village we had so long been seeking.

"We've found it, Tim," I said. "Spur on, old comrade. Another hour will see us safely under shelter."

"By the mortial, it's welcome it'll be," said Tim, urging the flagging pace of his horse to a gallop. "Hurroo! for the pretty Mexicans! Shure, I havn't seen a purty face for months."

"You'd better take a looking-glass on your next journey, Tim," said I, laughing, "and so that difficulty will be got over."

"Aisy now, Silvershot, avick," Tim replied. "Shure, if the tongue of yez has been sharpened on the grindstone, yez needn't be afther prickin' a frind with it."

"Never mind, Tim," I said, laughingly. "Let us reach yonder light to-night, and you can make love to as many of the pretty Mexican ninas as you like."

Tim Delany subsided, grumbling to himself, and we rode on again as fast as our jaded steeds would take us in the direction of the light.

Anxious as we were, it seemed to be neared very slowly, but at last we reached it, and dashed into the narrow, unpaved, and dirty street of the Mexican village. Reining up our horses before the door of a *rancheria*, from the window of which came the light which had attracted us.

The little town was bustling with anima-

tia, and grouped around the door of the rancheria were native Mexicans of both sexes, and representatives of the English, Scotch, and French nations, all more or less dirty and villanous in aspect. There was hardly a respectable face to be seen.

Tim and I, however, were not just then in the mood to study physiognomy, and quickly dismounting, we gave our horses into the charge of the most decent-looking Mexican we could see, and entered the house.

It was filled with the remains of the very band of guerillas between whom and the Crows so deadly a conflict had taken place, and whose trail we had so successfuly followed.

The men were regaling themselves after the fight and long ride with deep draughts of *aguardiente*, and relating to a crowd of eager listeners how they had thrashed the Indians, who only escaped through their superior numbers, and the freshness of their horses.

This, of course, was their account; Tim and I could have told a different story, but we did not wish to draw upon ourselves the enmity of the guerillas, especially as we should have to travel some distance through the Mexican country on our way to San Juan Campestrano.

We pushed our way through the throng of men, and ordered refreshments; for, after our long ride, we stood greatly in need of some.

A pretty, dark-eyed poblana soon supplied our wants; and we, having satisfied the wants of the inner man, as some one expresses it, began to look with interest upon the men grouped around us.

They were all native Mexicans, without a single exception, dressed in the picturesque, although gaudy guerilla costume.

Some were remarkably fine-looking men, all were, if not powerful, at least lithe and active, and my present close inspection made me wonder greatly at the comparative cowardice they had exhibited that day in the encounter with the Crows.

Tim's thoughts evidently coincided with my own, for he said, after a lengthened stare at the Mexicans—

"Shure, avick, it's moighty throublesome customers they'd be if they had the laaste taste in life of the ginuine old Irish pluck."

"You're right, Tim," I replied; "but I cannot imagine how so many men, although they are Mexicans, can be all cowards."

"By the mortial, avick, ye're right, but, faix, they're like sheep, or that dacent cratur, the pig, when one runs, the others foller."

"That's it, Tim; I wonder who's the captain of the band. If he were a brave man something might be done with these fellows."

"Faix, avick, I don't see the smallest sign

in life of a captain o' any sort whatever. Shure they're all mixed up like the Widdy McCallaghan's childher, whin——"

"Hush!" I said, suddenly, to my loquacious comrade. "Listen!"

A knot of the guerillas had collected near us, and were conversing eagerly together in Spanish.

I knew the language well, and it was the word *capitano* that arrested my attention.

I scarcely knew why I listened, for both the guerillas and their captain were or ought to have been matters of indifference, but I obeyed an irresistible impulse to speak to the men.

"Your pardon, senors," I said, when a pause in the conversation allowed me to speak with some show of civility; "but you seem to have had a tough ride to-day."

"*Carramba*," replied one of the guerillas, a tall, black-bearded, swarthy man, with a dark, sinister expression in his eyes that did not impress me very favourably. "*Carramba*, I should think so indeed, we have galloped full thirty miles after the accursed Indians."

As he spoke, he twisted the ends of his moustache with an expression of pride and triumph which would have become a general, after gaining a battle.

The fellow's conceit annoyed me; his boast of having pursued the Indians when the latter had so thoroughly beaten the guerillas was more than I could bear.

"*After* the Indians!" I repeated, laying a stress on the first word.

The guerilla frowned fiercely upon me, and laip his had menacingly on the pummel of a pistol, as he replied—

"Yes, after! *Corpo di Christo*, do you imagine they ran after *us?*"

"Pardon, senor," I said, mildly, for I wished to avoid a quarrel with such odds, for the guerilla seemed remarkably pugnacious in the presence of his comrades. "I but wondered that such a body of men as yourselves have left any Indians alive to run after."

The guerilla swallowed every compliment, extravagant as it was. The frown immediately left his face, and he looked complacently upon me.

"True, senor," he replied, amiably. I thought you could not have meant to charge the Mexican Rangers with cowardice. *Carramba!* if you could have seen us as we made the red vagabonds gallop off!"

I thought to myself that I must have possessed remarkably good eyesight to have seen anything of the kind, and with difficulty repressing a smile, I continued—

"Did you lose many men in the fight, senor Capitano?"

"But three or four, camarado, and one

was our captain; so you see you have made a bad guess."

"Your pardon. There was something in your manner that impressed me with the belief that you were the leader of these brave men."

Tim Delany could hardly restrain his laughter as he heard me address the Mexicans as brave men, when we had so lately seen them run like a flock of startled sheep.

The guerilla, however, luckily, perhaps, did not notice Tim's bursting cheeks and shaking sides as he bottled up his merriment, and bowing gravely to me, said, complacently—

"Your words may be prophetic, senor. To-morrow we elect a new captain, and as I am, without flattering myself, the best shot in the band, I think I stand a tolerably good chance."

"So," said I, "you elect, as a captain, the best shot amongst you?"

"Si, senor," replied the guerilla; "and as the competition is open to all, we choose to admit you and your comrade. If it so please you, you can try your fortune to-morrow."

"Gracias, senor," I replied, "I will consider your kind offer."

"Then, turning to Tim, I said, in English, "What do you say, old comrade? If I win the good-will of the band to-night, and am elected captain to-morrow, we may be able to prosecute our search better than if we were alone."

"Thrue, avick," said Tim; "and if we meet that ould divil, Bill Buckskin, by the mortial, we can take it out of him illigant!"

I turned to the guerillas again, decided upon the course I should take.

"It is agreed, senor," I said, offering my hand; "my comrade and myself will try our fortune to-morrow."

CHAPTER XLV.

UWATO'S PRESENT—GOLD DUST VERSUS DOLLARS.

THE remainder of the evening after my acceptance of the guerilla's challenge was passed in one of the noisiest debauches of which I had ever been witness.

I say witness, as I was but a seeming participator in the revelry. Such dissipation was never to my taste, and it was an easy matter to deceive the already half-intoxicated Mexicans, who were too much occupied at drinking themselves to notice whether I did so or not.

Tim, however, was not so self-denying. The Mexicans had the start of him by two or three hours, but in half an hour after we joined them, he was as noisy, and, if the truth must be told, as tipsy as the guerillas.

I wished, for my part, to keep my head clear. I had made up my mind to be elected captain the next day, and I was unaware whether the Mexican competitors were skilful or not.

It would have required a much stronger reason to prevent Tim from indulging in the strong aguardiente, the nearest approach to the mountain dew of his native land then procurable.

I had, before it was too late, made an appointment with the guerilla to whom I had first spoken, and he had told me where and under what conditions the election was to be conducted.

It was midnight before the revellers had drunk themselves into insensibility; others with stronger heads led their less fortunate companions away, and the rancheria was once more quiet.

Tim and I obtained quarters in the house, and it did not take us long to stretch ourselves upon the rough couches, and sink into a profound slumber.

It was broad daylight when I awoke, refreshed; for my sleep, after the fatigue of the previous day, had been very deep. Tim was still snoring, the aguardiente had been strong, and he had drunk deeply.

I quickly donned my own habiliments, and then sought to rouse my comrade. He paid no attention, beyond a complaining grunt to the rough shakes and kicks I gave him; something more persuasive was needed to wake him from his insensibility.

A pitcher of water stood near. I took it and emptied the contents upon the head and shoulders of the somnolent Tim.

The unaccustomed contact of the cold fluid produced an instantaneous effect. Tim Delany started up with a howl of disgust, shaking his dripping head as the water ran down in streams.

"Be the mortial, Silvershot, avick! what are ye after, bad cess to yez!"

"All right, Tim," I said, speaking as well as my laughter at his ridiculous appearance would allow me. "I only did it to wake you."

"Faix, then, couldn't you wake me gintally, instead of trating me like a pig that wants washing?"

Tim was quite angry; the sudden shock had disturbed him. But I could not help saying—

"I'm sure, old comrade, you want washing quite as badly as any pig in Tipperary."

This was true, for Delany's features still retained the traces of our fight and flight of the previous day, and the orgie of the night before had not improved his appearance.

"Be the mortial, Silvershot, if any other man than yerself had done that same, it's a sound larruping I'd be after givin' him."

Tim was wiping his drenched face and head upon a rough buffalo hide, that had served for a bed covering, growling and muttering the while, like an angry bear.

"I'll go, old comrade," said I, "and see what we can get in the way of breakfast, though I don't suppose you have much of an appetite, after getting so tipsy last night."

"Tipsy!" ejaculated Tim, with the most profound contempt, "faix, don't be afther insulting me, Silvershot. Shure, do ye think them yeller-bellied Mexicans or their 'okkartinty' could make an Irish jintleman who's been used to the 'crathur,' the rale potheen—do ye think that 'u'd make him tipsy? Yah!"

Delany turned away disgusted, and I went below to see if anyone was stirring, and whether we could get any breakfast, for I had not forgotten my appointment with the guerillas, and remembered that the election was to take place at mid-day.

I found the keeper of the rancheria and his daughter busied in clearing up the wreck we had made of the rough furniture that had adorned the scene of our revelry.

The host, a swarthy, stout, but not ill-looking Mexican, greeted me with a "Buenos dias, senor," as I entered the room. The pretty poblana, his child, glanced quickly up, then down again; she looked disappointed, and I recollected that the irrepressible Tim had been making violent love to her the previous evening. Delany was not, strictly speaking, a handsome man, but he had an irrestible, dashing manner with the fair sex which took them by storm. He had evidently made a conquest of the dark-eyed, pretty Mexican.

"What can you give me and my companion in the way of desayuna?" I said, returning the greeting.

"Que quiere v., senor, what do you want? A taso of chocolate, some fowls, and fruit."

"That will do," I replied. "Gracias, amigo, as soon as you please; for I tasted but 'ittle yesterday, and I have the appetite of a famished prairie wolf."

"Anda, quick, Margarita," said the host to the pretty poblana. "You hear, stir up that idle vagabond, José; carrai, he is not worth his chocolate."

"You shall have your desayuna soon, senor," said the Mexican, with a bow. I was puzzled for a moment to account for the unusual civility showed me, but a moment sufficed to disclose the real reason. I recollected having, on the preceding evening, pulled out and displayed the little bag of gold dust, Uwato's present.

I had done this purposely, as my stock of ready money was very small, only consisting of a few dollars, whereas the possession of a few gold onzas is absolutely necessary to inspire respect in the breast of a Mexican.

Some of these men, I knew, also were possessed of tolerably large sums of ready money, and were always willing to do a stroke of business; my host might not feel indisposed to change a few of his solid onzas and dollars for my bag of glittering dust.

In its present state the gold was of really no use to me; converted into coin it would prove of great service now we had arrived on the Mexican frontier, where the necessaries of life had to be bought, and food was no longer to be had for the catching.

I saw that the Mexican's thoughts were running upon my gold dust, by the way in which he glanced from time to time at the protuberance it caused in my hunting shirt; but I did not wish to appear in the least desirous of parting with it, as I knew it would greatly lessen the amount he might think it worth while to offer me.

Seating myself carelessly, I said—

"Any news of the Indians?"

"No, senor, none," replied the Mexican; "a curse upon them. Carajo, they yesterday killed one of my best customers."

"Indeed!"

"Si, senor, the captain of the guerillas who were here yesterday. Holy Virgin! dollars were as plentiful with him as thorns in the mesquite thicket, and he could drink more mezcal than any two of his troop. Santissima Maria, it was worse than sacrilege."

"What—the mezcal drinking?" I said, with a smile.

"Carrambo, senor; no, the killing so worthy a man. But you, senor, are going to shoot for the post, are you not?"

"Si amigo," I replied, "and I hope to win it, too."

"The Holy Virgin grant you may!" said the Mexican, fervently.

"Why do you wish that? I should have thought your sympathies would have been with your countrymen, rather than with a stranger."

"Carral, senor; it is soon said. Most of the guerillas have as little money as modesty, and as they are all-powerful here, I am obliged to supply them with what they require, whether paid for or not. The capitano was a generous man, and"—here he looked meaningly at me—"I trust his successor will be the same."

I repressed a smile, which the Mexican's disinterested words had called up, and said, gravely—

"If I am elected, amigo, you shall have no cause to complain of me, or make disparaging comparisons between the late noble capitano and your humble servant."

My host's features beamed with a happy smile, and he looked benignly at me as he said again—

"I do not doubt you, senor. Carrambo! generosity is written as plainly on your face as was ever ladrone on the features of those rascally Indios."

I bowed gravely to the compliment.

"If there is any way in which I can serve the illustrious capitano, I am ever ready at his service."

I knew what the artful Mexican meant, but merely said—

"Gracias mil gracias! A thousand thanks, nothing except my breakfast, for I am most terribly hungry, and I hear my comrade coming.

"Anda Jose, Margarita el desayuna! The breakfast, quick!" shouted the host. Then he turned to me again.

"In one moment, senor, and if you wil pardon my officiousness I saw that you had a quantity of gold dust. Perhaps I can serve the senor by changing them for doubloons."

And again the Mexican glanced at the protuberance in my hunting shirt.

"No—thanks," I replied carelessly. "I have enough money for the present."

"But, senor," said my host, eagerly, "jt will be more convenient to have money than gold-dust, which is of no use to you. I can offer full value, money down, senor."

Although I desired nothing more than to convert Uwato's present into shining dollars, I pretended, for motives of policy, to hesitate.

"Will senor allow me to look?" said the Mexican.

I reluctantly drew the pouch from my shirt, and threw it carelessly on the table.

"There it is, amigo, but I do not care to sell it. Gold dust is more compact and less likely to attract unwelcome attraction than a heavy bag of dollars."

My host had clutched the bag, and was greedily examining the contents, "hefting" the bag, feeling the yellow grains, his eyes glistening, his fingers trembling. I saw at once that I should have a good bargain of the man if I could only summon up a sufficient amount of indifference.

After revelling for two or three minutes in the delight of handling the gold, the breakfast was brought in, and at the same moment Tim Delany entered, looking much better for his involuntary bath.

My comrade wore a sulky look when he entered, but this vanished at sight of the breakfast, and, without saying a word, he drew up a rough stool and attacked the chocola's and fowls with such an appetite as only one who passes his life on the prairie can feel.

I set to work, too, keeping one eye fixed upon the Mexican, who was wholly absorbed in his interesting pursuit.

At length he looked up from the precious contents of the bag, and turned his attention to me

"Well, senor," he said, hesitatingly, "I will give you a hundred dollars, all new, for the gold."

I shook my head vehemently, and helped myself to another piece of the fowl.

"No, no, amigo, I do not wish to part with the gold at all; and if I did, should certainly not accept a sum so far below the real value."

"But consider, senor," continued the man, half imploringly, "a hundred bright dollars."

I shook my head again, more decisively than before; and Tim, at the mention of the money, looked up from his plate, and paused in the act of conveying a chicken's leg to his mouth.

"Bedad, avick!" he said, in a loud whisper, "don't be afther refusing such an offer—a hundred dollars! Be the mortial! I'd sell myself to the naygur for half as much!"

"Hush!" I said. "I'll get twice as much out of him. Wait.

Tim was silent, and the Mexican resumed his examination of the gold dust. I verily believe he counted every grain.

"Well, senor," he said, again, in desperation, "a hundred and fifty, though, Santissima Maria! I know not where I shall find the money."

I shook my head again.

"No; I tell you again, I do not want to part with the dust.

Tim gave me a powerful kick on the shins, and winked furiously at me.

"Two hundred, then!" almost shouted my host; "not a cent more, by San Trinidado! I shall lose by the bargain."

"Then don't make it, amigo," I coolly replied. "I did not ask you, nor do I care to take the money at all."

"Pardon, senor, said the Mexican, more mildly; "say, is it a bargain? Two hundred dollars—carrambo! it is a fortune."

"Well, since you seem to wish it, the gold dust is yours upon those terms," said I, as coolly as I could, for inwardly I felt delighted at making so good a bargain.

"When do you want the money, senor?" asked the Mexican. He did not seem nearly so eager now that he had gained my consent.

"Immediately," I replied, "or it is no bargain. Do not inconvenience yourself. If you have not the money it matters little to me."

The avarice of the man's nature again broke out at the prospect of losing the bargain, for I had stretched out my hand as if to take up the purse, and he said, hurriedly—

"It is well, senor. You shall have it immediately. But, Madre de Dios, two hundred dollars!"

He turned and left the room. No sooner had he done so than Tim looked at me with wonder and admiration expressed in every feature.

"Shure, Silvershot, avick, is it thrue? Will the fellow give you two hundred dollars for that?"

"Yes, old comrade, and make a good thing of it too, though I have had a better bargain than I thought."

Tim stared again in wonder, and stared still harder when the Mexican returned with a big, heavy bag in his hand, and slowly untying the mouth, proceeded to count the dollars, Tim counting after him with much unction.

As the last dollar fell from his fingers I swept the money up and shovelled it into my pouch as if I had been the possessor of thousands, though, to tell the truth, I was never so pleased at a "swop" in my life.

I saw the host's eye brighten as he looked at Tim. He was thinking of that gentleman's predilection for mezcal and aguardiente, and of how many of the dollars he had just parted with would find their way back.

So it was in a rather more cheerful tone that he wished us success at the approaching contest, and then left the room.

Tim had finished his breakfast, and drawing a cigarette from his pocket, lit it, and puffed away in silent enjoyment.

I followed Tim's example, and we were enjoying the fragrant vapour and the unwonted repose, when suddenly the door of the rancheria opened, and my swaggering guerilla friend of the previous evening stalked in.

He greeted me with the nearest approach to a smile his surly, lowering features could assume, and, with the customary "Buenas dias, senor," placed himself by my side.

"Well, senor Capitano," I said, affably, "ready for the shooting, I hope; though last night's adventure was not well calculated to give any of us a clear head and a steady hand this morning."

"Carrai! senor, you are right," he replied, with a loud laugh; "but we guerillas are used to that; and it would take more than a night's drinking to make my eyes see less clearly or my nerves shake—bah!"

"Doubtless," I said, humouring the boastful guerilla; "but we prairie men are unused to your fiery aguardiente, or our heads are less able to withstand its effects."

"It is possible," replied the guerilla, grandiloquently: "but, carrambo! senor, if you join our troop, you will soon get used to it; and, by the way, it is the very thing I came to talk to you about. Holo! José."

José, a bright-eyed Mexican lad, appeared, and the guerilla commanded a dozen cigarettos and some mezcal, which he obligingly allowed me to pay for.

"The conditions, senor, under which you will join our troop are these :—You and your companion will be first admitted in our ranks as privates, and then can compete for the post of capitano"——

"Then, senor," said I, interrupting him; "if we should fail?"

"You will, of course, remain with us. Carrambo, senor! you cannot expect to risk nothing for so much."

In my inmost heart I thought but very little indeed of the position of capitano of such a set of poltroons as the guerillas were; but it suited my purpose, and I felt so confident of my capabilities as a marksman that the risk was very small.

"Agreed," I replied; "I will abide by the conditions. Here is my hand upon it."

"Buen, senor, in an hour hence you will find us at the appointed place; be punctual, for the shooting will commence directly all are assembled."

Coolly pocketing the remainder of the cigaritos, and draining his cup of mezcal, the guerilla departed.

"Well, man alive," said Tim, "I couldn't understand all the naygur sed; but, by the mortial, a more consayted, ignorant baste I niver met wid in all me life."

"You are right, old comrade; but we will presently, if I am not very much mistaken, take some of the conceit out of him."

"How so, avick?"

In an hour from this they elect a fresh captain. Have you forgotten, Tim, that we are to try our fortunes?"

"Hurroo!" shouted my companion. "Faix, where's me rifle? If I don't bate every mother's son to-day, Silvershot, barring yer own illigant self, may I be turned into a yallar-bellied Mexikin!"

Half-an-hour afterwards, Tim Delany and I, with our rifles over our shoulders, stepped out for the rendezvous.

CHAPTER XLVI.

RIFLE PRACTICE.—THE ELECTION.

THE place appointed by the guerilla lay about half a mile from the Mexican village, near to a clump of trees that stood isolated upon the llano.

The single street that ran through the centre of the collection of houses, called by courtesy a pueblita, opened directly upon the trees, and in the clear, pure prairie atmosphere we could see that the guerilleros had already assembled. A few natives of the town, through motives of curiosity, were also walking towards the place of meeting.

Young and strong as we were, a very short time sufficed to bring us within speaking distance of the guerilleros, who were dismounted and drawn up in line, evidently waiting our approach. The black-browed gentleman, who seemed already to have assumed the command, shouted, as we drew near—

"Alto? quien va? Halt! Who goes there?"

"Amigos," I replied.

This little piece of formality having been passed through, we joined the Mexicans, who looked up us with some curiosity, as volunteers to their ranks were scarce, and opponents to the skill of the big guerilla were still scarcer.

Our old acquaintance slipped out and saluted us. There was a confident smile upon his face, as he gave the usual greeting.

"All is ready, senor. Give your names, and promise allegiance to the Mexican Government, and we can begin. My name is Juan Ramorez; the others you will soon learn."

Tim and I did as we were requested, and then followed Senor Juan Ramorez to the spot from whence the competitors were to fire.

A tree at about one hundred-and-fifty yards' distance from the standing-place, had been selected for the target, and upon the bark, six feet from the ground, a circular piece of paper, as large as the crown of a hat, had been fastened. This was the mark.

To an ordinary shot this would have been a sufficiently difficult one; but to Tim and I, trained as we had been, it was little more than child's play, and either of us could have struck the exact centre nineteen times out of twenty.

As I removed my gaze from the mark, I met the eyes of Juan Ramorez with a look upon his face that plainly said, "Confess yourselves beaten already.

However, I did not intend to do anything of the kind, but coolly examined the priming of my rifle, and adjusted the lock.

"Well, senor," said Ramorez, "what do think of the mark? Do you think you can strike the centre?"

"I will bet fifty dollars," was my reply, "that I fire half a dozen shots in as many minutes and leave but one bullet-hole."

Ramorez turned pale; he was unused to such shooting as that; but he soon recovered, evidently thinking I had been boasting.

"Carrambo, senor, you are jesting."

"Not at all. Will you bet?"

"I should be robbing you."

"I will risk it. Is it a bargain?"

"Done. Corpo di Christo! there is no man in Mexico who can perform such a feat."

"Your pardon, senor, I will show you you are mistaken."

"Carrai! I hope not; but my dollars are safe enough. Will you shoot first?"

"No, senor. With your permission, I and my comrade will try our skill last. The sight of your shooting will give us courage."

The guerilla bowed, and signed with his hand.

The Mexicans had ranged themselves opposite the target, and the first man stepped out and levelled his piece.

Taking a careful aim, he pulled the trigger a flash, a puff of smoke, and we saw the bullet chip a piece from the bark of the tree, quite a foot from the paper target.

"Bah!" ejaculated Tim, in a tone of disgust. "By the mortial, Silvershot, avick! I'd shoot better nor that wid me two blissid eyes shut."

Another and another of the guerillas followed, and fired, but with little better success than the first had had. At last it came to the turn of Juan Ramorez.

He stepped forward with a confident air, and raised his weapon to his shoulder, first glancing at us, as if to say, "Now you will see something better."

I could see by his attitude that he knew something of the use of his piece, and the way in which he handled his rifle, so I was not surprised when the report was followed by a shout from the Mexicans, and saw a bullet hole in the centre of the paper.

"There, senor," he said, triumphantly, with a wave of his hand, "now it is your turn."

"An excellent shot, indeed; but I shall win my wager. Tim, you will shoot first," I added, turning to my comrade.

"Right, avick. Here goes for the glory of ould Ireland!"

Tim raised his rifle, and fired. When the puff of smoke cleared away, but one bullet-hole was to be seen.

"Santissama Maria, he has missed it!" exclaimed the guerillas.

Tim chuckled grimly, and smiled at me, as, in my turn, I levelled and fired.

Another exclamation from the Mexicans, and a shout of delight from Juan Ramorez. There was only the single bullet hole to be seen.

"I have won, senor," he said exultingly. "The captaincy and the fifty dollars are mine!"

"One moment," I said. "Let us examine the target."

"I walked towards the tree; Ramorez and the Mexicans followed, wondering.

The tree was reached, and the guerilla looked on suspiciously as I pulled off the paper, and coolly drawing my hunting-knife, picked out not one, but three bullets.

"Sorcery!" ejaculated the guerillas.

"Carajo!" hissed the guerilla, between his clenched teeth.

"It is very simple," said I, coolly; "the bullets from my rifle and that of my comrade entered the hole first made by you."

"You have not won yet," said the guerilla, "as yet we are equals."

"True," I replied, "and as shooting at such a target and such a distance would be child's play to us, I propose a mark that will take all our skill to hit."

Juan turned away with a scowl of hatred already upon his face. He feared me and saw that his chance of being elected capitano was getting dangerously small.

I regarded him not, however; but taking from my pocket three large flat-headed nails and a strip of paper, I walked up to the tree, and with a stone hammered the nails into the bark, placing them about four inches apart in a vertical line.

I then coolly walked back to the firing point, and said to the discomfited guerilla, who had mechanically followed me—

"There, senor, is a mark that will require a steady aim and well-trained hand to hit at this distance—will you try a shot?"

Juan looked at the nails, which were scarcely visible at that distance, and then turning, frowned at me with envy, hatred, and every malicious passion strongly marked in his features.

"Carrambo, no! I will not shoot at a mark that I can scarce see; only chance and the devil could enable a man to do it."

"I will engage, senor, and chance the fifty dollars I just wagered upon the issue, that with three bullets I drive in those three nails —do you accept?"

"Carrai, yes!" replied the guerilla, as a gleam of hope sparkled in his eyes; he thought it impossible that I could do what I had said.

All looked eagerly on as I raised my rifle, and took a steady, careful aim; my eye glanced along the sights, the swerving of a hair's breath would spoil the shot; a touch upon the trigger, the sharp crack of the rifle, then the thud of the bullet, as it struck into the tree.

A murmur of admiration from the guerillas, a muttered curse from Juan Ramorez, a cry of "Hurro, avick!" from Tim.

One of the nails was gone. My bullet had struck it fairly on the top, driving it inche deep into the wood.

Another shot, with the same result—a third, equally steady, equally sure—I had won.

The murmur amongst the guerillas broke out into a shout of admiration at the final shot.

"Viva el capitan!" was the cry.

Juan Romarez alone did not join in it. He stood a little apart, leaning on his rifle, glancing at me from time to time. I have, in my career, seen many evil looks and faces, but I never saw so horribly malignant an expression as that of the guerilla.

I took no notice of him at the time, but, lifting my sombrero in acknowledgment of their cheers, said—

"Mexicans, I have complied with all the conditions imposed, and have competed fairly. Do you acknowledge and accept me for your leader?"

"Si, senor; viva el capitan. Dios y Guadalupe!"

Juan alone remained silent. I was determined, however, to make him acknowledge me as his leader, and equally determined to enforce my orders should he prove refractory.

CHAPTER XLVII.

EN ROUTE FOR SAN JUAN CAMPESTRANO— THE COMANCHES.

I COULD understand, to a certain degree, what the guerilla's feelings must be at having so suddenly snatched from him the object of his ambition, for which, perhaps, he had been scheming and plotting for months past.

But I was determined to exert my authoriy, and to bend the man into subjection. I was now master, and I meant to make the guerilla feel that such was the case.

I walked up to him and said quietly, but firmly—

"Senor Juan Ramorez, have you any opposition to make to my election, or do you agree to what your comrades have just said?"

He lifted his eyes to my face with a fierce scowl, but the firm, steady glance with which I met his gaze quelled him, and he muttered in a low, hissing voice—

"Carrambo! since I must—yes."

"It is enough," I said. Then, turning to the guerillas, "we will celebrate my election as captain at the rancheria, and at my expense. Andela—anda—forward."

I waited until slowly, reluctantly, Juan Ramorez took his place in the ranks, and then, with Tim by my side, marched my men back to the rancheria.

"Well, Tim, old comrade," said I, "what do you think of it all?"

"By the mortial! Silvershot, it's all the same to me, anyhow. But, shure, now we're sojiers we'll not be able to do as we like, avick!"

"Oh, yes we shall, Tim," I replied; "the general in command troubles the outposts very little. So long as he hears that there's fighting going on we shall not receive any orders from him."

"Faix! it's but little o' that he got when the last captain was alive."

"I believe you're right, Tim; but I'll make a change now. Some of the men have pluck, I believe, if they only had a leader to follow."

"Shure, Sllvershot, it's more than satisfied they'll be now, anyhow; for a greater divil for fighting than yerself it 'ud be hard to find in county Tipperary."

"That's a doubtful compliment, Tim," I replied, with a smile.

"The divil a betther, man, will yez git from me, ye ongrateful blaygaird. Faix! I hold a Tipperary man fit to thread on the tail of the coat of the best man that ivir tuk a weapon in his fisht!"

Tim began to gesticulate violently with his rifle, and from experience I knew that he was getting excited and angry, as he invariably did when the least insinuation was cast upon his countrymen. A very little more would have sufficed to put him in a violent rage, but at that moment we entered the plaza of the village, and I commanded a halt.

The host appeared at the door of his house almost instantly. He had been, doubtless, on the watch, anxious to finger again some of the dollars he had so reluctantly parted with in the morning.

The keen-sighted Mexican saw at a glance that I had been successful, and that his hopes were in a fair way of being fulfilled.

He was right for that night, and that only, for I had determined, for many reasons, that my stay in the wretched little village should be a short one.

"Welcome, capitano," said the Mexican. "Santissima Maria, my prayers have been heard. Welcome."

"Gracias," I replied, though I knew quite well the selfish source of my host's congratulations. "You have well guessed. I am captain of these brave men, and we have come to drink to my success."

The host fairly beamed with smiles, standing aside to let us pass in, and bowed profoundly as he did so.

My men were almost as pleased as themselves. It was not very often that such an opportunity for a carouse presented itself, and they were proportionately grateful.

When we entered the sala, we found that everything had been prepared. The Mexican was undoubtedly keen-sighted, and had by instinct divined that I should be the victor in the contest.

The liquids had been our host's principal care, but the solids also had been well provided, and my guerillas, nothing loth, attacked the viands with true prairie appetites.

Although the sala was uncommonly large, occupying the whole of the basement of the house, my men—for there were more than a hundred of them—were crowded closely together; and we had been seated some time, and the meal had progressed far towards its completion, when Tim said, suddenly—

"Shure, avick, I don't see that big ugly yaller-bellied varmint ye polished off so handsomely this blissid mornin'."

I looked up. It was as Tim had said; the man whose hopes I had so completely defeated was not present.

I felt an angry flush rise into my face; my pride was hurt; I was determined to conquer the rebellious spirit of the stubborn guerilla.

I rose to my feet, and in a tone sufficiently loud to be heard over the sala, called—

"Juan Ramorez!"

In an instant every eye was fixed upon me. Although I tried to control my voice, the anger that was in my heart found expression in its tones.

But no one answered, and a second time I called—

"Juan Ramorez!"

The eyes of the guerillas wandered round the apartment, in wonder at the absence of their comrade, who was usually the first at a carouse, and the last to leave it.

At length one spoke up and said—

"He is not here, capitan. It is strange, too—carrambo!"

"Let him be found," I said, sternly; "two of you go in search, and do not return until you bring him with you. Tim," I added, aside, "go with them, and see that they do their duty. Use force, if necessary."

"Aisy, avick," replied my comrade, with a wink. "I'll kick the blaiggaird iviry inch o' the way if he don't come mighty willin'."

Tim and the guerillas departed, and I resumed my seat; but the men no longer conversed or drank with such freedom as before. I could see that my angry tone and decisive action, perhaps, too, a certain amount of fear, had checked their gaiety.

This was going far beyond my wish. I was not unwilling that they should fear me to a certain degree, but I did not wish them to be uneasy or constrained in my presence, and in order to remove any such possible effect, I rose and said—

"Mexicans! obedience is a soldier's duty. In avoiding your company to-night, Ramorez has disobeyed me aud insulted you. For that he shall be punished; but do not let this untoward circumstance mar your enjoyment, for it will displease me greatly if a disappointed bully's caprice should spoil the pleasure of a hundred better men."

I had the pleasure of seeing that my speech produced the desired effect. With a chorus of "vivas," the guerillas resumed their former occupation of drinking, for the eating department was already closed. I alone waited for the arrival of Tim with the refractory Ramorez.

I had not long to wait. Scarce a quarter of an hour had elapsed, when Tim and the guerillas returned triumphant.

They had the Mexican by the collar, and were pushing him along with no gentle hand. As Ramorez thus unceremoniously entered, or rather was forced to enter the sala, he raised his eyes and encountered mine, which were fixed upon him half angry, half amused.

The guerilla stopped suddenly, his swarthy features flushed, and a scowl, black, malignant, and threatening as a thunder-cloud, swept across his face.

Tim observed it, too, and angered by the Mexican's sudden pause, which had brought the latter's foot heavily upon my comrade's, seized Ramorez tightly by the collar of his jacket with one hand, grasped a handful of the tight-fitting calzonerous with the other, and ran him up to me in an instant.

"There, ye ondacent blagguaird," said Tim, angrily; "thread on me toes agin, if ye dare. I'll tache ye manners?"

The Mexican's face was perfectly livid with rage, as he heard a laugh break from his companions, and saw an ill-repressed smile upon my face; he scowled alternately at Tim, the guerillas, and myself, as the blasphemous "carajo" hissed from between his pale lips.

"None o' yer bad languidge now," said Tim, threateningly; "another word like that, and I'll stop yer talking for a month to come."

"Silence, Tim," I interposed, authoritatively; "this is my affair."

Most of the guerillas had now risen, and, now advancing, grouped themselves round us. I saw that the moment had come for establishing my authority, when it was absolutely necessary that I should show myself master in fact as well as name.

"Juan Ramorez," I said to the guerilla, who was visibly trembling with the violent passions that agitated him, "why did you absent yourself without leave? Remember that I am captain, and that I will be obeyed. This once I pardon your offence, but if it is repeated I shall exact a heavy punishment. You may go."

I waved him away with a motion of my hand, and a murmur of admiration passed round the assembled guerillas. The fault was, in reality, trifling, but the obstinacy and anger of Ramorez had made it seem of far greater importance. I felt that I had made a hit.

The feelings of Ramorez may be more easily imagined than described. His eyes blazed with unnatural fury upon all around, his lips quivered as he tried in vain to give vent to his pent-up passion. I could hear the noise made by his clenched teeth, as he ground them together.

I saw that in another moment the Mexican's anger would break forth, and anxious to avoid further disturbance, especially as my object of enforcing authority was already gained, I signed to Tim to remove the man.

Delany, nothing loth, seized the guerilla by the arm, and moved him right-about-face in an instant.

That sufficed. Shaking off my comrade's hold, as a wet dog shakes the water from his hide, and uttering an oath, the Mexican drew his long, keen knife, and darted upon Tim, who had staggered back from the violence with which Ramarez had repulsed him.

The motion was so sudden and unexpected that before I, or any of my men, could make a motion, the glittering knife was raised high in the air, and another instant would have seen it buried in Tim's heart.

But the brave Irishman was equal to the emergency. Sudden as the guerilla's movement had been, and great as was the danger, he was prepared before the knife could descend. Tim's right fist shot out like lightning, and landed, with a crash, full between the Mexican's eyes.

He fell like a log, stunned and bleeding. The knife flew from his nerveless grasp, and fell at my feet. Tim coolly wiped the blood from his knuckles, and examined his enormous fist with critical approval.

The Mexicans stared in wonder. Ramorez was one of the most expert in handling the deadly knife, and it seemed to them almost miraculous how Tim could have escaped, and conquered his opponent with no other arms than those Nature had given him.

But they had no pity for their fallen comrade. Two of them raised him from the ground, for he was quite insensible. Tim had struck with full force, and he could have felled an ox.

"Carrambo," they muttered, "he was well served. Santissima Maria, it is wonderful!"

I was not ill-pleased at the turn events had taken. I had formally established my authority, and Tim, whom I determined to make my lieutenant, had created a prestige for himself amongst the guerillas.

"Carry him away, amigos," I said to the two who were supporting Ramorez. "I will see him in the morning; meanwhile watch him carefully. I shall hold you responsible for his safe custody."

The guerillas carried the insensible form of their companion away, and then returned; but the repose of the evening had been too much disturbed to think of detaining the rest of the men any longer, and I decided to dismiss them at once, while the memory of Tim's bold act yet impressed them.

"Mexicans," I said, as coolly as I could, "you will meet to-morrow on the plaza, at ten o'clock. Let the bugler sound 'to horse' at that hour precisely. Now, amigos, one parting glass, and then away, for you will have work to-morrow."

The guerillas tossed off each a glas of mezcal, and, saluting Tim and I with the utmost respect—almost reverence—passed out one by one.

Tim and I were alone; neither spoke for several moments, till, looking gravely round at my comrade, he burst into a hearty fit of laughing, doubling himself up, and rolling so from side to side that I almost feared he would go into a fit.

"Hush, Tim!" I said seriously, for I felt little inclined to partake of his merriment; "this is no laughing matter."

"By the mortial, Silvershot, avick! would yer have me cry? Faix, now, didn't I tumble the yaller-bellied schoundril over nicely? Shure it was fit for Donnybrook."

"That's all very well, Tim," said I; "but we have the consequences to think of. This fellow may influence the troop against us—"

"Influence yer grandmother!" ejaculated Tim Delaney, contemptuously. "Faix he udn't influence the tail o'a Tipperary pig. Influence, bah! If I thought such a spalpeen could influence thim fellers, I'd think less ov 'em than I do at this presint—and that's sayin' a considerable deal, Silvershot, avick!"

"I hope you are right, Tim," I replied; "all the better if it is so, for I am determined to be captain in fact as well as name. I know how loosely disciplined these Mexican guerillas are, but I mean to keep a tight hand over them."

"Shure, it's aisy as dhrinkin' whisky. All ye've got to do, Silvershot, is to knock 'em down once a week or so all round, and if that isn't enough, give one of 'em a lead pill to assist his digestion, and remind the others that they'd betther kape mighty quiet."

I could not help laughing at Tim's prescription for keeping unruly guerillas in order —there was sense in it, however. An occasional exhibition of force and a determination not to stick at trifles was an excellent plan to follow with such rough characters as I had now to deal with.

Discussing and arranging plans for the future, calling up reminiscences of old times, guessing the whereabouts of the chart which indicated the way to the treasure-cave of the Comanches, and vowing vengeance upon the head of Buckskin Bill when we caught him, the time slipped rapidly away, and the dusk of evening had closed upon the Mexican village before it seemed to us that an hour had passed.

"Well, Tim, old comrade," said I, "we had better turn in; there is a long ride before us to-morrow, and we have need of rest."

"Thrue, avick!" was the reply. "Faix, it's meself that feels ready for the arms of Murphy; so as soon as ye like, Silvershot."

I needed no second invitation. Another ten minutes saw us both firmly locked in the embraces of "Murphy," as my comrade phrased it.

CHAPTER XLVIII.
I MEET WITH AN OLD FRIEND.

It was late in the morning when Tim and I awoke from a long and refreshing sleep. The people of the village were already astir, and I could hear the clattering of horses' hoofs on the plaza.

"Up with you, old comrade," I called to Tim Delany, who, sitting up in his rude couch, was rubbing his eyes, and gaping fearfully.

"Right, avick," replied Tim; "but, by the mortial, it's mesilf that feels inclined for another spell of Murphy. Shure it isn't half enough I've had yit."

"Not another moment, Tim. Come, up with you, or I shall be obliged to give you another cold bath."

"Ugh," muttered Tim, grimacing, springing out of bed; "anythin' but that, avick! I'd never forgive ye if ye did that same agin."

My companion was as brave, generous, and true-hearted a man as ever set foot on the prairie; but, like most backwoodsmen, he had a holy horror of washing.

Keeping one eye on me, and the other on the pitcher of water, Tim soon donned his clothes, and, together, we descended to the sala, where our Mexican host, all smiles and courtesy, was awaiting us.

He had no idea of my intention to leave the town so soon, and I took good care not to inform him until the ceremony of settling his "little account" had been gone through.

That done, Tim and I took a hearty and affectionate farewell of him; but the ungrateful Mexican did not seem to return our greeting with the warmth we expected. He muttered something very like an oath, and his face lengthened visibly.

"Carrambo, senor!" he ejaculated. "You do not mean to go yet?"

"But, indeed, I do," was my reply. "I start with my troop for San Juan Campestrano this morning."

The man's face grew yet longer, and he muttered something anything but complimentary to me.

"This not fair, senor, I——'

"Not fair!" I repeated, angrily, for I saw that I should have to frighten him into submission. "Have I not paid you?"

"Si, senor, but—but," he stammered.

"Nonsense," I said, going towards the door, "buen dias, amigo. I have no further time to waste. Come, Tim."

The Mexican fell back with a look of almost agony upon his features as Tim and I passed him. He had reckoned upon fingering the dollars he had given me for my gold dust, and most probably considered them as safe as if they were already in his pocket.

We made our way quickly to the plazo, for the appointed time had already arrived; and just as we reached it, the shrill, clear tones of the bugle rang down the street.

"Come, Tim," I said to my comrade, "time is up, and we must not set a bad example."

Scarcely had the echoes died away than the narrow street became suddenly alive with the guerillas, hurrying from their quarters to the plaza, where all the horses were picketed.

When we reached the spot, we found that many of the guerillas were already there—some mounted, others tightening their horses' girths, or looking to their arms and accoutrements.

They presented a very respectable and warlike appearance, and a feeling almost of pride sprang up in my breast at the sight.

"Look there, avick!" said my comrade, suddenly.

Following the direction indicated by Tim's finger, I caught sight of Juan Ramorez, seated on his horse, and fully armed.

The guerilla had taken up a position apart from his comrades, and he wore a settled sullen, gloomy frown upon his face, yet marked by Tim's blow, that plainly showed he had neither forgotten nor forgiven the events of the preceding night.

He did not observe me, and I took no further notice of him than the passing glance at first, merely observing to Tim—

"Keep a sharp look-out on that man, old comrade. The Mexicans are revengeful, and this one evidently means mischief."

"Trust me," replied Delany. "Faix, I'll let daylight into his skull, if I see the laste sign in life o' the blagguaird's treachery!"

We mounted our horses, and I gave the bugler the word to sound.

The Mexicans are famous horsemen; used to the saddle from infancy, they attain a skill which would be envied by the most famous circus-rider in Europe.

Now all was ready; the men formed, and with Tim and I at their head, passed from the village at full gallop, to the great joy of the inhabitants, with the exception of our late host and the Mexican "ninas," who many of them lost a lover when the guerillas departed.

On we went, clattering down the narrow street until the vast, unbroken monotony of prairie lay before us, with only an occasional clump of trees, a mound, or a rock to guide us to our destination.

One of the guerillas acted as guide. He had been to San Juan Campestrano before, and, by the few landmarks on the plain, led the way with the utmost certainty where an European would have been utterly lost.

Ramorez had taken up his position in the rear, never speaking a word to his companions, and preserving the same moody silence. Tim left me as soon as we had reached the open prairie, and, riding at the side of the column, kept a careful watch upon the man.

"When shall we reach San Juan Compestrano?" I said to the Mexican who rode by my side.

"If we keep on at this rate, to-morrow night, Senor," was the reply.

This would suit my purpose admirably, and I felt more pleased than ever at the strange accident which had placed me in my present position. I felt certain that I should now be certain to carry out my object, and discover the plan of the Comanche treasure cave.

For five hours we galloped on without drawing rein, and then I commanded a halt, for both men and horses needed a rest.

Fortunately there was a spring of pure clear water on the very spot, and the only thing necessary was food, for we had brought none with us.

Game, however, is very plentiful on the southern prairies, and, selecting a dozen of the best shots in my troop, we started on foot, leaving Tim behind in command of the rest.

About half a mile distant some dozen or so black specks dotted the undulating surface of the llano. For these we made cautiously; they were too far off to make out whether they were buffalo or deer, but either would have been equally welcome. We should not, indeed, have been above a slice of nicely broiled mustang; prairie appetites are not particularly nice.

Before long we could see that the specks were deer browsing on the long prairie grass. The sight excited our appetites wonderfully

THE TRAPPER FIRED AND SENT HIM TO HIS LAST ACCOUNT.

I separated my men, and, ordering them to lay flat on the ground, we crawled in the herbage until within range.

Marking down a fine fat buck, I fired. The shot served as a signal to the others, and in an instant a dozen reports rang out, and as many deer fell to the ground; the rest sped away with the swiftness of light, and with a shout we jumped up, and ran towards our prey.

Before we could reach it, the shout was echoed from a hundred throats, and, as if by magic, a war party of Indians leapt from the grass, and charged towards us.

I was bewildered by the suddenness of the attack. We had had no idea that Indians were in the neighbourhood; but, collecting my guerillas, I formed them in a line, and advanced towards the foe, reloading their guns as they went.

The Indians were not a hundred yards distance, and, fortunate for us, were on foot. They had doubtless been in pursuit of the very game we had shot. The leader was a yard or two in front of the Indians, attired in full war panoply of feathers and paint.

Something familiar in his aspect thrilled through me with lightning rapidity. He came nearer, and the conviction became certainty.

I knew the dress—it was that of the Comanche tribe—and then I recognised the wearer—it was Uwato!

CHAPTER XLIX.

THE BLOODLESS VICTORY—SAN JUAN CAMPESTRANO.

MY astonishment at the sudden appearance of Uwato and the Comanches was intense; but there was no time for hesitation. I decided upon my course of action with the quickness of light.

Tim was by my side. The report of my rifle had brought him to me. He had not recognised Uwato, and, with a whoop of triumph, levelled his piece at the Comanche chief, and pulled the trigger.

Fortunately for Uwato, I saw the movement, and caught the barrel of the weapon just in time. The ball whistled over the head of the Indian chief, and, with a terrible shout, the Comanches levelled their pieces.

Another instant, and they would have been fired. Then a collision would have been inevitable. This I determined to avoid at all risks, and yet I dared not reveal my friendly connexions with the Indians to my guerillas.

Just then one of my men, whose back was towards the Indian, raised his riding-whip as a signal, the comrade of Uwato, whose costume betokened that he was a trapper, fired, and sent him to his last account. I had dreaded something like this, so instantly made up my mind.

I leapt forward in front of the deadly, glittering rifles of the Comanches, and called to Uwato, in his native tongue—

"Hold, my brother, I am Silvershot!"

In spite of his stoic Indian nature, Uwato started back, and his dark eyes flashed as he glanced at me. It was but for a single moment; the next he uttered a command to his warriors, waved his rifle above his head, and turning, sped swiftly away through the long grass, followed by the Comanches.

The surprise caused by the flight of the Indians, and the unexpected change in the aspect of affairs, was great indeed. The guerillas paused for a moment, staring in wonder at the dusky forms retreating over the prairie. Then, with a triumphant shout—

"Alto!" I said, arresting them suddenly. "We will not pursue them, amigos; there is not time. Collect the deer, and return."

A murmur of disappointment passed among the Mexicans. It was not often they gained so easy a victory, and they did not like to be robbed of the fruits.

Tim stared, open-mouthed, at me; and then, putting on a determined look, he shouldered his rifle and said—

"Well, Silvershot, avick, you're the quarist crittur I iver come nigh. Stop, is it, avick!

Faix, not for Tim, till he's had a pop at those thaving redskins."

So saying, Tim prepared to start; but I caught him by the arm.

"You don't know what you are doing, old comrade. That was Uwato, and the Comanches."

Tim started now in bewilderment, and uttered a low whistle.

"Uwato! The divil! And I tried to shoot him!"

"You did," I replied, "and would have succeeded had I not, luckily, thrown up the barrel of your rifle."

Tim grasped me by the hand, and shook it fervently.

"By the mortial, Silvershot! I feel grateful to ye. Shure, if I shot Uwato, I should niver have forgiven meself."

I knew that well, and I breathed more freely now that the danger was over. Then I reflected upon the strange chance that had brought Uwato so far from his country.

A little reflection made the reason plain to me. Alarmed at our long absence, the Comanches had become alarmed, and Uwato had come out in search of us.

Another safeguard, for I knew well that the noble Indian would watch over my safety until the dangers of the prairie were passed.

The guerillas were busily at work, skinning and cutting up the the deer. It was a heavy task, but working with a will, for hunger gave them vigour, it was soon done, and each taking a portion, we returned to the encampment.

Hungry men are not too particular about cookery. Our appetites were enormous, and we soon each had a skinful of broiled venison.

The instant the meal was concluded, I ordered the men into their saddles, and we started again at full speed, never slackening speed until the approach of night compelled us to halt.

We had taken a considerable quantity of the meat with us with an eye to our supper. A blazing fire was soon lit, and the smoking steaks cooked for the hungry Mexicans.

Then there was a short spell of repose as the guerillas assembled round the blazing fire and smoked their cigarettos, talking over the victory of that day.

I was the subject of much admiration, not to say wonder, to the Mexicans; they, judging from experience, had expected a hard fight, and most probably a defeat, when the Comanches charged down upon us, and I had with a few words caused them to take flight. It was incomprehensible to them, and partook of the character of sorcery. I cared not, as this belief of the guerillas heightened their respect for me.

Tired as they were with their long ride, the men now left off talking, and stretched themselves round the fire, and sought in sleep fresh strength for the next day's work.

Tim and I followed their example, first appointing two of the guerillas to keep watch and relieve each other during the night.

With the first beams of the bright sun lighting up the vast level of the llano we awoke, and finished the remainder of the deer meat—for, large as was the quantity we brought with us, it took a great deal to satisfy the appetites of eighty-three full-grown men, for such was the number of our party, all told.

Then, in the saddle again, without a moment's unnecessary loss of time, the ground shaking under the tread of our horses' hoofs, the pure western breeze blowing in our faces, and the bright sun flinging fantastic shadows on the green herbage.

We took no precautions to hide our trail, for, confident in our numbers and our arms, we knew that it was unlikely that we should fall in with anybody likely to prove dangerous.

Tim kept faithful to his task of watching the surly guerilla, for, from the man's looks I felt confident that he intended mischief if he could only get an opportunity. But my comrade's vigilance effectually prevented him from making any attempt upon me.

The guerilla who acted as a guide had well calculated the distance and speed. Just as the sun set, the red gleams of the departing rays gleamed upon the church spires and white-walled rancherias of San Juan Campestrano.

"Hurroo, avick!" shouted Tim, waving his cap in the air. "Faix, Silvershot, avick, we're at the ind of our journey!"

"Of our journey forward, Tim," I replied, "but remember, old comrade, that we have to get back again."

"There ye go, growlin' and grumblin'!" said Tim, with an expression of disgust on his face. "Shure, couldn't yez let me injy me own reflections?"

"All right, old comrade. Go into the looking glass business, by all means, if it suits you."

The deep glow on the western sky had faded into the grey shadows of night before we galloped into the town, and reined our horses up in the centre of the plaza.

The town seemed in a most unusual state of bustle and excitement; the square was full of people, talking and gesticulating violently. I saw at once that something unusual had occurred.

This opinion was confirmed when the people greeted our arrival with cheers, and crowded round us—a most unusual thing, for the guerillas, as a rule, were anything but favourites with their countrymen.

The alcaldé came up to me, and dropping his huge sombrero, with profound politeness, bade me welcome in the name of the inhabitants of Don Juan Campestrano.

"Your arrival is most welcome, senor," he said, "a band of Tejanos, the accursed ladrones, were to-day, pillaging and plundering the poor people; and, senor," here the round, good-tempered face of the of the alcaldé became almost fierce with anger, "the villains, not content with robbing me—the curse of St. Stephano attend them!—stole from me my daughter, 'ay de mi, senor,' she was my only child."

I pitied the poor old man, for his grief was deep and unaffected. A murmur of indignation burst from the crowd, for most of the people had suffered in person or property at the hands of the Texan rangers.

"What can I do, senor?" I replied, after a pause. "How long is it since the men were here?"

"Full five hours, senor."

"Nothing can be done to-night; we must follow their trail to-morrow."

"There is no need, senor," replied the alcaldé, "they promised to visit us again to-morrow, and they will doubtless keep their word; no fear of their leaving us until everything has been forced from us—the accursed ladrones!"

"Ladrones!" echoed the crowd, who, when then heard me promise aid, gave a lusty "vivas."

"Well, senor," I said to the alcaldé, "if you can give me and my men quarters for the night, we will repay you by thrashing the Tejanos to-morrow."

The Mexicans almost fought for the honour of having my men in their houses, and in a remarkably short space of time the guerillas had disappeared.

Tim and I were left with the alcaldé, who had reserved to himself the pleasure of entertaining at supper the captain of the men whom he trusted would do him good service on the morrow.

His house was built on the plaza itself. It was a small, but very neat and compact little dwelling, of only one storey, with the inseparable azotea, or flat roof, where, in the cool of the evening, the alcaldé would take his taso of chocolate and cigar.

The old man gave us a capital supper, some excellent wine and cigars, and did all that was in his power to make us comfortable: in which effort he was admirably seconded by his wife, a stout Mexican matron of five-and-thirty.

We naturally felt tired with our ride, and

soon proposed to our host that we should retire to rest.

The alcaldé rose, and with many apologies regretted that the smallness of his house prevented him from accommodating us, and offered to conduct us to a podesta, where the host could attend to our comfort.

I declined his offer to show us the way, and merely asking to be directed, Tim and I muffled ourselves in our long Mexican cloaks, and taking a hearty farewell, started along the narrow street, all unconscious of a dark figure silently following in our track.

The podesta, or inn, was close at hand; but when we reached it we found that it was nearly full, many of the townspeople, whose houses had been sacked by the Texans, had taken temporary refuge there.

"I have only room for one, senor," said the host, "but if you do not mind roughing it for one night, I have an out-house at the back."

"That will do," said I, closing with the offer at once, for I was terribly tired, and could have slept anywhere.

I turned over the room in the podesta to my comrade, and followed the host to the out-house.

A miserable place enough, under ordinary circumstances—two or three rough wooden stools and some barrels constituted the entire furniture of the place.

I stretched myself upon a pile of skins, and went to sleep directly, all unconscious of a hideous danger lurking near.

For, as I slept on calmly, the rude door slowly and silently opened, and the moonlight lit up a face black with evil passions, the eyes gleaming with the horrible glare of murder.

Noiselessly and stealthily the form stole towards me, the bare blade of a knife gleaming in one hand. Nearer and yet nearer it crept, and I still slept on,

The knife was raised. An instant more it would have descended, and I should have passed from the sleep of life to the wakeless slumber of death; but, at that moment, a second figure appeared in the doorway—a tall, spectral, weird form, armed with a rifle. The figure pulled the trigger. There was no flash of fire, no sound; but the murderer in thought threw up his arms, dropped his knife, and fell back—dead!

CHAPTER L.

SAVED BY THE SPECTRE WARRIOR—DEATH OF THE GUERILLA.

THE noise of the falling body aroused me from the deep slumper into which I had fallen; and, struggling yet with the semi-unconsciousness of sleep, I was dimly conscious for a moment of the presence in the rude hut of someone beside myself; but before my dulled faculties had regained their energy, the figures had gone, and I was alone.

Then, thoroughly awake, I started up and gazed around me, the mental and physical energy that sleep had temporarily deprived me of, restored, and, for the first time, I became instinctively conscious that I had escaped some great danger.

Through the wide-opened door the moonlight still streamed coldly. I knew that the host had closed it when he left me. What could have happened?

At that very moment, my gaze fell upon a dark stain in the centre of the hut, gleaming horridly red in the pale light—it was blood!

Darting forward instinctively, scarce knowing what I did, I followed the horrid trail to the door, and from thence, step by step, round the building into the plaza, lit up by the ghastly bluish moonlight.

Just then a cloud for a moment obscured the light, and I lifted my eyes from the track an instant, and the obscurity vanished; then I started back, uttering an involuntary cry of horror.

It was no trifle that caused a cry of fear to break from the lips of a man who daily—almost hourly—risked his life in the deadly perils of a hunter's existence. It was no ordinary cause that sent the life-blood rushing from my cheeks; for there, in the centre of the square lay a rigid, motionless form, with ghastly features upturned to the starlit sky, and standing over it was a tall, weird form, a form that I knew well, and had hoped never to see again.

It was the Spectre Warrior!

Although I must have been at least two hundred yards distant from the dread apparition, it heard the involuntary cry that I uttered, and slowly lifted up its head, and looked at me.

I could see its eyes bent on me for a moment with a fixed, glassy stare, as it raised its fingers in warning; then, for a second time, a cloud veiled the moonbeams, and when it passed away, the Spectre Warrior had disappeared.

Then a sudden giddiness and sickness seemed to come over me—a film passed before my eyes, I tried to stagger towards the still form that lay in the open plaza, but uselessly. Horror had deprived me of the use of my limbs, and I fell fainting to the ground.

When my senses returned I found myself in the podesta, with Tim standing over me, a flask of what he believed to be the best medicine in the world—whiskey—in his hand.

As I slowly opened my eyes, and stared at him, he uttered a cry of joy, and put the neck of the flask between my lips.

"Hurroo, avick," he said, gladly, "faix,

it's rubbed out I thought ye wur when I found yez lyin' out yonder. Drink, me boy, drink."

Tim tilted up the flask as he spoke, and a quantity of the fiery liquid filled my mouth and throat, nearly choking me.

When I had recovered sufficient courage to relate the terrible scene which had taken place, I told him in as few words as possible.

"Shure, this is dreadful!" said Tim, aghast. "The ghost, though, is a gentleman ivery inch of him, avick; for it's mighty sartin that blay-gaird of a Don John Ramrod meant to murder you."

"Who?" I said, startled for a moment.

"Ramrod, avick—that black-faced thafe I knocked down so nately a while ago."

"Ramorez!" I ejaculated. "You are right, Tim; if it was he, then indeed the Spectre Warrior has saved my life."

"There's no doubt of it at all, Silvershot."

"Where is the body, Tim?"

"In that place where ye slept last night, avick," replied Tim, "wid a lot of the yaller-bellied Mexicans round it, kicking up a hullabaloo."

"Why, Tim, do they think I killed him?"

"Sartint they do; shure I thort so meself till ye told me different."

"I'll go to them, Tim, and explain; though the man did intend to take my life, I don't want the guilt of his murder upon my soul."

I made my way to the outhouse, where I found the dead body of the guerilla with a number of his companions round it.

At my entrance they all looked up and I saw, in a moment, that they believed me to be the murderer. He was no favourite of theirs, but the feeling of nationality made them resent his death at the hands of a foreigner.

They uttered not a sound as Tim and I made our way to the side of the body. It had been laid out upon the floor, and the blood marks washed away from the ghastly white features.

Without taking any notice of the guerillas, who looked on in stern and sullen silence, I knelt on the floor and examined the body.

If any doubt had remained in my mind as to the author of the guerilla's death, it would have been instantly removed, for there were the sure signs of the Spectre Warrior's dreadful work—the bullet-hole in the throat, the scalp gone, and the teeth marks on the neck.

I pointed them out to Tim, and shudderingly he nodded assent. He as well as I had good cause to remember the death of poor Jenny Heywood.

I rose and confronted the guerillas, who still preserving the same threatening silence, waited for us to speak.

"Mexicans," I began, slowly and calmly,

"it needs no words of yours to convince me that I am suspected of killing this man; but, as I am a true man, you are mistaken."

A sullen murmur of incredulity broke from the Mexicans.

In the same calm, deliberate voice, I then narrated all that I had seen, aided by sundry interjections of Tim's, but my audience were not convinced; they knew that the guerilla and I were at enmity with each other, and nothing seemed more likely to them than that I should have killed him.

I pointed to the dead body with my finger, and continued—

"Look there, amigos, is that the work of a Christian man? I might have killed him, but is it likely that a white man would have taken his scalp, or made those ghastly teeth marks in his throat? Can you believe that of me?"

This produced more effect than I had hoped.

The Mexicans seemed to hesitate, and one or two of them advanced, and, stooping, examined the terrible signs the Spectre Warrior had left upon his victim.

Then, one by one, they all advanced and looked. I saw now that they hesitated; but my story of the Spectre Warrior was almost more than they could believe, it was so much easier to think me the murderer.

"Come, now, amigos," I spoke, after a short pause, "the unfortunate man shall be buried to-day, and, with him, all your mistaken suspicions. I will have a dozen masses said in the church of San José, and we will go to the podesta and drink confusion to the murderer."

The promise to have the masses said went a long way to restore me to the confidence of my men—further even than the offer to regale them at my expense, for the Mexicans are most devout Catholics.

With this temporary suspension of hostilities I was forced to be content. I did not wish for an open breach with the guerillas; my purpose was not yet served, and if it had, as at first seemed probable, ended in a fight, the odds would have been terribly against Tim and I, unarmed as we were at that moment.

I did not spare my money when the inn was reached, and, under the influence of the liquor, the Mexicans banished the anger they had felt at the death of their comrade.

I knew, however, that it was more than probable that when the effects of the spirits had passed away they would be more resentful than ever, unless all traces of the unfortunate occurrence were removed.

I quietly gave Tim a hint to this effect, and he departed, promising to see the body interred, a matter of little difficulty, provided the way was paved with a few dollars

All the events had taken place at a comparatively early hour; and before my guerillas had finished their potations, the alcaldé arrived to demand the fulfilment of my promise.

I think the worthy alcaldé must have been a little astonished at the fervour of the reception I gave him, and the eagerness which I showed to be upon the trail of the Tejanos, and recover his stolen daughter.

"The Holy Virgin bless you, senor!" he said grasping my hand. "All I have is at your service if you will only bring back my child."

"That I will," said I, returning the pressure of his hand. "I will only await the return of my lieutenant, who has gone to see the interment of the unfortunate man who was murdered last night."

"Murdered! Santissima Maria!" ejaculated the alcaldé. "By whom?"

I related what had happened as briefly as I could, only suppressing the fact that I was myself suspected.

"Holy Virgin! what a terrible affair!" said the Mexican, aghast; but he did not seem nearly so affected as I thought he would have been—his own trouble seemed to have absorbed his whole attention.

After a moment's pause, he said—

"If you will, senor, I will arrange the interment of the unfortunate man, and you can start at once upon the track of the accursed ladrones.

"Gracias," I replied, "I accept your offer;" then, turning to one of the guerillas, I despatched him in search of Tim Delany, and communicated to the rest my determination to start at once after the Texan rangers.

The men were willing enough. Stimulated by the aguardiente they had consumed, their courage was up to fighting-point.

Ten minutes more saw us in the saddle, and galloping in the direction taken by the rangers on the preceding evening.

We hold on a north-easterly direction, guided by the horse tracks, which were yet fresh and plain. The ground, trampled down for yards, showed that there must have been a considerable body of them.

We followed the trail in this way for more than three miles without coming upon the object of our pursuit.

Suddenly Tim caught me by the arm, and pointed to the horizon.

"There, avick! d'ye see? That's them, shure enough."

I looked, and saw a number of dark specks, at least two miles ahead. I should have at first sight taken them for deer or buffaloes, but a keener survey convinced me that they were horses—and mounted.

To approach them by stealth was impossible; the open prairie afforded no cover; we could only charge them openly. There was not much fear of their avoiding us. The Texan rangers possessed at least the quality of courage.

Spurring my horse to a faster pace, I waved my rifle above my head and shouted—

"Forward, men! For the glory of Mexico, death to the Tejanos!"

CHAPTER LI.

THE RESCUE.—FATE OF THE ALCALDE'S DAUGHTER.

As I had anticipated, the Texans did not make an attempt to fly; on the contrary, when our wild shout and the thunder of our horses' hoofs upon the turf first gave indication of our approach, they reined up, and instantly wheeling about, faced us.

I had no time to count them, but I saw that they were at least equal in numbers to my own party, while their arms were superior; my guerillas having only the native escopettes, the Texans to a man had the long, brown-barrelled rifles, which they knew well how to use.

When we had galloped to within three hundred yards of the Texans, I gave the word to halt. I could not depend well enough upon the guerillas to charge at once the rangers, who had now placed their plunder-laden horses and the captive girl behind themselves, ready for my attack.

There was no need to declare hostilities on the broad prairie—every man's hand is against his neighbour. Besides, the Mexican uniform was enough for the Texans.

"Faix, avick," said Tim, as he pulled up reluctantly, "what are ye goin' to do!"

"We must pick off a few of these fellows, Tim," I replied, "before we charge them. These guerillas of mine have not grit enough; we should be routed in five minutes."

"Thrue, avick," said Tim. "But how are ye goin' to do it, thin?"

"You'll see, old comrade. I'll serve these Texans as the Indians did these very Mexicans when we first met them."

Tim looked puzzled. But I had no time to explain, and turning to the guerillas, I gave the order.

Instantly half-a-dozen shot out, and galloped towards the enemy.

Tim clutched my arm, exclaiming—

"Shure now, Silvershot, thim there are niver goin' to tackle the lot?"

"Wait, Tim," I said; "look to your rifle, and let us see if we can't plug one or two of them from here."

Delany was eagerly and curiously watching the operations of the six guerillas, who were circling round and round the Texans, gradually drawing nearer and nearer, until they had arrived within a hundred and fifty yards or so of the Rangers, who, with their rifles ready in their hands, waited an opportunity to get a shot.

But it was no such easy matter; for just as my guerillas arrived within range, one and all slipped from the saddle, and disappeared behind the bodies of their horses, leaving no mark for their opponents' rifles but the toe of their boots projecting just above the saddle.

A moment, and half-a-dozen sharp reports rang out over the prairie, and three of the Texans fell from their saddles dead, while by the confusion in the ranks I could see that more than one had been wounded.

Delany, carried away by excitement, now dashed at the enemy, and, seeing the danger he was in, I ordered my guerillas to charge.

Another moment we were upon them. Their disorder gave us a great advantage, for many of their rifles had been discharged and not reloaded, in the excitement which Tim's unexpected entry into their ranks had caused.

We fell like a thunderbolt upon them. The sheer force of our charge bore several to the earth, and the remainder, confused and broken, fought but feebly, and were soon overcome or sought refuge in flight.

Our victory was complete, and almost bloodless, so far as we were concerned; but two of my guerillas were wounded, and that but slightly, while the greater part of the Texans lay on the prairie, dead or dying, leaving us masters of the field.

The daughter of the alcaldé, a pretty, dark-eyed little girl, of about sixteen, had remained, trembling, where she had been placed by her captors, in company with the plunder-laden horses.

She was pale with fright, and trembling violently in every limb, as I approached her, and it is certain that my appearance, grimed with gunpowder smoke, and stained in more than one place with blood, was not much calculated to inspire confidence in a timid girl.

"Somos amigos! We are friends," I said, as persuasively as I could. "Do not be frightened, senorita, I have come to restore you to your father."

She looked timidly at my disordered apparel, my rough hair and beard, as if but half reassured by my words, and then, suddenly gaining confidence, she stepped forward and laid her hand in mine.

The day was too far advanced, and our party too tired to undertake the return journey then, so it was determined that we should encamp for the night on the prairie. A rude sort of hut was constructed for the accommodation of Rosina, the alcaldé's daughter, and having lighted a fire and refreshed our-

selves with a hearty meal, we stretched ourselves out to sleep.

CHAPTER LII.

A PERILOUS SITUATION.

I AWOKE suddenly at an early hour the next morning, as if I had been startled in my sleep, and with a strange presentiment that something terrible had happened, sprang to my feet.

There was no apparent cause, all around was deep in the silence of repose, but, nevertheless, it was with an awful dread in my heart that I advanced towards the fire.

The red gleam of the dying embers, now and then flashing into fitful sparkles of light, showed me the still form of Rosina, lying where I had left her but a few hours before.

Something, I know not what, impelled me to stoop down to the graceful figure lying there motionless, the long hair, escaped from its confinement, shading the face and neck, the small hands folded on her bosom.

I called her gently by her name, but she stirred not; then again more loudly, but I obtained no answer.

The same apparently causeless impulse made me lay my hand upon her shoulder and gently shake her.

Her head, which had been turned towards the fire by the motion of my hand, fell backwards, just as a brighter gleam than usual lit up her features and her neck.

Never shall I forget the sickening horror that thrilled through me at that moment—the indescribable awe and fear that seized me, as in that brief moment, I saw the eyes fixed in the glassy stare of death, the bullet hole in the neck, and the ghastly teeth marks that showed the fell work of the Spectre Warrior.

One moment I stood transfixed, petrified with the dread horror of the sight; then I started up, and a stern resolve to fathom the terrible mystery came over me.

I was not superstitious, but in every man's heart there lurks a dread of the unknown and mysterious, and the dark, silent deeds of this awful apparition were sufficient to cause the stoutest heart to quail.

Running back to where I had been lying I seized my rifle, and, without awakening my comrades, took a few steps towards the trees, determined to face the Spectre Warrior, and, man or devil, try whether a bullet from my rifle would not put an end to his hideous career of blood.

I had not far to go, for the unspoken wish to face the fiend was gratified on the instant, for there, his tall, weird form revealed by the fitful flashes of the fire, stood the Spectre Warrior.

I set my teeth firmly together, and cocking my rifle, raised it to my shoulder, and took a steady, careful aim.

The Spectre Warrior was not more than thirty yards from me, and at that distance I could have hit with unerring certainty the smallest mark it was possible to see.

The apparition moved not an inch. It seemed like a statue of mist looming dimly through the semi-obscurity. One instant I glanced along the sights, my aim was true— then I pulled the trigger.

A quick, bright flash, and the sharp report of my rifle rang out upon the still night air. The smoke for a moment hid the figure from my view, and when it cleared away the Spectre Warrior had vanished!

I darted forward to where the figure had stood, but not a trace remained.

Almost before the echoes of the rifle had died away into silence amongst the trees, I was surrounded by Tim and a number of the guerillas, who, awakened by the report of my weapon, came hurrying to me, their rifles in their hands, thinking that we had been attacked by Indians.

Fifty questions were put to me at once by Tim and the excited Mexicans; but, sick at heart and bewildered, I comprehended them vaguely and returned no answer, only gazing now in the direction of the trees, and then toward the fire, by which lay the still form of poor Rosina.

Tim Delany clutched me by the arm, and stared wonderingly in my face.

"Faix, avick, what's the matter wid ye? Is it the thaving red-skins?"

"The Spectre Warrior!" I replied, in such a low, hollow tone that the very sound startled me.

"The Lord have mercy on us!" my comrade exclaimed, starting back, and looking wildly around him. "Where, man alive?"

"Gone," I said; "but he has left a trace of his deadly presence behind him. "Look there!" and I pointed to where the poor Mexican girl lay motionless in death.

With a low cry of mingled rage and horror, Delany rushed to the body: the guerillas could not understand my words, but they did my gesture, and instantly followed Tim.

One of them threw more wood upon the fire, and a bright blaze was mingled with the dull grey glimmer of the morning.

Then arose a succession of cries of rage, horror, and lamentation, as they comprehended the fearful deed that had converted a pretty, light-hearted girl into a hideous, ghastly, lifeless thing.

They had withdrawn from the body, and stood together in a group, conversing in low tones, and ever and anon casting dark, threatening looks towards myself.

The Irishman, brave as a lion in war, was as tender-hearted as a woman, and I saw that his eyes were glistening with a moisture to which they had been strangers for many a long day.

"Well, Tim," I said, laying my hand upon his shoulder, "it is useless staying here. We must go back to San Juan Campestrano, and break the news as best we may to the unhappy parents of the girl."

"Thrue, avick," replied Tim, sorrowfully.

I turned then to the Mexicans who were still grouped together, and looking ominously threateningly at me.

"Mexicans!" I said, "our presence here is useless, and only recals the awful deed done this night. The Spectre Warrior is beyond our reach. Time only can unravel the secret. To horse."

To my surprise, the guerillas did not move an inch. A low murmur only of incredulity came from the group.

Tim now joined me, and observed, for the first time, the angry, threatening looks of the guerillas.

"What is it, man alive?"

"I can't make out, old comrade; wait, and I'll speak to them again."

I addressed the men once more, infusing more of sternness and authority into my voice.

"Why do you not obey me?" I asked. "To horse at once, and the last man mounted shall feel the weight of my displeasure."

Still no movement was made; and now, really angry, I stepped forward, determined to enforce obedience, when one of the guerillas came to the front, and I paused to hear what he had to say.

"We have decided, senor capitano, not to leave here until the murderer of the senorita has been secured. We will not return to San Juan Campestrano without him."

"Willingly," I replied, re-assured now that their motive was explained; "but where is he? Who amongst you can battle with a spectre?"

Again, the low, mocking laugh broke from the band—a laugh of unmistakable contempt and incredulity.

"He is no spectre," said again the man who acted as spokesman; "and we will secure him without going very far from here."

The Mexican stamped his foot on the ground as he spoke, and as if by a preconcerted signal, the rest of the band advanced and surrounded Tim Delany and I.

The real truth of the matter had not yet dawned upon me, and I looked wonderingly at my comrade, who stared vacantly at the circle of dark, angry faces round us.

"I do not understand you," I said again, impatiently.

"And yet my words were simple enough, replied the guerilla. "I say the Spectre Warrior exists but in your fancy."

"Is that a fancy?" I asked, pointing to the body of the unfortunate Mexican girl. "Who has done that?"

"You!" thundered the guerilla, raising his right arm in the air. "And, by the Holy Virgin, you shall pay dearly for it! Down with the accursed murderers!"

The Mexicans rushed furiously upon us. Tim and I sprang back and levelled our rifles; but before we could fire we were seized from behind, and thrown to the ground, and firmly bound hand and foot.

It was now quite light, and the bright blaze of the morning sun lit up the broad bosom of the prairie, flooding it with golden light; the guerillas were busily preparing for departure, some unpicketing and saddling the horses, others, and I could not help giving an involuntary shudder, placing the body of the pretty Rosina upon a rudely-constructed litter.

The preparations were brief and soon finished. Then the guerillas advanced towards Tim and I, with such a look of fierce hatred upon their countenance, that I feared for the moment that they contemplated administering summary justice upon the spot, and leaving our carcases for the prairie wolves.

Such, however, was not their intention. Three of them raised Tim from the ground, and staggering under the heavy weight, bound him to the back of his horse.

Three others paid a similiar attention to me; and all being ready, the horses were headed for San Juan Campestrano at full gallop.

During that ride, short as it was, I suffered intense torture. The thongs with which I was bound cut deeply into me at every fresh jolt of the horse; and I knew, by the muttered execrations of Tim, that he was as badly off as myself.

But the tortures my body suffered were slight compared to those endured by my mind. Sorrow at the horrible death of the poor girl, the remembrance of the terrible vision of the Spectre Warrior, and fearful apprehensions of worse to come rendered my condition anything but enviable, and I groaned in the very bitterness of despair.

CHAPTER LIII.

THE RETURN TO SAN JUAN CAMPESTRANO—THE ACCUSAL—BILL BUCKSKIN AGAIN.

IN a time that seemed terribly short, the town was reached, and our melancholy cavalcade reined up before the door of the alcalde's house.

The approach of the party had been noticed by some of the inhabitants long before it reached San Juan Campestrano, and nearly the whole of the population had assembled to greet our return, little expecting the awful event that had occurred.

The poor alcaldé was among the first, and the crowd made way for him as he advanced eagerly to welcome us, and catch a glimpse of his daughter.

The Mexican who had taken the post of leader dismounted, and respectfully doffing his sombrero, said, with unaffected feeling and commiseration in his voice—

"I hardly know, Senor Alcaldé, how to break the sad news I bring with me. Your daughter"——

The man paused, and the alcaldé's look of amazement deepened into one of horror and despair, as the conviction of the dreadful truth dawned upon him.

The Mexican leader made a sign with his hand, and the guerillas fell back, disclosing the litter and its ghastly burden.

The unhappy father caught sight of it, and with such a cry of utter, heart-rending agony as I hope never to hear again, ran forward, took one look at the body of his daughter, then passed his hand over his eyes, and staggered back as if he had been struck.

"Who has done this?" he said, in a low, hoarse tone—such a tone as might come from the lips of a dead man, were such a thing possible.

The answer was short and explicit. The guerilla simply moved his hand, and pointed to Tim and myself.

The alcaldé started back. He must have suspected it from the manner in which we were bound; but the open accusation startled him when it came.

"Madre de Dios!" he said, in the same tone; "it is impossible!"

"It is true, senor," replied the Mexican, gravely. "They were taken in the act."

"It is enough," he said, averting his gaze from the remains of his unfortunate daughter; "take them away and keep them securely until the morrow. I hold you responsible for their safe custody."

"One word, senor," I said, imploringly, to the alcaldé, as, with his head bent, and hands clasped, he turned towards the door of his house. "I——"

The old man turned and regarded me with a look in which sorrow for the fate of his daughter was mingled with aversion and hate for those whom he supposed had caused his bereavement.

"Not a word," he said, abruptly and sternly. "You shall have speedy justice. More you cannot hope for."

As he concluded he turned and walked slowly into his house.

I heard the groans and muttered execrations of Delany close by me, but I could not, from the manner in which I was bound, see him, until the four guerillas appointed to guard us placed our two horses in the centre, and started for the prison.

Being close at hand it was soon reached, and we were unbound and led into the place.

The place where we were destined to pass the next few hours of our existence was a gloomy hole enough, dark, dirty, and dreary, with no accommodation except an old fur rug or two, which were immediately appropriated by our captors.

The instant they let go their hold of me I sank upon the floor of the cell. Tim did the same, only taking the precaution of dragging a Mexican with him to fall on.

With a fierce carajo the man got up and bestowed a furious kick upon poor Delany, who, too tired and sore to resent the action, grunted inaudibly and instantly fell asleep.

Soon afterwards I dozed off into a sort of half swoon, produced by the anguish of my mind and the intense pain of my aching limbs. The guards looked stolidly on, leaning upon the barrels of their escopettes.

I must have remained in that semi-insensible state for a long time, for it was not until the shades of evening deepened the gloom in the cell that I was awakened by someone shaking me roughly.

"Get up—anda," said the voice of the guerilla leader; "all is ready for the trial."

I complied mechanically, staggering feebly to my feet. I felt sore and bruised, and as weak as a child.

A similar, though stronger shaking, roused Tim from his sleep, and then we were marched out of the prison into the street.

There was a mob of infuriated Mexicans outside; the story of the murdered girl had got about, and, curious as all mobs are, of whatever nation, it had assembled to see the man who had done so fearful a deed.

A volley of curses came from the men, and a volley of stones from the women and children. They were mean in their hate, but it was, unfortunately for us, mistaken.

The guerillas would willingly have consented to the stoning; but, as they were in close proximity to us, several of the stones struck them, and, in self-defence, they were forced to stop the demonstration.

The town-hall of San Juan Campestrano was close by the alcaldé's residence, and a few moments sufficed to bring us there.

Tim and I were hurried in, and we found the alcaldé and a motley collection of rangers, guerillas, and Mexicans eagerly awaiting our arrival.

The poor old alcaldé was seated at the and of the hall, waiting to pass judgment upon those whom he supposed to be the murderers of his daughter. Several of the guerillas were in readiness to bear testimony against us.

The alcalde's face was as pale and stern as I had seen it on the preceding evening; but there was a touching trace of sadness in his features, and every now and then his mouth would quiver and the muscles of his face relax as he gazed upon the mutilated form of his daughter, which was placed upon a bier in the centre of the hall.

Only for a moment did his eyes blaze up with sudden fury, and I saw him clench his hands; it was when Tim and I were brought in and led to our places to be tried.

I glanced mechanically at the assemblage of curious faces, all of which were unknown to me—save one, there was an assemblage of curious faces, with the eyes all turned in one direction, eager to see the man who had perpetrated so horrible a crime in such a manner; and there, in a corner—I started with sheer astonishment when I saw it—was the burly form, and stolid, resolute features of Buckskin Bill!

His eyes were fixed upon me with an expression of the greatest triumph and delight. I saw at once that he had heard of the affair, and had come to rejoice in Tim's and my downfall.

Tim Delany was placed at some little distance from me, with a couple of guerillas between us, to prevent any intercourse taking place.

All was now ready for our trial, and the alcaldé motioned with his hand for the proceedings to commence.

The guerilla, who had assumed the leadership since my accusal, now stepped forward, and a priest swore him over the dead body of the unfortunate Rosina.

Then, in a clear, distinct voice, he gave his version of the murder. The man spoke sincerely, and with a full belief in the guilt of my comrade and myself. But this very belief made him so colour and heighten the suspicions against us, that no one who heard his statement could have done otherwise than believe we were the murderers.

When he had concluded, four others of the guerillas came forward and gave their evidence, each one adding something to the previous statement which tended more and more to strengthen the chain of evidence.

Then there was a pause of a few moments. I looked towards my old enemy, Bill Buckskin, and saw a grin of malignant triumph on his features, as he stepped forward to the centre of the hall, and addressed him to th alcaldé.

Bill spoke Spanish fluently, and there was a great deal of rough eloquence in his nature.

I feared the effect, lest he might say more than anything which had been previously stated; for his evidence would surely and beyond doubt fix the crimes of the Spectre Warrior upon us.

Then Bill Buckskin's deep voice, solemn and impressive in the dead silence, and in the presence of the murdered girl, spoke out—

"What I have to say, Senor Alcaldé, will soon be said, and I am thankful that an accident brought me here in time to see justice done upon two of the blackest villains that ever trod the prairie."

CHAPTER LIV.

THE TRIAL—THE SENTENCE—THE SPECTRE WARRIOR SAVES US FROM DEATH.

THERE was the deep and breathless silence of interest as Bill Buckskin finished his speech.

The Mexicans did not understand a word he said; but the stern, menacing tone was unmistakable, and they waited eagerly for the dénouement.

Then he, who had once been my friend and tutor in the wild sports of the prairie, turned again, and addressed the alcaldé, who, stern and irrevocable, sat upon the judgment-seat, waiting to deliver the sentence that was to avenge his murdered child.

Buckskin Bill told the story of poor Jenny Heywood, and how she had been murdered.

"Now, Senor Alcaldé," he said, in conclusion, "I leave it to you to decide whether or no these men are guilty of the crime. The circumstances are the same, the same marks are found upon the body, and these murders have never take place but when these men are near. Judge, then, decide whether or no there stand those who have personated the Spectre Warrior!"

A long, deep-drawn murmur rang through the assembly at the conclusion of Bill Buckskin's speech, but the end was not yet come. A sentence fitting our supposed crimes had yet to be passed. All eyes were turned towards the alcaldé.

It was some time before he spoke, a mingling of conflicting emotions prevented him uttering the words that longed to escape his lips—the words that were to be the signal of our death, for but a short time elapses in Mexico between the sentence and its execution.

"Prisoners," he said at last, "your crime has been fully proved—proved beyond a doubt, for what the last witness has said fixes the stain of many murders upon your soul. The story you have told of the Spectre Warrior is a fable which even credulous children would be ashamed to believe. How, then, can you expect the men you have wronged to do so? You have committed many crimes; you can suffer but one death; but that shall be as long and painful as your guilt deserves."

The alcaldé paused. Tim and I shuddered. We knew well by hearsay and experience to what refinement the Mexicans had brought the art of torture.

"You," he continued, slowly pausing and emphasizing each word, as if weighing the misery they would cause us. "You are sentenced to be stripped naked, smeared with honey, and suspended from a tree outside the city until the wasps have stung you to death."

Hardened as I was, and inured to scenes of death, a cold shiver ran through me, and my whole frame was paralyzed at the thought of the horrible punishment awaiting me and poor Tim.

Well I knew the torture we should suffer, exposed to the broiling Mexican sun for two or three days, until heat and the poisonous stings of the insects gave us relief in death.

Bill Buckskin was looking at us with an air of the utmost triumph on his hard-featured face. He felt that at last his hour of triumph had come, and his revenge would be satiated together.

Raising my head, I looked at the Alcaldé, who received my reply to the sentence before giving orders to have it carried into execution.

"Senor," I began, and I knew that my voice trembled as I spoke, "the fate to which you have consigned us would be all too merciful were we indeed guilty of the crimes laid to our charge; but by the Holy Virgin, I swear I am innocent. You have said that I have personated the Spectre Warrior. It is false; the demon is a dread reality, and to him alone must the guilt of these murders be laid."

"Ha, ha!" laughed Bill Buckskin, mockingly regardless of the solemn drama of life or death that was being enacted; "the Spectre Warrior indeed! he is a myth, and exists but in your murderous fancy."

And then a voice, deep, clear, and sonorous, but which yet sounded as if coming from the inmost recesses of some cavern, rang out in the midst of the assembly, pronouncing the words—

"You lie!"

And then a shudder of awe chilled and horrified me, as I saw, in the centre of the hall, the tall, weird form of the Spectre Warrior, by the very side of his last victim.

How or whence the apparition had come, I could not tell. I only knew that it was there, leaning on the deadly rifle; its eyes fixed upon Bill Buckskin, who, ashy pale, and his strong limbs trembling like reeds, seemed paralysed with horror.

The effect upon the Mexicans is beyond my power to describe. Always superstitious, and their feelings now worked upon by the mystery of the murders and the trial, the awful and sudden appearance, in their midst, of the dread spectre itself, paralysed them with fear.

The alcaldé was leaning forward, his eyes dilated not so much in fear as in wonder and fierce anger. I saw him rise slowly from his seat, his eyes never wandering from the apparition. Then he took a rifle, which one of the guerillas had placed near him, and, taking aim, fired.

What followed seemed like a dream. I saw the flash, and heard the report which followed, then the whistle of the bullet, as, apparently passing through the spectre, it struck against the wall; then the mocking laugh of the demon as he slowly turned and faced the alcaldé.

The old man's anger turned to awe, and I saw his face pale with fear.

The rifle dropped from his nerveless grasp. He was unable to move. The spectators of the awful scene seemed changed into statues, only their deep breathing could be heard.

Until now my whole attention had been fixed upon the Spectre Warrior, but a sudden movement at my side caused me to turn, and I saw Tim Delany take a rifle from one of the guerillas, and aim it at the demon.

My comrade was not twenty yards from the Spectre Warrior, and to miss at that distance seemed an impossibility. I waited breathless for the result. I saw the jet of flame dart from the muzzle, and then a cloud of smoke hid the apparition from our view. When it cleared away, the Spectre Warrior was gone!

Dropping the weapon on the ground, Tim darted to the place where the Spectre had stood, but not a trace of its presence remained. It had vanished as mysteriously as it had come.

Then the silence was broken, and the guerillas crowded round the bier, exclaiming in wonder and awe at the vision. One thing was certain—the Spectre Warrior had saved us from a dreadful and imminent death.

Bill Buckskin was the first to come up and speak to us. He had not recovered from the fright. His features were pale, and his strong hand trembled like a leaf as he held it out to me.

"There, Silvershot," he said, fervently, "take that. Darn me, if ever I thought that we should meet again in friendship."

I took the proffered hand, and gripped it heartily. I could readily forgive him all he had done, for I well knew that he had only endeavoured to punish me for a crime of which he believed me guilty.

Tim received a similar attention from the burly trapper, and then the alcaldé came forward, and by the dead body of his child, begged of us to pardon him for the injury he had so unwittingly caused us, and the horrible death to which we should have been doomed had it not been for the timely appearance of the Spectre Warrior.

"Say no more, senor," I said. "We have escaped, and that is sufficient. This awful mystery is as yet beyond our comprehension; time will, perhaps, solve it; until then we must wait."

I then shook hands with the grief-stricken old man, and with Tim turned to depart.

The guerillas, though they had assembled round us, had not as yet testified otherwise than by looks their shame and regret at the manner in which they had treated us; but as we were departing, the leader came up, and, with many protestations of sorrow, offered, in the name of his comrades, to again place themselves under my command.

I scarcely knew how to reply. Bill Buckskin was once again my friend, and perhaps he might be induced to give up the map of the Comanche treasure-cave, which it had been the object of my journey to recover.

My resolve was quickly made. I decided at once to have an interview with the old trapper, and tell him my object. In his present state of mind, there would be little difficulty, I thought, in inducing him to comply.

Making a promise to meet the guerillas the next morning and give my answer, I asked Bill Buckskin to accompany me to the podesta, and in company with Tim, started at once, full of hope and gladness at the lucky turn my affairs had taken.

CHAPTER LV.
THE MEETING—A PERILOUS RIDE ON THE WILD HORSE OF THE PRAIRIE.

My intercourse with the alcaldé was not so favourable as I had anticipated. The old man was so borne down with grief that he was forced to seek retirement, and so I left the podesta with a heavy heart.

"Cheer up, Silvershot," said Tim, when he saw me looking so downcast. "Avick! now, look there," he added, pointing to a man mounted on a strong black steed that was galloping swiftly towards us.

"Ike Brushton!" I exclaimed, as soon as I recognised the man's face. "What are you doing here?"

"Well, I've come to congratulate you on your lucky escape, and to give you a chance of letting this affair blow over. Come with me for a few days; by that time things will settle, and the girl will be buried."

ON A SWELL OF THE PRAIRIE STOOD THE SPECTRE WARRIOR BEFORE US.

"Not at all a bad plan," said I; "but where do you intend going?"

"Well," replied he, looking me full in the eyes, "I am the head of a party of mustang hunters. You like sport, Silvershot; come with me, and you shall have it."

Bill Buckskin and Tim joined him in his persuasion, and soon we were mounted and on the way to the hunting ground.

Fortunately we soon sighted a herd after reaching the range.

The night before, a fine shower had fallen, and the animals were so much occupied in feeding upon the new, green, and tender grass that they had not noticed our approach.

The old leader was nowhere to be seen, and Ike Brushton, suspecting that he was in search of water in yonder barranca (ravine) directed his two best vaqueros, with their lassoes, to dismount, and to move cautiously under cover of that little clump of timber, and, with the wind in their favour, to reconnoitre the place.

The men reached the timber, and then drawing themselves noiselessly along the ground, reached the edge of the barranca without being discovered by the mares.

Finding a suitable place, one of them crossed the gulley, and gained the top of the other bank, and the two passed cautiously along, one on each side.

From where we had halted I could see all the motions of the men.

I was observing them with excited interest, when I observed the one on the opposite side of the barranca rise suddenly to his feet, and swing his long leathern thong over his head, gave it a wide cast out over the gully.

At the same instant the other man also threw his lasso, and we could see by the tugging at the ropes that some animal had been ensnared.

A glad shout now told of their success, and sinking the rowels into the sides of our animals, we were soon upon the edge of the ravine.

Below there, by the edge of a water-hole, the vaqueros had discovered the leader of the herd.

The noble creature was struggling in the coils of the two lassoes, both of which had been skilfully thrown over his beautiful, arching neck, and the captured horse essayed in vain to escape their fatal embrace.

With wild cries of terror and rage, the old horse gave the alarm, and the excited mares, with ears erected, and manes and flowing tails upon the breeze, gathered from every direction, and rushing together, like a body of mounted cavalry, approached the edge of the barranca at a little distance, and gazing a moment upon the fierce struggle of their leader, uttered wild cries of alarm, and then, in one compact troop, bounded away over the plain.

After a severe struggle with the desperate and vicious animal, whose strength was not a match for the skill of his captors, we succeeded in getting him out of the barranca upon the level ground.

But when once there, and he caught sight of the beautiful harem, as it continued to sweep in a wide circle about the spot, all his efforts to escape were redoubled, and the fierce cries of the baffled creature were painful to hear.

For a time it required all the cunning of the Mexicans to prevent his escape; but when at length they managed to throw him upon the ground, and slipped a close bandage over his eyes, it was but the work of a moment to bind the secure wooden saddle to his back, and force the terrible jaw-breaking bridle into his mouth.

This was done,—and Ike Brushton turning to me, bid me tighten my sash, and prepare to mount the panting and furious horse.

"Come, Silvershot," said he. "You have been long anxious to break a wild mustang; and now is your chance. You shall have it to boast, that you have ridden, for the first time, the noblest animal on the plain! Ready, my men!"

So saying the old hunter made a sign to the vaqueros to slip the lassos quietly from the still prostrate horse. As he felt his neck and limbs relieved from the pressure of the ropes, the horse sprang trembling to his feet. But no sooner had he risen from the ground, than I was securely seated in the saddle, with bridle reins firmly grasped in my hands.

At that moment Ike approached the head of the horse, and with a skilful motion relieved him of the bandage which had been covering his eyes.

No sooner had the blinder been removed than I felt the gallant mustang swell beneath me, as he inspired a breastful of the free air, and then, with an exultant neigh, which was heard by the still circling herd, and fiercely answered back to him, he gathered his feet together beneath him, and threw himself with a sudden bound at least ten feet into the air, then he threw his head aloft, and switching his long, beautiful, glossy tail from side to side, darted like an arrow over the plain.

Bracing myself firmly in my stirrups, and closing my teeth, while I grasped the bridle, I gave him free rein. As I felt myself borne swiftly through the yielding air, at a rate I had never before experienced, my pulse leaped within me with a wild joy.

Without swerving an inch from his course the flying horse bore directly towards the rising ground, where the mares had halted; and forming themselves into an extended line, were gazing with elevated heads and straining eyes upon their approaching lord. As he drew nearer he seemed to increase his speed; and filling the air with neighs of glad recognition, had already reached the foot of the slight ascent, when, for the first time, the herd discovered the strange object upon his back. But an instant only did they stand their ground after making this discovery, for now they wheeled suddenly about, and fled away again towards the horizon.

Still the noble animal pressed after them, scarcely touching the ground as he flew, and we were again gaining upon the herd. So much excited was I by this headlong rush, that I was not aware of the distance that lay between me and my companions till, on ascending another eminence of the gently rolling prairie, I cast my eyes over the plain we had passed, and was surprised to find that I had left them out of sight.

I now determined to retrace my steps, and rejoin them; and for this purpose began to bear upon the powerful lever of my mustang bit, an instrument so constructed that the ordinary force of a child's arm is sufficient to break the jaw of the strongest animal. It was necessary to check my horse's speed before I attempted to turn his head in the opposite direction.

But no sooner did I exert a little pressure upon my bridle reins for this purpose, than, to my horror, I saw the knot that confined the headstall at the top of the head slip from its fastening, and dragged apart by the weight of the heavy iron bit, fall over each cheek of the flying horse.

I now became alarmed, but still retained my presence of mind, and endeavoured, by a continued strain upon the reins, to keep the bit in his mouth. But, as if aware of what had occurred, the animal, regathering all his energies, threw himself into the air, and tossing his head till it came in contact with my own, with an almost stunning blow freed its mouth entirely of the bit, which fell uselessly upon his muscular breast.

I was now entirely at the mercy of the frantic brute, and it is impossible to imagine a situation more terrible than mine was then. Unless some providential interference should come to my relief, I was certain a fearful death awaited me. Onward rushed the horse with redoubled speed—a speed that made it almost impossible to catch my breath; and with such force did the air impinge upon my face that it seemed as if the blood was starting from the skin. A few more flying leaps, and we were in among the kicking and snorting herd!

My friends must have been miles away, for I could see no signs of their approach, if, indeed, they had mounted and given chase after me. This, however, I could not doubt; and this thought encouraged me to cling to my firmly-girthed saddle.

At length an idea occurred to me. It was this: I might kill the noble brute beneath me; I might let out his hot blood upon the plain, and as his glorious strength should desert him by degrees, safely free myself from him. Inspired by this new-born hope, I felt for my knife; but I uttered a cry of disappointment as my hand came in contact with the empty sheath—I had lost the blade. But, as if directed by some good angel, my silken sash now becoming loose, and its ends streaming behind me, attracted my eyes.

"Thank God!" I exclaimed, as I caught at it, and hastily unwound it from my waist; for another plan of escape had suddenly suggested itself to my mind.

Not a moment did I lose, but burying my long rowels in the lathery flanks of the horse, which caused him to throw his head suddenly upwards, I threw a coil of the sash about his neck, and hastily knotting it tightly, grasped the circlet with one hand, and with the assistance of my sheath, twisted it with a vice-like grip about his throat.

The effect was instantaneous; for as the animal felt the painful pressure upon his windpipe, he suddenly checked his speed, and in another moment broke into a staggering and undecided trot; and as I took another turn in the ligature, came to a dead halt; and by desperate efforts, endeavoured to free his throat of the choking circlet.

His bloodshot eyeballs protruded from their sockets; and as I took still another turn in my sash, I felt his limbs tremble convulsively beneath me, and he fell first upon his knees, and then, with a gurgling choking groan, tumbled over upon his sweat-reeking side.

Without an effort, I sprang to my feet, still, however, retaining my hold upon the twisted sash.

The noble creature was now completely conquered; and relaxing a little the strong grip I had upon his throat lest he might die of suffocation, I restored the bridle to his mouth, and knotting the headstall securely to its place, snatched the sash entirely from his neck.

In another instant he was upon his feet, I was once more securely seated upon his back. The frightened mares were still scudding away, as I turned my already half-broken mustang upon the back-track, and gave him the sharp points of my spurs. Again we went flying over the prairie; but not at the rate we had come; and by the time I met Tim Delany and Ike, who were in search of me, the beautiful creature might have been safely mounted by a child.

CHAPTER LVI.
THE SIOUX INDIANS AND THE VICTIM AT THE STAKE.

IT was a wild spot, and why Ike Brushton had chosen it for our encampment I could not for the life of me imagine, until he led me through a dense scrub, and showed me as beautiful a patch of pasture land as ever my eyes beheld.

It was shut in on the three sides by the tall heavy timbers, and on the fourth was a pure rippling stream, that bounded from rock to rock, on the hilly slope of which, on the other side, we could see the red deer grazing unconscious of our presence.

As I stood watching the noble creatures, I was surprised to see Tim Delany and two of the vaqueros creeping up the hill side. Tim with his rifle slung across his shoulder and his hunting knife clasped in his hand; the vaqueros with their lassos ready for use, so soon as they were near enough to do so without startling the herd.

Already some dried wood had been gathered and was fast kindling into a flame. After my long and perilous ride, I needed some refreshment, and indeed so did the whole of our little party.

"Well, Silvershot," said the old hunter, who noticed that I was nervously twitching the stock of my rifle, "you doubtless think our manner of hunting queer and tedious. One false aim and the deer would be out of sight——"

"Indeed, I do," said I, interrupting him. "I could put a bullet through the heart of either one of the creatures at this range; but "——

"I have a motive for what I do," replied he. "One shot from your rifle might cost us our scalps. Large parties of the cut-throat Indians are always prowling about these parts. Hark! did you hear that?" he exclaimed, clutching my arm.

I listened; what I had heard made me shudder for the moment.

"The death-chant of the Sioux Indians," I replied.

"Yes," said he, "they are at their fiendish work; some poor wretch has fallen into their devilish clutches."

I turned to Ike. "Shall we let them carry on their bloody work without interruption?" I said, "and so near to us, too?"

"We can mount and leave them," replied he, carelessly; "my scalp is too valuable to lose in the cause of a stranger."

I turned from him in disgust, and I noticed Tim's face suddenly assume an angry frown.

"We will go alone, Tim," I said, addressing the plucky Irishman.

"Bedgad, so we will, Silvershot. Arrah! who knows but what it may be one of our old chums they've got a howlt of? St. Pathrick! how the devils howl; come on, boys, at oncet."

Ike Brushton, on seeing that we were resolute, offered to accompany us; he led the way, and we followed.

Louder and louder sounded the death-song, and we quickened our pace, heedless of the dense foliage and tangled brush-wood that barred our progress, until we came to an opening in the timber, and then we caught sight of the half-naked monsters in a deep hollow, flanked by precipitous rocks.

A band of some fifty Sioux Indians were collected there, and they were under the command of Owl Wing, a chief of that tribe. A maiden, just verging into womanhood, was to be the victim. She was clad after the fashion of a forest-queen, but her face gave evidence of the fact that she was of white origin.

So tightly had she been lashed to a mountain-pine that she could not move. She was listening to the words of the chief, but she exhibited no fear.

She was bound with green thongs, and a score of rifles were pointed at her heart. They were waiting the word of command, and the bloody work would be done. The old chief stood near. The expression of his face was calm, although his eyes denoted anger. Then he spoke—

"Let her not die the death of a warrior. We fall in battle, our hearts pierced with bullets, and the death is a glorious one, for we die in defending the graves of our sires and our homes. The only pang we feel is, that we must receive death at the hands of the accursed paleface. One who has proved herself a traitress to her race should not so perish. Throw aside the rifle, and take up the bow and arrow."

A wild yell broke from the lips of the dusky band as the command of their leader was spoken, and the captive watched them. They threw aside their rifles, and, seizing their bows and arrows, stood awaiting further orders. They came.

"A traitress should die by torture. Pierce her body with your shafts, but do not strike a vital part. Let her death be a lingering one, that she may feel her punishment."

The bows were bent, but the chief continued—

"Let not an arrow fly until I give the word of command.

Then, as if speaking his thoughts, Owl Wing muttered—

"She does not flinch. She is fit to live. But can I save her now? I fear it is too late."

Then, approaching the maiden, he said—

"You have broken our laws, and death must be your portion. I must pronounce your sentence. I must see that sentence executed. Can you forgive me?"

"Need you ask me?" replied the maiden, scornfully. "Does the squaw mourn for her child when she has sacrificed it to the great Manitou? Answer Azalu this, and then say whether the chief of the great Sioux nation would heed the chidings of the prairie flower."

"He would not. Owl Wing is too bold a warrior to shed tears like a squaw."

"Then I forgive you all, and with my last breath will pray the Great Spirit to bless and protect you."

The chief appeared to be deeply moved, and turning to his warriors said—

"You see, I give up all for your sakes. She has merited death, and she shall have it, if such is your decision. Shall she die, or will you spare your prairie queen?"

"She must die!" was the general response.

"I will keep her a close prisoner. She shall not again betray us to the palefaces. Owl King has said."

"She must die!" again echoed the savage wretches.

For some time the old chief did not speak. At length, turning to Azalu, he said—

"My child, you have always been faithful to us until you committed this last act of treachery. Will you tell me what prompted you to do so?"

"Yes, I will tell you all, and in the presence of the Great Spirit before whom I shall soon appear. Will you believe that Azalu speaks truly?"

"I will."

"From my earliest recollections I have been among you, and I have always been treated kindly. I loved you all, but I did not love your deeds of blood. The tiger and the wolf will destroy the poor antelope, and we hate them for it; the serpent will devour the little bird, and we kill the reptile. Why should we, who can count our warriors by the thousands, seek to destroy the palefaces, who are few in numbers and weak?"

"You are mistaken. The palefaces outnumber us a thousand to one. Their homes are beyond the great waters. If they come here to seize our lands, we must drive them back. We must do this before they arrive in great bodies and crush us, or drive us back into the ocean."

"My father is mistaken, the Great Spirit has turned his face from him, or else why does he try to steal upon the palefaces by night? I love the palefaces, and for what I have done I fear not to suffer a just punishment."

"Waugh!" growled the old chieftain, "the red man hates his foes. You are a traitress, and you must die, die with the pleasure of knowing that you are not my child; but the daughter of one of the accursed race—your father was a settler."

"And you were his murderer. Ah! I know all this."

"Ugh!" vociferated the old chief fiercely, "Azalu speaks falsely; the torture and the stake shall make "——

"I fear it not," said the brave girl, defiantly. "Let your red-skinned warriors do their worst. Azalu will not flinch."

"Brave girl!" I heard Tim mutter, and I could see by his looks that he was already in love with her.

I caught his arm, as I heard the lock of his rifle click.

"Tim—Tim," I whispered, "for heaven's sake, lay quiet!"

"Be me sowl, I cannot, Silvershot," he replied, in an agitated voice. "Avick, do ye not see what the blaygairds are about? Och, Saint Dinnis, jist let me have a slap at that ould curmudgeon!"

I had a hard job to keep Tim from gratifying his wish—in fact, I had some difficulty to restrain my own desire of putting a bullet through the ould chief's carcase; for I saw

him sign to the two naked savages, daubed with the war-paint, who stood near the stake, and they prepared to obey his horrible mandate.

I and Tim shuddered, and old Ike Brushton, who was not so accustomed to Indian brutality as we were, almost fainted at the sight.

I have seen many a brave man die, and many a bold warrior suffer torture at the stake in my time, but never before had I seen so much heroic devotion displayed by a female as on this occasion.

Pale, but resolute, she stood, facing her fiendish executioners, or torturers, rather, for the death that Owl Wing had doomed her to was a thousand deaths in itself.

I knew what the wretches were about when I saw them draw their sharp knives, and strip off small pieces from a knob of resin pine. They were about to thrust the sharp splinters into the girl's tender flesh, and then set fire to them.

By this means her body would be burning all over at once, inflicting horrible torture, yet doing but little vital injury. In this manner I had seen the victim writhe for hours, therefore it is no wonder that my very marrow seemed to crawl.

CHAPTER LVII.

THE MYSTERIOUS RIFLE-SHOT—WHITE EAGLE TO THE RESCUE—AZALU IS SAVED BY MY GUERILLAS.

TIM DELANY was now in a fever of anxiety.

"Tare an ouns!" he burst out, "I can bear it no longer, Silvershot. See how the murthering villains are tearing off her delicate clothing, and exposing her tinder white limbs."

I snatched the rifle from him as he levelled it at the old chief's head.

"Wait your time, Tim," I said. "See! the old man relents. Hark now! listen to his voice."

The old chief faltered. He made a sign for the painted barbarians to desist; then he said—

"Draw your bows, now; let your arrows pierce her flesh, but strike no vital part. She must feel what it is to die the death of a traitress."

This command had scarcely been spoken, when a single rifle-shot rang out, and with a wild yell, the chief leaped into the air, and fell forward upon his face, dead.

For an instant the savages were thrown into confusion; then, with terrific shrieks they dashed towards a rocky ledge, from whence the messenger of death came.

Two more shots were fired, and a savage fell at each; then the avenger was discovered

He fought desperately with his knife, but he was soon overpowered and bound. He was so covered with blood as scarcely to be recognisable; but as the red monsters gazed upon him, they exclaimed as with one voice—

"White Eagle, the hunter!"

"My father!" echoed Azalu, "then you are not dead?"

"Yes, Annie, I am your father, murmured the old man. "These fiends stole you from me years ago, and I have sought for you in vain. But a few moments since my eyes first fell on my child, but I should have known her, even had I not heard the words of Owl Wing."

"But he told me you were dead."

"He struck me down, but I was not killed. Heaven has spared my life for this hour, and for this meeting."

"Father, we meet but to die together."

"Courage, my child."

And the old settler swept the plains with his eye, but nothing could be seen to give him hope, and he murmured—

"O, will they come? They should have been here before this."

The savages had given little heed to their captive after having bound him, but they were busily engaged in collecting combustible materials. It was evident he was to be burned at once. The preparations were complete, and White Eagle was lashed to a tree, while the brushwood was heaped around him. Their yellings were constant and fearful.

Suddenly another single shot rang out from behind the same rock from whence the first had come. The fiends turned in that direction again, only to receive a volley from our rifles. The Indians became panic-stricken, and such as were able fled from the spot with all their speed.

But too late; we pursued them hotly, and a party of my guerillas dashed down from the steep rocks and joined in the chase.

The fight was a desperate one. The Indians, seeing that escape was hopeless, turned upon us like a pack of howling wolves, shouting their war-cry, and fighting desperately with their tomahawks and knives.

It was a hand-to-hand struggle, for there was no range for the rifle. The Indians were hemmed in on all sides, so that those who escaped had to cut their way through a wall of men that compassed them about.

Those that did escape were few. Forty dead bodies of Sioux we counted lying on the ground, and several others wounded, past the possibility of recovery.

The captives were then liberated. A couple of powerful mustangs were placed at their disposal; but before starting for San Juan Campestrano we sat down to refresh ourselves, and a hearty meal we made of the deer Tim had brought in.

It was then that we learnt from the White Eagle the cause of what we had seen, and I will repeat his story in as few words as possible.

It was shortly after the Texans had made a raid upon San Juan Campestrano, and carried off the alcaldé's daughter, Rosina, that a band of Sioux Indians, numbering some five hundred strong, hung about the outskirts of the town, with the intention of attacking it and revelling in bloodshed and plunder.

They had kept themselves carefully concealed; so those in the town did not dream that so powerful an enemy was near.

It was the close of a lovely autumn day when they collected on the southern bluffs overlooking the stronghold and in plain sight of the place. But a short time before there had been a large number of troops present, but it was known to the savage that many of them had just been removed to different points.

How large a force remained he could not tell, so he resolved to send Azalu forward to ascertain. The presence of one Indian maiden, he was aware, would attract no especial attention; and, at tattoo, she could gain the required information.

Little did Owl Wing imagine that my hardy guerillas were in the town; for the regular soldiery he cared but little, but guerilla warfare was too hot for him to stand against.

It was with an expression of pleasure that the poor maiden set out under the pretext of performing her mission. But other thoughts filled her mind and controlled her actions.

Scarcely had she departed when an Indian scout came in, and reported to the chief the fact that the soldiers were gone.

A midnight surprise was almost sure to be successful.

It was resolved to make the assault without waiting for the return of Azalu, unless she should make her appearance before they were ready.

"She will not return—she intends to betray us!" exclaimed one of the warriors, addressing the chief.

"Then follow her. If she proves herself a traitress, bring her back alive if possible. If you cannot do that, leave her lifeless body behind you."

The savage needed no further bidding.

He mounted his pony, and rode over the bluffs, down the northern slopes.

He passed on towards the town, and at length reached the building, which was used as the head-quarters of the alcaldé.

One solitary light was burning, and attracted the attention of the savage.

While he was thus watching, he saw Azalu

cross the plaza. She mounted the verandah, and thus gained the open window, through which she shortly after disappeared.

It was the work of a moment for the Indian to follow.

The room which Azalu had entered was that in which the alcaldé slept; but he had not yet retired to rest. He started, just as if the Spectre Warrior had made his appearance again, when the brave girl stood behind him.

The Indian ground his teeth savagely when he saw the alcaldé's countenance change, and he rose to give the alarm upon the information he had received.

The Indian determined to prevent him from doing so. Clutching his tomahawk, he leaped into the apartment, and then he raised the weapon with both hands above his head; but, before he could deal the fatal blow, the alcaldé sprang to his feet and raised an alarm.

The savage knew that instant flight was necessary now, in order to save himself. He seized Azalu in his powerful arms, and, passing through the window, sprang to the ground, and ran with the speed of a deer towards the wood.

He found his horse secure, and, mounting, he dashed out of sight, with the maiden still in his arms, while his wild whoop of defiance rang out upon the night air.

The alarm thus given, the night attack was abandoned, and the majority of the band sent in different directions upon missions of blood. About fifty remained with the chief; and these took up their temporary quarters at the base of the ragged peak which was about forty miles from San Juan Campestrano, and where, had it not been for the timely arrival of my guerillas, she would have suffered a most horrible death.

CHAPTER LVIII.

THE LOG CABIN—THE INDIANS SEEK TO BE REVENGED.

HAVING finished our repast, and refreshed ourselves with a horn of brandy, we prepared for our homeward journey, as we did not like the idea of camping so near the scene of slaughter for the night.

"Well, Tim, what do you think of it now?" I said, as Tim and I, side by side, fell in at the rear of the cavalcade.

"Don't ask me, shure; I'm just wondering whether old White Eagle will object to me having his daughter."

"You will not ask him, unless you are mad," I replied, laughing. "Whatever ails you—are you going crazy?"

"I'm in love, Silvershot, and I can't help it; that girl's eyes seem to haunt me. Did you not see the look she gave me, shure? Faix, she's in love wid me, or—"

"Tut, tut, man. You remind me of the sailor who had a wife in every port. Have you forgotten the lovely Comanche maiden?"

"St. Denis! I'd forgotten all about her. But there, she is a long way off, and maybe I shall never see her again. How confoundedly dark it's getting, Silvershot."

"My friend capitano," said White Eagle, approaching me, "we shall have it down upon us like a thunderbolt presently. Hark! do you not hear how the wind is rising?"

"We must strike in among the thick timber," I replied; "there is no chance of any better shelter hereabout."

"We shall see. Let us push on, all depends upon the progress we can make while it is light."

For some time after we had entered the forest I was buried in deep thought, reflecting upon the strange adventure that had brought us to the rescue of Azalu, when the voice of the hunter, who had undertaken to be our guide, commanded a halt.

Through the gloom, I could just make out the dim outlines of an old log hut, and very glad were we to find such a shelter for our weary limbs.

We made up a bed for Azalu with our furs and blankets and she laid down to rest awhile until supper was ready.

Of course, we were all anxious to hear how it was that Azalu had fallen into the hands of the Sioux Indians, but the rustling of the foliage, and the creaking of the old pine logs, which threatened to come down about our ears, prevented us from hearing each other speak.

We smoked our pipes in silence until the fury of the whirlwind had passed, and then the moon shone out, and we were enabled to see to the horses and to look round the hut and see what damage the storm had done.

Towards morning we heard a mysterious noise outside the hut, and after a little deliberation it was agreed upon that two should go out and reconnoitre. Tim Delany and White Eagle were chosen; the rest of us waited anxiously for their return.

White Eagle, however, came back alone, and I, alarmed for Tim's safety, went in search of him.

I had a guerilla with me, a timid sort of a fellow he seemed to be. He said—

"I could ha' swore that I seen an Ingin's face when I glanced up. But when I turned my eyes there as quick as I could think, nothin' of the kind appeared."

"Most likely it was fancy," I observed, and he seemed to feel the same conviction. Still both of us kept up a stricter search than before, fearful in proportion as the dawn brightened.

Our worst fear was that poor Tim was in the hands of the redskins, and that they had taken him away, to put him to the torture, perhaps to make him confess where the girl was hidden, and that I knew he would not do, even to save his own life.

CHAPTER LIX.

WE DISCOVER TIM DELANY—THE INDIANS COMMENCE THEIR WORK.

IT was a time of fearful suspense to me as Jack Linchling and I pursued our way through the dense forest, trying by every means to strike the trail of either Indian or hunter.

At last, however, we succeeded. On a soft piece of earth we found the impression of a man's boot.

It was Tim Delany's. I could swear to it among a thousand.

But what was the light impression that caught my eye now and then?

It was the mark of an Indian mocassin. Tim was assuredly followed—not at all unlikely he had been lured away by some crafty stratagem.

With our eyes ready to catch the slightest object moving, and our eyes strained to catch the least sound, we threaded the mazes of the dense forest, unmindful of the distance we were placing between ourselves and the log-cabin.

At length we found ourselves ascending a narrow pathway between thick bushes; and, as we proceeded, the ground became hard and rocky, and we had some difficulty in keeping the trail we had so carefully followed.

The guerilla did not follow me so wilingly now. He seemed to have a sort of dread upon him. He fell back; but I pushed upward until my way was completely blocked up with the tangled undergrowth.

If Tim had come that way, where could he have gone to? He could not have gone back again, or we must have met him.

I had been in the bushes but a few minutes when I heard a confused scrambling, which announced that some one was entering the retreat.

Presently the form appeared, and, from the wild beard, I knew it to be none other than Jack Linchling.

"Ah, Jack, you are here," I said, when he was within speaking distance. "All right?"

"Yes. Have you seen Tim?"

"No," I replied.

After this we retraced our way some distance down the steep path, when all of a sudden we heard a strange noise.

"Lay quiet," I whispered to Jack; "the Indian skunks are concealed somewhere about here; let us hide."

We did so, but the place into which we had crawled was hardly large enough for two, and so we crept back into the daylight, and with careful woodcraft prepared to make our way back to the cabin.

"I wish I could discover poor Tim, and learn, if nothing else, what has been his fate," I muttered unconsciously aloud.

"Faix, thin, you can have your wish," replied a voice. It was evidently somewhere near to us, but where, that was the question.

Presently I saw a head thrust up through a hole in the rock, and pleased enough I was to see the face of my old companion.

"You are there, Tim," I exclaimed; "are you all right?"

"Hold your whist, avick, unless you want a bullet through you. The spalpeens have got on the wrong scent, and now they're trying to correct their error. Och, blood an' 'ouns, look out, Silvershot!"

CHAPTER LX.

THE EXPLOSION.—TIM HAS A NARROW ESCAPE.

I HEARD Tim's caution, but before I could reply there came the report of a rifle not far away, and the bullet went crashing through all that opposed it, a foot or two above our heads. While the first blank look of dismay remained upon our faces other shots followed, and other balls flew, not so far away from the main mark as the first.

Luckily we were between two large fallen trees, so that by dropping upon the ground we were completely sheltered from shots coming in any direction.

In a little while the firing was discontinued, and we instinctively knew that some more dangerous demonstration would speedily follow.

A dull hissing and crackling soon came to our ears; the scent of fire and smoke to our nostrils; while by looking below us we could see a column of smoke winding upward.

"Great heaven!" cried Jack, "they are going to smoke us out!"

"Quick! quick! We must escape from this place," said Tim.

But how? The flames would travel through that thicket faster than we could hope to make our way, and of course the watchful savages would stand in readiness to shoot us down whenever we might appear.

To add to our distress, the vapour from the damp leaves, mingled with flame and smoke, almost choked us, for the crafty savages had fired the bush to windward of the little eminence on which we stood.

There was but little time for reflection, however, one hasty glance I took of our position, and I cautioned Delany, who was coolly loading his rifle, not to expose the powder too much, as the sparks were falling in a scintillating shower around us.

Either Tim did not hear me, or my warning was unheeded; a few grains fell from his pouch, there was a sharp phizz, and the rest of the powder exploded in his hand, sending the rifle whirling through the opening in the bushes we had made with our knives.

The shock for a moment staggered us all; but a shout from the exulted Indians restored us to our senses. And when the smoke partly cleared away, I found that my friend Tim was unhurt.

Jack, who was standing near him at the time of the explosion, was less fortunate; his clothes took fire, and every bit of hair was scorched from his head and face, as clean as though he had been shaved.

To extinguish the fire was an easy matter, my hands were certainly blistered a little; but of that I took no heed; I would not have cared if they had been more severely burnt, could I have extinguished the flames that were making our ambush too hot for us.

"Bedad, Silvershot, this will never do; we must move out of this or be roasted alive, shure. Look ye, the very stones are cracking under our feet," said Delany.

"What can we do?" asked the guerilla, looking at me as though he expected an answer, "must we face the red-skinned varmints, or"——

"Stay here till the fat's fried out of us," chimed in Tim.

"Face them, of course," I replied, sternly. "Are you afraid of the cowardly skunks?"

I said this rather boldly, though I must own that I did not relish the idea of exposing my body to a score of rifles; but there was no alternative, go we must.

The fire was gradually urging forward; in single file we passed through the gap, and concealed by the dense cloud of smoke that even set our strong lungs coughing, we dropped cautiously down the side of the rock.

Fortunately there were plenty of stout timbers at hand, and behind these we sought shelter, before the Sioux Indians were aware of the move we had taken.

"Bravo, avick! we are safe now!" exclaimed Tim. "But what's this, avick?"

He stooped down and raised something from the tall grass. It was his rifle, and fortunately it had escaped damage.

So far we were safe, as Tim expressed it; but how soon we might be placed in danger again there was no knowing, the Indians were between us and the log hut where we had left our companions, and to get back to them it was necessary that we should make a circuit open prairie.

I could see that Jack Lindley was growing disheartened, the loss of his hair and whiskers was enough to make him feel sad, yet I could not help eyeing him with a look of mingled pity and disgust.

"Well, lads," I said, after we had remained some moments in silence, "what shall we do? I propose that we make our way back to the log hut, and brave all risks."

"Then you'll not have my company," said the guerilla, "you can go by your two selves. I shall not move a peg from these trees until the red varmints are gone."

"Very well, we shall leave you," said I, "and I warrant you'll regret having parted from our company. Come on, Tim, hark how the demons are whooping, I daresay they fancy they can smell the sweet savour of our roasted carcases."

"Bedad, ye are just right—now look there," exclaimed Tim, and he pointed to a group of the fiends, who were just visible through a clearing in the smoke.

CHAPTER LXI.

THE SPECTRE WARRIOR AGAIN—WE MEET WITH RED HUGH, THE BACKWOODSMAN.

"Come on, Tim," said I, "we have no time to waste; our friends in the log hut may need our assistance, and, besides, I have mentally resolved to clear up the mystery of the Spectre Warrior."

"God help you to do it!" replied Tim, solemnly, and then he gave a cry so startling that, for the moment, I feared the bullet of some skulking Sioux had pierced him."

"Tim, are you hit?" I exclaimed, as he staggered back, and I stretched out my hand to save him from falling, and then I cast an anxious glance through the misty smoke.

That glance revealed the cause of Tim's alarm. On a swell of the prairie, his legs hidden by the long grass, stood the Spectre Warrior before us. Then a dense cloud of smoke and sparks hid him from our view, and when it cleared away the spectre had vanished.

"Bad cess to the varmint, it's the very divil, shure. I hope you won't mention the spalpeen, again," said Tim seriously. "Be me soul, no matter when or where we spake of the horrible craythur, he's sure to pay us a visit."

I thought of Tim's favourite saying whenever anyone turned up suddenly. "Talk of the divil, he's sure to appear," and the strange appearance of the spectre whenever our conversation turned upon it, certainly went far to confirm the suspicion that the Spectre Warrior was in some way connected with the Evil One, were he not the very gentleman himself.

My reverie was disturbed by my companion, who urged the necessity of our getting back to the log-hut, and taking advantage of the smoke and the tall grass, we dismounted and crept stealthily past the Indians, who never dreamed that two of the three men whom they supposed were roasting in the flames were passing within a spear's length of them.

Silently we proceeded, carefully watching every bush, and eagerly scanning the thickly interwoven branches above us as we glided from tree to tree.

Tim's eagle eye, however, seemed to have lost its keen perceptibility, for he failed to notice a slight movement of one of the bushes, so slight, in fact, that none but a well-trained woodman would have heeded it.

"Back, Tim," I whispered, as I caught his arm, and drew him behind a huge cactus. "We're watched; look out for the skulking hound, whoever he may be."

I had scarcely uttered this warning, when I heard a well-known voice, and the head of Red Hugh was thrust through an opening in the bushes.

"Ah, Silvershot," he said, "you are safe. I was afraid that you would not get out of this mess alive, and Tim, too—by the hookey, he looks pale enough over it."

"He is in love," I replied, laughing, in the hope that by treating the matter lightly, I should turn Tim's thoughts from Azalu, but I was mistaken, for he replied—

"Indeed, I am, Hugh, and with as purty a girl as ever you saw; and I want to get back to her, for we've seen "——

"Hush; did you not chide me for using that name? Why not let the subject drop?" said I, sharply.

I saw Hugh's face turn pale.

"You have seen the Spectre Warrior again, I suppose," remarked he.

"Troth, and we just have, and a mighty cuss that same has been to us wheriver we go. I don't like the look of the varmint, at all, at all."

CHAPTER LXII.

THE NIGHT-WATCH—I TRY A BRACE OF BULLETS ON THE GHASTLY SPECTRE.

WHEN we reached the log cabin, we found it well guarded; and within it, White Eagle, surrounded by a dozen of the guerillas, was holding council.

The old trapper was pleased to see us again. He shook me and Tim heartily by the hand; but Red Hugh, who was a stranger to him, he treated rather coldly.

"Well, camarado," said White Eagle, "have you seen the red-skinned devils? We have learned sufficiently to know that they have blocked us in, and I very much fear that our scouting party that left us two hours ago has been cut off."

"Then we must stick to the log hut," I replied. "We have seen some of the demons, and I have no doubt they muster several hundred strong."

"And their treachery and craft doubles their number," said White Eagle; "but we might force our way through them, if it were not for my daughter."

He cast his eyes towards the dark corner of the hut, where Azalu was seated, and sighed.

"Be me sowl, the red divils shall not harm her!" exclaimed Tim, vehemently. "Tare an ouns, it's Tim Delany that will watch over her, shure. Faix, it's mesilf that is as good as tin Indians when a lady's in danger."

Tim seated himself on my right, the best position he could get to obtain a look at Azalu, and Red Hugh squatted down on my left, saying very little, but looking, as I thought, unusually gloomy.

"Now, look here, my lads," said the old trapper, breaking the monotonous silence, "we all stand in need of rest, for there's no knowing how long we may be imprisoned here. I vote that we take it in turns to sleep, so that we may be better able to repulse an attack, if one should be made."

"I am of your opinion," said I. "We will divide our number equally, and arrange which party shall first keep watch."

"That is already arranged, Silvershot; I am the father of Azalu; she is my treasure, and White Eagle is the proper one to guard it. You and your friend, Silvershot, can remain in the hut; the men can lay down near the door ready for the first alarm of danger."

At first I would not agree to this; the old man, I knew, was nearly worn out. I offered to change places with him, but he was inflexible in his purpose.

The men composing my party threw themselves wearily on a heap of leaves and brushwood near the door, and soon fell asleep, leaving me, Tim, and Red Hugh, in the log cabin with the girl.

Tim laid and smoked, until the narcotic weed and exhausted nature bore him to the land of dreams, whilst Red Hugh and myself chatted until I fell asleep.

The smouldering embers of the fire were still burning when I awoke, and by the fitful light I saw a figure leaning over me. A giant form it appeared to be, and then a voice aroused me to consciousness.

It was Red Hugh's voice.

"Wake up, Silvershot," he said, in a hoarse whisper, "the Sioux are upon us. Come on, follow me."

Mechanically I followed Hugh out of the hut, scarcely knowing, much less heeding whisper he was leading me, until my foot suddenly became entangled with a shrub. I was precipitated forward, my head struck against a sharp piece of rock and I became insensible.

How long I laid there unconscious I had no means of determining; as soon as I recovered I crawled to my feet and made the best of my way back to the hut.

The task was difficult, but I accomplished it, wondering all the time what could have become of Red Hugh; but before I reached the door of the cabin I fancied I heard a low wailing cry, and to my surprise I saw the Spectre Warrior glide noiselessly from the hut.

This sight restored me to my senses at once. Bringing my rifle to my shoulder, I fired point blank at the breast of the spectre, who turned and faced me as I levelled my piece.

"Ha! ha! ha!" laughed the hideous fiend, as I cocked the trigger of the second barrel, to make certain of my aim. "Ha! ha! ha!" and both bullets were hurled back at me, and struck me in the face.

The blows of the lead on my cheekbones compelled me to close my eyes. Wild with rage, I clubbed my rifle, and made a dash at the spectre, but the blow met with no resistance—the spectre was gone.

With a quick step, and almost mad with disappointment, I entered the hut, and stirred up the smouldering embers into a blaze.

"Tim!" Tim!" I shouted, "where are you?" and then I glanced wildly round.

"Here, Silvershot," replied Tim's husky voice. "Good God, comrade! here's a sight!"

CHAPTER LXIII.

DEATH ONCE MORE MENACES US—THE AMBUSCADE.

TIM DELANY was right. The sight that the log fire revealed to me I shall never forget. The Spectre Warrior had made another victim.

There, plain enough, was the red gash across the throat, the bullet hole in the neck, and the teeth marks in the delicate flesh of Azalu, who now slumbered in death on her couch of furs.

"What shall we do now, Silvershot?" Tim asked of me, through his clenched teeth. "How can we render account for this, think ye?"

"How?" I replied. "Did you not see the Spectre?"

"Faix, how could I in my sleep? I heard the crack of a rifle; and I could have sworn it was your piece that woke me."

"Perhaps it was. I fired at the demon.

But look here, Tim," and I held up the bullets as I spoke; "do you recognise them?" I asked.

Tim turned deadly pale. "I could swear to them," he replied. "Did the Spectre return them to you?"

"He did; but here come the men. Do you think they will believe our story?"

Tim had no time to reply; the report of my rifle had aroused the sound sleepers who were laying about the house; and, after running wildly about, they entered the cabin.

White Eagle and some of his party were among the crowd that flocked eagerly in.

His eyes glittered fiercely as he saw us bending over the couch where his daughter lay. Fiercer still they flashed when they beheld the horrid sight that had riveted our attention.

"Good God! what is this? My child murdered?" he exclaimed. "Fiends, which of you have done this foul deed?"

Neither of us could answer him for a moment, but at length I mustered sufficient courage to give an explanation.

I might as well have remained dumb.

"'Tis false!" cried White Eagle, interrupting him. "This is the third murder that has been clearly traced to you. Demons in human form, you shall not escape justice this time."

"Lynch them! lynch them!" was the unanimous cry. "The wretches are not fit to live!"

I began to think now that our last hour had come, but the return of a party of outscouts, who had, as we surmised, been cut off by the Indians, turned the tide of affairs.

They had been trapped in an ambush, and made prisoners by the Sioux; but, for some mysterious cause, the Sioux vanished and left them free.

There was now a clear path for us out of the forest, and after a short consultation it was agreed that we should be bound and taken back to San Juan Campestrano to be tried again before the alcaldé.

Our march was a severe one, for White Eagle wanted to clear the Indian territory before night, so that we might encamp on the Mexican frontier.

We halted on the banks of a stream we had to ford, to quench our thirst and fill our waterskins; then we proceeded, and did not stop until we struck across an Indian trail.

While we halted, White Eagle went forward and examined the trail, which was so cunningly contrived as to baffle every attempt of the trapper to discover in which direction the Indians had gone.

"Let us push on," he said, gloomily; "they have, doubtless, taken to the forest. We must avoid an encounter if possible."

He had scarcely spoken, and made a sign for our party to proceed, when a loud whoop rent the air, and about one hundred Indians rushed from their concealment in the thick underwood and surrounded us.

"Snared, by Jove!" exclaimed the old trapper; "look out, boys, sell your lives as dearly as possible. Make every shot tell."

CHAPTER LXIV.

RESCUED BY UWATO—DEATH OF WHITE EAGLE, THE TRAPPER.

WHITE EAGLE's speech was responded to by a loud shout from the guerillas, and a desperate fight ensued, in which we were not allowed to take part.

Our position was by no means pleasant. Shots and arrows were flying in showers above us, while the trampling feet of the combatants threatened to put an end to our existence.

"Go it, you spalpeens!" cried Tim, in his excitement, as he raised his head to get a view of the fray; but the blow from a spear-handle almost settled him, and he dropped his head with a groan.

Like Tim, I felt anxious to see which of the parties were likely to be victors, but his fate warned me to lay still and trust to Providence.

Presently a loud whoop, sounded above the rest of the din, caused my heart to beat wildly between fear and hope.

It was Uwato's voice. I could hear him shouting to the guerillas to give up their prisoners.

"Never!" replied White Eagle. "The murderers must die. They have shed innocent blood, and—"

"By the Great Manitou, I swear they shall not die!" shouted the old chief. "My white brothers are not so wicked as you paint them. Silver Bullet is—"

"A fiend!" shouted White Eagle, pointing to the body of his murdered daughter, and then he ordered his men to form a barrier around me and Tim.

I would have given anything at that moment to have been free.

The cords that bound my hands were cutting my wrists almost to the bone, and I was afraid to speak; for by the old trapper's tone I felt assured that he would not hesitate in dashing out my brains.

It was for poor Tim that I felt most, for I could see the blood streaming from his forehead.

If a chance of escape offered itself, he was not in a position to avail himself of it; but at present there seemed no prospect of our escaping.

Uwato's party, though the strongest, was not so well armed as the guerillas; but the old chief was not so easily beaten. He rallied his warriors, and the fight again commenced.

At length the guerillas began to waver. Their line became broken, and Uwato's tomahawk stretched White Eagle on the blood-stained ground.

A blow from one of the rifles partly stunned me, as one of the guerillas fell dead across my body; but the weight was instantly removed, and the keen edge of a knife glided swiftly across my wrists.

The stroke was so swift, and my flesh was so numbed, that I was a moment before I comprehended what had happened.

As my eye glanced around, I saw Tim being borne away in the strong arms of a Comanche Indian, and, with lightning rapidity, I was also carried from the scene of slaughter.

"Silver Bullet, you are wounded," said a friendly voice, as my preserver rested his burden on the edge of a small stream, and began to bathe my brow. "How came my brother in the hands of those merciless fiends?"

I was too bewildered to speak; my brow seemed on fire, and my brain whirled. The next moment I was insensible.

. . . . . .

When I returned to consciousness, some hours afterwards, I found myself lying in an Indian tent. Uwato was seated beside me, and Tim Delany slept at my feet on a bed of furs.

Gradually reason began to dawn upon me. One circumstance after another began to dawn upon my mind. I put my hand to my brow, and found that it was bandaged, and a stream of cold water was running down my cheek.

CHAPTER LXV.

A FIGHT WITH THE AMERICAN TROOPERS.

UWATO left me, and sent one of his braves to administer to my wants; and when I was sufficiently recovered to hold converse without exciting myself too much, the old chief explained how it was that he had undertaken the journey to that part of the country.

"My brother knows that Buckskin Bill holds the chart that would lead the hungry Mexicans to the treasure cave," he began; "and to see him and come to terms was the cause of my visit; for, knowing his treacherous nature and the animosity he owed to you, I was afraid he would lead you into some snare, and perhaps murder you."

I was anxious to learn how Bill Buckskin had effected his escape from the prison in which Uwato had confined him, and so I asked how he had managed to release himself from the living tomb in which the stern chief had doomed him to end his existence.

I LEAPED AT THE REDSKIN TO INTERCEPT THE BLOW.

"Ah, therein lies a mystery," replied Uwato, wreathing his lips into a ghastly smile. "I sent one of my braves to see that all was safe before we left, and he brought me word that he was gone." I afterwards learnt that he had followed you to San Juan Campestrano, so I followed with a small party to intercept him."

"Thanks—a thousand thanks!" I exclaimed. "You arrived in the nick of time to save us."

That night we broke up the encampment, and made tracks for the Comanche country to the delight of Tim Delany, who, in spite of all that had happened, thought of the Comanche maiden who had won his affections.

Uwato rode by my side, and he was remarkably silent. At times he would ride forward to the head of the cavalcade, and hold a hurried conversation with the young braves, who acted as scouts, and continually returned with some important intelligence. To me this was all mystery.

I felt certain that the Comanches were following the trail of an enemy; but whether that enemy was the Sioux, or a party of white men, I could not determine.

Suddenly the sound of a bugle startled us, and from a clump of timbers on a small hill to our right dashed a party of horsemen.

Uwato immediately he saw them dextrously turned his party back into the forest.

The horsemen were a light company of American cavalry, the leader being a tall Kentuckian, whose features, slight as was the glance I caught of them, appeared familiar to me.

Tim and I joined in the fight. The first two saddles that approached us were emptied by our hands.

My object was to reach the leader of the troop, and, with a quick glance, I singled out my man—a tall, herculean fellow, who bore down all before him.

For a moment our eyes met, and I fancied he recognised me, for he reined in his steed as we bore towards each other; but whatever were his thoughts or intentions, I know not —a swift blow from a sabre, or some sharp instrument, laid bare the back of my skull, and I fell forward, bleeding and senseless, upon the neck of my horse, who gave a deep snort of pain at the same moment, and then rolled over with me on the slippery, blood-stained ground.

CHAPTER LXVI.

IN PRISON—WE MEET WITH AN OLD COMPANION.

THE fall from my horse, added to the sabre cut, must have nearly killed me, for I remember nothing until I awoke, with a cold stream of water pouring on my face, and I found myself in a rude sort of building.

Presently a noise, like some one moving at the other end of the shed, startled me.

I felt for my knife. It was gone. Unconsciously I groaned again, and then I heard a voice.

"Och, be my soul! are ye alive now?" exclaimed the voice. "Bad cess to me if I didn't think they'd notched ye this time. Spake, man; spake, Silvershot, if you're not above talking to an old chum."

"Tim Delany!" I gasped, almost speechless with joy; "where are you?"

"Och, safe enough. Sure, the American varmints payed mighty great attention to us, they've put us in here just to fatten us a bit before they string us up."

I was about to speak to Tim again when the sound of footsteps caught my ear, and I saw a light glare through the chinks of the cabin.

Our suspense was abruptly terminated by the entrance of a soldier, bearing an oat cake and a pitcher of water for Tim's breakfast.

"Hallo, my crafty opossum, you've come round then," said he, giving me a fierce look.

"Come, none of your fox capers, I heard you talking."

I was shamming insensibility again, but I found that the fellow was too cute for me. He put me more in mind of some lynx-eyed trapper than a soldier. Finding that deceit would avail me nothing I turned over on my side and faced him.

I gave a start, and Tim fairly shouted.

"Paul Morgan, me bhoy, give me your hand, be me sowl!"

Paul Morgan was completely staggered when we made ourselves known to him, but we had no time to waste in congratulations, such as one would have supposed after being so long parted.

"Look here, comrades," said Paul, stifling the emotion which, for a moment, overcame us all; "to-day, at twelve o'clock, is fixed for your execution. If you stay here nothing can save you; the governor is a fearful tyrant. Dick Crosby is here with me; but we want horses. I think, however, I can manage that. I will assist you to mount, and you must do your best to keep your saddles. In one half-hour our escape will be discovered, even if we are fortunate enough to reach the wood unseen."

By this time I was seated on my horse, and owing to my weakness I had some difficulty to keep my equilibrium, but Paul handed me a small flask, and while I was fortifying myself with its contents Paul assisted Tim to mount.

During this time Dick had been pacing his post, so as to keep watch, and prevent suspicion, but now he joined us, he taking the reins of one horse, and Paul the other, which they led along a narrow path, that wound round the back of the hill on which the fort was raised.

That we should soon be missed, and would be pursued was quite evident, so we lost no time in making our way into the depths of the forest, where, being excellent woodsmen all of us, we could easily escape detection.

CHAPTER LXVII.

WE MAKE A NEW DISCOVERY.

THREE months passed when we stood once more beneath the withered branches of the old plane tree.

There was not the smallest mark to indicate that anyone had visited it since Tim and I were there, and with saddened hearts we partook of supper and laid ourselves down to sleep, thinking of our four missing companions.

We had not been asleep long when something awoke us, Tim instantly sprang up and went out to reconnoitre, when at the same moment, he was seized at the door of the hut by a gigantic Indian, who struck him with a dagger. I leaped at the redskin to intercept the blow, but too late, Tim fell at my feet with a loud cry of agony. To revenge the fate of my companion, I wrested the weapon from the Indian's grasp, and buried it in his heart, then I turned my attention to Tim; he was not so badly hurt as I imagined, he had received a flesh wound in the shoulder, which I bound up for him. Thinking that perhaps a tribe of Indians was on our trail, we thought it advisable to go further afield to spend the night, and it was nearly three o'clock in the morning before we again stretched ourselves on the green sward, to snatch a few hours' sleep.

Scarcely had the morning dawned, however, when we heard the gentle rustling of the bushes. The dry twigs began to crack, and the figure of a man appeared through the foliage.

"Well, stranger," said the man, eyeing me closely. "Who would have thought of meeting anyone in this lonely spot?"

Tim was busied in stripping the panther of his hide while I was conversing with the stranger, but I noticed him pause suddenly and listen.

"Did ye hear that, Silvershot?" he suddenly exclaimed. "I could swear it was"——

Here the stranger interrupted him.

"Silvershot!" he ejaculated. "What! is it possible?"

I looked at the man, and then I thought I recognized him.

"You are," I said, "Ben Brewster?"

"I am," he replied, stepping forward and grasping my hand. "God bless you, Silvershot. I never thought we should meet again."

Presently the sound that had startled Tim was repeated loud enough for us all to hear, and before I could ask Ben any questions, the sun-tanned face of Phillip Allan was visible on the other side of the clearing.

Our joy on thus meeting I will not attempt to describe. Six of us out of the eight breakfasted that morning at the foot of the old plane tree, and numerous were the questions asked as we discussed our pleasant meal.

Then it was agreed that we should start early on the following morning, and leave no means untried of discovering the fate of Bill Southern and Jack Walton.

When this was arranged, we lit our pipes, and as they were all anxious to hear some of mine and Tim's adventures, I told them the story of the Spectre Warrior, and the hairbreadth escapes it had led us into.

CHAPTER LXVIII.
THE MYSTERY EXPLAINED.

ANOTHER year was waning fast; sad and weary, we were once more wending our way to the old spot. We had arranged before starting, that, either separated or together, we should do so, until something occurred to sever the hunter's bond.

Little did we imagine how near that something was approaching. How should we? We were not endowed with the power of foretelling the future.

One night (we were just three days' journey from the old plane-tree), as I lay rolled up in my blanket, having talked Tim to sleep, I saw old Jip spring up from his warm berth near the fire, and take an uneasy survey of a clump of trees some distance away on our right, and then he commenced sniffing and uttering a low plaintive wail.

We were just in the right part to meet with any number of wild beasts; the day before we had shot no less than five different species, so that I attributed the dog's uneasiness to the presence of some midnight prowler, who was very probably reconnoitring our stronghold before attacking it.

The other dog, Ben, now began to be uneasy, and to add to my alarm, he came and licked my face, and tapped my cheek with his paw.

I aroused Tim, and consulted him on the subject, and he directly gave it as his opinion that there was a party of Indians in the wood, for, said he——

"Faix, I didn't tell ye that I fancied I saw some smoke climbing up from the trees yonder."

Such a thing might be possible, but I doubted it, for we had not seen the track of an Indian for more than a week; however, I quietly awakened the rest, and giving orders that no one should follow me, unless I signalled, I crept silently towards the wood, and hid myself behind the trunk of a huge chesnut tree.

From this position I could see anything or anybody passing from the wood towards our camp; but, for ten minutes, I neither saw nor heard anything at all indicative of life.

At the end of that time, I fancied I heard a leaf rustle, so gently that, if I had not been listening intently, it would have escaped my notice; as it was, it caused my eyes to wander in the direction of the sound, and, to my horror, I beheld the white form of the Spectre Warrior.

It was gliding along softly, but swiftly, as though bent on its horrible work, and as soon as I could recover my faculties, I determined upon pursuing it.

Without pausing to reflect upon the dangerous course I was pursuing, I made my way from tree to tree, almost as noiselessly as the spectre, and soon I found myself emerging from the opening on the other side of the wood.

I was right in my conjecture, for I again caught sight of the spectral object moving among the smouldering embers of a fire recently disturbed.

With one bound, I sprang forward, elevating my rifle, in order, if possible, to bring down the midnight murderer.

Suddenly I heard a dull click, like the sound of a mimic pop-gun; another second, and the fatal bullet had sped.

Another moment, and his ghastly work would have been complete. He turned and faced me, and my hand gripped him by the neck, and, quick as lightning, with my other hand I wrenched from his grasp a long hunting-knife, which he had half drawn from its sheath.

"Now, fiend!" I cried, brandishing the bright weapon before the spectre's eyes, "now, fiend, I have caught you, throw off all deception, for now I know that you are flesh and blood."

I felt the wretch tremble under my vice-like grasp, I heard him utter a moan of anguish, and then a current of air fanning the embers into a flame, enabled me to get a good look at the spectre's features.

A startled cry burst from me as I saw through the base deception—the features I viewed were decidedly those of Red Hugh.

My cry brought the hunters to their feet, for there were two of them, and surprised enough they were to find me grappling the strange figure by the throat.

This strange discovery drove from my mind the intention I had at first formed of taking the spectre's life.

Curious to know what motive could have put such diabolical practices into his head, I led him away with me, and then demanded an explanation.

His history was soon told. He reminded me of the massacre in Pine Valley, of the young girl betrothed to the hunter—she who had the bullet hole in her neck, her throat cut, and her silvery locks scalped, and——

"I remember all this," I said; "but what has it to do with the horrible deeds you have been committing, and which but for my timely interference, would have included in your list of victims these two noble fellows."

"All," he replied. "Did I not tell you that the young hunter went mad, that he made a vow to sweep from the prairie every living soul, white or red."

"Good heavens!" I gasped, "was this hunter and the spectre one!"

"Ay," he cried, his eyes flashing wildly. "Red Hugh was the hunter—Red Hugh was

the spectre, and the vow I had taken would sooner or later have been accomplished had it not been for your interference, which has broken the spell."

We all gazed upon him in horror.

Even now, with the most convincing proofs before me, I could scarce believe such a thing possible—the gun, too, there was a mystery about that I could not make out.

Red Hugh explained it.

It was a strange weapon, cleverly constructed; it had two barrels, one of ordinary make, the other so contrived that it worked with air instead of powder, and when fired, made only the strange, almost inaudible, report I have before explained.

Tim sat listening with open mouth to this part of the story, and then his face assumed a broad grin.

"Faix! how did he give us back our bullets? That's a mystery, anyway, ain't it?" said he.

"Not at all," replied Hugh. "While you were sleeping, I drew the bullets from your rifles, then, without waking you, I slipped into the forest and changed my clothes—a little bruised bark served to darken my skin, and when all was complete neither of you knew me; the bullets I returned to you were the same I had taken from your rifles, and the reason of my looking at my victims before sending them to their last account was to prevent me murdering my friends."

"But," said I, "you had no opportunity of drawing the bullet from Bill Buckskin's rifle when he fired at you in San Juan Campestrano."

"I did not; but I was determined to risk my life rather than you should suffer innocently. Even in my madness, I had sense enough for this, though your turn would have come in the course of time."

I will not weary the reader with the unpleasant reflections this open confession caused me. Although I could not willingly take the life of a man who had so considerately spared my own, I could not think of nourishing the companionship of one who had so recklessly sacrificed innocent lives, and there was no knowing when this strange passion for revenge might come upon him again.

This adventure, however, had led to a strange discovery.

The two hunters I had so miraculously saved were no others than the two companions we had so long sought after—Bill Southern and Jack Walton, the latter of whom had a nasty graze on his neck, caused by the bullet that had been fired at him by Red Hugh, the Backwoodsman; or, the Spectre Warrior.

THE END.